THE SOLITARY
APOCALYPSE

Jeff Haws

The Solitary Apocalypse

Printed in the United States of America

First Printing, 2017

ISBN: 978-1-945768-10-1

Publisher: Shifty Squid, LLC

P.O. Box 170392

Atlanta, GA 30317

Visit the author's website and blog at www.jeffhaws.com

1

Her lips wrapped tightly around the pistol's steel barrel, Theresa shifted her weight from her left knee as it began to ache against the frost-laded concrete on a cold February evening. Stretching her eyes to their peripheral limits, she tried to catch a glimpse of her friend Lucas, lying motionless beside her, a welt beginning to rise from his temple.

"It's time, Audrey!" Paul held the gun firm, swiveling his head to the left to make eye contact, trying to make his voice heard. "We can't keep pussying out. Say the word, and I'll take care of them. You can just go back to pondering life's mysteries, or whatever it is you do in your room."

Audrey took slow steps toward Paul, holding his gaze. Staying under control in situations like this was why she'd risen to where she was, holding sway over what might be the final organized colony of humans left on Earth. She'd taken them this far on smarts, some guile, and repressive, unquestioned control. Keeping Paul around was good for her, she thought. He wasn't afraid to challenge her, and make her think about why she was making the decisions she was making. At times like this, she questioned that, though.

"How can you crave death, Paul?" Audrey took two more steps and stopped, close enough for her frozen breath's billow to crawl up Paul's face as it dissipated into the air. "Have you not seen enough? We may be the last of God's children. We have to protect each other."

"They put everyone in danger. Everyone!" Paul punctuated the last word with a jab of the barrel deeper into Theresa's mouth, bouncing it off both rows of her teeth and leaving shards of enamel on her tongue. "It's fucking selfish. We can't just let people defy the rules in order to get a hand job or whatever crap they were trying to pull, and walk away. What kind of message does that send? The virus spreads through touch, and if it makes it in these walls, we're all fucked (dead). You want that? How about you, whatever your name is?"

Theresa shook her head and mumbled incoherently, as she shifted her weight back to her left knee. Both her hands were beginning to go numb from the ropes tied more tightly than necessary around her wrists.

Paul smiled and turned back to Audrey. "See? Princess here agrees with me. I think that settles it; you're outvoted, two to one. Pretty sure the big guy on the ground isn't gonna be weighing in right now."

"Take the gun out of her mouth." Audrey took a step back. "You know this isn't how we do things. Order without violence. Remember?"

Paul rolled his eyes and yanked the gun back; Theresa gasped for air, saliva dripping from her lips. Paul pulled the slide back on the pistol, loading a round into the chamber, then pulled her hair to lift her head back up and jammed the gun back between her lips. Her eyes grew, and she mumbled nervously.

"Remind me, which one of us was it who ripped families in this town apart?" Paul bellowed, his left arm sweeping in an exaggerated shrug. "Which one of us forced everyone to wear these ridiculous steel rings? And who made it a point to catch people like these two sneaking around together? Because it sure as hell wasn't me!"

Audrey glanced away and took a deep breath. There weren't a lot of people she could trust in this world anymore, but her brother was one of those people. She couldn't let this get away from her.

"I get it. I do. You're angry."

Paul shook his head. "Angry? You're damn right, I'm angry. Because I'm tired of your bullshit, that's why. You think you're all *noble*, but look at the society you've built. The people are zombies! Everybody's miserable. But you don't have the (guts) balls to just take all this to its logical conclusion. Do you want power badly enough to keep people isolated from one another? If so, this is the way to do it. Go big or go home, sis. I'm ready to go big, and so is Mister Semi-Automatic here."

Theresa murmured loudly, kicking the ground behind her and shaking wildly. Blonde strands of hair fell across her forehead and rested on the bridge of her nose, tickling her eyelashes. The long-sleeved red blouse she wore was cold with sweat.

Audrey rose her head up and met Paul's eyes, searching for humanity within them.

"I still believe there's another way," she said in just above a whisper. "Help me find it."

She took a step back toward Paul, her arms extended in front of her, her left palm turned toward the ceiling.

"If you believe that, you're fooling yourself."

"Then let me fool myself for a little while longer, okay?" Audrey pleaded with Paul. "I'm your big sister. You know I'm gonna make sure we're both all right. I've got this. Let me try it my way for a little while. You'll be here to keep me in check. Right?"

Paul stared into her eyes and nodded almost imperceptibly.

"Okay, then." Audrey nodded toward her left hand. "Can you give me the gun?"

Theresa's teeth stopped chattering. She didn't dare make a sound.

Paul ran his free hand through his dark brown hair, pitching his head forward and scratching the back of his neck. He grimaced and looked at the floor, shaking his head quickly back and forth. He sighed, expelling a plume of frozen air droplets into the air in front of him, then looked up at Audrey.

"How long do you think you can keep this up?" Paul's eyes narrowed. "This isn't gonna last. They're gonna come for you."

Audrey straightened her back and threw back her shoulders. She was tall, close to six feet, and she knew how to exude confidence when she needed to.

"When they do, we'll be ready."

"And in the meantime...?"

"We'll run this motherfucker. Together. You and me." She smiled and lowered her chin. "Without shooting people."

Paul closed his eyes and yanked the gun from Theresa's mouth, and she fell forward on her stomach, hacking out a dry cough and gasping for air. He smacked the gun into Audrey's open palm; she closed her hand around it, but he didn't let go.

"You better be right," he said.

"Let's hope you're not."

2

"Risking gruesome death to get laid is a bold move, my friend." Michael swirled a spoon through a bowl of tomato soup in front of him, sitting in a diner straight out of the 1950s. It was like a time capsule, not just to the '50s, but back to a time when civilization was something people could hold onto. It was comforting. It was also one of just two restaurants in the town. Going out was a tradeoff—you had to wear your bulky steel ring whenever you were out in public, so that was a hassle. But it was also a chance to have some human contact, to commiserate over a meal. If you were caught having people into your house, quarantine awaited. No one knew what quarantine entailed, but the threat was plenty to make cooking for two not worth the risk.

The rings were an unorthodox solution to the problem of needing to keep the virus from spreading if it hit the town, but they kept the town somewhat functional even under constant threat of a deadly, highly contagious pandemic. Steel had been a heavy choice to lug around, but Audrey went with it because the town had already acquired a few dozen ten-foot steel beams for various construction projects—most notably, the renovation of the old courthouse on the square. So they had the material, and the furniture manufacturing plant where Michael took over as foreman had the pipe bending and cutting machines, along with the welding and compressor machines they needed to shape the steel. Michael led the effort, and it had required plenty of help from the community to finish the job quickly, making 223 of them—one for each citizen of Alessandra who remained. It created a sort of forced separation between individuals, and it took awhile to get used to the extra weight. People talked about the past a lot, and hoped to return to their normal lives once the virus threat passed.

"Remember Tara Dernier freshman year?" His friend Nick took a bite of his grilled chicken sandwich, mustard smearing his cheek. He wiped clumsily with his napkin. "That chick was at least three fifty. Pretty sure you risked gruesome death to get laid with *that* chick."

Michael laughed. Bits of chicken sputtered from Nick's mouth as he smacked his leg with an open palm. His ring clanged against the bottom of the table as he jostled on the bench.

"Come on. She wasn't three fifty." Michael smiled and held his arms straight out, a few feet apart. He brought them toward each other a bit. "Two fifty, maybe."

Nick rested his elbow on the table and pointed at Michael. "Aw, don't give me your Bizarro fish story, man. That chick was probably four bills."

"Naw, man. No way." Michael shrugged his arms above the table, nearly knocking over his soup with his left elbow. A few tablespoons sloshed over the edge and spilled onto the table. He slid right to avoid it trickling onto his pants, then wiped it up with his napkin.

"Thinkin' about that sweet ass of Tara's really gets you out of sorts, doesn't it?"

Michael grinned and looked across the table at Nick. "Shove it up your ass, will ya?"

"Is that what *she* said?"

Michael rolled his eyes and went to sit back, but there was no back to the seat; it was still easy for people to forget public seats can't have backs when all the customers are wearing big rings of steel around their midsections. As the foreman at the town's furniture-manufacturing plant—which had been Alessandra's signature export other than drunkenness and swerving speedboats—part of his job was to know which places needed new pieces that would work for their business. As he made a quick mental note, he grabbed the table just in time to keep from flipping over the back of the bench. Nick laughed harder this time, opening his mouth wide to reveal a large bite of chewed corned chicken.

"You're a clumsy son of a bitch, you know that?" Nick put his sandwich down and smiled.

"Hey, man…Do I have to remind you who was the starting free safety and who was the fat kid riding the pine back in high school?"

Nick sipped his glass of water. "We're a long way from high school."

"Ain't that the truth?"

They both ate silently for a few minutes, neither feeling the need to say much. Michael and Nick had been friends since third grade, when they both had an affinity for playing checkers in Mrs. Hartsell's class. For awhile, they would organize tournaments for the class. But after the ninth straight time they met up in the finals, the other kids got to be pretty scarce when playtime came along. That was okay by them. They'd just as soon play by themselves anyway. Nobody could beat them except each other, and there was nobody either of them would rather beat.

By sixth grade, they were best friends, and played every sport they could get a team together for when they weren't playing Nintendo. Checkers was left behind, but their competitive streak wasn't. Baseball, basketball, and football—it all came down to a grudge match between the two of them, no matter how many other kids were involved. In high school, they both made the football team and were competing for a lot of the same girls. Michael was the more traditionally good-looking one, but Nick's personality more than made up for his plus-sized frame. In adolescence—much like in adulthood—confidence could carry a guy a long way with women, and Nick had it.

When Michael got the Homecoming Queen to go to senior prom with him, he rented a limo and had it pull up to Nick's house to gloat on his way to the recreation center that night. He leaned against the car with his right arm wrapped around the Homecoming Queen, grinning widely. He had the limo driver call Nick's house, and ask him to come out front. When he did, he walked out with two girls—the two closest runners-up in the Homecoming court, dressed in matching royal blue dresses. Nick opened his mouth wide and made a finger gun toward Michael, pulled the trigger, and walked toward his dad's Mercedes, his arms around the girls flanking him.

Now, they were in their mid thirties. Both divorced. Nick three times. And this was a tough age for people at what looked like it could be the end of the Earth. When you grew up thinking this was a time when you'd have a loving family and a nice-paying job, it was tough to accept that, by the time humanity recovered from this massive blow to move forward—*if* it recovered—you'd probably either be dead or too old to ever have any of those things. And now something as simple as a companion, someone to share your life with, was stripped from you because of this plague that could wipe out what was left of the human race. Depression was common. So was suicide, when people could find the means.

But Michael and Nick weren't near that point. They'd endured a lot over the previous year in this colony, from surviving the plague that started like any other flu outbreak but turned into a global pandemic, and then somehow spiraled even further out of control, leaving families torn apart, cities empty, and hospitals overwhelmed. Alessandra was fortunate, though—it was isolated enough in North Georgia to be less traveled by people from the overrun cities, and have a low, easily contained population, along

with being located along the banks of the large Lake Chatuga.
That meant both that they only had to protect themselves from
three sides from any potential hordes, and they had a convenient
source of fresh water at their disposal, bringing food right along
with it.

Michael and Nick grew up there, graduating from Towns
High, getting odd jobs well into their twenties to afford whatever
cheap pot and beer met their agenda on Friday night. They'd both
fallen into marriage at various periods in that decade, but never
fully committed to it, and never had any children. Nick married
women seemingly just for the party he got an excuse to throw,
along with the week of honeymoon sex, and his follow-through
showed that. He was never violent, but he could be a piss-mean
drunk when he wanted to be, and he let that demon of his roam
free once the ring was on. It never took long for his most recent
wife to wise up and become his most recent ex-wife.

Michael was far more judicious when it came to women. He
rarely got serious in relationships, and had a tendency to keep
everyone—not just women—at arm's length, except Nick. When
he met Stephanie at the local flea market, it didn't seem different.
They'd fought over buying the same coffee table, setting off a
dual auction while the seller rocked lazily in his chair, grinning
and sharpening his hunting knife on a whetstone. After she wore
him down and was carrying the table to her truck, he told her she
should buy him a drink to make up for stealing his table. She told
him to hop in the cab. He didn't ask her out for any reason other
than he liked watching her ass as she walked away with the table.

This was far from love at first sight. That night at the bar,
they had a hard time even finding common interests beyond
trolling flea markets for odd items and the occasional hiking trip.
Too much of that first night was spent sipping their beers to
avoid being the one who had to talk, and making small talk about
how stupid expensive gas was getting to be.

But they exchanged numbers and went out a second time. Then a third and a fourth. The first "I love you" snuck out of his mouth one night when he was grilling burgers on the back deck and the light caught her crimson hair in a way that silhouetted her against the falling sun. He proposed on a whim eight months later as they walked toward their car from the local Quik Trip, sipping slushies on a bright summer evening.

Everything about their relationship seemed to sneak up on him, but he was undoubtedly in love. It didn't end how he'd planned, but he had certainly been in love. Nick was another story. What love meant to Nick, it was hard to say. He loved women, in his own way. Or, at least, he loved having women around. And the feeling was pretty mutual. Not being able to sleep with women—or even feel their velvet touch on his skin—was driving Nick borderline mad. Michael was hanging in there okay; he was completely on board with the regulations, having known Audrey well for more than a decade after occasionally crossing paths growing up, and trusting her leadership. If she said this was the way it had to be, he wasn't going to argue. He wouldn't necessarily call Audrey a friend, but they were reasonably friendly. They'd exchanged pleasantries here and there through high school, but officially met through Stephanie, who was a medical assistant at the time for Audrey's doctor. Michael had been to Audrey's house for dinner a number of times, and she impressed him as she moved up the local political ranks, from city accountant to comptroller, council person to chairman.

She'd been the deputy mayor when the plague struck. Mayor Charles Handy was in Atlanta for a week-long conference, and no one understood the ramifications of what was happening at first. It spread so quickly, especially among thousands of state leaders shaking hands and coughing on each other over a week's time. He fell ill before he made it back to Alessandra. By the time he was shuttled back to town, they had no choice but to place him in quarantine. They brought in the most experienced doctors they could find—including Stephanie, who had become an internal medicine specialist and researcher after the divorce—but he couldn't be saved. Audrey was the leader the town had left standing, and she recruited Michael as one of her community deputies—helping to monitor the people they lived near—and he took the role seriously.

That was part of why he was sitting in the diner right then, trying to feel out his friend. Nick had met Rachel at Walt's Bar one Thursday night. They'd hit it off, as people do, but that was a dangerous game under the colony's tight regulations. Since the plague spread by touch, even the temptation of a hand on the thigh had the potential to destroy what they'd built. It wasn't just about protecting the individuals involved; if the virus made it through the town's walls uncontrolled, it could ravage the population in days. Discipline was hard, but it was vital, and Michael knew that. Whether or not Nick did was yet to be seen.

"But, seriously," Michael sipped the last drops of soup from his bowl. "What's going on with this girl? I know she's hot. I mean, I get it, man. I've met her. But this is dangerous ground. This ain't the world we used to live in. Are you guys…*doing* anything?"

Nick wiped his mouth with his napkin, balled it up and tossed it onto the table. The sound of waitress's shoes tapping the tile floor in rapid succession and orders being called rang out from around them.

"Who's askin'? Michael the childhood friend who wouldn't think of fucking me over, or Michael the wingman for Audrey's gestapo?"

"Come on. Don't worry about all that shit. This is just friends talking."

Nick tilted his head to the left and rested his chin on his balled-up hand. "I've gotta worry about it, man. Even if not for me, I can't put *her* in any danger. And what if they have this place bugged?"

"Bugging this place would be fun," Michael laughed. "They'd learn a lot about what sort of fish Table Four was ordering, and not much else."

"Ooo…It's Ben, and he got the trout." Nick looked over at Table Four, and saw Ben slicing into a flaky pink filet on a bed of white rice. "I totally should have gotten that instead."

"Sure, sure. You getting fish," Michael said. "You're still upset you can't get a big bloody hamburger anymore."

"Yeah. Like you wouldn't order one too if you could, Mister 'I'll just have a soup.'"

They both laughed, enjoying the way they comfortably slid into their needling banter, even if they didn't see each other as often as they used to. Living in Alessandra was an isolating, repetitive existence. Home. Work. Home. Rest. Then start again the next day. With only a couple of hundred residents, everyone knew each other's name, but it seemed like there were few friends. Something about wearing that ring just kept people in their little personal bubble, the lack of physical touch—shaking hands, hugging, kissing—turned people inward, so they avoided everything beyond a friendly wave. So Michael and Nick knew how fortunate they were to have the bond they had, even if they didn't always think about it. Among all the cacophony of sounds in the diner that day, theirs was the only laughter.

"Okay, I get that you don't want to go into too much right here." Michael brought his elbows up to the table, leaned forward and glanced quickly left, then right. "Just know this isn't a game. This isn't casual sex, or another future bride you're playing with here. All right? This is life and death. Not just for you, but potentially for all of us. So, while I get wanting to get your dick wet and all, think about what that means. And think what happens when they catch you."

3

"Take them down to the pen with the others." Audrey turned and walked away from Paul, in the direction of her bedroom. "I think I'm gonna lie down and take a nap."

"I'll get them set up." Paul crouched in front of Lucas and lightly smacked his cheeks a few times. "Big guy here seems to be coming around. He'll have a nasty knot on his head, but I'm sure he'll recover like a champ."

Paul grabbed Lucas's bound arms from behind him and hoisted him onto his knees. Then up again to help him get his feet under him and stand.

"Ladies first." Paul gestured his gun toward a path ten feet away, leading them to a large fence surrounding the quarantine camp. "And can you handle a bit of a walk, big guy? One step at a time. Wouldn't want you to fall down and crush the young lady."

Audrey stopped at the top of an adjacent set of stairs and turned back toward them, her hand on the doorknob to the mansion.

"Paul!" Audrey yelled to get his attention. The three of them stopped and looked in her direction. "Either hold onto Lucas, or put him out in front and go slowly. Don't fuck around."

Paul threw his hands up to his sides. "I was just joking! Come on. You knew I was joking, didn't you, big guy?"

Lucas looked at Paul and winced.

Audrey narrowed her eyes. "And remember…"

"I know, I know. Set them up with one of the nice tents. Make sure they get water and food. Yada yada yada…" Paul poked Lucas in the back with the gun barrel. "Let's do this. Get movin'."

Audrey sat on the edge of her bed and slipped off her shoes one by one. They were a basic pair of loafers, her go-to shoe for every day around her sprawling, 3.5-acre compound on the western edge of town, overlooking one of the main sections of the town's wall and guard towers, along with the town square they used to call "historic," but none of that history seemed to much matter anymore.

In her "former life"—as she called her first fifty-one years on Earth, before the plague ravaged human civilization and left her tiny band of survivors to pick up the pieces—she was a shoe hoarder of sorts. Back then, it was a luxury, born of her wealth growing up with a state senator father and lawyer mother, and a simple pleasure in her life. In post-plague life, these shoes were her most prized possessions—sets of pointed pumps in suede and leather that glistened in the sunlight, sandals with ankle straps almost as thin as a shoelace, sexy black leather boots that nearly touched her knees, snakeskin heels that made her feel exotic and dangerous, flat boots that could deal with the harsh weather they sometimes saw in this part of Georgia, and dozens of others. They reminded her of a time when the world seemed full of possibilities, and allowed her to forget it had all changed quite so much. When she could walk into that closet and look at those shoes, pick out the pair that was perfect for that day, she felt ready to confront whatever challenges lay in front of her.

In a day when caring for clothes was difficult—new designer ones weren't coming, and rationed water meant precious little could go toward keeping that little black dress clean and lacking in funk—shoes could stand the test of time. Put an ounce of care into them, and they'd repay you with a pound of longevity. Life had suddenly become arduous; this was her simple rebellion, her chance to connect with a past that had left them far too quickly.

As she spun her legs onto the bed and lay back, resting her head on the pillow, she thought about how this had happened around her. How did she end up denying people something as basic as human touch? How had it all come to this? It wasn't something she'd planned out, exactly. But when the plague struck, nobody knew how it spread. That was one of the main reasons it gained momentum so rapidly—its method of transmission puzzled the scientists who studied it. There was little evidence that masks worked; the only option they found that was effective was quarantine.

So, once the mayor returned as the town's first victim, Audrey acted quickly, establishing a quarantine area and warding him off from the rest of the population. And, when he died, she knew it was up to her to protect the town from further damage. Researchers around the world had studied the virus, and all the studies on transmission had been inconclusive. But they had their own mayor's body to study, and she didn't want him to die in vain. Maybe some good could come from Mayor Handy's death if it could help them save the town, if not the world.

By that time, though, it was becoming more and more clear that they were isolated, and the world around them was crumbling away quickly. As populations dwindled, communications broke down, and media got increasingly difficult to both produce and distribute. So she ordered one of the doctors at Alessandra's St. Francis Hospital to research how the virus was being transmitted; she felt like they were uniquely positioned to conduct this research away from all the worldwide chaos, and contribute to the knowledge surrounding the outbreak.

Within two months of the virus taking hold, whole cities started going dark; within four months, federal and local governments had lost control of what populace was left. By the six-month mark from the first mentions of the plague in the media, that same media was mostly blacked out around the world; in Alessandra, they were either alone or forgotten by the rest of civilization.

It was at this point that Dr. Richard Giles told her he completed his research, and determined that the virus was spread via physical touch. He said he thought other doctors were missing this because they were probably too overwhelmed to study touch in a comprehensive manner. He also said his study determined there was reason to believe the virus could lay dormant for some period of time, so people could be asymptomatic but still contagious. Audrey hailed this as a major breakthrough but, by this time, they had no way to communicate with anyone else. Still, the information had the potential to save Alessandra. She determined that keeping people from touching each other might keep the town safe. With cities and towns throughout the world being decimated and abandoned, anything was worth a shot.

She found, though, that this was an impossible policy to enforce. How do you tell people they can't touch the ones they love? Even if you tell them, what do you do to prevent it from happening? She knew almost immediately it would require a series of changes that would be received harshly by the citizens, and could crush whatever mandate to leadership she had. But she also knew it was absolutely necessary, and she could be a hero if she could sell them on that idea.

"I know this isn't what you all want to hear," she said from a podium in the town square one chilly January evening, as the plague's progress brought it closer and closer to their isolated town. "But I'm tasked with maintaining order in this town and protecting its citizens from threats, and sometimes that means telling you difficult truths. The fact is we're still here right now, and that's more than most of the world can say as I stand before you today. Remaining here is going to be trying on even the strongest of us. It's going to take collective sacrifice. It's going to take cooperation and brotherhood. Determination and grit. You're going to have to want a life more than you want this particular life, for the time being. You're going to have to accept changes you never thought you'd have to accept, and be part of something greater than yourself, greater than your family, greater than everything you already know. That's the price to be part of a rebirth. I want you all to follow me there.

"What doesn't kill me makes me stronger. My friends, I believe that's true, today more than ever. I stand before you today to bear witness that we can do this. We can live. We can fight another day, and come out the other side of this nightmare stronger, more together than ever before. Will you follow me? Will you be a part of this?"

Many would. Some wouldn't. That day, children were taken from their homes—the ones who remained in the town were placed into a special kids' quarantine center, where they were monitored around the clock by workers who were tested multiple times daily for the virus. Marriages were dissolved. Families were torn asunder. But when Audrey told everyone she knew of a secret location, protected from the virus, where she could send a limited number of women and children, that helped some people come to grips with it. Some families actually separated enthusiastically, thinking this was the best for everyone. The women and children would be isolated and safe until the virus was dead. Many of the men were willing to endure whatever hardships Audrey laid upon them to keep their wife and kids from being infected. And she told them they'd all be reunited as soon as was possible.

Each person who remained in the town was fitted with their own steel ring that connected to their bodies via a custom-made belt, surrounding them to separate them from one another. The rings defined each individual's personal space in brutalist fashion, leaving no question as to where each person's line was crossed.

She required that everyone wear these whenever they were in public; the rule was followed first with anger and skepticism, and eventually with a sort of sadness and forced resignation. There were exceptions—doctors, childcare workers, and police officers among them—but the rule was enforced strictly for basically everyone else. That made any sort of physical contact a risk that, for most, wasn't worth taking as long as the threat of this plague hung heavy over their heads.

With Audrey still lying in her bed, staring at the ceiling, golden light from the hallway slowly crept across the floor as the door to her bedroom creaked open. She didn't move, her eyes barely registering any change.

"I keep saying we need to get that door oiled," said Danny, the town's chief of police. "I'm always afraid the damn thing's gonna wake the dead."

Audrey lay still, holding her stare above.

"That's nothing compared to how noisy I'm gonna be in a few minutes." She lifted her head slightly and cracked a crooked smile, then curled an index finger toward herself. "Now close the door and get your sexy ass over here."

4

Michael stood at a podium in the auditorium of what used to be Towns High School and knocked three times with his fist.

"Okay, guys, let's bring this thing to order. Gotta get started if we're gonna get out of here at a decent hour."

The community watch group was made up of eight men, along with Michael, whom Audrey assigned to lead the meetings. She wanted someone she knew and thought she could trust to help keep an eye on how well people were sticking with the rules down on the street level. They weren't going to make arrests; they were mostly snitches, and everyone knew it. They did have a certain bit of vigilante immunity, though. Audrey had no problem letting them figure out ways to keep people in line, if it allowed her to keep her hands from getting too dirty.

For Michael, it was a way to continue to feel important in this new world order, and to have some semblance of control over what happened around him. Maybe he could make a difference. Or maybe he just liked having authority over people, illusory as it might be. Whatever it was, this was a role he relished, and he enjoyed having people know he held it.

"Andy, let's review what we talked about last time," he said.

Andy stood up and cleared his throat as he dug in his right jeans pocket. He came up empty and switched to the other pocket, finding a slip of paper inside.

"Hank suggested we find out from Leadership if we can get clearance to do some patrols in the area, so we can help monitor more closely what's going on. Benjamin wanted to set up some late-night patrols among the guys here for down by the lake, because we could be vulnerable to a water attack if there's somebody out there. And we talked about putting together a fishing group for Sunday mornings."

Michael nodded. "Good. Thanks, Andy. So, I guess those first two are on me to check. Nothing yet, but I'll keep running those up the flagpole to see if we can get any traction with it. As far as fishing goes, I'll never drag my ass up as early as some of you guys, so I'll leave that up to you. If anybody's interested in drinking beer at 5:30 in the morning, see Zac over there. Pretty sure he's your guy. He'd rather drink beer and clean fish than sleep."

Zac rolled his eyes, as some of the guys chuckled lightly. Michael stood up straight at the podium. "Okay, guys. I think that takes care of last week. Any new business? Hank?"

Hank lowered his right arm and stood up. "Thanks. So, I don't know if this is a big deal or not. Maybe it isn't, but I thought it was worth mentioning. The other day, I saw Trevor Kites out on his front lawn. It was pretty late at night, probably eleven or so. I mean, it was strange enough for anyone to even be outside at that time. Who just wanders around in their yard that late? I was only even up because I couldn't sleep. I've been having all sorts of issues lately. It sucks. It really does. Anyway, so I notice him standing there and peek out the window, right? And the guy's not wearing his ring. Just him out there in his boxers, practically naked to the world."

A couple of audible gasps came from the group. Michael stayed stoic, keeping his hands on the podium.

"You're sure about that?" Michael said. "It had to have been really dark."

"I swear to God, man. I mean, it was dark, sure. But these damn things are tough to miss." Hank patted his ring several times, sending a heavy metallic "clonk" bounding through the quiet air. "I could see plenty well enough to see he didn't have a ring on."

Michael paused, scratching the back of his head. He leaned hard against the podium.

"So what do we do?" Zac said, looking around at the rest of the group. "We can't just let him do this."

A chorus of "Yeah" echoed through the group of men, some of them pounding on their rings. Michael rested his chin against his right hand. He opened his mouth, then closed it again and turned his head to his right.

"We're not just letting this go, Michael," Benjamin said. "Any ideas?"

Michael looked sideways at Zac, and cocked his head in his direction.

"I just want us to be smart, okay?" Michael pulled back from the podium a step and stood straight up. "I recognize that we can't just look the other way. Let's just not be a mob. All right? Let's just a couple of us go over there and chat for a few minutes. Keep it friendly. Find out what he's thinkin'."

"This better not be your way of letting him get away with this shit," Zac said. "Because we all have to deal with this ring shit all the time. No fuckin' way is Trevor just taking the damn thing off and leaving it inside."

Several of the men clapped. Two stood and pointed angrily at Michael.

"Look, fellas…I get that you're angry." Michael put his hands up in front of himself, stepping back nervously from the group. "Nobody's getting away with anything. Okay? Is Trevor really the first person to maybe just forget? It's easy to forget what it was like before these contraptions, when you really *could* just walk outside whenever you wanted, practically naked. Maybe he was sleepwalking. Or maybe he thought it was okay since nobody was around. It was after eleven o'clock. Right, Hank?"

Hank's eyes shifted quickly left and right, then landed on Michael. He nodded slowly.

"There ya go, then," Michael said, shifting his gaze to Zac. "Lots of reasons not to fly off the handle quite yet. Hank, why don't you and I go pay Trevor a visit after this meeting? We'll figure out what was going on. How's that sound to you guys?"

The room was silent. Zac remained seated, his arms crossed tightly across his chest, meeting Michael's stare. Michael knew that the first man to speak in a situation like this was often the one who lost the room. He needed to be able to wait out the loud silence. *Maintain eye contact. Back straight. Shoulders rolled forward. Don't let him intimidate you*, he thought. *Just a few more seconds.*

Zac unfolded his arms and placed them on the ring in front of his body, leaning toward Michael.

"We'll do it your way—*once*," Zac held his index finger up at Michael. "You'll need an army bigger than whatever you've got to hold that line, though, if there's a second time."

5

With each patient step Nick took, he wanted to reach out and feel Rachel's cheek, her beside him on an evening stroll under a brilliant canopy of stars.

What does her skin feel like? What would it be like to have her fingers interlocking with mine? These sorts of simple connections were lost in Alessandra and, less than a year after the walls cut this colony of survivors off from whatever remained of the rest of the world, it was easy to forget what it was like to feel another person's touch. For Nick, it was the absence of the touch of a woman. And not even in a sexual way. That mattered, of course. What he wouldn't have given for a blowjob, or even a quick handie, but the idea of something as simple as running the back of his hand across the brim of her jawline, or nibbling on the nape of her neck, sent shivers down his spine.

That desire was part of what made us alive. Forget "human." It was one of the few drives that truly transcended humanity. No matter how many world-renowned paintings humans produced, or how many of our sonnets made others weep, or how many remarkable ways we came to understand and appreciate the vastness of the universe in which we lived, we still craved those physical connections—just like our chimpanzee cousins, like the gazelles on the plains and the frogs in the swamp. It was what drove our species more than any one behavior ever could. Nick took glances at Rachel as they walked and wondered if she was feeling the same way.

Nick turned his gaze skyward. "Beautiful night."

"Yeah. That's been one great thing about surviving through all this." She smiled and stopped walking, running a finger along her ring. "I never knew how amazing the sky could look at night until all the light was gone from on Earth. There are so many stars now."

"I know. It's incredible. It can make you think about how insignificant we all are. Not just me, or you. Everyone. Those stars are an impossible distance away. Thousands. Millions of light years, even. And yet, we see them as we stand here. They don't care about all the shit that's happened here, ya know? They couldn't be further removed from it all. But we connect with them all the same."

Rachel looked at Nick and paused for a second. "Right. And if there are more people left on the planet. If some city in China or India or Bangladesh made it through this and is thriving, but we have no way of knowing it, maybe another couple is standing outside looking up at the same stars and spouting a lot of this same clichéd bullshit that we are."

She tilted her head and smiled at Nick, then they both burst into laughter. Bent at the waist, Nick nodded, then straightened back up and looked at Rachel.

"You win. Would it be too clichéd if we sat down on the rim of the fountain over there?" He motioned toward the fountain.

"Seems a little romcom-ey, but I'll allow it."

Rachel spun gracefully and skipped toward the fountain, twenty feet away. She stopped quickly at the base, planting a foot and spinning, then flopping down on the concrete base. Nick had barely taken a step yet.

"What's taking you so long?" she yelled, cupping her hands around her mouth.

"I don't skip."

"Maybe you should start. Get movin'. I'm getting lonely."

Nick shook his head as he walked toward Rachel, sitting on the fountain's rim. She was leaning back slightly, her hands resting beside her. The fountain was more than a hundred years old, built to honor Alessandra's legendary mayor Al Richmond, who relentlessly sold the town to outside investors, bringing major dollars and business interests into Alessandra for the first time. He took Alessandra from being a sleepy mountain town into being, for a time, one of the state's most lucrative tourist towns. "The Gateway to the Appalachians," he liked to say. And the town went from nearly dead to rich in a whiplash-inducing amount of time.

The Richmond Fountain was a work of art, with waterfalls spraying in four directions, high into the night sky, flanking a trumpet-playing angel whose wings used to light up brilliantly and be seen from anywhere in the town. Today, the angel was dark, but Rachel was beaming, a broad smile below flowing water while Nick came steps closer to joining her at the fountain. The light from the Square around them threw her shadow behind her onto the flowing water, her silhouette seeming to climb into the fountain to play. He pictured them stripping down, carelessly letting their rings clang to the ground at their feet, and climbing into the water, splashing each other and making love as the stream rained down on them.

A few steps away, Nick could take it all in—her scarlet hair was fire upon her shoulders, flowing onto her back and engulfing the nape of her neck, a frame on the face that was a shining beacon beckoning him near—before he took his place beside her, settling down just outside the range of her ring. No one else was around. The world was theirs. At that moment, Nick might have considered the Earth opening up and swallowing him whole if it meant he'd get a chance to press her lips to his, just to know what she tasted like. If the elixir brought death, then he was ready for it.

He slid back onto the seat and rested his hands in his lap, turning to look at her, practically shaking. She swung her leg and spun toward him, meeting his gaze.

"Glad you could make it," she said, twirling some strands of hair around two fingers on her right hand. "I love this fountain. It's so beautiful and relaxing."

He turned and looked at the water rising into the air and splashing behind them, a never-ending cycle.

"Yeah, my mom used to bring me and my brother up here when we were little. Back then, they let kids splash around in there if they wanted, and we'd always go scrounging around for the change people tossed in. My mom never let us take it, though. She'd say, 'That's somebody else's wish, not yours. If you take the coin, the wish will never come true. How would you feel if somebody tried to steal your wish?'"

"Did you ever make your own wish?"

"I tossed a few in there," he said.

"Any luck?"

"Not even once."

"Why don't you give it another try?"

"Well, coins aren't exactly plentiful these days."

Rachel dug into the back pocket of her jeans and pulled out a penny, then pinched it between her index finger and thumb.

"Been saving this for something important."

"Is tonight important enough?"

"I think it qualifies." She held it in front of his face. "Make a wish, Nick."

She flipped the coin to him and he caught it, placing it in his right palm and closing his fist around it. He pressed his eyes together hard, his face tightening. After a few seconds of silence, he opened his eyes and tossed the penny into the water. It splashed softly and wobbled to the fountain floor.

"What'd you wish for?" she smiled.

He matched her smile, then closed his eyes and leaned toward her, trying to push past his ring and hers, feeling for her face. His heart was thunder in his chest, pounding with an incessant drumbeat. He was a virgin again, stealing a peek at his first pussy, peeling the panties slowly down until tufts of hair appeared, then the curve of thigh drawing his every desire. This kiss was going to be taking back something denied to him for so long, something he never thought he'd need to get back so much.

"Wait."

He heard, but it didn't register at first. He continued leaning forward, feeling desperately for contact, for that reciprocation he expected surely would come. But it didn't, and he heard it again.

"Wait! Hold on, Nick."

He opened his eyes, and she wasn't sitting there anymore. She had moved back several feet and was starting to stand, her hands up in front of her as if trying to push him the other way.

"I…I'm sorry. I just—"

"No. No, it's okay." She sat back down as he caught himself and straightened back up. "It's just not gonna happen tonight. Not here."

"But when? Where?"

"Look…We have to be careful. Okay? We've got to really *think* about this."

Nick was starting to wish the Earth really *would* swallow him whole now.

"I've thought about it plenty."

"Yeah. Well, I haven't. This isn't a makeout session in the back of your dad's Chevelle, Nick." Rachel ran her fingers across her scalp. "This is life and death. I *like* you. Hell, in a different world, we'd probably be fucking in the woods over there right now. But that's not the world we're in. And you know it as well as I do."

Nick sighed and rocked backward, throwing his head high in the air.

"What I know and what I'm willing to accept may be two different things."

"Hey…Hopefully our time will come. Let's just think about it a bit, okay?"

"Oh, I'll be thinking about it. You can bet that much."

Rachel smiled. "I'll see you in your dreams, then."

6

Audrey's sandy brown hair a tangled mess lying limp against her bare shoulder and back, she laid on her side, her right arm thrown across officer Danny's hairless chest. He smiled slightly as he ran his fingernails across her back.

She told herself she didn't have to feel guilty; this is what anyone would do in her position. They didn't have the time to test everyone in the town for the virus every day, but she could take the blood test—along with doctors, child care workers and anyone else who had to be in contact with people—as often as was needed to make sure she was clean. So could Danny. Or whoever else might catch her eye on any given day, for that matter. But Danny was the one she felt connected to, who she could see having a real relationship with if the town could ever move beyond this fear and isolation. Until then, though, she could make sure they were as safe as possible, and still blow off steam a bit from the stress of having to protect what might be the last people on Earth. Of course the people of Alessandra would like to do the same, but it wasn't practical. It was just too much to ask for each person to submit to testing as often as would be needed. A carrier could still be out there. Given the number of people in the town, in fact, it might even be likely.

Back before the walls went up, scientists figured the carriers lasted for a while. Eventually, though, the virus got them too. Eventually, it got everyone. But Audrey was going to keep her people alive as long as possible. And, if it was going to take her down in the end, she was going to be damned if she was going to spend the last months of her life—the last months of humanity

—in an isolated, sexless stupor. Not when she had a better option, anyway.

So, no. Lying here next to Danny, slowly rubbing his chest, with its curves and swells right where she liked them to be, didn't cause her guilt. It felt exactly right. She needed to be of sound mind to make the right decisions for the people of Alessandra, and this was essential in order to make sure that happened. Even if the people of the town found out, they'd surely understand that much.

"How'd it go with Theresa and Lucas?" Danny ran his fingers through Audrey's hair, massaging her scalp like he was kneading a lump of dough.

"Everything's fine." She closed her eyes and leaned her head into the motion of his fingers. "They're down with the others."

"That's good. Theresa's cool. I've known her for a while. When do you think all this stuff is gonna end?"

"What stuff?"

"The plague. All the worry. People wearing the rings, being quarantined for holding hands. All that. Are we ever gonna go back to being normal again?"

Audrey propped her elbow up on the bed and lifted her head, strands of hair falling across her face. She tucked them behind her right ear.

"Maybe this is just what 'normal' is now, if we want to survive, anyway. I don't know. I really don't. All I can do is push through from day to day, and I wake up every morning terrified *this* is the day someone in the town starts coughing and sneezing. Then, the fever. Then the suffering really begins. We still don't have anything approaching a cure, or a vaccine. Our only defense is a good offense, and I've got to do everything in my power to prevent this killer from breaching those walls out there. I feel that weight. I really do."

"So does it just go on…forever? Can we really keep stashing people away like this?"

Audrey paused and looked down.

"We've got good doctors and researchers working on it, trying to find out what they can. When they say the virus is dead, we won't have to do this anymore. If they tell me the virus doesn't spread through skin-to-skin contact, a lot can change. But so far, everything we know tells us it's probably still lurking out there, and touch is the chief way it spreads. As long as that's the case, I don't see much choice."

Audrey let herself fall onto her back, a smooth satin sheet covering her legs and resting across her stomach. Danny turned toward the nightstand and picked up a half-full glass of water. She bent her right arm onto the pillow and rested her head in her hand. The sun thrust bright rays of light through the window to their left, casting them through the trees outside like shards of glass shattered across the bed. In the summer, the trees would mostly blot out the morning sun in her room, but the leafless trees allowed the light to pass through, letting them feel a taste of February warmth.

"Mornings like this are nice, aren't they?" she said. "All I need now is a waiter with breakfast."

The door began to creak open, and Audrey bolted upright, not bothering to cover up her breasts, which bobbed upon her sitting up. Danny spilled water down his chin and onto the sheet.

A man's head peeked around the door frame and into the room, one hand still on the knob.

"Sorry to disturb you, Ms. Reese," the man said, before seeing she was topless with Danny, and spinning his head back toward the hallway. "But there's a man approaching the south wall. We need to know what to do."

"Is there just one?" Audrey asked as she met George Yates, her head of wall security, the two of them walking briskly toward the north wall, where the only gate was set up. George had been Mayor Handy's chief of security before the world turned to chaos, so he'd been one of the first men Audrey trusted to fill an important role in the new version of Alessandra. Danny was in charge of the police force inside the walls, but George dealt with any issues that arose outside them.

He took to the job immediately, organizing first the building of the wall, raiding concrete, rebar, and other materials from some of the town's abandoned buildings to put together enough material for 2.5 miles worth of a wall that was six feet high and two feet thick. Then he set up an around-the-clock watch team, along with protocols for when a threat approached. They hadn't seen many other people, but they always figured their setup along the water would put them in a prime position for any straggling survivors that were wandering around. And their structured society with sufficient food and water would make them a target for people who might want what they had. The people within those walls might be struggling with Audrey's isolationist mandates and strong-armed approach to enforcing them. But the nomads beyond the walls who were fighting just to live from one day to the next would wear whatever heavy steel adornment they had to in order to go back to a more comfortable existence that didn't involve picking at dead, fly-ridden carcasses for food, and drinking brown water that reeked of raw sewage to stave off dehydration.

So, George knew they were at risk whenever any desperate-looking tribe approached their perimeter, and he was going to make sure they were ready to deal with it.

"As best as I can tell, it's just one guy," he said. "He looks fairly strong from a distance. He looks like he's carrying something that could be a weapon, and he's walking at a decent pace."

"Okay, good. How long until he actually reaches the wall?"

"At this point? Less than ten minutes."

"Let's not let him get much closer." Audrey grabbed the ladder and pulled herself up as she reached the wall. "Do we think he can hear us yet from the bullhorn?"

George climbed up below her, and crawled into place beside her on top of the wall. "He can hear us, but it'll be a little bit of a one-way conversation at this point."

"I'm okay with that." Audrey put her right hand out toward the wall guard beside her, and he handed her the bullhorn.

"Whoever you are, we see you coming, and we're prepared to defend ourselves!"

Her voice boomed through the bullhorn and echoed through the barren trees that littered the landscape in front of her. She knew everyone in the town would have heard her, and it would draw attention. But there was little way around that. This was a problem that needed to be dealt with immediately.

"Is he stopping?" she asked. "I can't tell much from here. He's too far away still."

George pulled up the binoculars that were around his neck.

"If he stopped, it wasn't for long. He's moving directly for us."

"Shit." Audrey held the bullhorn just below her chin, debating what to say next. "How far out is he now?"

"Less than five minutes, I'd say." George brought down the binoculars. "Look out there. You can probably see him yourself now."

The man emerged from the trees less than a half-mile away, and it was clear that life fending for himself hadn't been kind. Audrey imagined he'd once had a normal job. Maybe he worked on a construction site, making a solid middle-class wage; he had a wife and a couple of kids. Maybe a Cavalier King Charles named Skip. Then, one day, the world basically blew up around him, and here he was, in a position he never would have expected—tired, dirty and beaten down, trudging weakly but steadily toward a small town, hoping for a second chance.

Audrey's heart went out to him. She had a complicated relationship with God, but "There but for the grace of God go I" came to mind in moments like this one. It wouldn't have taken much for her to end up in much the same position as him. But she'd had some political luck in what happened to be the right small town to keep her just isolated enough to make it this far. Whatever problems they had in Alessandra, she tried to never lose sight of how lucky they were, and she tried to make the people of the town feel the same. And if this man making his way toward their walls had the virus that had ravaged the world, she had a responsibility to make sure he never saw the other side of Alessandra's walls.

7

Michael stepped softly onto Trevor's porch, Hank close behind him. It was dusk, and crickets chirped their Southern melody in the background. Michael wore a black peacoat he'd purchased six years before at a military surplus store. Its stiff collar could be propped up against his neck on particularly cold winter days like they often had in these months. The coat was warm, sturdy, and hid its age about as well as any clothing item he had. Given the turn society had eventually taken, he considered it one of the most astute buys of his life.

He cast a glance at Hank, to his left.

"Why don't you step up front here and knock? You know Trevor better than I do."

"Sure."

Hank stepped around Michael, and stood between him and the front door. He brought his hand up, paused and spun his head around toward Michael. "Do you know Trevor at all, by the way?"

"In passing. We're not exactly childhood sweethearts or anything."

Hank looked up at the grey-purple sky and blew a fog of breath into the air.

"Something I should know?" Michael said.

Hank lowered his eyes back toward the door. "That's what I'm trying to figure out."

He paused another couple of seconds, then pounded the door three times with his fist. Then he turned his head back over his shoulder to look at Michael and smiled.

"You'll see."

Michael wasn't sure what to make of that, but there wasn't any time to do psychological mapping on this guy. He just hoped there wasn't going to be much drama here. There didn't have to be. Michael preferred they have a brief chat, Trevor acknowledges he was just blowing off some steam, he won't do it again, and everybody could move along. Since it was so late at night, there was virtually no chance he caused any real problems, so they could likely leave it at that. The key was not to make Trevor feel like he was cornered. That was why Michael wanted Hank with him—and, more importantly, *didn't* want Zac there. Hank was the neighbor, and was a familiar face. Hopefully, that would put Trevor at ease. The last thing Michael wanted was to march the cavalry up there to talk with a man who was doing something crazy out in front of his house for the world to see. Hopefully, it was a momentary lapse in judgment. But Michael really didn't know this guy. Who knew what else he might be doing behind closed doors?

Waiting fifteen seconds after Hank knocked, there was no sign of anyone coming to the door.

"Maybe he's not home," Hank said.

"It's possible. Let's try him one more time."

Hank raised his arm to knock. As his hand rocked forward, the door flew open; Hank almost fell forward into the house. Trevor stood, holding the doorknob and smiling widely at them. His eyes were the kind of deep sky blue you felt like you could tumble into and keep falling, big and welcoming. His sandy brown hair was slicked back in a careful pompadour, a striking look in a post-apocalyptic world where most people were doing well to own a hairbrush. He wore a slim-cut button-down shirt under a midnight grey sport jacket that looked tailored, and a dark-washed pair of jeans with a pair of thick-soled burgundy Red Wing boots. No ring either, because it wasn't required when you were in your own house. Michael quickly scanned him; when his eyes returned to Trevor's face, he was still smiling. And those eyes.

"Trevor, this is Michael." Hank gestured a thumb over his right shoulder. "I'm sure you guys have met at some point."

"Absolutely!" Trevor said, stepping forward into the door opening. "A pleasure to see you again, Michael. I hope everything is well with you."

"Getting by day to day," Michael said. "Thanks for asking."

The three of them looked at each other for a few seconds.

"So, to what do I owe the pleasure of your visit, gentlemen?"

Hank glanced back over his shoulder at Michael, then turned back to the door.

"Just wanted to have a quick chat. Do you mind if we come in?"

Trevor's eyes widened, and he looked back into the house behind him. "I…didn't think we were supposed to—"

"It's fine, Trevor. We're with the Watch," Michael said. "We're authorized."

"You'll just have to put on your ring, of course." Hank nodded toward Trevor's waist.

Trevor looked down. "Oh! Yes. Of course. Give me…just a moment."

He closed the door but left just a crack open. Michael and Hank stood on the porch, crossing their arms to help shield themselves against the gathering winter breeze. Bulbous grey clouds were amassing above like soldiers gathering for battle, coalescing into a dark gray mass.

"Snow might be comin'," Hank said.

Michael looked up, straining his neck against the collar of his coat. "Sky's getting ready for something. Whatever it is, it ain't gonna be fun, and it's moving in quick."

The door swung back open wide, and their heads swiveled toward it.

"Okay, guys! Come on in," said Trevor, his ring now strapped to his sides. "But please excuse the mess. Have to admit, I wasn't expecting company. Follow me."

Both of them slipped off their rings and carried them at their sides as they stepped through the doorway. Michael came in behind Hank, and they both strapped their rings back on after Trevor closed the door behind them. Hank and Michael followed Trevor through the living room toward the back of the house. Out of the corner of his eye, behind them, Michael saw a sparse room with ivory-colored walls countered with odd splashes of color—greens and yellows and blues and reds. He couldn't immediately pick up any pattern to them; perhaps they were just a form of expressionistic art. Michael stopped and turned while Hank and Trevor stepped silently ahead.

Almost as if transfixed, he walked back toward the colorful room, looking at the color swatches—a swipe of a brush here, a spray of a can there—and wondered what Trevor was expressing. It was chaotic, almost to the point of madness. This post-virus world wasn't one particularly full of bright colors, literally or figuratively. The colors people had in their clothes had faded with time, and makeup wasn't common even for women when surviving from day to day was the priority. Color had largely descended into the background, with no reason for its existence. The only time bright colors entered their lives was in the fall, when the trees of North Georgia would burn brilliant with reds and yellows, so bright against the gray backdrop it was like a cartoon being drawn into their real-life world.

As he walked closer, he turned the corner into the room and saw a wall at the far end that had been out of his field of vision. On it, there was a corkboard with dozens of photos of people tacked up, enough for them to crowd each other off the board itself. He squinted to see who was in the photos, and could quickly identify the ones with faces—they were people who lived in Alessandra, people Michael knew. Many didn't show faces at all, though. Several appeared to be taken from very close behind what appeared to be women, in shots that probably would have been up their skirts if women wore short skirts anymore. Others were just of women's breasts, or at least the shape their breasts made beneath their clothing, with the faces cut off. Skinny women, larger women. Michael thought he might recognize some of them, but it wasn't easy to say when you were just looking at their chest.

He reached the board and lifted up the corner of a photo to see the one underneath it. He could tell there were several layers of these, at least five or six before you reached the board itself. It looked as if they had been haphazardly re-arranged. As he dug further down, the images evolved from mildly creepy to pornographic. Getting closer to the surface of the corkboard, there were pictures of women stepping from a bath, the curve of their ass straddling the rim of the tub as they dripped into the floor. He saw women changing clothes, pulling bloomers up over the swell of their bare calves, their breasts hanging limp as they bent to step into the underwear. He saw women touching themselves, their eyes closed, their mouths frozen wide, hands sliding between their spread thighs.

Michael knew these women. There was Ellen, who helped organize the farmers market, and knew exactly when okra would be perfect for frying. And Rebecca, his neighbor from three doors down who was obsessed with keeping her hedges neatly trimmed. Said it was her connection to another time, before their world was ripped apart. Even a shot or two of Nick's girl Rachel, her breasts peeking out from beneath an open nightgown as she stretched to pull something down from a kitchen cabinet, her dark red hair curling off the swell of her shoulders.

But his mouth fell open when he saw Stephanie, his ex-wife who he'd purposefully avoided since everyone gathered in Alessandra. Sweat beaded on his forehead, staring at the photo of her, naked from the waist up, her head turned to the right, hair matted to her forehead, muscles rippling with tension. It was a look of pleasure both familiar and foreign, one he hadn't seen since their divorce three years earlier. Her back was arched, sucking her breasts back against her body, her ribcage pushing out from her midsection. Michael examined her shape, still familiar after these years.

He wanted to reach out and touch her, but he knew he couldn't. That bridge was burned. The memory still seared, his indifference even in marriage, pushing her away, taking for granted that giving her a ring meant she belonged to him. He hadn't been mature enough to handle the rigors of marriage, of living with and sleeping with the same woman every day. He didn't cheat on her—if he was honest, it'd been because the opportunity never presented itself in Alessandra with any woman who he didn't think was too ugly or too crazy for him to justify— but what he'd done was maybe even worse. He'd done nothing to show he cared once they were married, nothing to show she was important to him, that she really mattered as more than just a trophy. He regretted it now. If he could go back and change it, he would. It was funny how facing a near-extinction of your species forced a certain bit of perspective into your life, and you realized how much you didn't appreciate about the world around you, and about how fortunate you were to have people in your life who loved you. He touched the photo and remembered what her skin felt like, milky to the touch, smooth and supple. She was there in front of him again, begging for him to take her, to connect with her.

A hand landed hard on his shoulder, pulling him backward; his stomach dropped, electricity like needle pricks in his chest. He jerked his head around, his eyes dancing wildly.

Trevor was standing behind him, a wide smile across his face. "Find anything you like?"

8

Walt wiped down the bar with a rag that used to be white, while Nick nursed his fourth beer of the night. Walt's had been a local fixture since the 1940s, and it was one of the first places that re-opened after supplies from the outside dried up and Alessandra had to start producing everything on their own. It may take a bit of time to set up agricultural supply lines to local farmers who have to figure out life without just heading down to the feed store, but there are people brewing up beer and moonshine in every little town in this country. Walt knew them all in North Georgia—hell, he *was* one of them. Plus, Jack Daniels has a shelf life of pretty much infinity.

So, with Rachel still doing laps in his head, there was no question in Nick's mind where he needed to be. Sitting at home was only going to make the questions run in a loop. What could he do here? Did he have the strength to pull back? Did she? If he couldn't find the answers at the suds-filled bottom of a glass, maybe Walt would have some advice.

"You young'uns have it rough today," Walt said, as he swirled the gnarly rag around the rim of a glass. "I was born in nineteen thirty-eight. I've had enough pussy for two lifetimes. I've lived, and then some. If that devil's plague comes and grabs me tomorrow, I say fuck it."

"Yeah, well, I'm starting to wonder if that's the right attitude myself."

Walt put down the glass. "Eh, don't act like you're an old coot like me. I've seen some shit. Been around the world. Had me three gorgeous young brides—"

"Me too," Nick interrupted.

Walt looked around the bar, pausing a few seconds. "You're what, Nick? Thirty? Thirty-one?"

"Thirty-six."

"Thirty-six…You know what I was doin' at thirty-six?"

"Besides running this shitty bar in this shitty town?"

"Hey…This shitty bar's the only bar you got left, so don't be shootin' it down. And my brother was runnin' this place then. Ya know where I was at thirty-six? Viet fucking Nam, that's where. I've been in the jungle. I've crawled through muddy troughs and bogs that stink of shit and death. I've killed children running toward me across an open field, and I've fucked women on four continents. What have you done?"

Nick slammed his glass down on the bar. It sloshed around, spilling a bit over the edge onto his hand.

"I've *lived*. You don't have to go to some third-world country to be an expert on life."

"No, ya don't. And I don't know what the answer is for ya here. But from where I stand, I see a guy who's been comin' to this bar for fi'teen years, sitting in that same damn barstool, and now you're *really* stuck there. You're walled in now. They're tellin' you how to live, what to wear. They're even telling you who you can fuck. Or, more to the point, who you *can't* fuck. Which is everyone. You've played it safe your whole life. Probably never left Alessandra except for a weekend at the fucking beach.

"Now, look at these goddamn rings they've got people strappin' to themselves," Walt pointed over the bar at Nick; an exemption had been carved out in the law for Walt to not wear his as long as he was behind the bar. "I'm eighty-three years old. I can't fight this anymore. I'm not that guy full of piss and vinegar, marchin' off to Nam like I was gonna save the world. Like I was some invincible superhero. I know now I could have died. I know I didn't have no S on my chest. But back then, the world was mine. Nobody was gonna tell me what to do, and nobody was gonna tell me I had to sit at home and do nothin' while my brothers were dyin' in some god-forsaken mud pit.

"But you're sittin' here whinin' about what to do when an attractive woman wants you? *That's* your war? *That's* your Nam? I ain't had a woman look at me like she wants me in twenty years. Some days, I wonder why I'm here at all. There's a reason, though. That much, I'm sure of. Go figure out yours. Maybe it's her. You gonna let that slip by?"

Walt pounded an open hand on the bar and walked toward the end by the door, where another regular had just sat down. Nick stared ahead, his mind racing. Walt had hammered home to Nick his dilemma—he was scared as hell to do anything physical with Rachel, and he was scared as hell not to. It seemed clear most everyone in the town had decided it just wasn't worth it. The potential consequences of just touching—forget about sex —were so great, whether they came from a ravenous plague destroying their town, or from the town's enforcement teams snatching you away into whatever purgatory they had set up for people who violated the code.

Could one fling possibly be worth all that risk? He didn't see how it could be. Still, the feeling in his gut was unshakeable. How could a desire this strong not be right? Why would any god worth believing in put this sort of temptation in his heart, if it was so wrong to act on it? He didn't know the answers. Even more than that, he certainly didn't know if Rachel knew them, and he had no idea if she was doing anything other than being a flirt before. The opportunity would be there to find out, though.

Nick got up from his stool and threw his glass against the concrete floor, sending glass shrapnel in every direction. Walt and the other man at the bar jerked their heads in his direction, Walt staring with a furrowed brow.

"Sorry, Walt. Slipped."

Nick walked across the bar and out the door into the cool evening air.

9

Walking within 100 feet of the outside of Alessandra's gates, the man trudged a bit slower, maintaining his gaze on the waist-high grass in front of him.

"He's not stopping," George whispered, leaning his head toward Audrey. "What do you want to do?"

Audrey looked up and grimaced against the purple-hued, sun-setting sky.

"Audrey?"

"Yeah, George. I know. We'll figure something out," she said. "It's one guy, and he looks tired even if he may be strong. I don't think he came here to start shit with us. I'll talk to him."

At about fifty feet away, the man stopped and raised his head. He cupped his hands around his mouth and looked at Audrey on top of the fence.

"Hello! I don't mean you any harm," the man spoke loudly with a voice that sounded strained and dry. "I could use some food, medicine and fresh water. Can I enter?"

Audrey hung her head, then looked back up at the man.

"Did you not hear when I addressed you a few minutes ago?"

He looked at the ground in front of him, then back up. "I heard. But I thought you'd have sympathy once we spoke."

"My only sympathy is with the people of this town. You see what's here in front of you? There's a reason you want in here. You want a piece of what we have. You want to bring another mouth to feed, another person to house. You have to know I can't let just anyone in here, particularly when you could be infected."

The man shook his head. "If I were infected, wouldn't I have been dead a long time ago?"

"There's reason to think some people are carriers. Basically time bombs for the virus. We're surviving by keeping this population clean as long as we can."

The man blinked and took a deep breath, sweat dripping from his forehead despite the chilly evening. "Is there *anything* you can do for me? I'm not gonna make it long out here at this point. I've got a cut on my leg that'll probably get infected, and I haven't eaten in…four or five days. I've lost track, to be honest."

Audrey felt a tap on her shoulder, swung around and saw Paul standing behind her.

"What are you doing here?" she said.

"Half the fucking town can hear you. I'm making sure you know that."

"Fine. I know. Anything else?"

"Let me go out and talk to the guy."

Audrey raised her eyebrows and cocked her head to the left. "*Go out?*"

"Yeah. Seriously. Do you really want to have this conversation with him while everybody in the town listens? Let me go talk to him. I've got some water to take with me as a goodwill gesture."

"Well…But what are you gonna tell him?"

"I just want to figure out where he's coming from. What does he need? What can we do for him? I think we both know we're not gonna let him come live here or anything. Right?"

Audrey nodded. "Right. Yeah."

"Okay, then. We're on the same page. So just let me go talk to him and get the lay of the land."

Audrey put her right hand on her head and craned her neck to look back at the man, still standing in the dormant grass, looking up at her in the dimming evening light.

"Sure," she said, still facing the man.

Paul turned and climbed onto the ladder to get back down to the ground.

Turning back around, Audrey looked down the ladder. "And, Paul…Don't do anything stupid. Okay?"

Paul stopped climbing and looked back up. "You can trust me, sis. Be back in a few minutes."

Audrey turned back in the direction of the man; she noticed it was getting harder to see him. She couldn't make out as many features as she could earlier. She guessed he was maybe six foot two, thin but not frail, considering what he'd probably been through to get there. His hair was long, falling in sickly strands across his shoulder blades like bristles from a broom. He was hunched over a bit, and he had a small brown knapsack that likely held whatever possessions he had left.

In the fading light, though, all she could see was the outline of a man, huddled against the cold, leaning against a massive, twisting oak tree outside their little kingdom. It never failed to surprise her when someone would occasionally wander up to the walls. It was a reminder that they weren't the only ones left in the world, and that they had it pretty good, imperfect as the circumstances might be.

She also worried what would become of this man, along with the handful of others that had been turned away at their gates. She knew it had to be a harsh world out there beyond Alessandra's walls, but she had no idea how harsh it really was. None of the people who lived there had ever had to fend for themselves as nomads in an indifferent, cruel world. They'd been protected by the walls, by their own isolation as a community, and that was what Audrey was sure was going to continue to keep them safe.

Audrey heard the gate creak open beneath her, and Paul walked out, carrying a blazing wooden torch and a jug of water. The fire from the torch sent waves of light fluttering into the sky

around him, dissipating in the night air as it carried its way closer
to Audrey. She remained enveloped in an increasingly dark night,
while Paul carried the light with him, making his way to the
huddled mass of a man who stood before him.

As Paul reached the man, he laid the torch down in a dirt
patch beside him, letting the darkness blanket them both. Audrey
couldn't see much. Paul's back was to her, and she could see his
head moving in a way that suggested he was talking. She could
only pick up the faintest of noises from the two of them; she
leaned forward, trying to turn toward them with her better left
ear to make out any words. Nothing. Just the distant sound of
voices in the dark.

She wondered if she should have gone out there with him.
But the fact was, the idea terrified her. She hadn't stepped foot
outside the walls since they were built, and she couldn't stand the
thought of doing so. It was as if the walls formed not just a
physical, but emotional barrier for her, and likely did the same for
many others in the town. It was a separation, both literal and
figurative. It separated the sick from the well, the before from the
after. Walking to the other side of it stripped you of that
protection. She had been burned by the outside world once, and
she wasn't going to let it happen again. She was happy within
these walls, and she didn't want anything to do with those who
might puncture that safety and contentedness.

Even seeing her brother walk outside the walls made her
squirm. What if something happened to him out there? What if
this were a trap? Could this guy have others, and he was luring
Paul into an ambush? Audrey struggled with Paul sometimes, but
she didn't know what she'd do without him. He was the person
she trusted most. Even if he didn't always do what she expected,
she knew that—in the end—he did what he thought was best,
and he loved her. Most people in the world didn't have that
anymore. Parents had lost children, husbands had lost wives,

sisters had lost brothers. In a worldwide plague, no one is spared. For some, it had turned them more toward God, searching for answers in a world that had turned into nothing but questions. But for Audrey, it had only made her question her faith more—if there were a god, he was either testing or punishing them. Either way, that wasn't a god she felt was worthy of unquestioned worship. That didn't mean she didn't try, though.

Glancing back down toward Paul, it looked to Audrey like they were still talking, and she was worried. Why was this taking so long? She wanted Paul back behind the walls, back where everything made sense. Not out *there*, exposed to whatever elements had destroyed the world as they knew it.

Then she saw a glint of something shiny there, picked up by the light from the crescent moon. It was near Paul and the man. She had no idea what it was, but she saw the glint of light again. At this point, she couldn't even make out the silhouettes of the two men. She scanned for the shiny object again, but couldn't spot it. Had it moved? She wasn't sure.

She stayed still and listened closely. She heard what sounded like a long, guttural groan from one of the men, and then footsteps pounding the ground rapidly, headed her way.

The gate swung toward him, its rusty hinge wailing, and Paul stepped out from behind the gate. This was the first time he'd left Alessandra's walls in close to a year, and it was an odd experience. Standing inside the fortress city, he never gave that much thought to how much peace of mind that protection gave him, but he now felt exposed. The slight breeze even felt colder to him, perhaps freed by the open world around him instead of being buffeted by the walls. It was the chill of a lake wind, funneled between trees and gorged on the winter air. It prompted Paul to cinch his coat nearer his body, and hold the warmth of the torch's fire a little lower toward his face as he walked.

The man who had approached was standing ahead, leaning against a large tree. His image became a bit clearer as Paul got closer, with the dark seeming to accelerate beneath the tree cover. Paul still wasn't sure what exactly he was going to do with the man. One thing was for certain—he wasn't getting any closer to Alessandra than he already was. *Audrey never should have let him get this far*, he thought. *This isn't a risk worth taking*. But, the way Paul saw it, everything beyond that was up to the man. Paul was open to having a short conversation and sending him on his way.

Walking within a few feet of the man, Paul switched the torch to his left hand and extended his right toward him.

"Good to meet you." Paul stopped a few feet in front of the man. "Paul. What's your name? Where you from?"

"Frank. Came up here from down Atlanta ways. Had a small group for a bit. Wife and daughter died from the illness. Just tryin' to make it from day to day now."

Standing close to Frank, Paul noticed the stark contrast between how the two of them were living. Paul had a wool topcoat with a pop-up collar to help protect his neck from the harsh winds, a pair of Levi's jeans that was worn through the back pockets but had served him well for nearly ten years, a knit ski cap, and a pair of burgundy Wolverine boots that would probably outlive the cockroaches. The man he gazed upon barely had enough rags to cover his body, with a plaid work shirt riddled with scratches and holes, some cargo pants in tatters below the knees, and a pair of basketball shoes with the toes nearly rotted away to the point of being tissue paper. There was dirt caked in random patterns across his cheeks, criss-crossing like tributaries off a large river, and it lurked under his fingernails, black and uninviting. And the smell, like being downwind of a speeding garbage truck on a sticky summer morning, invaded his nose and swamped his head, nearly sending him staggering. He laid down the torch.

"So, tell me, Frank, what are you doing here?"

"Well, like I told the woman there, I just really need some water. Maybe some food and medicine. I'd love to come inside."

"Water I've got," Paul said, handing the jug over to Frank, who snatched it with both hands, tore off the lid and ravenously poured it down his throat, splashing drops down his chin. "But you want to come *inside*? Inside *the walls*?"

Paul laughed, smiled, and licked his upper teeth. "You think you can just waltz into the world we created? Look around you. Civilization is a dust pile. But we survived. And we're going to keep surviving. We don't do that by throwing open our doors to every random homeless guy who begs for sympathy."

Frank lowered the jug and set it on the ground at his feet. "I'm not a charity case, though. I know I'd have to pull my weight. I'm pretty good with my hands, I know a little about electricity and plumbing. I could help you beef up a lot about this town."

"What do *you* know about our town?"

Frank looked back over Paul's shoulder, at the walls of Alessandra.

"Well…Not much. I just felt like I owed it to m'self to check it out."

"Fair enough. Just know this: Right here is as far as you get."

Frank nodded, grimacing a bit, then rubbed his chin.

"Yeah, I figured as much. What about the supplies? Could you at least look those up for me? I'd appreciate it."

Paul glanced back over his shoulder at the town, and turned back to Frank.

"It's possible," Paul shrugged. "What can you do for us?"

"What can I *do*? From out here?"

"Yeah. Do you have something to trade? Maybe you can dance and entertain us. Know any good jokes?"

Frank cocked his head to the left and looked at the ground.

"Well, I…I don't know any jokes. And I've got nothin' to spare. It's cold, man. I'm out here on my own. Can't you help me out some? Don't you care *a little?*"

Paul straightened his back and looked at Frank, his mouth flat, his eyes steely.

"Does this look like a world that *cares?* Seriously, look around you. Does this world look like it gives a half a damn about you being cold, or hungry, or lonely? Do those trees look like they have sympathy for you?"

Frank cleared his throat, and rubbed the back of his neck.

"I…think God will find—"

"*God?*" Paul interrupted. "After all this carnage that's happened, and where you're standing right now, you still think *God* is going to help you?"

"He helped me find you. And that's why I know you'll help me. Because you're good people. That's why God led me here. That's why I've walked all this way. That's why my feet are bleeding, and my skin is like sandpaper. I could hear His voice, leading me in this direction. And, when I saw the walls of your town rising on the horizon ahead of me, I knew it was a sign, a gift from God. He brought me all the way here, and now all you need to do is bring me the last few steps."

Paul licked his lips and crossed his arms, guarding himself against the growing chill in the air.

"There are people in our town back there who think like you," Paul nodded back over his shoulder. "Lots of 'em, actually. They think this is a test of their faith, that believing in something bigger is part of what keeps 'em going. And, frankly, I'm sympathetic to that. I get it. In a world that spiraled out of our control in a big damn hurry, it's tempting to think someone who's smarter, more generous, more powerful than us is still in control, and has our best interests at heart. That there's a plan to all of this."

Paul took two steps toward Frank, and stood with his ring pressed against his midsection, Paul's chin thrust forward.

"But I'm standing here in front of you to tell ya it's all bullshit. *All* of it. This is not a world that's planned. There's no good that's coming from this. Nobody's in charge. We live in a pitiless universe, and we wait for help to rain down from the sky at our fucking peril. There probably *is* no god. And, if there is, he gave up on us a long time ago. This is no test; it's just the world we live in. Shit happens. Deal with it. Take care of you and your own. Survive. Live to see another day and—if you're lucky—another one after that. Call it tribalism. Call it amoral. But when it comes to the people of that town behind me—my family—there's nothing I won't do to keep them safe. No code I won't break. No amount of sympathy great enough. So whatever it was that led you here, I'm sorry it did."

Paul yanked a bowie knife from the back waistband of his pants and jabbed it hard into the man's stomach with his right hand, then pulled it back out and stabbed him once more. The man bent forward, wailing loudly from the pain. Paul put his left hand on the man's back and used it to help him slowly fall to the ground, blood quickly soaking through his shirt and rushing between his fingers.

Paul stuck the knife back in his waistband and ran toward the gate.

10

"I…I'm not sure," Michael stuttered, with Trevor smiling widely, still holding his hand on Michael's shoulder.

It had been so long since Michael had felt anyone touch him. He hadn't anticipated the next time would be from the calloused hand of some guy who might be insane. His eyes glanced warily at Trevor's hand.

"Oh! Yes, I'm sorry," Trevor pulled his hand away and took a step backward. "I wasn't thinking. We're not supposed to touch, right? It's just been so long since anyone has been in my home. Michael, was it?"

Michael stood stock still, except for his eyes, dancing around and searching for any sign of Hank.

"That's, um, right." Michael could feel sweat beading on his forehead, and his heart thumped in his chest. "Um, where's Hank?"

Trevor's smile seemed to get even wider. His eyes said nothing. They were hollow, vacuous, and *so deep*. Michael thought it was like staring into a blue void that he was spiraling into.

"Hank?" Trevor's back straightened. "He's just sitting back in the living room, waiting on us. I thought we were gonna chat. Come on. I already feel rude, leaving a guest alone out there. I lost you once; I don't want to lose Hank too. Let's go."

Trevor turned to the side and started to walk back toward the hallway, motioning with his right hand for Michael to follow. But Michael stayed still, trying hard to listen. *Is Hank really there? How long was I staring at those crazy pictures?* He wanted to hear *something* to confirm it was safe. With someone who was capable of taking those photos and posting them proudly in his home, who knew what he was capable of doing? All Michael knew for sure was Trevor was creeping him out, and he wanted out of that house.

"I…" Michael exhaled loudly. "I think the talk can wait."

Trevor paused, put his hand down at his side and raised his head to look Michael in the eyes. The smile slowly faded from his face, morphing into something rounder, more quizzical. He bit his lip and dug uncomfortably with his teeth. Michael winced watching him, biting down hard, grinding his upper teeth into his lip until the skin burst and blood trickled down his chin in two little streams. It slowly crawled through Trevor's stubble, worming its way toward the end of his chin before dripping molasses-like to the floor below. Michael turned away, squeezing his eyes shut against what he saw.

Trevor lifted his teeth apart and pulled them back into his mouth, blood still flowing from two half-circle wounds in front of his bottom lip. He didn't wipe the blood before speaking, then broke into a wide smile once again.

"Why don't you want to talk anymore?" Trevor asked and took two steps toward Michael, lines of blood still trickling from Trevor's bottom lip. "I was looking forward to it."

Michael's body tensed up, and he instinctively moved back toward the wall with the pictures, trying to keep space between him and Trevor. With the ring on, he'd only be able to get so close to the wall, though. He didn't ever want to feel that hand again. Trevor took two more steps closer.

"Hank!" Michael yelled, cupping his hands around his mouth. "Hank, are you there?"

Trevor immediately stopped, his smile fading then returning quickly once again. There were footsteps in the hallway; Hank stepped into the room, ten feet behind Trevor.

"Yeah, man. I'm here," Hank said. "Where else would I be? What are you guys doing?"

Trevor continued looking at Michael, grinning and seeming to stare through to the wall behind him.

"We're, um, gonna go ahead and go," Michael said, stepping sideways to his left and giving Trevor a wide berth.

"Go?" Hank said. "We're supposed to talk to Trevor."

"I think we've talked enough." Michael began moving fast toward the hallway and the front door. "Let's get out of here."

Hank was confused, but he shrugged; they both quickly stepped out of their rings, and Hank walked out behind Michael. Trevor never turned around.

"What the hell was that?" Hank said, as he caught up to Michael on the sidewalk, walking crisply away from the house.

"That was getting the fuck out of that place," Michael said. "That's what that was."

Hank looked around. "Why? What happened?"

"Is he following us?"

"*Following* us?" Hank glanced back over his shoulder. No one was there. "Why would he be doing that?"

Michael ran his left hand through his hair. "I don't know. The guy. That whole place. It was weirding me out. Did you see those pictures on the wall?"

"What pictures? The ones that were behind you when I came over to you guys? I couldn't really see them."

"He had dozens of pictures of women from Alessandra naked," Michael said, still walking fast away from the house without looking back. "He's apparently been stalking them. The dude's fucked up."

"Shit. But, I mean, what should we do?"

Michael abruptly stopped walking and turned to Hank.

"I don't know! I really, really don't. I was just expecting to feel the guy out on why he wasn't wearing his ring, not find a collection of Peeping Tom skin pics all over the wall of his house. And that smile he gave me. I swear, I thought the guy was gonna tie me up and shove me in his basement or something."

Hank rolled his eyes. "Oh, come on, Michael. The guy's harmless. A little horny, maybe. But he's not—"

"No!" Michael interrupted, pointing at Hank's chest. "You are not excusing this shit. This is *not* okay. I don't care if he's your neighbor. I don't care if he's your fucking *brother.* I control this neighborhood, and I'm not dismissing this as, 'Oh, he just misses his Pornhub fix.' That's *bullshit*, man! And you know it."

Michael began walking again, his back hunched forward. Hank followed just behind.

"Look, I'm not excusing it. But it's just a few pictures. Nobody's gonna see them. We wouldn't even know they were there if we hadn't gone in his house. And we could have taken them down if you hadn't had to rush out of there so damn fast."

Michael stopped again and swung around. "What'd you say?"

"You're the one who wanted to leave, man," Hank said, his face unmoving, looking into Michael's eyes. "If this was so bad, why didn't we confront him about it? What are you scared of?"

"Fucking *Trevor's* what I was scared of. And you should be too."

"Why? I've known him for years. He's a friend of mine. He's always seemed like a decent guy to me. A little unusual at times, maybe. Might like to get off, assuming those pictures were even there, but—"

"Are you suggesting I'm making this shit up about the pictures?" Michael's eyes narrowed.

"Hey, I'm just saying I didn't see 'em. All right? And I'm saying it's weird that you're so scared of that skinny blonde dude back there who's never hurt a fly. He likes to get his rocks off. Who doesn't? It's not like we've got a lot of options for that in this godforsaken town. But you need to fucking *relax*."

Michael shook his head and looked at the ground at his feet. Then he snapped his head back up at Hank.

"The *hell* I do. You didn't see what I saw. Maybe you're covering for the guy. I don't know. But I'm getting the group together and telling them. You want to tell your side of it? Fine. Do it. We'll see what *they* wanna do."

"So, mob rule? That's your solution?"

"This is what I've been trusted with, okay? This is my turf. Audrey put me in this position for a reason. *She* trusts me to keep an eye and a goddamn lid on everything that's happening here. Got that?"

Hank said nothing, pursing his lips tightly.

"And I'm not gonna let some creep and his butt-buddy neighbor put my reputation on the line. We'll take care of it. You want to die on this hill? Go right the *fuck* ahead. But it won't stop me from doing this job."

11

When Rachel heard banging on her door, her eyes opened. Still in that fugue state between asleep and awake, she rolled over to see what time it was, sliding the book she fell asleep reading down the sheets and onto the floor. The wristwatch she kept by her bed read 11:47. With no TV, and electricity heavily rationed, there was little to keep most people awake too much past dark. Being on the streets past 11:00 was borderline unheard of, outside a few drunks the town officials would prod back home from Walt's Bar. Rachel still felt a little bit in a fog, and there had been no banging for several seconds.

Did I really hear that, or was I still dreaming? she asked herself. *Who would be knocking on my door at this hour?*

She lay still, listening, the covers pulled tight up under her chin. With solar and hydro electricity sporadically released among the townspeople, the winter could be tough, with the temperature in people's homes rising and falling with their ration schedule. And she couldn't sleep with much clothing, so she was only wearing a pair of cotton panties under the covers. She didn't look forward to the chilly air in her room hitting her body if she had to roll out of bed to answer the door. Even though she kept a nightgown right beside the bed, it'd still be a jolt, and she wasn't sure about answering the door in just a nightgown either.

After ten seconds of lying motionless, just her eyes scanning around the room, she still hadn't heard anything. *Maybe I really did dream that. Or maybe whoever it was went away. Either way, I'm—*

Then she heard it again, louder this time, fists rattling the door on its hinges. It almost sounded like the person was trying to knock *down* the front door, not just knock *on* it. The knocking seemed nearly frantic. Did someone need help? What were the odds of someone who really needed help happening to end up at her door this late at night? And, if they *did* need help, what could she even do for them?

As the banging continued for ten seconds, then fifteen, Rachel nudged the blankets to the side and snatched the nightgown from the foot of the bed, deftly whipping it around her back and cinching it tight at her waist as she stood. It was made from a blend of cotton and rayon, making it silky soft, and one of the nicest garments she still owned from the pre-plague world. There were plenty of days she made it a point never to put anything else on.

The knocking having subsided, she slid into her slippers and trudged over to her bedroom window, which faced out over the front of the house. There was a small, pitched roof over her front porch, so she wouldn't see much from the person if they were still at the door. But she wanted to look out to see if there was any clue who might be there. Maybe someone's bicycle, an official electric car, a crazy mad man yelping and wielding a hatchet. Whatever. Any hint might ease—or ramp up—her fears before she went down to confront whoever it was.

Pressing her nose to the window, she looked down, stretching her neck to the left to try to catch any sort of glimpse of the person who had been knocking—shoes, a sleeve of a shirt, the cuff of a pair of jeans. Anything that might give a clue of the person's gender, or why they were there. But there was nothing. She scanned the front yard, but everything was cast in shadows, sitting dark and formless across the lawn. There was only stillness in the air. And quiet. There had been no knocks for thirty seconds or so. Still, though, she didn't see anyone walking away. That meant whoever it was hadn't given up yet. They were still there, waiting for her, knowing she'd be home.

Her heart pounded urgently, as if making up for the overwhelming silence and anticipation, the sound crawling up her chest into her throat, arriving heavy in her head. Could she wait this person out? Maybe they already decided they wouldn't knock again. Rachel didn't dare make a noise. Everything that created sound seemed amplified. She could hear the tinny ticking of the wristwatch that sat on her nightstand and the subtle creak in the floorboards of her room when she'd shift weight from her left to her right foot, and back again. She remained looking down, hoping to see a figure come down off the porch, walking slowly back toward the street.

Thirty seconds turned into a minute. Then two. Still, no knocking. No sound at all. Her mind tumbled and looped over itself.

Is it possible I missed the person leaving? she thought. *No. No. I mean, they'd have to hop off the side of the porch into the prickly bushes and practically crawl out. Why would anyone do that? That doesn't make any sense. No. The person is still there, for some reason.*

Neither answer made much sense to her. Either this person had taken the most unorthodox route possible to leave her porch, avoiding her detection, or that person was still there, at least three minutes after the last knock. Waiting. Silent.

Then a thought leapt into her head, a lightning bolt blasting throughout her body, causing her to shiver.

Did I lock the door?

She typically did, right before she went to bed. But it was an easy thing to forget. Particularly if she had dozed off on the couch and was half asleep as she swayed up the stairs, like she had on this night. And it wasn't an urgent issue, for the most part. Everyone knew each other in this town, and that tended to dramatically cut down on the crime rate. Still, she thought she had locked it. The door was directly across from the foot of the stairs. Just before she turned to go up, she reached over and flipped the switch up to lock it. Right?

Then, an unmistakable sound. Heavy-soled boots. The stairs moaned beneath her. Her blood turned to ice.

Walking away from Walt's Bar, Nick didn't know where he was headed.

It was well after dark and, by all accounts, he should be walking home. Where else was there to even go at this hour? It was after 11:30. It's not like this was New York City. Or, well, what *used to be* New York City. Bright lights. Subway running twenty-four hours a day. This was Podunk, and nobody was doing anything except drinking or fucking after 11 even before the plague. Now? You were lucky if you even had power to run in the evening. Seeing a guy wandering the streets this late, you could get better than even money that he was drunk, and Walt was the best supplier in town.

But Nick didn't find himself walking in the direction of his house. Almost against his will, he was going the other way. Instead of taking that right on Taylor Street, he went left. There were no streetlights. No passing cars to illuminate his path with their headlights. At this point, he couldn't see his hand in front of his face; everything was one dark, amorphous blob in front of him as his eyes slowly adjusted to the night.

He hadn't made this walk at night before, but he knew where he was headed. Rachel lived at 982 Market Street. It was a two-story shotgun-style house with white trim on a navy blue paint job that was beginning to peel. He had memorized it as he watched her wave to him while he wandered back toward the sidewalk each afternoon when he walked her home from her job at a small convenience store down the street. They'd met there, him stopping by during the work day to grab a small afternoon

snack—everything there was made by someone in the town now
—and it eventually turned into a regular walk.

He'd never been inside, but he wanted to step through that
door one day. He wanted to laugh while they made dinner
together, drinking a glass of Cabernet and listening to Billy Joel
while he smashed garlic and she tended to the simmering broth.
He wanted to sit beside her on the couch, her head in his lap,
running his fingers through the tangles of her hair. He wanted to
know what it was like to sleep next to her, to see her chest rise
and fall as the night turned to morning.

He knew that his patience would have to be rewarded—some
day, surely. This insanity couldn't continue. Eventually, they'd be
allowed to be together, when this plague was stamped out of
existence. It was going to happen.

When, though? He had no idea. And his patience was
running on empty. Had Walt been right? Was he letting other
people run his life, and scare him from doing what he really
wanted to do? Was he taking Rachel's desire for granted, that it
would continue indefinitely if he didn't make a bold move?

That was a chance he wasn't going to take anymore. This had
to be the night. He couldn't wait any longer. He was going to her
house, and he was going to lay his cards on the table. Make her
listen to him. Convince her there was nothing Audrey and her
goons could do to them. They'd have love, and their friends
would stand up for them. They could do this. Life was too short
to keep waiting for tomorrow when today was right here in front
of you.

As he took a left onto Market Street, his eyes were adjusting
to the light, and he could just make out the shape of the house
four doors ahead. From the side, it looked like it could be a
mansion, pushing deep back away from the street, and stretching
high into the air. Once you got to the front of it, though, you

could see it was only maybe thirty feet across, making for some evidently tight quarters.

Each step filled Nick with a sense of nervous anticipation; his steps came more quickly now, his calves beginning to burn as they propelled his legs forward. The ring around his waist added close to twenty pounds to his weight, so his legs—and everyone's in this town—were working even harder to move fast than they used to. Despite the cold, his forehead was becoming clammy, with sweat beginning to bead around his hairline. His mouth was drying up, making his tongue feel wooden, and his throat sandpaper as he swallowed. The combination of heat and nerves was making this walk seem longer than it was.

Another few steps, and he came even with the near edge of the house. There were no signs of movement or candle light, which was no surprise. He'd most certainly be waking her up, but he didn't care at this point. It was time.

He turned up the walk toward the front porch, and he noticed something strange. It looked like he could see inside the house. It was very dark, so he wasn't certain, but the front door appeared to be open. As he reached the stairs to the porch, there was no doubt. The door was standing completely open, pushed against the far wall. He stopped on the second step and crouched down carefully, his ring resting on the stair above him. He swung his head right, then left. No one seemed to be around. Then he remained still and listened. Could she have left the house and forgot to close the door? Or perhaps someone broke in while she was gone, and *they* left the door open? But it made no sense that she'd be gone. There was nowhere to go. People didn't have sleepovers. There were no vacations to take. She should have been home. If she was, though, why was the door wide open, with no sign of her or anyone else around?

He crept up one more step, then onto the porch. His feet landed softly, guarding against any noise the aging wood might make. At the door's opening, he stopped and slipped off his ring to make sure he could get through the doorway if needed. He reached inside and placed it carefully on the floor, leaned against the wall, then stood crouched, waiting for a sound. His heart pounded as he waited, trying to decide if he should walk right in, or go to find help. The house was dark and quiet inside. He could see the stairs just in front of him. The open door was the only sign anything might be wrong.

Something told him he had to do something, though. He couldn't just walk away from this. It was too strange.

Nick cupped his hands around his mouth and leaned across the doorframe.

"Rachel!" he said, in a hard whisper, loud enough for her to hear him if she were ten or so feet away, but not much more.

He waited several seconds, but got no response. Everything was quiet and very still. He took a deep breath.

"Rachel!" this time much louder, not quite at a yell, but easily strong enough for her to hear through much of the house. Maybe even loud enough to wake her up.

"Nick! He—" her voice came from up the stairs, panicky and muffled behind a closed door, but it was unmistakably her. Nick's hair stood up on the back of his neck, and he bolted through the front door opening, bounding up the stairs to the landing. He grabbed the doorknob to the room in front of him with his right hand and jerked it open. When he did, he saw a naked man writhing and thrusting on top of Rachel, whose nightgown was pulled up over her head, the man's hands pressing it against her face as she tried to scream.

Nick didn't recognize the man immediately. But, when the man paused and turned his head slowly toward the door, Nick could see it was Trevor Kites, a man who lived a couple of blocks away. Nick charged toward Trevor, who rolled off Rachel to his right, hitting the other side of the bed and bouncing off to the far side of the room. Rachel yanked her nightgown back down over her body, and pulled the covers over herself, shaking uncontrollably, tears streaming down her cheeks.

Nick stood between the bed and the door, waiting for Trevor to stand up and make a break for it. He couldn't see Trevor, but he knew he had to be staying low behind the bed. There was literally nowhere else for him to go. Nick just needed some way to subdue him until he could get some authorities there. He slowly crept around to the foot of the bed, staying in a slight crouch so Trevor would have a hard time seeing him.

How dangerous is this guy? Nick thought. *I mean, he's not wearing a thing, so it'd be tough for him to have a weapon. But always be wary of the cornered animal. It's when you run out of options that you're at your most deadly.*

He took short shuffle steps with his back to the bed, first his left foot, then his right. Nick was leaning, trying to see what he could on the far side of the bed without completely giving away where he was. Each small step forward, though, and he saw nothing. Just an off-white carpet, and a few hairballs Rachel's cat left behind. When he got to the far edge of the bed, he paused and took a deep breath. Nick could hear Rachel sobbing, choking through tears under the covers just feet away; he wanted to go to her and comfort her, but he had to confront Trevor first. He exhaled, and spun around the bedpost, facing the bed, crouched with his fists raised in front of him.

There was no one there. Nick spun his head right, then left. There were no doors. Only a window overlooking the backyard, but Nick would obviously have seen him if he'd taken that route.

What is this guy? Fucking Houdini? Is there a goddamn trap door here?

Then he heard a noise, a scratching on the other side of the bed. A still-naked Trevor had crawled under the bed on his stomach, and was scrambling to his feet, moving toward the door on all fours. Nick pivoted to go back around the bed to chase him, and his ring slammed into the bed post, sending him spinning to his left as pain shot through his hip like being jabbed in the side with a police baton. He winced and fell to one knee, but caught himself. Rising back to his feet, he heard the bedroom door slam as Trevor ran out and toward the stairs. Nick sprinted to the door and had grabbed the doorknob when he heard Rachel from behind him.

"Don't."

Nick stopped and turned his head slowly toward her. "What do you mean, 'Don't'? I *have* to."

"Don't go," she said in a voice strained from crying. "I can't be alone right now."

Nick pulled his hand from the doorknob and stepped back toward the bed. Slowly, he pulled back the covers and allowed himself to fall, first his head and back, then swinging his legs up beside her. She pulled her head from beneath the covers and turned to her right side, then slung her left arm across his chest.

"What can I do?" Nick said, her head resting in the crook of his shoulder.

"Just be here. That's all."

He thought that this wasn't how he'd hoped to end up here, but this was most of what he had wanted. He was in bed with the woman he loved, and he was feeling the soft touch of a woman —of *anyone*, for that matter—for the first time in more than a year. The sensation was surreal. He wished it had come under better circumstances, but he couldn't help but smile. He felt bad about that, and tried to fight it. This was a moment when she needed him to be better than he knew he was, and he desperately wanted to be the person she hoped he could be for her.

Then the bedroom door slammed open violently, banging into the wall behind it. Nick snapped his head up to look in that direction, his muscles tightening and the blood rushing quickly from his face. There were two men dressed in black, with guns drawn toward Nick and Rachel.

"Hands up, and move away from each other, out of the bed!" one of the men demanded loudly. "This is the police!"

12

They swung the gate open, and Paul staggered through, his back arched forward, his labored breaths crystallizing in the air in front of him. As they closed the gate behind him, he stopped, leaned forward and dropped the blood-soaked knife on the ground at his feet.

Audrey reached the bottom of the ladder, turned and ran toward Paul, who collapsed to his knees. The solar-powered lights inside the wall shone behind him, tossing his shadow toward the darkened town.

"What happened?" she said, taking the final few steps toward him and reaching out for his arms. "Are you all right?"

Paul bent onto all fours and gagged. Nothing but spittle came out, rolling down his cheek and dripping onto the dirt.

"He tried to attack me," Paul took a deep breath. "I didn't have any choice."

"What did you do?" Audrey asked, the workers at the gate gathering around the two of them.

Paul's breaths were still staggered; he looked up at Audrey. "I'm sorry."

Paul began sobbing, covering his face in his hands, which were crusted in crimson; his chest heaved uncontrollably. He kicked the dirt, sending jagged pebbles scattering around the crowd that had formed.

Audrey stood frozen, looking down at Paul writhing in the dirt. George slowly walked over and got onto his knees, looking into Paul's eyes.

"It's all right. It's gonna be okay," George whispered. "You didn't have a choice. I know it can't be easy, though."

A couple of the other men walked in closer to Paul, who took his hands off his face. He wiped his sleeve across his nose and eyes, then tried to stand.

"God, I'm a mess. Shit," Paul said, grimacing and rubbing his eyes.

George looked back at Audrey, who stared blankly.

"It's fine, Paul. We understand. You did the right thing," George said. "Now, let's go get you cleaned up."

George grabbed Paul's ring with both hands and nodded at one of the other men, who came over and wrapped his hands around it on the opposite side. They pulled up and helped Paul get fully onto his feet.

"Are you okay to walk?"

"Y—Yeah, I think so," Paul nodded. "Could you come with me, though? I don't really want to be alone right now."

"Of course. Yes. Absolutely," George said. "Whatever you need. We can go back to your place, or wherever."

Paul stumbled forward, and they walked slowly down the street, back toward the main part of the town. The workers shuffled back to their posts along the wall.

Audrey's feet were still planted where they'd been when Paul told her what happened. Her eyes were closed, and she was shivering, her muscles erupting into periodic spasms. Slowly, she turned her head to look at Paul and George as they walked away toward the dark. Before he got completely out of the light, she saw Paul's head swing around to his right, and her eyes met his. He smiled and winked.

13

"So, what you're telling us is this guy's a pervert and a menace," Zac said, standing up and jabbing his finger at Michael.

"Hey, guys," Hank raised his arms, hoping to quiet the murmur that was growing among the Watch group. "Let's not get ourselves whipped into some sort of frenzy. I was there too, and I didn't see anything like that. The guy might be a little weird, but he's not dangerous."

Michael glared at Hank, then shook his head. He turned back toward the crowd.

"I know what I saw, guys," Michael said, narrowing his eyes at Hank. "For *whatever* reason, Hank feels the need to defend his neighbor. Maybe they're in cahoots on this. I couldn't say. But I know for *damn* sure what I saw."

"Whoa, now. Hey, if you guys want to break out the pitchforks on this, go for it. I won't be standing in the line of fire," Hank said. "I'm just trying to be a voice of reason. You fellas do what you have to do, but I won't be a part of it."

Zac motioned to a couple of guys near him to follow him, and they charged back through the doors of the gathering hall as scattered yells rose up from the group, fists pumping in the air. Michael stood and kicked Hank's stool out from under him, knocking him to the ground, and driving his ring into his stomach. Blunt pain rocketed up his torso and through his back like being hit with tasers. He rolled over to a sitting position, wrapped his arms around his legs and bit his lip hard. Michael leapt down off the stage, and weaved through the crowd to catch up to Zac and his friends.

Fifteen minutes later, Michael was back on Trevor's front porch, this time flanked by Zac, Andy, and Benjamin, with a small crowd of other Watch members waiting and watching from the front yard.

"Okay, guys. Let's be cool," Michael said. "We don't want to spook him, and make this harder than it has to be. If we're calm, we can take those pictures down, and put enough of a scare into him that he'll never pull that shit again. Got it?"

Zac rolled his eyes, and looked at Michael.

"We got it, man. We know what we're here to do. Let's do this."

Michael raised his fist and banged on the door four times, then waited. The crowd, which had been frenzied earlier, was quiet enough to hear one of them scratch his leg. Another kicked the dirt at his feet. None of them knew what was next.

After several seconds, Michael heard footsteps from inside. The knob turned, and the door opened a few inches. Trevor was using a gold chain lock, and it caught in place. He peered out through the opening.

"Ah, Michael. Good to see you again," Trevor smiled. "And I see you brought some new friends this time."

Michael swung his head left, then right. "We need to come in and talk for a minute. You okay with that?"

"Well, it's really a bad time. Could you come back later?" Trevor said. "Next week might work better. How's Tuesday?"

Zac looked at Michael and threw up his hands, then unstrapped his ring, letting it fall hard to the porch. "The fuck is he talking about, Tuesday? We're going in now. Get outta the way."

"Hold on, now. Wait," Michael put both hands in front of him. "Trevor was just kidding before. Weren't you, Trevor? Now, undo the lock so we can have a little chat. Won't take long."

Trevor's eyes shifted to his left, but he kept his head pointed at the opening in the front door.

"I don't think that's gonna work," Trevor said. "I really am in the middle of something h—"

"Oh, fuck this," Zac said, as he slid past Michael's ring and lowered his shoulder into the door, shaking the chain lock on its hinges. He reached his right hand through the opening in the door and grabbed Trevor's neck. Trevor gurgled and made slurring noises as he struggled to breathe, and Zac's fingers dug into the sides of his neck.

"Undo the fucking lock, Trevor."

Zac squeezed his hands with each word, pulsing against Trevor's veins. He could feel Trevor's pulse picking up its pace rapidly.

"Undo the fucking lock, or I swear I'll suck away every last bit of sad, sorry little life you have left."

Trevor's face grew ashen, the color draining slowly as he nodded. Zac pulled his hand back, and Trevor rocked the door just enough to pull the lock out, and he started to open the door fully. When he did, Zac threw himself against the door, slamming it out of Trevor's hand and charged for him. Andy and Benjamin, already out of their rings, followed closely behind him, and Michael reacted last, leaving his ring behind and coming in last.

Trevor was backtracking, and his legs hit a table behind him, tripping him up and sending him crashing through the glass top. Zac stalked after him, reaching into the table frame and grabbing him by the shirt collar. Michael slid past Andy and Benjamin to get into the living room to Zac's right.

"Oh, god. No. What do you want?" Trevor said, his feet kicking for solid ground to stand on. "I don't know what you're here for."

"Your balls," Zac tossed Trevor like a sack of potatoes, his head banging against the plaster wall. "That's what we're here for."

"My...balls?"

"You're fucking right. Andy, get this pervert's pants."

Michael felt frozen in place. What was happening? This had escalated far beyond what he'd planned, and he was regretting what he'd done. Maybe Hank had been right. Maybe telling Zac and his crew was lighting a fire that couldn't be unlit. He just hadn't expected it to be taken quite this far. Still, *something* had to be done. Trevor had to be dealt with. Michael just wasn't sure castration was the best way to do it. He rattled his head to jolt himself back into the present, and quickly shuffled toward Trevor, standing between him and Zac.

"Whoa, guys," Michael said, his hands held out in front of him. "Let's think about this. Do you know the amount of blood that would cause? It's substantial. This isn't fun and games. You're talking about castration here."

"He damn well deserves it for what he did!" Zac said.

"I'm with ya. But we've gotta be smart. We're given a good bit of leeway in this town, but I'm pretty sure the line's drawn somewhere between here and vigilante balls removal. It's messy, and impossible to explain away. On the other hand, a good, swift kick—"

Michael spun around and swung his round-toed boot into Trevor's stomach, eliciting a grunt as Trevor rolled over on the floor.

"—could come from practically *anything*. Maybe it was a fall down the stairs. Or he tripped on some ice. Is that what happened, Trevor? You slipped on some ice?"

Trevor clutched his stomach with both arms and groaned. "No!"

Michael turned again and slammed his boot into Trevor's back, sending him crashing flat onto the floor. Then he landed a hard kick into Trevor's side. Michael crouched beside him.

"What do you think now?"

"I tripped," Trevor spat, clutching his midsection as the words tumbled clumsily from his lips.

"You're a smart man. Okay, then. You guys satisfied?"

Zac narrowed his eyes and shrugged.

"I won't be satisfied 'til that *perv* gets what's comin' to him."

Zac stepped toward Michael, pointing over his shoulder at Trevor on the floor behind him.

"Chill out for now, man," Michael said, turning his head around toward Trevor. "I don't think we'll hear much from this guy anymore. Will we, Trevor?"

Trevor said nothing, just wrapped his arms around his waist and gritted his teeth.

"That's what I thought. Let's go. Hey, Benjamin, you got the pictures?" Michael yelled back toward the other room down the hall.

Benjamin came around the corner holding a stack of printed photos.

"Got 'em all," Benjamin said. "That's some crazy shit back there."

Michael and Andy began to walk toward Benjamin and the front door.

"You comin'?" Michael said, stopping to look back over his shoulder at Zac, who was still standing a few feet from Trevor.

Zac shook his head and pursed his lips. "Yeah. Yeah, I'm coming."

He followed them toward the door, and Benjamin, Andy and Michael walked through the open door onto the front porch. The men waiting outside swarmed toward the porch, nearly tripping over each other and blocked the stairs to come down. Finally, one of them yelled, "What happened? What'd you do to him?"

"You won't have to worry about Trevor pulling this crap anymore," Michael said. "Let's just leave it at that, guys. Okay? Can we go?"

A few of the men raised their fists and let out a grumble before turning around and walking back to the street.

As soon as Michael stepped out the door, Zac stopped. He took three large steps back toward Trevor and crouched beside him. He stuck Trevor's forehead into the crook of his right arm, snapping his head up toward the ceiling. He leaned his head up against Trevor's left ear.

"This is exactly what you deserve, you sick bastard," he whispered, and slid his knife across the width of Trevor's neck, sending blood in spurts onto the floor beneath him. Zac let him fall to the floor, gurgling and gasping for air, then walked to the door and stepped out just as Michael was talking. When Michael finished, he turned and looked at Zac standing behind him. Zac smiled and nodded.

14

Hands cuffed, Nick had the three-foot stick prodding him in the small of his back as he walked out the front door of the house, Rachel a step behind him with the same sharp poke. A large white sign hung around their necks with the words *QUARANTINE — STAY BACK* scrawled in red ink, a signal for everyone in the vicinity to keep their distance. Audrey's officers nudged them toward the two solar-powered electric vehicles they used to navigate the town—the only two cars in Alessandra. Nick and Rachel's rings were left lying on the bedroom floor upstairs.

A man ahead of them opened the rear doors and quickly scurried away from the vehicles to give Nick and Rachel a wide berth as they approached. If one of them had a dormant version of the virus, they could both have it now, and no one was taking any chances.

From a few blocks up the street came a crowd, spilling off the sidewalk into the road. Michael—out in front, alongside Zac, Benjamin and Andy—noticed the cars and put his arms out to his side.

"Hold up, guys," he stopped and squinted ahead. "The cop cars are up there. Looks like they're taking some people away."

"Hope she was the best lay that guy ever had, 'cause he's fucked now," Zac laughed, and a chorus of men bellowed behind him.

Michael was trying to tell who it was. He knew he recognized them, but everybody recognized everybody in this town. That didn't help. There was something about the man's gait. He was afraid he knew who it was, but he was hoping he was wrong.

"Hey, is that Rachel Iles' house?" It dawned on Michael where they were, and his heart plummeted in his chest. It pumped rapidly.

"Rachel? Um, yeah, pretty sure that's right," Benjamin said. "That chick's hot as hell. Maybe there's a picture of her in this little gift set from good ol' Trevor."

Several of the guys started gathering around him as Benjamin flipped through the photos he'd grabbed off the wall, but Michael stood still, staring ahead. *Could it be them? Did they get caught already?*

Then Michael started moving, first slow steps, then jogging, then a full sprint, arms pumping like pistons, feet pounding the pavement. When he got within fifty feet, Nick and Rachel spotted him before the police did. Their eyes turned toward him, but their heads mostly stayed pointed toward the cars. Michael's head bounded wildly as he ran, so his friend seemed to bob around in front of him—up and to the left, down and to the right, over and over. As they made eye contact at thirty feet away, Michael slowed his sprint, and Nick's face steadied in his vision. He could see Nick mouth the word "Stop." He did, and bent over, hands on his knees as the officers came into view behind them. Michael's heart was a set of razor blades, slicing into his chest, making his breath short and painful. He gasped as he bent at the waist, trying to suck in air in short bursts.

Michael glanced up as they were turned toward him to be placed into the cars, and he caught a glimpse of the word QUARANTINE before they settled into the back seats. It was exactly what he'd feared, from the first time Nick had told him about Rachel. Michael pounded his knee with his fist several times, trading the pain of his chest for the pain of his leg. He wanted to feel something different, wanted to inflict new pain on himself. How had it come to this? How had Nick let this happen? Why hadn't he been stronger? *My best friend threw his life away for sex.* Michael pounded again and again, his anger pouring through his forearm and driving through his knee. After nearly a minute, he could barely stand anymore, and he collapsed to the pavement, waves of pain tearing up through his thigh and almost to his waist. He sat, yanking his knees up into his ring and wrapping his arms around his legs. The pain roared through his body; he laid his head in his arms and cried.

"Sir! You need to leave," one of the officers said. "There's been an incident here, and we can't have you being this close. Please proceed south down the street."

Michael looked up, and there was a uniformed man standing over him, pointing a long stick at his head. He narrowed his eyes against the sun that shone from over the man's shoulder, and he wiped the tears from his face with the back of his right hand.

"I don't understand what happened," Michael said.

"That's not of your concern. Please move along. Do you need help standing up?"

Michael looked down at the pavement between his legs and sighed. "Probably so."

The officer stepped back and held the stick out in front of him. Michael grabbed it with his left hand and pulled himself to his feet.

"I'll trust you know your way back to your home," the officer said.

"Yeah. Yeah, I can make it."

"Good. Walk that way." He pointed in the opposite direction Michael was facing. "And don't look back."

15

Glassy-eyed, Audrey stared at the back of Trevor's lolling head, his torso slumped forward and his tousled hair dipping slightly into a glistening pool of blood on the floor beneath him.

"What happened?" she asked, crossing her arms below her chest.

"We're, um, not sure, Ms. Reese," said Danny, who had begun the previous morning next to Audrey in bed, and was now standing beside her looking down at a murder victim. "Obviously, he was killed. There's no murder weapon anywhere around here. Beyond that, we'll need a little time."

Audrey closed her eyes and shook her head slowly. "I just don't understand what's going on. This doesn't happen in my town."

"No, of course it doesn't." Danny lifted Trevor's head a bit to take a closer look at the wound. "We're all as shocked as you are, Ms. Reese."

"You'll catch whoever did this." Audrey said it without a hint of question. It was more of a command.

Danny stood from his crouch and looked her in the eyes. "One hundred percent, we will. You've got my word."

"Not a word of this leaves this room," Audrey said. "Got that?"

"Absolutely."

Danny signaled for one of the other men to come over and help him with something, while Audrey slowly stepped toward the hall by the front door.

This isn't supposed to be happening. Not here. Not while I'm running this show. Pacing the floor, Audrey's mind couldn't let go how she'd let this happen. What could she have done differently? How could she have prevented this?

She'd made this her life's work—keeping these people safe from the dangers of the outside world. She'd instituted whichever draconian rules and regulations she had to, building the wall to keep out anyone who might do them harm, but now perhaps the harm was coming from within. She knew her brother was a problem, but she believed she could contain him. She at least *understood* him. And he could help her to get what she wanted. She knew, though, that this wasn't his work. She'd been with him much of the evening, and he wouldn't have had time to get to the house and do this.

She almost wished it had been him, though. Because if it wasn't him, that meant there was at least one more Alessandrian who was willing to kill, and she had no idea if it was someone she could keep under her thumb.

This had the potential to get ugly. She knew nothing about this person, whoever it was. She didn't know if this was a cold-blooded murder, or just an argument that got way out of hand. This wasn't something she'd had to deal with. This was a sleepy little town. Everybody knew everybody else. What crime they had prior to the plague was mostly some petty theft, the occasional stolen car, and the random assortment of drunken fights at 2 a.m.

Since the plague, they'd coasted by without much in the way of real crime. The people of the town seemed to understand they were in this together, and a sharing economy ruled the day. People worked with each other. They knew no one was coming to help them; it was up to them to be a family, to take care of each other. She'd fostered this atmosphere, and she was proud of the results. She'd had to get tough with the rings, and the enforcement of keeping people separated from each other, and that had been hard. But it had worked beautifully up to this point. And she wasn't going to let one problem deter her from a governing strategy that had kept them alive—and safe—for this long.

Now, though, she faced one of her biggest tests as the leader of the town. People were going to find out about this. She was certain of that much. And, when they did, they were going to expect action. There would be rumors and suspicions. There was no way to halt that, especially in a town like this. The best they could do would be to make an arrest as soon as possible. She needed to prove that she was in charge, and that justice could be served with her leading the way. Could she be judge, jury and executioner? She was ready to do it.

Audrey slumped into a beanbag chair on the floor against the wall, which turned out to be one of the most comfortable spots she'd found to sit outside her own home in a while. One of the drawbacks of the rings was how difficult it was to just relax when you weren't at home in your pajamas. You were constantly in backless seats—from stools to long benches to regular chairs with the backs sawed off—and so you were always having to lean forward. Given enough time, she figured almost everybody would have back issues. It always made Audrey miss being around her compound, where she could roam freely. The beanbag chair gave just enough support to make her feel almost at home.

Leaning back, she began to look around the room and was transfixed by the colors. It was mesmerizing. She couldn't remember the last time she'd seen such brilliant reds and blues and yellows, strewn in what may have been patterns across the walls all around her. It was hard to remember a time at this point when their existence hadn't seemed gray and drab, but this room stirred something in her. It had life. It had some sort of purpose. So close to the death that laid down the hall, this room was on fire with the man's expression. What did it all mean? She wished she could ask him.

She noticed several holes punched in the one wall that wasn't painted in wild, thrashing colors. It looked like dozens of pinpricks had been there at one time. There was no way of knowing what they might have once held up. She pushed herself up to her feet and walked closer to get a better look. She crossed the room, past the walnut coffee table and two stools that sat in front of it. Beneath the pin holes in the wall sat a medium-sized dresser, pushed not quite flush with the wall.

She grabbed the dresser from behind with a few fingers and yanked it away from the wall. It didn't move freely, but it budged, shifting the near leg a couple of inches toward her. She could get her full hand behind it now and pulled with both arms. It moved six inches out, and she could see behind it now.

On the floor there, she saw the back of what looked like an old Polaroid picture that had fallen behind the dresser. Maybe this was one of the items that had been pinned to the wall? She reached back and grabbed it, then flipped it over and brought it out where she could see it.

It was a photo of a woman, sitting nude on the edge of her tub, bending over to shave just below her left knee. The photo appeared to be snapped through a window, as she could see the fuzzy reflection of trees between the camera and the subject. It took a moment for Audrey to recognize the woman, but then she realized she'd seen her very recently. She got up and walked back into the other room, taking the picture with her.

"Danny!" Audrey said. "You need to see this."

Danny looked over from talking to one of the other officers. "What is it?"

"Didn't we just take in Rachel Iles for a major touching violation with Nick Dyerson earlier this evening?"

"Yep. What about it?"

"I just found this behind a dresser in the other room," Audrey held up the photo. "That's Rachel, which may give us a suspect *and* motive here."

16

Thin lines of sunlight danced across Michael's forehead and neck, as he squinted and rolled over to his side. He reached over and grabbed the watch he kept on his nightstand—7:14 a.m. Sleep had come in fits. Thirty minutes here, maybe an hour there. Michael kept telling his mind to shut off. Stop thinking about Nick and Rachel. Stop thinking about *everything*. His mind was a steamroller, bowling through topic after topic. He could stand in front of it with his hand raised and be a momentary distraction, but it was going to flatten him. And now it was morning.

Would he ever see his friend again? He had no idea. No one outside Audrey's innermost circle knew what happened once someone was taken into quarantine, and those people weren't talking. What Michael knew, though, was he'd never seen anyone emerge from the quarantine. Up to this point, everyone who'd been quietly taken away like Nick and Rachel hadn't come back to the community. There would be no formal announcement. No official ceremony. The people of the town were encouraged to go on about their lives, as if nothing had changed. Audrey didn't want people focusing on the loss; she said this was for the best. Hopefully, the quarantined people would recover, the virus would be comfortably eradicated, and everyone could be reunited at a later date. In the meantime, it was business as usual. There was a town to run, a community to protect. And if they didn't work every day to protect it, no one was going to do it for them.

While Michael was on board with that idea, it was going to be hard this time. He had to put it out of his head. He'd known Nick as long as he could remember, but he'd also known Audrey almost as long. And he had unwavering faith in her judgment. It was why he'd signed up to be part of her team at the neighborhood level. It was why he'd defended her decisions whenever his Watch team questioned them. And it was why he would swallow his sadness the morning after watching his best friend taken away. He'd go to work and do his job, like any other normal morning.

He enjoyed the work, too. Leading a furniture-manufacturing team wasn't exactly his dream job back when he'd dropped out of college, but he'd been more than willing to give it a shot when Audrey came to him and asked him to keep the plant running. During the plague, many people fled the town, hoping to join up with family or friends who lived elsewhere, or just trying to stay ahead of the virus's spread. So the population of Alessandra dwindled from more than 900 prior to the plague all the way down below 300.

Many of those 900 had worked making furniture at the large plant, and there was little hope they'd be able to keep it going. But much of the work had been done by hand, with tools and other machinery helping out with the process. Despite the town's isolation, Alessandra had two main things going for it—the lake, and the abundance of white oak trees in the forest surrounding it. White oak was a heavy, strong hardwood that worked perfectly for well-made furniture. It had the benefit of being relatively easy to work with, complimentary to a wide range of decors, and extremely durable. With some care, a white oak table would be something a person could pass down to his grandchildren.

It wasn't grandchildren or exports Audrey had been concerned about, though. It was seating. With the ever-present rings in public, it was important to produce unique chairs and other seating for public spaces. Michael didn't have a lot of workers—only eight people came in regularly to help, making the 50,000-square-foot plant on the west side of the town feel cavernous and empty much of the time—but it was rewarding, challenging work. He hadn't known much about furniture when he started, but he studied psychology in college, and Audrey said they just needed a leader. The work had brought out his creative side, which he enjoyed. He'd learned the basics fairly quickly, and his outside perspective let him take a fresh look at what was possible. In addition to classic stools and benches, Michael came up with designs for seating, including some chairs with wraparound backs that included a cutout for the ring. Prior to the plague, Michael had done some work with his hands, building lawn mowers and some woodworking; he found the skills he'd learned through several years in actually building things helped him when thinking of the end product when the town needed unique pieces of furniture. It'd been a good fit.

And, on this morning, he welcomed the distraction of it. He couldn't continue to torture himself about Nick's mistake. He'd known the consequences; they'd talked about it. Michael knew he'd tried to warn him. Still, he wondered if he could have done more. The Trevor problem had distracted him. He felt like it was something he had to deal with, and he left his friend on his own. What could he have done, though? It wasn't like he was going to tie Nick up in his basement or something. The guy was an adult. He could take care of himself.

Michael knew Nick, though. Knew him better than anyone. He knew Nick was impulsive and immature at times, and often looked to Michael for guidance, even if he wouldn't admit it. Michael wanted to think he'd done everything he could, but maybe that was just an excuse he was making because, deep down, he thought some of the blame for this lay at his feet. He wasn't there when his friend needed him, and Nick was gone because of it. If all Michael could do was sit at home and sulk, that would have taken up most of his day. But now his team at the plant needed him, and he needed to put his mind on anything but whatever was happening with Nick.

He took off his ring and walked through the door of his office, then hung up his coat and sat down, more ready than he'd been in a while to put in a full day's work. Almost immediately, his door swung open, and his floor manager Vance walked in carrying his ring.

"Mornin'" he said.

"Yeah," Michael looked up from his desk and nodded, then put his head back down. "Good morning. How's it look out there?"

"Not bad, not bad. Chris is out today, it looks like. Oh, and did you hear about what happened to Trevor? Holy shit, man. Everybody's talking about it."

Michael's head snapped up quickly, his eyes darting left, then right.

"Trevor? What about him?"

17

"We know you killed Trevor Kites," Audrey said, standing over Nick in a small, windowless holding room at her compound.

Nick looked up.

"You what?"

"We found the picture of Rachel in his house. I assume that's what started it? You found out about the picture?"

"I...Trevor ran. I never touched him."

"Well, your knife apparently touched him pretty good. Plenty well enough to kill him."

Nick ran his hand through his hair and rubbed his eyes with both hands. Sweat began to bead on his forehead. The events of the previous night ran through his head—opening the door to see Trevor raping Rachel, stalking him to the opposite side of the bed, then watching helplessly as Trevor scampered down the steps and out the front door. He had hoped to deal with Trevor later, but apparently someone else had done it for him.

"I don't understand what's going on. I thought you brought us in for a touching violation, and we were in quarantine."

"Oh, we did. But then we found Trevor's body, and that picture we found of Rachel gives you motive to kill him," she crouched in front of him. "Look, I get it. You found out he'd been taking nude pics of your girlfriend, and you got angry. Went to confront him, and it got out of hand. Overreaction, but you're not the first."

"What the fuck are you talking about with a picture? The guy *raped* her! I saw him do it!"

Audrey's eyes widened, and she stood back up. She laughed slightly, then smiled.

"Well, that's an even better motive than the picture. Thanks."

"No, but he got away! I never even left the house," Nick leaned forward, his arms outstretched.

Audrey crouched again.

"It's okay, Nick. This is good. We can spin this as a crime of passion, probably even justifiable in many people's eyes. That helps us. It also helps you, because we don't have to hang you in the square, or perform some other silly public showing of justice. You caught him raping Rachel. He escaped the house. You comforted her but, in a fit of passion, went to his house during the night to confront him. When you did, you guys got in an argument, maybe a fight, and you ended up slitting his throat. You had to defend Rachel's honor. You're a hero, really."

"That's not what happened!"

Audrey smacked the concrete floor with the open palms of both hands, the sound echoing through the gray room.

"Yes, it is! Yes, it is, Nick! That's *exactly* what fucking happened. And that's what you'll tell anyone who asks. We'll get Rachel on board too. Your life probably depends on it."

As far as detective work went, they were back into the dark ages in post-plague Alessandra. There were no labs to do DNA tests for them. Their fingerprint database had been digitized a decade before by the police department at the county seat of Blairsville, but they hadn't figured out how to get access to that information since Blairsville was abandoned.

So, for the most part, they were back to finding witnesses, defining motive, and following leads. It was about as inexact a science as it gets, but that's what much of detective work was for millennia. There were no magic bullets, and Audrey knew that. How many wrongful arrests and convictions had been made over the years in law enforcement? Countless. But when someone was murdered—especially in a small town—the people of the town needed peace of mind. They needed to feel assured that this wasn't going to happen again, that justice was being served. The last thing Audrey needed was a town of people worried about a killer being loose, and also questioning whether she and her men had the ability to catch someone who committed a major crime, and keep the rest of the people safe.

Did Nick do it? Probably. He certainly had the motive. He even admitted to seeing Trevor in the act of raping Rachel. If that wouldn't drive a man to potentially kill another man, what would? He said he didn't do it, but that's what everyone says. He was trying to save his hide. What Audrey knew he needed to understand was this was the best outcome for him. Unless someone else came out and confessed, she was going to have to pin this murder on Nick. She was either going to have to do it behind a combination of evidence flimsy and conjured out of thin air, or she was going to do it with solid evidence assigning understandable motive to him. This was a near-perfect motive, and the people of Alessandra would buy it easily.

The possibility nagged at her, though—what if he really didn't do it? She had been ready to send him down for the crime just on the basis of that picture, and even *she* wasn't completely buying that. If he actually *didn't* do it, that meant the person who did was still out there somewhere. In that case, she had to hope this was some sort of crime of passion. Maybe it was just an argument that went wrong.

Of course, there was also the possibility that something darker was out there in the shadows. There was the possibility that the people of Alessandra should be scared, that there really was someone capable of that kind of violent at seeming random. She needed to hope that wasn't the case. She needed to hope that she was right about Nick. If so, this set up very well for her. If not, she wasn't ready to think about that possibility.

18

Yesterday, Trevor was alive, and now he's dead. His throat was slit. Michael's mind raced as he sat at his desk, the clock crawling past 10 a.m. *What the hell happened? When?*

Michael knew Trevor had been alive when he walked out that front door. Vance said they found Trevor's body just a short time after they left the house. *And everyone was with me when I walked out, right?* Yes, he was sure of it. Benjamin had been in the other room; he walked out just ahead, with Andy and Michael walking out together and Zac right behind them.

Or is that right? Zac wasn't anxious to leave. I remember calling back to him, prodding him to follow us out the door. But he came. I'm sure of it. He was walking behind me toward the door. Yeah, he was right there when I turned around. Everybody was there.

He was starting to question it, though. There was no doubt Zac had wanted to do more to Trevor. Hell, he'd been ready to castrate the guy. But Michael stepped in and stopped that. Maybe Trevor deserved to be knocked around a little bit, but it wasn't worth doing something drastic. He just needed to know that he couldn't hide what he'd done, and get a taste of what the consequences were. If he continued, maybe they'd have to be more forceful, but Michael felt like he had the right approach.

Zac clearly didn't agree, but this had been Michael's show, and Zac had gone along with that. When Michael told him to stand down, he had. He followed Michael out the door. That was the part, though, that Michael wasn't entirely sure about. When he looked back at Zac, he saw Zac's eyes glaring at Trevor writhing on the ground in the adjoining room. Maybe he was thinking about what he wanted to do, but Michael had figured Zac was mostly bluster. Surely he wasn't capable of something like this. And, even if he were, when would he have done it?

Michael kept running through the events in his head. Had Zac really been right behind him on the way out the door? He'd thought so, but the fact was he didn't watch him the entire time. Michael turned toward the door, and then was distracted for a few seconds by the rush of men to the porch. He wasn't sure what they were going to do, and he felt like he needed to step forward as the leader of the group. When he turned around, Zac was right there. How long had he been there, though? How long had that taken? Ten seconds? Fifteen? How long was enough time to kill a man? Trevor had only been a few steps away, and he was probably too hurt to put up much of a fight.

Could Zac have done it? It seemed improbable, but was there even another possibility? Some other random murderer happened upon Trevor's house in the short time between when they left and when his body was found? Michael already knew Zac had the motive, and the desire to do it. He also knew Zac had been in the house with Trevor, and Michael couldn't account for where he was for at least ten seconds. Could he have done it in ten seconds?

Step, step, step, crouch, grab, slash, drop, step, step, step. How long would that have taken?

That was what Michael figured it would take for Zac to do it. He looked around his office. He had plenty of room to test this out. How far had it been from near the front door to where Trevor was lying? He guessed about ten feet. He pulled a measuring tape from the top drawer of his desk and laid it on the wood floor by one of the desk's legs, then pulled out the yellow strip to ten feet. He grabbed a pencil from the top of his desk and drew a small mark on the floor at the ten-foot mark.

He let the tape snap back, and placed its casing back on the desk. He stood by the front right leg of his desk and sucked in two large breaths. *Step, step, step, crouch, grab, slash, drop, step, step, step.* He ran through the sequence in his head. His watch had a stopwatch function on it. He pressed buttons and listened to it beep until the clock digits turned to all zeroes. Two more breaths in.

As he took the first step, he punched the stopwatch button with his thumb. One big step. Another. And another. His heart was beginning to pound. He crouched, picturing the gasping Trevor lying beside him, perhaps pleading with his final few breaths. What went through Trevor's head at that moment? He was nearly helpless because of the beating Michael had given him, clutching at his midsection at what may have been broken ribs. When ribs break, they can feel like shards of glass in your abdomen. Every time you breathe, it feels like someone stabbing you, then rubbing sandpaper over the wound. Nauseated and aching, Trevor had been easy pickings.

Michael quickly grabbed the imaginary Trevor's head, ripping it upward to expose the fleshy neck, with veins that are the gateway to the heart and brain, the life trail for the body. Sever that, and there's no hope of survival without rapid intervention by trained professionals. And in post-plague Alessandra, there would be virtually no hope of that help arriving no matter what happened.

He pictured a blade gleaming in his left hand, scraping it across the neck just below his right hand, which was pressed against the forehead; Trevor's mouth lay open, a murmur of fear emerging from deep in his throat.

Michael stood and pivoted back toward the desk leg where he began, slipping the imaginary knife into the waistband of his pants. One big step. Two. Three, and he was back. He pressed the stopwatch one more time, and turned his wrist. He lowered his head to look at the number.

8.7 seconds

He ripped his coat off the rack by the door and slid one arm in as he opened the door and jogged out toward the exit.

19

"I, Nick Dyerson, mu—murdered Trevor Kites last Thursday ni—Why am I reading this, Audrey?" Nick said.

"You're reading it because we need a confession to calm nerves in this town, and we're recording this," she said, holding up a battery-powered electronic voice recorder she'd kept since long before the plague to keep personal notes to herself. "And because Paul's a pretty good shot. Isn't that right, Paul?"

"Damn straight, it is," said Paul, with a pistol held in front of him, pointed at Rachel's temple while she fought to hold back tears. "But, to be fair, I'm pretty sure anyone could hit from here."

"Don't sell yourself short, little bro."

"Love ya, sis."

"So," Audrey said, smiling at Nick. "We ready to do this for real?"

Nick sighed heavily and then looked at the ceiling of the large room with hardwood floors and basic drywall painted a taupe-like color. For being part of a large estate, the room was nothing to look at. He was kneeling and the floor was cold; the room itself was drafty, letting the February winds waft in like the walls were made of Swiss cheese. Wearing the same navy Henley shirt he'd had on for three days now, Nick began to shiver against the cutting air, then looked back down as he held the paper up to his face.

"I, Nick Dyerson," he paused and looked up at Audrey, his eyes begging for a reprieve, but none came. He looked back down. "Murdered Trevor Kites last Thursday night, February twenty-eighth. Some might say it was self defense, but it was more complicated than that. Yes, we were in a fight at his house, but it's what led up to that confrontation that explains how Trevor's life came to an end that night. Earlier in the evening, I walked in while Trevor was forcing himself upon Rachel, a woman I'd been very close to. I admit I shouldn't have been in her house. It was a violation of the law, and I'm sorry for that. But I saw the door open, and I sensed something was wrong. If I hadn't taken that chance, who knows what would have happened to her? I caught him in the act, and I wanted to beat him then and there, but he slipped out the front door before I could get to him. I felt like Rachel needed to me to console her, so I stayed and held her for hours, listening to her cry and massaging her head. Once she fell asleep, though, I slipped away, down the street to Trevor's house. When he saw me, he tried to act like nothing happened, but I knew, and I called him out for it. When he tried to deny it, I couldn't take it and took a swing at him. We struggled for several minutes until I found a knife on the living room table. I grabbed it and quickly sliced across his throat, and let him fall to the ground.

"It was difficult, taking another man's life. I'll never be able to forget the horror that's going to live with me, and the nightmares it will bring. But I believe Alessandra's a better place without a man like that living amongst us, and I did what I felt like I had to do. I hope you can understand that, and perhaps forgive me in time."

Nick let the paper fall out of his hands, fluttering to and fro before sliding onto the floor. He knew the story was mostly a lie, but what was he going to do? Audrey was more ruthless than he'd known, and her brother might have been even worse. He had no doubt that the only thing keeping him and Rachel alive was reading that confession. And, in the end, who was really hurt by that? It probably *was* a good thing that Trevor was dead, whoever did it. There was no shortage of people that guy might have pissed off in town. It wasn't Nick who killed him, but maybe it was someone who was similarly wronged by him. This easily could have been a justifiable homicide, and that helped Nick feel better about taking the fall for it. Hopefully, whoever did it wouldn't have any interest in doing that again.

"That's great, Nick," Audrey said. "You did a good thing, ya know. This was the right move, and not just because you saved Rachel here. Think about the people who won't be afraid now, because of you. You're gonna be a hero to a lot of people in this town. I just did you a huge favor. You're a hero and a martyr for Alessandra. You sacrificed yourself for the good of the town. It's noble. I think a lot of people will see it that way."

"It's not true, though, is it?" Rachel said, looking over at Paul, who held the gun at his side. She then looked at Audrey. "You know it's a lie, and you don't care. You just want somebody to blame this on."

Audrey stood up and spun toward Rachel, then took large, deliberate steps in her direction.

"You don't know the *first* thing about leadership, do you?" Audrey said. "You don't understand what I'm trying to do here at all."

"I understand that you're lying to the people of the town. *He* didn't kill Trevor. We all know that!" she held her arms out from her body and pointed around the room.

"I don't know that at all," Audrey said. "He *says* he didn't, but that doesn't mean a thing. What I know is he has a clear motive, and opportunity. And I also know that this is a fragile social order I've built here. The slightest spark might set off a powder keg. Is that what you want?"

Rachel looked down, then mouthed the word "No."

"That's the kind of stuff *I* have to worry about. *You* don't. *You're* just another person living in the world I built for you. That wall outside wouldn't be there if not for me. The places you live, the places you work. None of that would be there if I hadn't made it happen. These people needed order, and by god, that's what I was going to give them. If that means I 'lie' every now and then, so fucking be it. But this town is a way higher priority to me than any two people in it. You guys can play along and help me with that, or you can burn for all I care. We're out here all alone, battling a killer we can't see, and I have a town full of people relying on me to figure out how to rescue us from this island we're stranded on. Must be nice to be able to afford high-minded ethics. But this is the solitary apocalypse, Rachel, and those of us with responsibilities don't have that option."

Rachel looked at Nick, who looked back and shrugged. What were they going to do? Their backs were against the wall, and Audrey wasn't showing any signs of letting up.

Behind them, they heard a door creak open, and footsteps echoed onto the floor.

"Audrey, there's a visitor for you at the front gate," Danny said, as he walked up behind Nick and Rachel.

"Who's the visitor?"

"It's Michael Sloan," he said. "And he says it's important."

20

Michael sat on a plush couch that was a rich chocolate brown leather and embraced the shape of his body like it was cashmere, with carefully cut spaces for his ring to fit into. Sitting down on it felt like falling into a cloud, with a feeling of near weightlessness, as if he was going to hit the floor below. The golden chandelier above was almost intimidating in its elaborateness. He'd never seen anything like it. The arms jutted out tentacle-like in all directions, sprawling across the ceiling, casting wild, criss-crossing shadows, beckoning his eyes to follow them. The room's white walls had gold, swirling shapes, mesmerizingly dancing from floor to ceiling, between windows that spanned nearly the entire side of the house.

This was far beyond anything the people in town had in their homes. Clearly, Audrey was living well. To be fair, though, she was the leader who had saved them from certain death, and she had kept them safe this long. It was hard to want to deny her too many of the spoils of that work, though he wondered where all this came from. Had Mayor Handy been living like this as well, or had she brought these adornments in after the plague, when she took over the compound? If so, did she loot some guy's mountain mansion? Or have some of her people do it? Maybe it didn't matter, but he never expected to see this level of opulence in Audrey's home. The last time he'd been there, shortly before the wall was completed, it'd been far more sparsely decorated. It wasn't a choice he thought she'd make.

Behind him, he heard footsteps on the marble floor. He turned around as they got closer.

"Ms. Reese will see you now," said a tuxedo-wearing bald white man Michael didn't recognize.

Michael began to push himself up, but his feet were dangling above the floor.

"Do you need some help, sir?"

"No. No, I'll be fine."

Michael pushed up from his shoulders, and his toes tapped the floor, but his ring hung up on the back of the couch. He pushed again, but it held, and the front of it dug into his sides, sending bolts of pain through his back. The man hurried around to the front of the couch.

"Let me give you a hand, sir," he reached both arms out, but Michael paused and held his hands above his head.

"It's f—fine. Just back away, please."

The man nodded and stepped back. Michael shoved back against the couch with both hands and felt his momentum move forward. He wobbled onto his feet and got his balance, standing straight up.

"Are you okay, sir?" the man asked.

"Yeah," Michael said, still looking at the couch, and seeing a tear where his ring had caught. "Sorry about that."

"It's no trouble, I'm sure. Come with me?"

"Sure. Lead the way."

The man opened a large wooden door, and motioned for Michael to follow him through it. As he did, he saw Audrey sitting behind a mahogany desk that looked like it was probably built in the mid twentieth century, neat with not a single scrap of paper on it.

"Always great to see you, Michael. How have you been?"

"Um, things are going well," Michael nodded. "Thanks for giving me some time."

"Anything for an old friend and such a tremendous help out in the field," she smiled. "What can I help you with? I'm told it's important."

"Well, yes. I just heard about Trevor."

She frowned and bowed her head for a moment, then raised it to meet Michael's eyes.

"Yes, that was very sad for us all. We mourn every life we lose here. We're all in this together, as you know."

"Right, right. Yeah. Well, I was wanting to know, do you have any idea who killed him?"

"Ah," she nodded and grimaced a bit. "You heard he was a victim of murder?"

"Yeah. That's apparently what's going around."

"Okay, then. I'm going to be frank with you, Michael," she said, then sighed and placed her hands in front of her on the desk. "It's true. He was murdered. That's not something we prefer got out until we're ready, but yeah."

"Uh-huh. So, do you have a suspect, or any idea who did it?"

"Look, Michael, I'm not trying to keep you in the dark or anything like that, but we're just not in a position to talk about that right now. I'm sure you'll understand. I'll make sure you're one of the first to know when we are. Okay?"

"That's actually where I might be able to help."

"Oh? How's that?" she leaned forward in her seat.

"I know who did it."

Audrey straightened up and stared at Michael. There was something in her eyes Michael didn't like. He had hoped to see relief. Gratitude, perhaps. But what he saw was like staring into frost-covered glass on a cold winter night. He couldn't read it. What was she thinking? He'd known her for twenty-five years, and he'd never seen this in her before. The hair on the back of his neck began to stretch out, bringing goosebumps with it. He shivered slightly. She was silent for almost ten seconds before she finally spoke.

"You know who did it?" Her lips pursed as she finished the sentence.

"Yes. I know who killed Trevor."

"Tell me who it is, then."

"It was Zac. From the Watch group."

"You're sure about that? Did you see him do it?"

"Well, no. I mean, I was there, but he did it when he was out of my sight. He's the only one who could have done it, though."

Audrey stood up, maintaining Michael's gaze, then spun and began pacing the room behind the desk.

"How can you be so sure if you didn't see him do it?" she walked to the wall, keeping her back to Michael.

"He wanted to kill the guy. Trevor had been taking all these nude photos of women around town. He was a weird guy, and Zac didn't like it. None of us did, really. Zac was just...I don't know. Angrier than most, I guess. Or more violent, maybe. I didn't know he did it at the time, but now I'm sure of it. And there were a bunch of other guys there who can probably back me up once I explain my theory."

Audrey kept facing the wall, cupping her hands behind her back. Michael saw her head tilt toward the ceiling, then fall back down. She sighed loudly. She reached inside the front of her jacket and pulled something out. She looked down at it as she hit some buttons. It looked like something electronic, but Michael couldn't tell what it was. Then he heard a familiar voice.

"I, Nick Dyerson..."

"Wait! That's Nick!"

Audrey hit pause and raised her left hand in the air.

"Quiet! Listen."

She punched play, and Michael *did* listen. He heard his best friend since childhood confess to a murder Michael knew he didn't commit. Michael's forehead became clammy, and his head pounded, thinking of what this meant. When the recording finished, Michael stood up at the desk.

"But he didn't do it! I'm telling you it was Zac!"

Audrey turned around and walked around to the front of the desk, stopping within a foot of Michael's ring.

"You have no proof. You have nothing. And you're going to forget you even have *that*."

"But why? There's something wrong with Nick's confession. I don't know why he said that, but Zac is the one who did it."

"No he didn't, Michael," she bumped her body up against his ring and raised her chin. "No, he didn't. I've got a confession, and I'm giving Nick to the people. I'm not going into some investigation that'll probably lead nowhere, while people get scared there's a murderer on the loose. Nick's the guy. That's the end of it."

"He's not, though! And I think you know it."

"It doesn't matter what I *know*. And it sure as hell doesn't matter what *you* know. What matters is keeping these people safe and happy."

"I think what matters to you is keeping this comfy setup you've got going here."

Audrey pulled back a half step.

"What'd you say?"

"This fucking Shangri-La you've got up here. You just want to keep us all going about our business, accepting whatever crap you shovel our way so we don't question anything, or anyone. I think you've forgotten what it's like to be one of us."

"You might want to be careful how you speak to me, Michael," she stepped back toward him.

"And why's that?"

"I'm not someone you want to be your enemy."

"I'm not trying to make an enemy. But this 'I'm lying to them for their own good' stuff is bullshit. That's what you tell yourself to feel better."

"You don't know what I deal with up here. You don't know how hard this is. You get to do your 'Neighborhood Watch' crap, and act like you're doing tough work? Please. I have the weight of a whole town on my shoulders every fucking day, while you're making shitty furniture. You wanna do this job? You think you can do it better than me?"

Audrey raised her arms, then picked up a vase off a table by the wall and threw it, shattering it against the desk. Breathing heavily, she stood, looking at Michael. He sighed.

"I don't want your job, Audrey. I just want you to be better at it."

Her eyes got big, and she took a large breath.

"Get the hell outta here before I do something I'll regret," she pointed back the way he came. "You know where the door is."

Michael looked at the floor. "Yeah. I do."

He walked to the door, opened it and went back into the hall. Walking back toward the exit, he wondered if he'd been wrong about Audrey. To find out, he needed a good plan. And he knew who he needed to reach out to in order to put that together. It was someone he hadn't spoken to in awhile, but he knew just where to find her.

21

Paul was sitting ring-less and sideways in a leather recliner, his arms holding a dog-eared paperback book and his legs tossed up over the opposite armrest, when Audrey walked into his room and slammed the door behind her.

"Michael knows Nick didn't kill Trevor," she said, spitting out the words.

Paul paused a moment before lowering the book.

"He what?"

"He knows somebody else killed Trevor. He knows Nick's confession is bullshit."

"How does he know that?"

"He was *there*, Paul. He was fucking *there*! He says it was Zac. Shouldn't surprise us. Seriously. That guy's a hothead. He's carrying a lot of baggage since the virus went through."

"He was *there*? Why was *he* there?"

"I don't know," Audrey flopped down on the bed, staring at the ceiling. "They were confronting Trevor about those pictures we found. Apparently, there were a lot more of them. I guess that didn't go so well."

"Whatever. Does this really matter? Who cares what Michael thinks? What's he gonna do?"

"I *don't know*, Paul. That's the point. And he's not a guy we can just take without causing some issues. He's a prominent member of the community. Scooping him up would make a lot of waves."

"Is that even necessary, though?" Paul spun around and sat forward in the chair, his elbows on his knees. "This is a guy you've known for thirty years or so, right? And he's a friend. He knows the good you've done here. He's not gonna screw that up over this."

"Maybe you're right. I'm just not sure."

"Well, let's say I'm wrong. What's the worst he does? He tells some people what he saw? We've got an *actual confession*. Nick's got motive. Nick's got opportunity. What does Michael have? His word? Hell, unless Zac comes out and gives us competing confessions, we've got a hell of a lot better case than he does. At the very least, we've got plenty of justification for *thinking* we're right. Nobody's gonna hold that against us, even if it somehow turned out that Zac did it in the end."

Audrey looked between her legs at the floor.

"Michael will," she said. "*Michael* will hold it against me. That's his best friend we're pinning a murder on. He's not gonna let that slide. No way."

Paul stood and took a couple of steps toward the door, then stopped. He turned back around and licked his lips.

"Okay. Let's put eyes on Michael for a bit, then."

Audrey looked up at Paul, her arms still hanging between her legs. She didn't speak.

"What do ya think?" Paul said, stepping closer to her. "Nothing too extreme. Just have some of the guys do their best to watch where he goes, what he does, who he talks to. We'll get a handle on what he's thinking. I know he's a friend of yours, and I know you don't want to make the people nervous. I get that. We can do this pretty quietly. It's a precaution. That's all. If he's acting normal and going about his everyday routine, we'll back off after a few days. If not, well, we'll know there might be something to worry about."

Audrey hung her head again, then raised it and stood face to face with Paul.

"This isn't a guy I want to do any harm to," she raised her chin. "You know that, right? This isn't just some random person."

"I know, Aud. I've known the guy for a long time, too. Not as well as you, but I've known him all my life, pretty much. I remember him coming over when I was a little kid, and you guys building forts out of pillows and blankets in the guest bedroom. I know you guys have been close. I don't have any interest in hurting Michael. I'm just talking about giving you a little peace of mind. Hopefully, there's nothing to be concerned with. But if there is, don't you want to know about that?"

"Of course. But—"

"Then let me do this. I'll handle it. Just go relax. Forget this is even happening."

"No," Audrey lifted her head and looked Paul in the eye. "No, you just sit back in your chair and go back to your little book. I'll get this. The last time I let you handle something, a guy ended up dead."

"Oh, come on. You're still worried about that random guy in the woods? Who cares?"

"I guess I'm not ready to be quite as cavalier about life as you are," she jabbed her finger into his chest.

"That's not fair, and you know it."

"Whatever, little bro. Just sit down in that chair. I'll get some eyes on Michael, okay? We'll see what he's up to. But don't you dare make one fucking move toward him without coming to me first. You got that?"

Paul maintained his stare and opened up a half-smile.

"You got that?" she repeated.

Paul's smile remained as he nodded.

"Good," Audrey said. "I'm taking a shower. I don't want to see anyone the rest of the night."

22

Michael walked through the main hall of St. Francis Hospital, his footsteps echoing off the walls around him. It had been a coup for Alessandra to get the funding for this hospital in the first place. The county leaders in Blairsville wanted to build it there, but they couldn't find quite the right parcel of land. Mayor Handy and his team came in and made their pitch on why it made sense to put it in Alessandra. Blairsville eventually figured out where to build their own medical center when some businesses shut down near the town's core, but St. Francis and its sixty-two beds had already been established as the county's leader in medical science. Doctors and researchers from other small towns around the northern part of the state often came for visits to observe how work was done, and to look at the surroundings.

It was a beautiful building, with a sleek, modern gray facade lined with windows and stark lines. The inside had wide, spacious hallways with wood floors, along with glass partitions alongside doorways for an increased feeling of openness. The hospital had been fitted with its own networks, making it the only post-plague building in Alessandra outside of Audrey's compound with wireless intranet and telephone service. That helped doctors communicate between rooms and floors, and helped patients alert nurses if there was a problem.

While Audrey had established rationing on everyone else for electricity usage, she'd mostly left the hospital alone to do what it needed to do. Post-plague, the beds were rarely full, but the research unit they'd set up long before had become a valuable source for keeping track of the virus. It had been a mad scramble as the virus was first ramping up, dealing with panic while remaining vigilant and focused on the job at hand. They'd been responsible for gathering data from other towns around the county and region to try to figure out a plan of attack for how to deal with it. Sick people had been rushed there by the thousands, eventually being shuttled in through their back entrance with their own wing, cordoned off from the rest of the patients. Without a good handle on how the virus was spreading, doctors and researchers wore hazmat suits when going into the room or touching the patients, and had the patients in a secure bubble whenever possible.

In the end, they hadn't been able to stop its spread, though. Their colleagues at Grady and Emory in Atlanta—along with the Centers for Disease Control—had also been powerless to get it under control. All those patients who flooded into St. Francis became victims, statistics among the billions that had fallen at the hands of the deadliest virus outbreak humanity had seen. For some of the staff at St. Francis, the trauma of seeing that many people die while they were helpless to do anything about it had stayed with them, making it difficult to do their jobs going forward. For most, though, they soldiered on, still trying to fight a villain they couldn't see, hear or feel, couldn't even know for sure if it still existed. But that was part of their purpose, many of them felt, to determine when it was safe to breathe again. When the people of Alessandra could be confident this virus wouldn't claim more victims, and they could move forward with their lives, maybe even venture out and connect with people elsewhere who also thought they were the only community remaining. Maybe begin to rebuild humanity. They were determined for that day to come, and soon.

For the time being, though, their research supported Audrey's conclusion to take drastic measures to keep people apart. Physical contact seemed the most likely way the disease had spread, and

Doctor Giles confirmed that theory as best as he could. Their main goal following that finding was to determine how to test for the virus. Doctors can only test for one virus at a time; normally, they take a drop of blood and look for antibodies specific to whichever virus they're looking for. But, with this particular virus, the human body never produced antibodies. They believed something about the virus was arresting that part of the process. That made tracking it exceedingly difficult for doctors and researchers, and it was a major reason it spread and killed so quickly. Until they could test for it, the threat was always going to exist. And even once they did figure out how to test people, identifying a signature white blood cell reduction that came alongside the virus, the possibility of some people being asymptomatic carriers still kept everyone on edge.

Michael reached the main concierge desk, which had a slot cut out of the front to allow people's rings to slide in as they pushed close.

"How may I help you?" said a woman with short, curly red hair and a pair of pearl earrings.

"Is Stephanie Sloan in?"

"I believe Doctor Sloan is in, yes. Would you like me to ring her office for you?"

"That'd be great. Thanks."

The woman punched a few numbers on a phone in front of her, then picked up the headset. As they waited for Stephanie to pick up, Michael looked around. The hospital always seemed to be buzzing with activity. It was in contrast to much of the town, which could feel deserted at times; people often locked themselves in their homes alone so they didn't have to strap on the ring. Some of them would wander into the darkness of Walt's Bar and down some homemade beer or moonshine. But, except for occasional events Audrey organized, there wasn't much that seemed to happen. There was just the general inertia of day-today life. In the hospital, though, people were busy. Some of the staff just chose to never leave, sleeping in their offices and working almost constantly, trying to regain a handle on the world around them as if by brute force.

It was also jarring to see so many people without rings on in public. Doctors and nurses were some of the few people authorized to not wear them, as long as they were at work in the hospital—it wasn't practical to help a patient if you had to stay separated from them. So there was an air of normality to the hospital, as if time hadn't stopped a year before when the virus destroyed everything Michael had known about the world. Standing in this building, it was as if life had never changed.

"Doctor Sloan?…Yes, it's Trish…How are you?…Oh, that's wonderful…I'm great, thanks…Well, there's a man here to see you.…What?…Who is it? Oh, yes. Hold on."

Trish placed her right hand over the mouthpiece and leaned toward Michael.

"What's your name, sweetie?"

"Michael. Sloan."

She started to take her hand off the mouthpiece and bring it back up to her, then paused. She leaned toward Michael again.

"Sloan? Any relation to the doctor?"

"Um, yes. I'm her hus—ex-husband."

Trish mouthed an emphatic "Ohh," then put her right index finger to her lips, as if promising to keep a secret. Michael smiled and nodded. She brought the receiver back to her mouth.

"It's Michael Sl—yes.…Yes, that's right.…Oh, well, I don't know. Would you like me to ask?…Certainly. Just a moment."

Trish repeated her earlier routine.

"She wants to know what it is you want. I hope the divorce wasn't ugly, hun."

"No, no. It was fine. Um, can you tell her I just need ten minutes to talk? Tell her it's important."

Trish smiled and smacked some gum in her mouth, then went back to the phone.

"He says it's important, Doctor. Life or death," she looked at Michael and winked. "Okay. I'll tell him. Thank you, Doctor Sloan. Have a great day!"

She placed the phone in its cradle and looked up at Michael.

"Second floor, just up those stairs to the left," she pointed toward a glass staircase with an onyx metal railing. "She's in Room 227, through the double doors in front of you, and fifth door on your right. Fourth door's the women's washroom, so don't make a mistake!"

She laughed and smacked her gum. Michael smiled slightly and nodded.

"Right. I'll have to keep that in mind. Thanks, Trish."

"No worries, dear. Good luck."

23

The gate creaked as Paul pushed it open, stepped in and nudged it closed behind him, sliding the lock into place. Surrounding him was an eight-foot-tall fence, fully draped in blackout curtains, covering an area of the compound's courtyard that was 200 by 100 feet. Small tents were spread throughout much of the field, which was mostly dirt but had patchy brown grass like it had missed some spots shaving. The larger tents were big enough for one person to live relatively comfortably with a small bag carrying some personal items. There were also smaller tents scattered across the area closer to the gate, and those were a tight squeeze for anyone. The ones with people in them had a large "Occupied" sign affixed to both sides of the pitched roof.

In the center of the smaller ones was an iron pole its resident was forced to drive three feet into the hard-packed ground, to which the person's shackles were affixed. Paul and Danny were the only people Audrey authorized to enter the camp, and one of them would bring a bowl of water twice a day—if they didn't forget or get busy—and a tray of food that varied in quality depending upon who was bringing it and how lazy he was feeling that day. On the good days, it might include leftover fish or chicken from the house. On the bad days, it was either wet dog food or nothing came at all. Either way, the shackled prisoners were eating on all fours, their heads buried in a bowl with their feet chained together.

The shackled ones sometimes didn't survive a night, particularly if their fire went out and nobody brought them kindling to get it back going, or if it dropped well below freezing and a small fire wasn't enough with the linen jacket they were given. Those who survived lost thirty, forty pounds, maybe more. Their skin appeared almost purple from the clouds of red clay that attached to them when the weather got dry, and they lay in muddy pools of stagnant water when the rains came. They were rarely hosed down, and their teeth slowly browned from a lack of hygiene. They often stayed zipped in their tents to keep flies from buzzing around them, and out of embarrassment from showing their faces to the others. Sometimes, the noises they'd make could be haunting, though. Their campmates had to block it out to maintain their own sanity.

Nick and Rachel were two of the lucky ones. None of the people kept in the quarantine camp knew why some of them were treated humanely, with respect, while others had the existence of an abused dog. And sometimes, that treatment could turn on a dime. If you were in Paul's good graces, you could expect three meals a day, pretty consistently at nine, noon, and six, at a long wooden table under a large army mess hall tent. There were seven of them, dining on scrambled eggs, grilled chicken, lake trout, steamed broccoli, sometimes better food than they would have gotten on the outside. They had cast-iron wood-burning stoves by their tents to keep them warm in the winter, and wind-powered fans to cool them down in the summer.

All that could end, though, by saying the wrong word to Paul or Danny—though, really, it was Paul who set the boundaries. He always reminded the privileged group, there were eight single tents sitting empty, and their iron rod was waiting for them, stacked ominously against the fence near their dining table. The members of that privileged group were constantly on edge—cross an imaginary line Paul had no incentive to detail for them, and they could slowly wither away, wailing in a small tent while bugs crawled over their flesh. They'd seen it before. The most recent was a man named Victor. It was dark out and Nick was reading a book by candlelight in his tent when he heard Victor pleading, a panicked shriek coming from his mouth. Nick wanted to open his tent and see what was happening, but he stayed still, listening to Victor's screams become louder, then softer as he got further away, alongside the sound of shoes bumping and dragging across the dirty ground. When the noise stopped, Nick exhaled loudly, not realizing he'd been holding his breath as Victor was pulled away. Nick remained still on his mattress, not wanting to bring any attention to himself and hoping Victor would be the only target that night. He didn't hear a sound except for the crickets, as he lay awake. Sleep wouldn't come.

When they all emerged from their tents the next morning, they saw one of the large tents was missing, leaving just a dark spot on the dirt where sunlight hadn't penetrated for months. They turned to look at the group of smaller tents and began counting. The previous day, five had "Occupied" signs hanging on them. This time, in the light of the morning, they counted six, then looked around at each other. They were outnumbered. And what's worse was nobody had any idea why.

Soon after, Paul entered with a tray of food, and they all silently sat down to eat. Not a word was spoken about Victor; it was as if he'd never existed. They dined on eggs, biscuits and poached salmon, with dashes of cilantro and fresh apple juice. It was the best meal they'd had since the virus struck. Paul watched, pacing alongside the table as they enjoyed their meal, less than twenty steps from where their friend Victor lay, shackled to an iron rod, blood trickling down his chin from his right ear.

So when Paul would enter the camp without food, the privileged ones would try not to look alarmed, while also watching to see what he was doing. And when Paul shut the gate on that evening, he strolled past the small tents and into the area where Nick was finishing cleaning up after the dinner Danny had brought an hour before. Nick continued his work, even as his heart beat louder in his chest. He could swear Paul would be able to hear it as he got close.

Paul got near Nick, then kept walking over to the fence. He picked up an iron rod and held it in front of him with both hands, looking down at it like he was examining a bottle of wine at a nice restaurant. He lifted it, wrapping his hands around it and holding it up like a baseball bat, wiggling it just a little and looking ahead like he was waiting on a pitch. From ten feet away, Nick watched him out of the corner of his eye while he wiped down a plate.

Paul swung the rod like it was a bat, which didn't look easy when the thing was made of iron. As he finished his follow-through, he let one end of it touch the ground while he brought his right hand up over his eyes as if to shade the sun and watch his home run sail over the fence. Balancing the rod against his hip, he bent down and picked up some dirt, rubbing it between his hands and clapping, sending small puffs of dirt clouds into the air around him.

He picked up the rod again and began walking past Nick and toward the large tents. Nick stopped cleaning and stared, his muscles tightening, his fingers pressing hard enough into the plate he was holding to leave fingerprint marks.

Standing in the middle of the large tents, in front of Nick's, with three flanking him on either side, Paul held the rod by one end and let the other drop to the dirt in front of one of the tents that was the furthest to his right. Nick was the only one who hadn't gone back to his tent, since it was his night to clean up. He wondered if the rest of them knew what was going on outside, but there was nothing he could do to help them. Paul then picked the rod off the ground and turned it to land in front of the next tent to the left. He paused for a moment, then did the same one more tent left. Then to Nick's tent. He stopped, holding it there for a moment, and turned his head slowly. Nick could feel the blood run from his face as he stood, frozen in place. His heart pounded, and he felt nauseated, his stomach doing loops as his breath became shorter and more rapid. Paul looked at him and smiled, raising his eyebrows. Without taking his eyes off Nick, he lifted the rod again, then let it fall in front of the next tent to his left.

Paul turned his head back to the tents, grabbed the rod with both hands, then leaned down and unzipped the tent in front of him. It was Lucas's. Nick had gotten to know Lucas a bit, and he seemed like a good guy. Much like Nick, he'd been taken because he couldn't keep his hands off a woman, and he'd counted himself fortunate in a way that they'd taken him, since he now got to spend plenty of time with her. The couples who made it here without being chained in a single tent lived a pretty decent, if captive, life. Even the captivity could be excused away over time; they could convince themselves that everybody in Alessandra was captive in their own way. In the camp, they might be prisoners, but at least they got to shed those rings. They got to have sex, and eat well. All their needs were taken care of for them. Lucas had never said a bad word about Paul or Danny—at least, not to Nick. Why would Paul target him?

It seemed so random, which made it all the more terrifying when Nick heard the sound of the rod slamming into Lucas's side, him screaming, and then another blow from the rod. And another. Nick couldn't see the men, but he could see the shadows through the tent in the dying light of dusk. He could see Paul's silhouette raise the rod, then slash it through the air, meeting a silhouetted mound beneath him, eliciting muffled moans and screams. Five swings. Six. Seven. The rod cut heavily through the night air. Spots splattered haphazardly on the inside of the tent, a tiny bit at first, then larger globs, turning darker as they dripped lazily toward the ground.

Finally, Paul's shadow stopped, remaining still for several seconds before unzipping the tent, stepping out and zipping it closed behind him. He dragged the crimson-splattered rod along the ground behind him—it made a metallic sound like running a needle across a record, skipping through the barren dirt—and walked toward Nick.

"Do *not* open that tent," Paul said as he got close, barely above a whisper. "Never."

He walked back toward the gate, the rod tracing his path along the ground. Nick stared.

24

When Michael tapped on the door, he heard a voice he hadn't heard in awhile. It was both unfamiliar and very familiar.

"Door's open. Come on in."

Hearing it ignited memories, both good and bad. There was the divorce, obviously. Why had it gone south? There was no dramatic moment when the relationship went up in flames. Nobody walked in on the other in bed with their best friend, or got tired of having fresh bruises all the time. It probably just hadn't been the right time for either of them. They'd been high school sweethearts, her sitting in the bleachers watching him hurl fastballs for the baseball team, while he tried to pretend he knew something about volleyball when she talked about her matches. They started dating in tenth grade, then attended the University of North Georgia together in order to stay close to home. When Michael dropped out after three semesters, Stephanie transferred to the University of Georgia, seventy miles away in Athens. They tried keeping the relationship going long distance for nearly a year, but their lives were too different at the time, with Michael working odd jobs, fixing cars or painting houses, while Stephanie was working toward an honors degree and a scholarship for medical school.

They mutually decided they should end it, and Michael lost track of her for a while, as she finished her degree, then got a partial scholarship to Emory University in Atlanta to complete her doctorate. During her time in medical school, she used her connections in Alessandra to come back and get work experience whenever possible, particularly in the summer. And, of course,

Michael was still there, selling the occasional handmade bowl or handyman service. During those visits, they re-connected, usually finding time to sleep together when she could convince her parents she was working late, which she probably was.

And when it was time for her residency, there was little doubt she was coming back to St. Francis to stay. Six months later, she was Stephanie Sloan, and they were married at twenty-six years old.

It started well, as all but the worst marriages do. They were happy to be together, and they took a honeymoon to a small cabin a friend had in the Blue Ridge Mountains. They spent two nights there, and hardly left the bed. If she hadn't been afraid someone would see her when she went to the kitchen for a snack, they might not have put a shred of clothes on the whole time they were there. When they got back, they both enjoyed the novelty of being married. Michael even felt like it helped him in his work. When you were a twenty-six-year-old male college dropout, potential employers had a tendency to look skeptically upon your reliability. But put that ring on, and suddenly you have the stink of responsibility on you. You'd probably even be having kids soon. That meant you'd need a paycheck to support your family. And that probably meant you'd be a good, dependable worker. When it came to working with your hands, that was exactly what employers wanted: good, dependable workers. Fortunately, Michael *was* that.

The problem, though, was that he wasn't the best or most dependable husband, and that only got worse as he got bored with her long hours as a resident doctor at St. Francis. When you're in residency, you don't have a lot of say in your hours, or what you'll be doing. You strap yourself in for three years and bust your ass, night shift, morning shift, eighteen hours because that's what it takes. Michael felt like he never saw her. And when he *did* see her, she was too tired for sex, or even for a hike in the trails that surrounded Alessandra. There was also the jealousy, with Michael knowing that she was always going to be the breadwinner, that their future kids would look to her as the leader of the household. It was immature and petty, but it was also honest. He had a hard time with that, and he wasn't sure if it was something he could get past. In the abstract, he loved the idea of not having to work; she'd take care of the bills. His pride was going to take a hit, though, and he started silently sabotaging the marriage.

Once rot starts in a relationship, it's almost impossible to fix it completely. A couple either learns to live with the damage that's been done, or they put an end to it and go on with their lives alone. Eventually, Stephanie decided she had to take the latter approach. Michael didn't fight it when she did.

Now, for the first time since that August afternoon in the office of her divorce attorney, staring at a small stack of paperwork, Michael was hearing Stephanie's voice again. He turned the knob and pushed the door open a crack, sticking his head through the opening.

"Hey. Long time, no see. How are ya?"

Michael saw Stephanie in a white coat, her dark brown hair pulled up in a bun, large, wide-rimmed glasses around her eyes.

"I'm doing all right, Michael…considering," she took off her glasses and laid them on the desk. "Sit."

Michael walked over to the chair in front of her desk and sat down.

"So, what's important?" she asked.

He looked around the room to his left and right, examining the walls. There were pictures of Stephanie in happier times, one with former President Jimmy Carter. Another with her arm wrapped around U.S. Representative and Civil Rights leader John Lewis. Her diplomas were hung proudly, alongside an article from *Atlanta* magazine that appeared to put her in some sort of "30

Under 30" list for the state. It was impressive to see. She'd clearly made an impact with her life, and she hadn't needed Michael in order to do it.

"Nice pictures," he turned to look back at her.

She shifted in her seat and glared at him blankly.

"Look, Michael. I'm not trying to be rude or whatever. Maybe we can find some time to catch up at some point. But I'm pretty busy, and I'm seeing you now because you said it was important. Life or death. Remember?"

Michael laughed. "Well, she may have…*exaggerated* a bit there. I'm not sure."

Stephanie sighed loudly.

"Can you tell me what you're doing here?"

"Yeah. Right. Okay. So, what do you know about the virus?"

"The virus? You mean the one that basically wiped out human civilization? *That* virus?"

"Yeah. The very one."

"Not nearly enough, I'm afraid," Stephanie said. "But we're trying. Every day. What about it?"

"What do you know about how it spreads?"

"Does this have anything to do with why you're here, or—"

"Yes. It does."

She paused for a moment.

"We don't know *for sure* yet. But the one study that our Doctor Giles performed showed it was likely by physical contact."

"Are you going to confirm that?"

"That's not the easiest thing to do, when there's so much else that's a higher priority. A lot of those requests are coming straight from the mayor's office."

"What are they requesting?"

"Michael, I'm gonna have to ask that you just get to whatever it is you're here for. I can't answer any more of your questions."

He sat forward in his chair, and placed his hands on the desk.

"I think Audrey may be lying about the way this virus spreads in order to keep us under her thumb," he said. "That's why I'm here. You're the only person I trust to help me find out the truth."

She furrowed her brow. "Are you *insane?*"

"Hardly."

"This is ridiculous. Even if it were true, what would you want *me* to do?" Stephanie shook her head and shrugged. "Figuring this stuff out isn't a matter of snapping my fingers."

"I know. It's probably not even fair to ask. I just don't know where else to go with this. Who else am I going to talk to?"

"The benchmark study is done. As far as I'm concerned, that's the Bible until we have a comparable study. And I have no idea when that's going to be. That doesn't mean we can't question it, but it *does* mean that's all we have to go on for the time being."

Michael's head dropped.

"Why do you even think she's lying about this? What good would it do? Tinfoil hats aren't flattering on you, I've gotta say."

He leaned back, placing his hands on the bench beside him for balance as his ring brushed the slope of the wood. He looked at the ceiling for several seconds before responding.

"I came here straight from there," he said.

"Straight from *where?*"

"From Audrey's. From the compound up the hill."

"Oh. What were you doing there?"

Michael told her about Trevor's murder, and Nick being taken into quarantine. She was sympathetic to him losing his friend to an uncertain fate, but skeptical that Audrey would do that if there hadn't been good reason.

"Is that why? Because of Nick?" Stephanie said. "I get that you're upset because you guys were so close, but Audrey does these things to protect us. She has to make hard decisions like that so this town can function. We're here because of her."

"Yeah. Sure. That's probably true. And that's pretty similar to the conversation I just had with her earlier this evening, especially after I found out she's going to pin Trevor's murder on him."

"She's going to do *what?*" Stephanie blinked.

"It was kind of funny. I just didn't see that coming at all. I was convinced the same as you, that she takes these hardline stances, straps us up in these ridiculous heavy rings, to keep us safe. We've made it this far, and that has to be because of what she's done. Ya know, I bet if you took a poll of everyone here, she'd have an approval rating in the nineties. It's amazing.

"But there was something she said when we were arguing over this. She was talking about why she was going to give Nick to the town as the killer, when I knew who actually did it, and she said, 'It doesn't matter what I know. It doesn't matter what you know. What matters is keeping these people safe and happy.' And it dawned on me that she'll do and say practically anything to keep this going. Maybe it's 'might makes right.' Or maybe it's just the ends justifying the means. But I'm convinced she'll lie, cheat, steal, maybe even kill if she has to in order to keep this 'I saved Alessandra' trophy in her mind."

"And you think the rings might be part of that," Stephanie said. "You think she'd lie to maintain the status quo there."

"Yeah. I do," he nodded. "I don't know how, or even *if*, we can figure this out. Maybe we can't. But I see the toll these things, and the separation rules that go along with them, have done to the town. Hell, I see the toll it's all taking on me. The streets are empty. It's a living ghost town. But that works for her, because it means people aren't plotting anything. They aren't talking, or building alliances. They're just sitting at home, maybe reading *Oliver Twist* and then going to bed at eight o'clock. Would she lie to us to keep that going? I bet she would."

Stephanie sat forward and put her arms on the table. She twitched her fingers to gesture Michael to lean close in to her. She sighed, then began to whisper.

"Okay. I don't even know if we can be talking about this. If you're right," she looked up and around the room at the walls around her. "And I'm by no means saying you are. It could be dangerous to even be having this conversation. It might even be dangerous that you were seen coming up here."

She picked up a bottle of water from beside her on the desk and took a drink. She held it out to offer some to Michael, but he shook his head.

"I'm gonna have to think about this, all right? I'm not even sure what I'd do, if I decide to provisionally believe you and do something. But give me a day or two. Take this walkie-talkie with you. I'll let you know when I figure something out."

Michael lifted himself from the bench and stood. Almost out of force of habit, she stuck out her hand to shake, and he twitched. It was a casual ritual that had fallen by the wayside in most of Alessandra, but it was still common in the hospital, where doctors and nurses lived a much more intermingled life, but they were tested for the virus frequently, and maintained strict hygiene standards. Michael was just a visitor; she quickly pulled her hand back.

"Sorry. I just—"

"I know," Michael said. "It's a little gesture, but it's one of the things we're fighting for here. We want our world back. Our being part of one another's lives. If we have a shot at that, I think it's worth it."

Stephanie nodded and reached up to tuck her hair behind her right ear. It was a gesture Michael had seen her do a thousand times, but this time was like the first. It reminded him how crippling the loneliness he felt was, and made him wonder if much of this new crusade was being driven by that, instead of reason and logic.

He walked to the door. Grabbing the knob, he turned his head and gave her a slight smile. She returned it, then sat back down at her desk, pulling a stack of papers over and grabbing a pen. He walked out and headed toward the hospital exit.

25

Audrey woke up feeling rested for the first time in weeks. Retiring early and locking her door at eight o'clock had been the best decision she'd made for a while. Eleven or so hours of sleep had been exactly what she needed. She'd almost forgotten about her arguments with Michael and Paul the night before, and having to monitor a longtime friend to find out if more drastic measures were necessary. Almost.

While she felt physically refreshed, her mind was still a bit of a mess. She felt like she was living in a House of Mirrors at a third-rate carnival, where everything you looked at was a distorted version of reality. She knew who she was and—to a certain extent —this wasn't it. She knew how to play political hardball. You didn't rise to the leadership position she was in, even in a town as small as Alessandra, without having some political game. She could play dirty when she needed to. She told herself she was willing to do whatever it took to keep the people of the town safe.

But she couldn't help but question whether she was cut out for this. She wanted to do the right thing, but trying to hold onto her morality had never felt more like trying to hold onto a handful of sand than it had in post-plague Alessandra. What was right, and what was wrong? Was it right to kill a man who appeared to be no threat, but who was standing near the walls of your town? She didn't think so. But Paul saw situations with respect to the town as more of a zero-sum game; for the people of Alessandra to be completely safe, no one from the outside could be. Everyone from elsewhere was expendable if there was any chance they could cause harm to someone inside those walls. And if someone from *inside* the walls posed a threat to the rest of the people, he could be disposed of as well. Was that right? Was it moral? Paul would say it was. Audrey wasn't sure she entirely agreed, but she saw where he was coming from. She understood the burden. She just wondered if she was equipped to handle it.

On the other hand, maybe *she* was the one who was right. Maybe Paul's extreme approach really *wasn't* necessary. Maybe she could straddle that middle ground of being tough but fair. Of being only as ruthless and unforgiving as she had to be in order to maintain order. She had no taste for blood. She didn't want to hurt anyone, and she felt like that was a line she wouldn't have to cross.

After several minutes of rolling over, stretching and yawning, she decided she was too awake to fall back asleep, and she was hungry. She swung her legs over to the side of the bed and stood up, bringing her arms up over her head toward the ceiling and arching her back behind her. She pulled her robe off the far bed post and wrapped it around her body, cinching it tight in front, and walked into the hall toward the kitchen.

Barefoot, she walked onto the cold kitchen tile and jumped just a bit, cringing at the temperature on the soles of her feet. She opened the fridge and got a carafe of water, then poured it into a glass that was sitting on the counter. She put the carafe back, then grabbed an apple—still fresh and bright red—that was sitting in a bowl by the microwave. She walked out of the kitchen and to the dining room table a few feet to her right.

Audrey set down the glass, sat down and bit into the apple. In front of her was a wood-paneled den with a large set of windows that overlooked the courtyard. From the table, she could look out over much of it, though it wasn't a view she much enjoyed. There was little grass down there and—especially in the winter—it had a tendency to look dim and gray. She'd rather quietly enjoy her apple and stare at the table.

On the floor in the den, though, something caught her eye. She couldn't tell what it was, but there was definitely a long object lying on the floor in there, not far from the door to the stairs that led down to the courtyard. She stretched to try to get a better look, but she couldn't make out what it might be. She laid her apple down, got off her stool and walked around the table to get a closer look.

Walking into the den, she could see it was the shape of a stick, but it was far more substantial than that. It was what looked like a forged, wrought-iron rod. And, while most of it was a dark, metallic gray, there was another color draped across much of it, almost as if it were splashed with a large can of paint. The color was dark, but not as dark as the iron itself; it was a black-tinged crimson. Was it…blood? Surely not. How would a blood-covered iron rod have ended up in her house? She walked over closer and sat down beside it, picking it up to hold it near her face. Was she seeing what she thought she was? She ran a finger along the rod, and some of the crimson flaked off. It was dry, but it wasn't entirely hardened. If it was blood, it hadn't been there long. She scraped it with her fingernail, and more shaved off into her left hand, waiting below.

She held it up, and looked at it closely. It looked like it was probably blood, but she wasn't sure. She cupped it in both her hands, and brought it to her nose, then sucked in hard. She picked up that unmistakably pungent, metallic odor of human blood. She was sure this rod was a murder weapon.

She dropped it to the floor with a heavy thunk, as it rattled to a rest on the parquet. She knew neither the victim, nor who might have killed them. But the likelihood was high that there was a killer in her home, and she hoped it wasn't who she thought it was.

26

Michael usually showed up early for Watch meetings, because he liked to be the first one there to greet everyone as they entered the old high school gym where they met. But he showed up even earlier this time because he didn't care much about the agenda on this night. He was waiting on one particular guy to show up.

He needed to know if his hunch was correct. Zac wouldn't freely admit he killed Trevor, but Michael felt like he could read Zac well enough to tell the truth anyway. Zac always thought he was the smartest guy in the room, but Michael felt like he was mostly talk. Zac had shown there was some action behind his bombast, though, and that did unnerve Michael a bit. Maybe Zac wasn't just a blustery former frat boy wanting to assert his masculinity in a room full of men. Or maybe he *had* been that, and now he was morphing into something more sinister, applying his talk into action. He knew Zac has been through a lot, and maybe the guy was snapping.

That wouldn't shock Michael. He'd seen the way this town had evolved over the past year. People were getting more isolated and testier. He worried it could cause problems, as people in the town dug their personal holes deeper, their rings creating a bubble that they didn't want to pop. A lot of people didn't work; Michael was one of the ones who enjoyed going to an office every day. Audrey gave those who worked some perks when it came to rations and such, but there wasn't much she could do to force people to get out of bed and leave the house if they didn't want to. And, in the end, Michael wasn't sure she wanted to anyway. A lethargic public was a public that wasn't going to worry

THE SOLITARY APOCALYPSE   134

about the rights they were losing. If you had nothing, you had
nothing to lose. And lots of the people of Alessandra basically
had nothing.

That included Zac, a former Army sniper who had been
married prior to the plague. He'd been a family man in an earlier
incarnation of himself. Michael remembered him working as a
forest ranger, living a few towns over, and bringing his wife,
Karen, and two daughters to festivals in the Alessandra square.
They looked happy then, Karen's blonde hair billowing against
the summer breeze, and his daughters nipping at double scoops
of ice cream while skipping ahead. As the virus raged, Zac and
his family moved to take advantage of the safety of Alessandra.

From there, all Michael knew was that—like with many other
families—Audrey's officers took Karen and their daughters from
Zac during her roundup as the walls were completed. While some
families took solace in the fact that the wife and children would
be kept safe in a separate location, Zac wasn't willing to watch
them go. Michael didn't know all the details, as Zac refused to talk
about it, but he heard it had been an ugly scene. For a while, he
blamed himself for not doing more to hold on to them. Maybe
he never stopped. He became more irritable, less forgiving of
others. It was like he needed to lash out at something, so he
lashed out at everything. It may have been irrational, but people
aren't always rational when it comes to those they love. And
Michael thought that simmering resentment over his loss might
have pushed him further and further until he couldn't contain his
anger. Who really knew?

Of course, Michael had sympathy for that. It was
heartbreaking what had happened to him, and many others. But
Michael also felt like Zac should understand that this was just a
pause in his family's relationship; the virus would be killed soon
enough, and his family was better off where they were taken,
cordoned off from any danger. It was for the good of the town

and society as a whole. It was a sacrifice, but they were all making sacrifices. Killing Trevor didn't even some sort of cosmic score for the loved ones he temporarily lost. Michael was going to make sure that was clear, especially if Nick had to be the one to take the blame for what Zac had done.

The men started showing up, and Michael stood near the door, like usual, welcoming them, asking how they'd been, and what plans they had for the coming week. Typical mindless chit-chat. During every word of it, his eyes kept darting to his left, looking for Zac to walk in. Typically, Zac was one of the early arrivers too, but not this time. Michael had been hoping Zac would show up at least ten minutes early so he'd have time to get him alone, and still make it to the podium to open the meeting. But it was now just five until one, and there was no sign of Zac with just five minutes until the guys would expect the meeting to begin.

There was a low din of voices coming from behind Michael as the men filled the backless folding chairs on the gym floor, talking about sports memories, chili recipes, and the latest town gossip. Michael stood alone, leaning against a white plaster pillar, staring out the front door of the gym in the hope of seeing Zac step into the building. He glanced down at his watch: 12:58. Zac was about out of time.

Michael turned around and walked between the rows of chairs to the front of the room and climbed the stairs to the podium. Hank sat silently in a chair next to him.

"I heard what happened to Trevor," Hank spun his head toward Michael, standing beside him.

Startled, Michael looked at Hank.

"What?"

"Why did you guys have to kill him?"

"It's complicated."

"It's complicated, is it? Murder is complicated?"

Michael opened his mouth, and then the doors opened. Zac stepped through and walked into the main hallway toward the gym.

"Can we continue this later?" Michael said. "You're gonna have to get the meeting going for me. Give me ten minutes."

"What do you—"

But Michael was already walking away, hopping down from the gym stage and onto the floor, hurrying to catch Zac before he found a seat. He reached Zac just as he started positioning a seat beneath himself.

"Hey! Hold on. Walk with me for a second. We need to talk."

Zac froze in place for a second, then rose back up.

"Is this about Trevor?"

"I think we should talk about this in private," Michael pointed his thumb toward the door to the hallway.

"Sure. Whatever you say, boss," Zac began walking up to Michael. Then, as he reached him, in a low voice: "But they're taking your boy down no matter what you say to me."

27

Wiping the sleep from his eyes, Paul rolled over in bed. It was approaching noon, but he wasn't anxious to get up and start the day. He rarely was, but this morning he felt even more lethargic than usual. He was still pissed off from the argument the previous day with Audrey, and he'd found his violent outbursts becoming more common—and feeling way too normal—when he had to work out some anger. Still, as he rolled back the previous night's events in his head, he felt it was all justified.

It's not like I'm some sort of murderer. People drove me to it. What was I supposed to do? There isn't a damn thing to do in this godforsaken town. You can't exactly go trolling for chicks at the bars on weekends. And Audrey surrounded herself with men. They all get a piece of her, but she's my fucking sister, so I get nothing but jacking off to relieve my eternal blue balls. Sure, I don't have to live my life wearing those ridiculous rings around my waist, but what other benefit do I get for all the work I do for Audrey? A comfortable bed and a fancy chaise lounge in the living room? Fuck all that. I might as well be one of the commoners out there, holed up in their homes and mooching off everything we do for them.

So I let off some steam every now and then. What sort of life do these people have anyway? I'm freeing them from this goddamn prison when I end their miserable lives here. Maybe somebody will do it to me one day. I'll welcome it. Bash my fucking skull in. Let's see the brain matter fly all over the walls; we need to redecorate anyway. I mean, what the hell? Audrey doesn't appreciate what I do for her, and for everyone here. She's still consumed with morals and making the right choice. But in a world gone mad, there's no such thing. Morals only matter in how your actions impact others. Newsflash: everyone's fucking dead. We're the survivors, and what good is it doing us? We get to scrape by day to day in a meaningless existence that'll inevitably end with us dying anyway? We don't get to indulge in the whole goddamn reasons for living—sex, drugs, alcohol and great food?

I'm not a murderer. I'm a realist. I'm a bringer of freedom, and I'm in touch with where we all are. I'm ready to protect the people of this town, because that's the best way for me to stay comfortable alongside big sis there in this compound. As little as I get from being here, I'd literally blow my fucking brains out with whatever I could find if I had to live like the rest of these pansies for one damn day. But I'm not gonna pretend this is some moral crusade, and I can maintain some sort of high road in doing it. If this is the fate the non-existent god has bestowed upon me, so be it. I'll play the hand I'm dealt until I have to fold. But I'm gonna do what I think is necessary for my own sanity in the meantime.

Paul rolled onto his left side and stared at the wall a few feet in front of him, letting his mind go blank. He didn't feel any guilt; he just felt nothing. Literally nothing. Not happy or sad. Not energetic or tired. He felt hollow, like he was a tanker truck that'd been spilled empty and wiped clean. Pristine and sparklingly hollow. There was an instinct to fill himself with something, but he had no idea what.

His bedroom door flew open, slamming into the wall behind it, and he jerked into a sitting position, looking in that direction. There stood Audrey, holding what looked like the iron rod he had beaten Victor with the previous night. Where had he left it? He had been in a weird mental state and couldn't remember, but it apparently hadn't taken her long to track it down. She was holding it up above her head, as if ready to bring it down on someone.

"Oh, shit! You're here. Are you all right?" Audrey brought the rod down to her side and walked over to Paul's bed. "This rod is covered in blood. Something happened last night while I was in bed."

Paul grimaced, then sighed.

"*Something* happened?"

"Apparently. Do you know anything about it?"

He looked down at the bed and ran his fingers through his hair, which was turning into a thick, black bird's nest on top of his head.

"God damn it," she rolled her eyes. "You do, don't you?"

Paul looked her in the eyes and raised his eyebrows, then lowered his head again, saying nothing.

"Well?" she said expectantly, gesturing with both arms.

"What do you want me to say? Seriously. What? What will it take for you to leave me alone?"

"I'm not going to *leave you alone*. You're gonna have to tell me whose blood this is. *You* look fine."

"You don't *actually* want the answer to that question." Paul scratched the back of his neck. "I think we both know that."

"What do you mean? I damn well *do* want to know that."

"You *don't*. Come on. Let's be real. You've never been comfortable with the shit I have to do in order to clean up the messes you don't want to take care of. You set us up in this fucking Hilton here so we can pretend we're different. Or better than everyone else in this town. But we're not. This could all be taken from us at any time, especially if you're not willing to do what it takes to keep us here."

"That…That's a fucking—"

"Don't. Let's just not do this, all right? Let's not pretend like you're all tough, and you're gonna break me or something. And we go round and round, and I tell you some bullshit story so you can go on turning a blind eye to shit that goes on around here."

"I know *everything* that goes on around here! This is *my* town, and don't you lose sight of that."

"You know *everything* that goes on around here?"

"Yeah," she slammed the rod into the bed, and Paul jumped. "Yeah, I fucking *do*."

"Then tell me, when's the last time you went into the quarantine camp out in the courtyard?"

"Um…" Audrey looked at the floor and shuffled her feet. "What do you mean?"

"The camp, Audrey. The fucking camp out there. You remember, the one you handed over to me and said to take care of it. The one where Danny and I have been taking the people you've had brought up here for touching violations. *That* camp. The one you won't even look at. The one you don't even ask about."

"I've been in there."

"Yeah? When? Right when we first set it up? Before people were in it? Don't tell me you forgot it was even there. You're a fucking hypocrite. You want to be tough, bringing all these people up here, but then when it comes to actually handing down the consequences, you turn it over to your little brother so you can allow yourself to plead ignorance. That's it, isn't it? You want to be able to honestly deny you know what we're doing with these people once they get up here."

"I've ordered you both to treat those people with the utmost care and professionalism." She banged her fist on the headboard. "If you haven't done that, that's on you, not me."

"Yeah. Sure," Paul shrugged. "But it's on you too. You just want plausible deniability, in case all this shit goes south. 'They disobeyed my orders! They're the guilty ones!' You need scapegoats, because you think this whole thing is a house of cards you've built. You think it'll all come crumbling down, and you're playing the game.

"You want to know whose blood that is? Well, I'm not gonna tell you. You want to know? Go down to the camp. Won't take you long to get your answer. That is, if you really *do* want one, and you're not just posturing. Your answer's down there. Go get it. I'm going back to sleep."

28

Stephanie had wanted to be a doctor ever since following her mom to her nursing shift at St. Francis on a "Bring your daughter to work day" when she was six years old. She got to sit at the computer and help her mom enter records, talk to all sorts of different people, and wear a cool white coat that made her feel like a superhero. Being a nurse would have been fine too, but she was enamored with the respect people in the building seemed to have for doctors, the way they were all referred to as "Doctor" like they were royalty. And since she was, to be frank, unlikely to become an actual princess, she figured a doctor was the next best thing.

Of course, at the time, she didn't know much of anything about what it took to get there, or the breadth of disciplines you could go into. She didn't know about forty-eight-hour shifts and grueling residencies and cleaning up shit-covered sheets—*lots* of shit-covered sheets—and the misogyny that seemed built into the medical establishment, especially in the rural south. Throughout medical school and much of her early time at the hospital, someone almost every day assumed she was a nurse, not a doctor. She was asked to clean bedpans, something the male doctors never got tasked with. And when they accepted that she wanted to be a doctor, the doctors and nurses at St. Francis tried to steer her toward gynecology or obstetrics instead of the type of rigorous scientific research she had a passion for.

It wasn't an easy road to get where she was sitting, as the co-chair of the St. Francis Department of Medical Research, one of the most respected such small units in the Southeast. Of course, what that even meant anymore, she wasn't sure. They still told themselves that. They still talked about their reputation, as if the world hadn't changed. Within those walls, in many ways, it hadn't. It was their own bubble, where they could pretend everything was just as it had always been. Sure, they had fewer patients. And they didn't have instantaneous contact with other doctors across the world. But they also didn't have all the bureaucratic red tape they had before. They may not have had the funding to do nearly as much, but if they felt like something was necessary, there was nothing to stop them from doing it other than their means—and they had learned to stretch those means further than they ever expected they could.

So when Doctor Giles issued the report that said physical contact was likely the key driving factor in the spread of H6N1—the technical term for the viral infection that rapidly killed off most of the human population—that was a big moment for the hospital, and the research department in particular. Doctor Giles was the head of their department, and he had close to forty years of experience in research. This wasn't like the hand of God coming down and saying "I say it, so it is the truth!" but it was about as close as it gets to that in the scientific community. Certainly, people could question the results, but replicating the tests again was challenging as many of the subjects had subsequently died, and the virus wasn't known to be functioning in anyone they had contact with. It wasn't that they internalized the results as being unquestioned fact, but it was all they had to go on, so they were functioning as if it were true.

And, Stephanie thought, it almost certainly was. Doctor Giles had no reason to lie, and the methodology had been peer reviewed throughout. He was the only one who finalized and certified the final results, but his credibility was never in question. Why would it be? That seemed to be his crowning achievement too, as he retired less than a month after the report was released,

quickly winding down an amazing career at St. Francis, elevating
Stephanie to co-chair of the department with Doctor Frank
Lawry.

   Michael walking into her office and questioning Doctor Giles'
study had caught her off guard. Not only had she been sitting
there looking at a man she'd successfully avoided for a couple of
years—through most of the divorce proceedings, the H6N1
nightmare, the wall going up, and Audrey's rules for the town—
but he was telling her a story that didn't seem real. His depiction
of Audrey as a duplicitous, power-hungry despot didn't sound
right to her. She'd known Audrey for years, first as a small-time
comptroller for Mayor Handy, moving up in his ranks through
secretarial jobs, then Chief Financial Officer, Deputy Mayor, and
then taking over for him after he succumbed to H6N1. She'd
always been respectful, and selfless in her dealings with Stephanie
and the town. Why would she take this turn so suddenly? What
would have changed? It didn't sound right, and she wasn't buying
it. There had to be something else going on. Was this just
Michael's excuse to get back in touch with her after all this time?
What good would that even do, if so? It wasn't like people had
crazy flings in the town, when the fate of the potential final
humans on earth might depend upon them keeping their libidos
in check for a while.

   Still, though, there was a part of her that wanted to consider
at least looking into Michael's questions. Not even so much
because she thought he was right, or that his story made any
sense, but more because *somebody* probably needed to. Doctor
Giles was a brilliant doctor, scientist and researcher; there was no
question about that. But science wasn't built on appeals to
authority or intelligence. Science demanded fair inquiry, and peer
review. She wasn't sure what she could do, but maybe she needed
to look into it just for science's sake. And if she could also shoot

Michael's wacko conspiracy theory down in the process, so be it. That could never be a bad thing.

Of course, if he actually *was* right, then it was doubtful she could do anything without some sort of jack-booted thugs standing in her way. He couldn't be right, though. If she had to bet on someone trying to play her between Audrey and Michael, she'd bet on Michael every day of the week. There was only one way she could possibly find out, but she did worry that she'd be encouraging whatever he was attempting by even indulging in it. Did she want to reward his lying and conspiracy mongering by giving him what he wanted? She really wasn't sure.

29

Audrey stood in the den, staring out through the large windows that looked over the courtyard. Had Paul been right? Had she avoided confronting this for months, allowing him and Danny to take care of it under her nose? Subconsciously or not, she probably had. Maintaining her distance from this made sense. She knew some ugly things might have to happen in there from time to time. It wasn't that she didn't have the stomach for it; it was that she had a reputation to maintain. It was a reputation she spent decades building. It was what allowed her to govern in the way she did, and helped keep the people of Alessandra alive. Right?

That's the story she told herself, at least. She wanted to believe it was true. The people needed to stay separate from one another. Without a strong, trusted leader, though, they'd never have the strength to do it on their own. She was the only one with the credibility to make this policy stick. People did it because they trusted her to do what was right, and only what was necessary for their safety. They knew she meant the best for them, and was making difficult choices.

If it was eventually found out that the quarantined people had been mistreated, though, how would that look for her if she'd been part of that? She might lose that benefit of the doubt. People wouldn't understand why it had to happen—why that show of force was necessary for control—and would doubt her commitment to peace. So, in some ways, yeah, she'd been setting it up to where she could say she'd been stabbed in the back by her brother, that he'd taken matters into his own hands. She'd pay

lip service to "dealing with him," talk about the punishment he
was receiving, have him say some words about being sorry, and
how he was going to do everything possible to work out his
aggression. And that'd be it. She could protect both the people
of Alessandra and her brother if she had control of the situation.
But there was nobody to protect her, if she was the one with eyes
upon her.

So, here she stared, down on the quarantine camp, with a dirt-
and mud-covered ground strewn with tents, some very small, and
others possibly big enough for a couple. There was what looked
like a dining table on the far side. It was the early afternoon, and
no one was moving around in the camp. There was no way of
knowing from here if *anyone* was alive down there, much less if
they all were. That bloody iron rod suggested at least one of
them wasn't in good shape.

Did she dare go down there? She was afraid of what she
might see. How bad could Paul and Danny have let it get? They
weren't bad men; she was sure of that much. But she had to see,
right? She had to see this for herself.

She walked a few steps to her left and opened the door to the
stairs that led down to the courtyard. They were black wrought
iron, not unlike a New York apartment fire escape, winding their
way down the side of the building. She'd like to have something a
bit more grandiose, but the courtyard had stopped being a
priority for her after they set the camp up. She carefully worked
her way down, spiraling in circles as she got closer to the ground.
At the bottom, she hopped off, her feet landing hard on the dry
ground, sending a cloud of dirt and dry, loose grass billowing
into the air around her ankles.

She turned to face the fence to the camp. From above, she
could see everything, looking down beyond this barrier. It felt like
something she could face—*had* to face—when she saw it from a
bird's-eye view. Standing on ground level, though, it was more

difficult to confront. The eight-foot fence had been draped on the inside with a large blackout curtain so there was nothing you could see. From here, it was easy to pretend nothing was in there. Certainly, no people were in there. You might hear some noises at times, but those could be coming from anywhere. Out of sight, out of mind. And from this vantage point, it would be easy for Audrey to let that literal wall serve as the proverbial wall in her mind.

Still, she walked closer. She knew what she'd seen from above. She wasn't going to pretend again. This was important for her to see first hand. She walked to the gate for the fence and lifted the lock to see the keyhole. She pulled out her key and unlatched it, tossing the lock aside. All she had to do now was shove it gently, and she'd be in.

It did occur to her, though, that maybe Paul was exaggerating. It was at least possible that he was messing with her, that he'd been slaughtering a pig or something with that rod. Maybe he had been *trying* to call her out on her attitude toward the camp, and this had been his way of doing it. He had left that rod in an awfully conspicuous place, where she was almost certain to find it. Maybe he *wanted* her to find it, so he could confront her. Maybe it'd force her to walk into the camp and see what was going on so that she'd be a part of it. He was trying to chain her to him—if he went down, she was going to go down with him.

But he didn't understand what she was trying to do. He wasn't as smart as she was. Never had been, and she knew it. She'd always been the one thinking steps ahead, and he'd always been the one acting impulsively, going all the way back to when they were kids. If she took one of his toys, he'd cry and scream until mom came to make Audrey give it back because her mom just wanted the screaming to stop, and she knew Audrey wouldn't do more than sulk. If she really wanted the toy, though, she'd take one of her toys and show so much interest in it, and talk so much about how great it was, that he'd have to have *that* toy. It might take a day or two of convincing, but she'd get him begging and crying for it. When her mom would come to make peace, Audrey would propose a trade for the toy she really wanted all along. In the end, everybody won because she'd been patient, and planned out a way to get what she wanted. He didn't have to know what was going on to benefit from it; she let him go on thinking he'd come out ahead in the deal. Didn't matter to her. She had the big red fire truck.

That was the same as what was happening here. He was screaming and crying, trying to get what he wanted from her. The stakes were enormous this time, though. This wasn't red fire trucks and ninja turtles. This was life or death, the fate of an entire town—possibly the last of the human race. She couldn't let him drag her down onto his level. She had to stick with the plan she'd been following. It would work, if it needed to.

She picked the lock back up and snapped it into place over the gate's latch, then walked back to the stairs.

30

With the din of Hank's voice in the background calling the meeting to order, Michael stopped in the hall next to the old concession stand, where he used to buy hot dogs and so-called "nachos" swimming in Cheez-Whiz at basketball games. He turned around to see Zac walking calmly toward him, several steps behind and with no apparent urgency. Michael crossed his arms as he waited for Zac to come closer.

"What do you mean by 'They're taking your boy down'?" Michael hissed through clenched teeth, leaning into the words as if to give them more force.

"I'm pretty sure you know exactly what I mean," Zac shrugged slightly and rolled his eyes.

Michael looked around, his face contorted into a pained grimace.

"You did it, didn't you?"

"Did *what?*"

"You murdered Trevor when my back was turned."

"'Murdered' is a pretty ugly term, Mike."

"Oh, go fuck yourself with that smarmy junk. You did it. We both know it."

"I really don't know what you're talking about," Zac said, frowning. "From what I hear, they've got a confession."

"From 'my boy'?"

"That's the word around the campfire, isn't it?"

Michael stared at him, searching for a hint of remorse or guilt; there was nothing there. Zac seemed distant, wearing a shield that protected him from the pangs that haunt an average man. Michael could hear Hank discussing trash pickup with one of the members in the gym.

"What do you want?"

"What do I *want*?"

"Yeah. What do you want?"

"Oh, I don't know. A nice warm blanket. The love of a good woman."

"Are you gonna keep playing dumb with me? You think this is a game?"

Zac stepped forward, his ring clanging loudly against Michael's.

"That's *exactly* what it is," Zac's eyes seemed to light up as he spoke. "This is *all* a game. Look around you, for Christ's sake! What do you think this is? It's all a fucking *game*. This isn't real life. You think this Watch nonsense makes you important? That it erases all the insanity that you're living in from day to day? The old rules are *done*, man. It doesn't matter what happened outside those walls. We're in *here* now. We're in this game, and I'm gonna goddamn *play* it. You can pretend this is just hunky-dory life as we all knew it, and act like I should give a shit that that asshole is dead. But I don't, and you shouldn't either. We're all in this for ourselves. You. Me. Trevor sure as hell was. But ya know what? He lost the game. And I'll tell ya one more thing—in the end, I'm gonna win it."

Zac stepped back and brushed his hands down the front of his coat. Michael stared silently.

"Now, if you'll excuse me, I've got a Watch meeting to pretend like I give a shit about."

Zac spun back around and walked toward the gym door to go back to the meeting. Michael took a deep breath and looked up at the ceiling.

That hadn't gone as he'd rehearsed it in his mind. Michael had a tendency to think he was more conniving and persuasive than he actually was. Whatever gifts he *did* have, though, simply weren't working on Zac. He could gain Audrey's trust, and take on a leadership role with this group of Alessandrians, but Zac seemed unreachable for him. They were constantly talking past each other, and there seemed to be no way for Michael to drag him back onto the same rhetorical plane; they were like two cars driving in the same direction on parallel highways, but without any exit ramp to meet up. Even if their ultimate destinations could be discerned and were similar, there was no way for them to communicate that to each other.

Now, Michael was even more worried about what would happen to Nick and Rachel. No one had officially been charged with murder in post-plague Alessandra. Trevor wasn't a beloved figure in the town, but Michael wondered how loud the call for justice would be once Nick was officially fed to the masses with the "murderer" label. In a small town like this, vigilante justice seemed like something they couldn't accept, though he hoped at least some people could be convinced to be sympathetic toward the situation Nick was in at the time. According to the story, yes, he'd followed the guy instead of contacting the officials to take care of it. But he'd done so in a fit of passion, after listening to a woman he had strong feelings for—maybe even loved—cry for hours after having been raped by the man. Most men would probably do something similar. It might not make it exactly right, but it was understandable enough to keep Audrey from having to take drastic action.

Of course, either way, Nick was stuck in quarantine purgatory for an indefinite amount of time, and no one knew what happened to the people who ended up there. That was a secret Audrey was keeping tight guard over, but the rumor was that there was a space on her campus where they kept these people. Theoretically, they'd eventually be released once it was clear they posed no danger to the rest of the people of the town. Michael wasn't sure if he bought that, though.

Lost in thought, Michael heard a burst of static from nearby and began looking around. Then he heard a faint voice. He stood as still as possible to try to hear it better and figure out where it came from. Then he remembered the walkie-talkie strapped to his belt on his back.

"Michael? Hello?" Stephanie said, getting impatient.

"Yes. Sorry. I forgot about this thing for a second."

Stephanie's eye roll could almost be heard through the speaker.

"All right. I've thought it over. And this seems like a really stupid thing to do."

Michael cursed under his breath.

"I really hope you'll reconsi—"

"Hold on. I wasn't done. This seems like a stupid thing to do, and I don't know why I'm saying yes. But I'm saying yes."

"Thank you. Thank you," Michael clasped his hands together and tossed a glance up. "I think we can do this."

"Right. About that. There's no 'we' here. At least not at first."

"But I can help. This is my idea."

"I'll let you know if and when I need help. For now, you need to let me do a few things on my end. Keep this thing on. I'll check back with you."

"Steph...I don't want you to do this by yourself. I want to be a part of it." Michael paused for a few seconds, and heard nothing. "Stephanie? Are you there? Shit."

31

When the morning sun rose over the lake, Nick could see splatters of blood in silhouette through Lucas's tent, like looking through a kaleidoscope. It was almost beautiful in the random patterns it made, striking the outside of the tent in spurts, some small and some larger, an artist choosing the targets of his vision carefully. Nick wanted to stare at it; maybe looking at it long enough would give him a deeper insight into what happened and why. If he could make sense of the seeming randomness of the thousands of scattered shadows of crimson, maybe he could gain an understanding of the seeming randomness of the murder itself.

Nick, Rachel and the others had lived in this camp for varying amounts of time—some for several months, others for barely a week. But there'd been a sense of control over their circumstances prior to Lucas's life coming to such a sudden and violent end. They'd felt that, as long as they did what was asked of them, they'd be okay, that the ones who were isolated had, in a sense, deserved their fate for breaking the rules. After Lucas met the butt end of an iron rod, though, they had to ask themselves if any of them were safe at all. And, in a camp where they were prisoners for an indefinite amount of time, with no trial and no jury, what did "safe" even mean? When there were no consequences for the guards, how long would it be before the power would get to them? And now that they were all potential witnesses to what Paul had done, what reason did they have to think he'd let them live long enough to tell anyone about it?

The only positive Nick had to take away from the situation was that they were, in fact, still alive. He was still breathing. So was Rachel, thank god. Theresa was still two tents over, and her sobs eventually stopped after Lucas was killed. Nick hoped she'd found sleep. There was Omar, in the tent next to Theresa. He'd been in the camp the longest of any of them, and was one of the first to be quarantined. His partner was sent to isolation months ago, though, and he hadn't said more than five words to anyone since then, Nick was told. He stood six-foot-four, Nick guessed at least two hundred eighty pounds, but he seemed scared to death of everything. He rarely saw the guy except for meal time. When Danny or Paul brought food, Omar would unzip his tent, sulk to the table with his shoulders slumped, slowly shovel food into his face, then shuffle back to his tent afterward. They'd stopped even bothering to try to get him to participate in cleaning; if they left it up to him, it'd never get done, and they didn't want to see what Paul's reaction to that would be.

And it was Paul who they had all been more concerned about. Even before Lucas's murder, Paul had been the one who typically dragged people to isolation. He'd been the one who would smile as he reached around Rachel from behind and ran his hand up her thigh, running a finger up the shape of her ass and then reaching under her shirt. He knew what she'd been through with Trevor, and Nick thought he was trying not to let her forget what that felt like, to have a man touch her in that way without consent. To have a man wield power over her, to try to own her body and take it as his property. She wasn't over that— might never be over that—and Paul relished taunting her about it. And, whenever possible, he tried to make eye contact with Nick while he did it.

If his assertion of power over Rachel was physical, his play on Nick was a psychological one. Nick may have "confessed" to murdering Trevor in a fit of rage but, in reality, Trevor had gotten away before Nick could even lay a hand on him. And, instead of following him and doing something about it, he watched Rachel's rapist flee down the stairs and out of their lives. She begged him to stay, and Nick knew deep down that had probably been the right move. Still, it ate at him that maybe he *should* have been the man to take Trevor's life, that some other man had finished the job he never started. Would he have been man enough to do that if he had caught Trevor? Should he have tracked him down and done it himself? It was one thing to be Rachel's comforter, but could he be a protector if she needed that? Now, Paul was continuing that, making sure Nick saw him violating her, and forcing her chin up so she knew Nick was there too. And yet, Nick still did nothing. He made no move to intervene. He played it safe, standing frozen without a word until Paul pulled back and walked away. Then, as he did that night, he would embrace Rachel and listen to her cry on his shoulder, patting her back and rubbing her head, telling her he was there, that it would all be all right. He knew she was strong. He knew she could be resilient. Still, though, it was emasculating to watch her be assaulted, and not be able to fight it. To watch other men do to her what he still never had, and have no recourse but to whisper softly to her as she wept.

Nick unzipped his tent and walked out into the chilly late-February afternoon, then tapped on Rachel's tent.

"Rachel…It's me," he said.

He heard a rustling from inside, and the zipper worked its way up.

"Hi. What's up?" she was on all fours, looking up at him.

"Can I come in?"

"Sure."

He crawled into the tent and sat down, crossing his legs in front of her. She contorted her legs underneath her, splaying her feet out diagonally behind her.

"We've got to do something," Nick placed his hands in his lap. "If we don't, this isn't gonna end well for any of us."

"Have something in mind?"

"I just might."

32

Stephanie turned her walkie-talkie off and laid it down on her desk, considering what her best move would be from there. Assuming Michael was being paranoid, this wouldn't be that tough to start with—just log into one of the computers in the Records Room and look through the documents associated with Doctor Giles' study. That'd get her started, at least. She could take another full review of the data and methodology to see if there were any holes in how the study was conducted. Once that was done, she could ask around the department about the need for a follow-up for confirmation. She'd be told that it would likely take years to get a representative enough sample of patients—if it was possible to do it at all—and she could pass that on to Michael as a best-case scenario. Hopefully, his dream would die there, and they could go on about their separate lives.

And what if he wasn't being paranoid? She didn't really want to think about that possibility, and she found it to be remote at best. But she knew the right person to help her find out—her childhood best friend, Anna Swafford, was the hospital's research clerk. If anyone would know much about getting access to the study, it'd be her. And, just in case this was going to be more complicated than she expected, it was worth checking with her before diving headlong into this mission.

The hospital's intranet and internal phone system both still worked well, because both were built to be entirely self-sufficient. It was important that communication channels within St. Francis weren't interrupted by any sort of problems elsewhere, so they set up the system to work without outside assistance. That had come in quite handy after the human race was basically wiped off the face of the Earth. Stephanie pressed the button on her phone marked "Anna" and hit Speaker. It rang three times before she heard a voice.

"Hey, Steph…We still on for grabbing some food later?"

"Um, maybe. Hopefully. Could you come up here first, though? I've got something to ask you about."

"Can't you just ask me while we're on the phone?"

Stephanie paused.

"I'm probably just being silly, but I'd rather talk in person."

Anna took the phone off speaker and put the receiver to her ear.

"What's going on? Is this bad?"

"Um, no. Nothing to worry about," Stephanie said. "It'd just be easier to handle face to face. Do you mind coming up?"

"I mean, I guess not. It's fine. Be there in two minutes."

"Perfect. You're the best."

"It's true."

Stephanie ended the call and leaned back in her chair, swiveling around to look out the window. From her third-floor office, she could see most of the town. To the east was Lake Chatuga, sparkling in the midday sun, the shadows of large oaks rippling with the silent motion of the water. Most of the homes were mid-century or older, and they were clustered on the narrow roads leading west from the lake. The old downtown sat below the hospital to the south, down the hill from the mayor's mansion on the western end of the town, but most of it was the historic square flanked by empty storefronts. There was Walt's bar down the road a bit, near the south wall, and Quinn still ran his dad's old convenience store just for something to do. There wasn't much to it, though. Just some fruit, vegetables and meats from the local farm, and small runs of handmade goods that people around the town made. There wasn't much room for mass production in Alessandra. Stephanie estimated the virus had set most of Alessandra back 150 years or so, technologically speaking. Everything had to be re-used now, and everything people had needed to last longer, because it wasn't as simple as going down to the corner market and buying more of almost anything. Looking out over the scaled-down town from her window tended to remind her of that.

Behind her, Stephanie's door opened, and Anna walked in, pushing it shut behind her. Anna sat down in the chair in front of Stephanie's desk.

"So, Miss Mysterioso, what was so urgent that we couldn't just talk about it on the phone?" Anna said. "Are you in the mob? You are, aren't you?"

"Don't mess with me, or you'll sleep wit da fishes," Stephanie laughed. Anna joined her.

"Okay," Anna said. "But, seriously, what's up?"

"Well, like I said, this is probably nothing. I'm just showing more than an abundance of caution here."

Anna nodded.

"So, Michael visited me yesterday."

Anna's eyes widened, and she leaned forward.

"*The* Michael? As in, the notorious, never-knew-how-good-he-had-it ex-hubby Michael?"

"The very one."

"Wow. Well, this *is* interesting. What'd that asshole have to say? Groveling to get you back?"

"Ya know, I'm not quite sure what his angle is. It was weird. He came in here babbling about a meeting with Audrey—"

"Audrey? About what?"

"He said it was about Trevor's murder."

"Oh yeah. I heard about that. Why was he talking to her about that?"

"I mean, he said he knew who did it. And he also said she's falsely pinning it on Nick."

"Jesus," Anna scratched her head. "What the hell?"

"Yeah, I know."

"All right," Anna said. "Let me try to get this straight. Michael walks into your office after not talking to you or seeing you in how long?"

"Oh, god. Three years?"

"So, three years. He says he met with the mayor about his involvement in a murder, and she told him she's pinning it on his best friend. And you fit into this how?"

"Right. Well, that's where I come in. And, I guess, you, if you can help," Stephanie said. "He wants me to review Doctor Giles' study on transmission of the virus."

"He *what*? Is he nuts? Why?"

"He says it's because he thinks Audrey may be covering something up, like she may be keeping the town wearing the rings and isolated in their personal bubbles because it helps her maintain power. Or something. I don't really understand. It sounds like an unhinged conspiracy theory to me."

"Uh-huh. Sure does," Anna shrugged. "And, since I assume you told him to fuck right the hell off, I ask again—how do you or I come into this?"

"I, um, didn't actually tell him to fuck off. I…" Stephanie fidgeted in her seat. "I told him I'd look into it."

"You what? Why the hell did you tell him *that*?"

"I think it's crazy as you do. Really. We know Audrey. She wouldn't do something insane like that, right?"

"Yeah. Right."

"But, from a *purely* scientific perspective, any study like that needs to be subject to peer review."

"Sure. But—"

"*And*," Stephanie interrupted, "when was the last time anyone took a really deep look at the full study, to look for any possible issues?"

"I honestly don't remember anyone doing that since it was logged into the system and announced to the public. But you checked the methodology yourself."

"Right. But not the results. Doctor Giles put those in himself. And where is he now?"

"Retired. Haven't seen the guy in a while, but that's not all that unusual. Probably keeps to himself, like a lot of people here. And, hell, it's not like I ever leave here anyway. Just finishing up a 1,568-hour shift. Think I'll pull a double."

They both laughed.

"Yeah, it's easy to find excuses to coop yourself up here. But, yeah, this is all about science, and being thorough. Screw Michael and his tinfoil hat. But it's still worth looking into, regardless. And, once I do, I can then tell him that there were no issues with it, and I'll look forward to his next visit in another three years."

"If that soon."

"I'll pencil him in on my calendar if he wants," Stephanie smiled.

"Okay. All right. Um, let me look into it, and track down the file for you in the system. I'll get back with you on it. Deal?"

"Deal. Now, how about that food date?"

"Great," Anna said. "'Cause all this sciencey talk has worked up my appetite."

33

The nave was quiet and empty when Audrey pushed open its glass doors and walked into the aisle. There was something about hearing the sound of her footsteps in an empty church that comforted Audrey when she was dealing with stress—the reverberating echo made her feel less alone. She still wasn't sure God was there at all, and the rampaging virus had only made that feeling more pronounced. The kind of god who would allow—much less *directly cause*—something like that to happen was, in her mind, a very complicated being to love, at the very least. They say the Lord works in mysterious ways, and humans aren't meant to understand his motivations all the time. At some point, though, was that just an excuse for why they had no evidence for him being there at all? When did faith stop being enough? When did "The Lord works in mysterious ways" give way to "Maybe this is what happens when there isn't anyone in charge"? She didn't know, but her Catholic upbringing didn't do a lot to try to squash such questions.

Slowly, she walked up the aisle of St. Catherine's Church, the only Alessandra place of worship whose priest survived the virus and still held services several times a week. At first, Audrey had gone frequently, seeking some sort of divine guidance and strength to deal with the challenges the town faced. In recent months, though, she'd mostly stopped going at all. The guidance and strength she'd sought, she didn't feel like she'd ever found. Surrounded by people and a mostly adoring town, she'd never felt more alone or lost. The pressure of having to protect possibly the last colony of humans on Earth was becoming more than she felt she could bear. She hoped she wasn't the highest authority left. But if there was no God, she might very well be. And that terrified her.

At the base of the altar, Audrey fell to her knees and rested her elbows on her ring, clasping her hands under her chin. She looked ahead at the crucified Jesus hanging behind the podium, dominating the back wall of the church. She almost felt like she could relate to the man who died at the cross. They'd both carried a heavy burden in trying to help their followers find a better path, to survive as best they could in a perilous world. They both faced criticism for the decisions they made, but they both felt those tough decisions benefited a higher cause. Maybe she was being too grandiose in comparing herself to Jesus while kneeling before his likeness but, in that brief moment, she felt she could understand some of that burden he'd known when he tried to help his people.

Sunlight fell in through the stained-glass windows to her right, cutting shattered streaks across the pews and the marble floor, warming her cheek as she knelt. She turned toward it and squinted into the brightness, broken by a scene from Bethlehem, as Mary cradled Jesus with the wise men looking on from behind the manger—a vision of rebirth, of purity and innocence. The sun's rays exploded around it, outlining the mother and son while flooding into the chapel in an unrelenting wave.

She turned back toward the altar and heard footsteps from down the aisle behind her. She quickly pivoted to look.

"I hope I'm not interrupting you," said Father Hayden, his cassock kissing the floor behind him as he walked, his stole affixed to his neck. His ring surrounded him conspicuously at the waist. "I was hoping I might join you, if you don't mind."

"Oh. Please, Father. There's plenty of room."

He walked up next to Audrey and kneeled.

"The need to supplicate oneself to a higher authority can be overwhelming at times, can't it?" he said, closing his eyes as he clasped his hands together in front of his face.

"I guess you could say that."

"It's human nature, I believe. We want and need to have someone to reach out to who is greater than us. It's humbling to allow ourselves to be the lesser, to allow our lives more meaning by accepting that we are flawed, and need the help of a higher power."

Growing up, Audrey had always felt like priests were superheroes, like they had powers beyond mere humans. Now, kneeling beside Father Hayden, she wondered about that again. It was almost like he'd known what she was struggling with. She was sure she hadn't spoken any of this out loud. Her heart pounded as he spoke.

"You falling on your knees here is a form of supplication. It's an important word. Did you know it's used sixty times in the Bible?"

Audrey frowned.

"It's typically referenced in relation to prayer and kneeling before God," he said. "Supplicating yourself before Him shows you accept that there is a higher authority than yourself. That higher authority is perfectly good and loving, without the flaws and personal conflicts you inherently possess. It's a good reminder that you aren't alone in your walk. God is always inside you."

"Thank you," Audrey said, looking at Father Hayden, her eyes watering slightly. He nodded, then stood up. She did the same.

"Thank *you* for letting me join you. You know, Audrey, we'd love to see more of you here. Seems like it's been a while."

"It has. I just…I'm so busy and stressed. It's hard to make time for it. You know?"

"Absolutely," he nodded. "I'm sure you have a lot on your mind. Just remember, you're loved and welcomed here. Whatever you seek, God will help you find."

"Yes. Thanks again, Father."

He walked back down the aisle and exited the chapel, the glass doors swinging shut behind him. Audrey stood in place, staring in that direction, and wept.

34

Michael slammed the gavel onto the podium, and the Watch members began shuffling out of the old gym. Most of them lived within easy walking distance, but a few would hop on their bikes to head back to their house for the night. There was some minimal socializing from the group, but Michael had noticed it decreasing as the months had passed. In the first months after the wall went up and the Watch group began, the guys would show up early and leave late. They'd reminisce and talk about their memories of sports and movies. As time dragged on, though, he saw far less of that. There were no sports or Hollywood anymore. No Braves fans wondering if this would be their year. No new Martin Scorsese movie to pick apart. Some DVDs and players were scattered about the town, but it took so much work and permitting to have a group of people together, and to use the electricity required for the film that few bothered anymore. So when people did get together, there just wasn't much to talk about once the meeting was over. It was sad to watch the men quietly walk home, single file, several feet apart.

As he gathered his papers, Michael remembered he meant to grab Hank for a quick chat, but now he didn't see him anywhere in the gym. Where'd he go so quickly? It wasn't a conversation he was anxious to have, but he felt the air needed to be cleared. He hadn't had a chance to talk with him about the Trevor situation, and Michael didn't feel like Hank knew all the details.

Michael stepped down from the podium and looked toward the back of the gym. There were two sets of doors leading to two sides of the parking lot. He had no clue which way Hank had gone, but the longer he took to make a decision, the more likely it would be that he'd have to go all the way to Hank's house to catch him. Based upon where Hank lived, he decided the left door made the most sense, so he jogged in that direction, hit the metal push bar to open it, and went through the concession area to the door to the parking lot.

It wasn't dark yet—to save on electricity, they always had these meetings during the day when the sun gave them plenty of light through the windows that sat high on the gym walls—so that helped him be able to see the men as they were moving away through the parking lot. He looked left toward the sidewalk and saw the backs of several heads, none of which looked like Hank's.

He glanced right but didn't think Hank would be going in that direction, so he jogged to the other edge of the school and peeked around the corner; there was Hank, swinging his right leg up over the seat of a bike.

"Hank! Hold up a sec!" Michael yelled and waved as he walked toward him.

Hank had been ready to pull away, but turned to see Michael. He swung his leg back over the bike and leaned it against the building.

"Hey," Michael said, panting slightly. "Had a tough time finding you."

"Wasn't especially anxious to be found, to be honest."

"Yeah," Michael rubbed the back of his neck. "I know you're pissed about Trevor. But I can explain."

"'Pissed' isn't really it, Michael. I'd get pissed if you punctured the tires on my bike. I'd get pissed if you tripped me while walking down the street. You *killed* a neighbor and friend of mine."

"Hey. Whoa," Michael stepped back and put both hands up in front of him. "I didn't kill anybody. I don't know where you got that."

"Who came up with the idea to go over there?"

"What difference does that—"

"And who fired up that goddamn *mob* to go get their pound of flesh?"

"That's not fair, Hank. I get that he was a friend of yours. I get that you're mad about what happened. But I didn't want him dead. I did everything I could to stop it."

Hank turned away and looked down.

"You really don't get it."

"What don't I get?"

"You and I both knew Zac and his little buddies were loose cannons. You were the only person in a position to talk them down, make them understand that a show of force wasn't necessary. But you led them out there like this was a fucking battle scene. It was irresponsible, Michael, and you should know that. You may not have slit Trevor's throat, but you killed him just as much as whoever did."

"You didn't see the pictures I saw. You didn't see the *look* Trevor gave me that day when you and I went over there. He was dangerous, whether you saw it or not. We *had* to make a move."

"Not like *that*, you didn't. Not with those guys salivating over the smell of blood. You marched them into that house like they had the blessing of God Himself to do what needed to be done. And you stood by and watched it happen."

Michael stepped forward and stomped hard in front of Hank.

"How do you know what I *watched*? You don't know what happened, because you refused to deal with it. Maybe if you had come, with your *superior morality*, maybe *you* could have protected your buddy. You knew just as well as I did the type of people we were taking there, and you stood on the sidelines. You just let whatever was gonna happen happen, so you could wash your hands of it and act like you were the bigger person. So don't lay your guilt on me, Hank. My conscience is clean."

Hank stood silent for a few moments, maintaining an icy stare with Michael. Finally, he glanced down, then back up at Michael.

"It shouldn't be. Mine sure isn't."

Hank bent over, picked up his bicycle and climbed on, pedaling toward his house.

35

"You really think he'd help us?" Rachel said, twisting her unkempt hair around her finger.

"I think he could be convinced, yeah," Nick said, shifting his weight up to his knees inside her tent. "Danny's never been the problem anyway, right? He isn't exactly the Welcome Wagon, but he's reasonably friendly when he brings us food. Sometimes brings us extra rolls. Seems like a decent guy. If he doesn't know what happened to Lucas, he needs to. If we show him, maybe he'll help us take Paul out and get the hell out of here."

"I mean, I get what you're saying and all. But it's one thing to bring us a couple of extra pieces of day-old bread. It's quite another to risk his life to help us break out of the quarantine camp. Even if he were able to get us out of here, how would he explain to Audrey that the people she'd quarantined to help stop the spread of the virus were now roaming the streets again? What would they do to Danny?"

"He tells her we overpowered him. Sneak attack. It's not like he's got a gun in his hand. He's carrying a tray of food; he's vulnerable, if we get our timing right. Audrey's not the type to do anything rash. I think she'd understand."

"What about Paul?"

"He's not in charge. He's just an overnight lackey who's drunk on power out here. He's probably practically neutered inside the walls of the compound. That's why he lashes out when he's with us—he feels powerful."

"Okay," Rachel sighed. "Let's say we do that. Let's say we convince Danny to help us. He lets us out, then gets us out of the compound and down the hill. And they buy the story that we overpowered him, and they don't punish him too badly. Okay. What then? Where do we go? We're in a small town surrounded by eight-foot walls. It's not like we can hop a plane to Timbuktu and start a new life. We're rats in a cage. You think they aren't gonna hunt us down?"

"I'm not saying it'll be easy. But we're healthy. At least, those of us who could go are. That'll help. And we've both got good friends out there, right? I think they'll be willing to hide us, or find us a place to hide until this blows over. It's also not as if Audrey has the FBI and CIA at her disposal. She's basically got a fairly small police force, and then a rag-tag bunch of citizens who might help, but have no real idea what they're doing. If we can't hide out in any of our friends' places, there are plenty of abandoned buildings we could explore. We could get Danny to bring us some food to get us by for a bit as well."

Rachel shook her head. "And we'd leave the small-tent people behind? I'm really not sure about this."

"Hell, neither am I. But what choice do we have at this point? There's a dead, bludgeoned body decomposing two tents over from you!"

"God, Nick. Do you have to bring that up?"

"Yes! Damn it, Rachel. Yes! We can't forget what happened. That was a random attack, and any one of us could be next. I know it's a risk, but so is waiting here until Paul decides he wants to crush somebody's skull again. Yeah, we might die if we try this. But we'll *probably* die if we stay. Do you really think they're ever going to just release us?"

Rachel pushed her hair out of her face and tucked it behind her ear, then pulled her knees in close to her chest.

"Yeah," Nick said. "I don't either. At least with this option, we're making an effort. We're not just sitting here waiting for our turn to die. I need you with me to sell the others on this. You with me?"

Nick held out his hand, but Rachel continued to sit, her arms wrapped around her shins, holding her knees into her chest. She rocked slightly, burying her chin between her legs. After several seconds, she slowly released her right arm from her legs, extending her right hand toward Nick. He grabbed it and shook.

"Okay," he nodded. "Let's call the others in here and go over the plan."

Danny pulled one more red apple out of the bowl on the table and placed it onto the large silver tray. He always liked adding a little bit of something extra beyond what was prescribed to take down to the quarantine camp when it was his turn to take the meals. He felt bad for them, especially the ones Paul ordered stuck in those single-tent torture chambers. Danny understood that, in this assignment, he largely had to follow Paul's orders, but he hated that. He hated all of it, except for the food. It wasn't like Paul was going to run him through a food checklist before he took it down to them. So this was one nice little thing Danny could do for them. After all the shit they'd been through, he felt like it was the least he could do.

This certainly wasn't where he'd expected to be ten years earlier, coming out of the police academy and looking for a job in Georgia. He grew up in Alpharetta, just north of Atlanta, and he had a dream of making it onto the Atlanta police force. He knew he'd have to work his way up, though, and a friend told him they were always hiring in North Georgia. He found a landing spot in Cornelia, mostly pushing papers and playing traffic cop for a few years as he worked his way slowly through the ranks. What he also found quickly was that he loved the pace of life in this part of the state. Alpharetta had only been a step or two removed from real city life in Atlanta, with the mind-numbing traffic and serious crime to go with it. That was what he'd grown up with, and thought he wanted. But in North Georgia, he could actually get to know the people of the community, walk the streets, have people know him by name, and rarely deal with anything more serious than a car being broken into. He even learned to enjoy fishing, as long as somebody brought a cooler full of beer and could scale the fish for him.

In Cornelia, he effectively went down with the ship. Having risen to Lieutenant prior to the virus, he took on the Captain role once the man who led the department for thirty years was one of the first in the town to succumb to the sickness. He immediately vowed to the people of the town that he wouldn't leave them behind, and they would do everything they could to keep them safe. It didn't take long, though, for him to realize this was an enemy the police academy didn't teach him how to fight. No amount of detective work, no show of force was going to arrest its momentum. They tried to set up quarantines, but the infrastructure wasn't there to do so effectively. They simply weren't equipped to deal with a pandemic of this size and ferocity. He dealt with some small-time looting, but suicides had been the hardest change to deal with. The suicide rate spiked in Cornelia—along with cities and towns across the country—as the virus ravaged communities. Seeing friends and family contract the virus, then die an agonizing death, often covered in boils and other herpes-like sores that spread all over their bodies in a matter of days or even hours, made people desperate to avoid the virus altogether. Some people started panicking at the slightest hint of sickness—sneeze, and they'd start contemplating sticking a gun in their mouth. Entire families—the parents assisting the kids first, like they were putting on oxygen masks on a plane— would sometimes end their lives together, in almost ritualistic fashion.

Those were the toughest for Danny, seeing four- and five-year-olds, their whole lives ahead of them, pallid and cold in their best dress or their Sunday suit, sometimes with a boil or two on their face. Sometimes not. Depending on how quickly he found them, they could almost be mistaken for being in a peaceful sleep. Almost, but there was something about the eyes of a dead child that gave it away. Something about the stare, like they could burrow through walls, deep into your soul. There was no mistaking that. Danny didn't even need to take a pulse.

For whatever reason, Danny never contracted the virus as his town's population dwindled toward zero. Whether he had a natural immunity or was just lucky, there was no real way of knowing. Either way, he wasn't sure whether to be thankful for the extra chance so many others didn't get, or guilty for the people he had failed to save. The only thing he knew was he didn't want to face the self-inflicted death of so many before him. He'd seen the aftermath too many times, and he didn't have the constitution for it. That stare haunted him.

When he heard that Alessandra—just four miles up the road —escaped relatively unscathed, he grabbed what belongings he could fit into an overnight sack and began walking. When he got there, they were gathering supplies to build a wall that would allow them to pick and choose who they let inside. He liked the plan, and Audrey was anxious to have an experienced officer to help organize whatever sort of small force she could put together to maintain order.

It had been exciting at first, training new officers, coming up with a new code almost from scratch. This was a brand new world, and Audrey wanted them to govern it in a way that would keep people safe and happy. Now, though, he was mostly confined to Audrey's compound, putting together trays of food for prisoners, and sleeping with Audrey whenever she got the itch. They cared for each other; he knew that much. She just had so much on her mind that he didn't know where that might go, if anywhere. They'd lie in bed and talk for hours, about their pasts, their ideas on how to make the town better, and what might lay ahead for them if the virus could be killed. Maybe they had a future together, one day. For the moment, though, it was a tough existence.

Danny lifted the tray with one hand and pulled the door open with the other, sliding sideways onto the landing, then down the stairs toward the courtyard. He got to the fence and pressed the tray against it with his body while he unlocked the gate, then swung it open, stepping inside. He pressed the tray against the fence again, and closed the gate behind him. He grabbed the tray, turned and walked toward the dining area.

It was six in the evening. On the tray, he carried five ribeye steaks, a large bowl of salad with balsamic vinegar and apple slices on it, a bowl of green beans with chopped grilled onions, eight dinner rolls, four red apples, and two bunches of purple grapes. Paul gave him enough latitude to use frozen food or cook, and he enjoyed making a big dinner. He used to do it often for his small police squad in Cornelia on slow nights, and doing it brought back good memories. Seeing people enjoy the food he made always gave him a warm feeling he didn't have much in Alessandra.

The people heard him and emerged from their tents to his left, walking quietly to the table and sitting down. As Danny was about to head back toward the gate, one of the people spoke to him.

"Officer, would it be possible for us to ask you for a favor?" Nick said, not looking up from his plate. "It's important."

36

"So, this is kinda weird," Anna said when Stephanie picked up her office phone.

"What? No 'Hey! How's it goin', old friend'?" Stephanie said.

"No time for that, jerk wad. I'm trying to help you. I'm looking into this study you want to check out."

"Yeah. And?"

"*And*...Well, there's something weird."

"Are you gonna tell me what's weird, or just keep saying something's weird?"

"I'm gettin' there. So, here's the thing. It's got a permission chain attached to it for viewing."

"Okay. What does that mean?"

"I've never seen this before, for one. And I've been here a while. The document e-verify program we use allows it, but I've dug through documents like a kid digs through a candy jar, and I've never seen anything in our system with this sort of stipulation added to it."

"Uh-huh," Stephanie nodded into the phone. "Go on..."

"The stipulation says it requires a password, but I can't get the password until I get a supplementary password from the office of someone you might be familiar with."

"Who's that?"

"Audrey E. Reese."

"The one and only?"

"You got it."

"Damn. And you say this is really unusual?"

"Couldn't be more unusual if it said an alien was going to beam the document to me via laser from Mars."

"That'll be the day, huh?"

"Tell me about it."

Stephanie turned her head to the side and rubbed her chin.

"Do you think they'd stop you from looking at it?"

"I can't know for sure, but there's nothing in this that indicates it's Top Secret or anything, just that I need permission to access it. I mean, if they really wanted to keep it out of everyone's hands, there's no reason for them to have left it in our system at all. So I'm guessing they're okay with people seeing it, as long as they know who's doing it."

"And as long as that person *knows* they know who's doing it."

"Yeah, that could be too," Anna said. "It'd serve as a nice deterrent if you thought that, I don't know, Audrey was participating in some sort of conspiracy to keep the people of the town from finding out that she's been lying to them all for a year or so. But that'd be crazy, of course."

"Of course," Stephanie's eyes raised to the ceiling. "So what do we do? Did you already tell them?"

"Hell no. Mama didn't raise no fool, Steph. That's why I'm calling you back, to find out if you still want to go forward with this."

"Do I want them to know that I'm looking at this file?"

"Yep. If you still think Michael's a loon—and we all know he probably is—then there's probably no harm in it. Maybe there's some good reason for this. But if you think Michael could accidentally be right, well, I at least wanted to give you the chance to say 'Fuck this,' and just, ya know, *tell* him you looked at it without actually doing it."

"I guess that would get him off my back."

"Sure. And, since he's probably certifiably insane, you haven't lost anything."

Stephanie paused for a few seconds, unsure what to do.

"Hey, um, give me just a minute to think," Stephanie said. "Can you hang on?"

"I'll just be here clipping my toenails."

Stephanie laughed lightly, then punched the Speaker button and hung up the receiver. She stood up and began pacing behind her desk. Anna was right that Michael was probably wrong about all of this. It just sounded like spectacular nonsense; he certainly wasn't a reliable source after the way he'd slow-gamed her in their marriage. And, generally, she'd have no good reason to believe him at all. But something about this permission structure for viewing the file bugged her. It was possible they had a viable reason for setting that up—maybe they wanted to track who was studying the subject so they knew who to contact for information on it, or perhaps there was some context they wanted to pass along in Doctor Giles' absence—but one scientific principle for validating any hypothesis was to make predictions about what to expect if it were true, and then follow up to see if those conditions existed. And this was the exact sort of thing you'd expect them to do if they *were* trying to hide something. It didn't mean Michael was right, but it did mean Stephanie couldn't rule it out based upon what she knew. The evidence so far supported Michael's thinking.

"Anna...Still there?" Stephanie said, leaning with her hands in front of her on her desk.

"Yep. Man, the little toe's always the hardest."

"I'm ready to do it. Go ahead and get the permission set up."

Anna stopped clipping and picked up the receiver.

"You're sure about this?"

"I can't just let this go."

"Okay, then. I'll give them a call right now."

"Great. Thanks."

"Oh, by the way," Anna said, "I'm also supposed to let them know what size cement shoes you wear."

Anna opened up her book of phone numbers and ran her finger down to find the right one. The only outside line in the hospital went to Audrey's compound, because you never knew when you might have to reach out to the almighty leader. But Anna had never had to call over there. She hadn't talked to Audrey in years, as far as she could remember. She never had a problem with Audrey, but they never ran in the same crowd. Anna had always been one of the geeks, with glasses, braces and a perm long after it had gone out of style. Anna's parents hadn't had much, but they tried hard for their only child. It hadn't been enough to give her the tools she needed to not be a socially awkward teenager who didn't kiss a boy until she was in her early twenties, but they did make an effort.

At one time, she would have been intimidated just from calling Audrey, worrying about what she'd say, and whether Audrey would make fun of something she said the next day in class. She'd have stressed over it for hours, writing out topics to talk about, rehearsing the conversation in a mirror, imagining Audrey thinking she was really interesting. Maybe they'd even become friends, and Anna would get that firm grip on the social ladder that she'd tried so desperately to gain throughout adolescence.

By the time she was reaching for the phone while sitting in the Research department of the St. Francis Hospital, though, all those stressful years had faded into distant memory. All she was thinking about was what might happen to her best friend if this call went south, and how she needed to do whatever she could to present this in the calmest, most reasonable way possible. She was willing to not bring Stephanie's name into it, and she wouldn't if she didn't have to, but she wasn't sure. Part of her wanted to sabotage this whole situation. Get them to reject the request. Not only might that feed into Michael's notion that they have something to hide, though, but it might even put Anna herself in danger if Michael was right. And, skeptical as she was, she wasn't anxious to tempt fate quite that much.

So, as she dialed Audrey's number, she felt like she was ready to take this on, come what may. A man greeted her after one ring, and she started talking.

"This is Anna Swafford, Chief Research Clerk at St. Francis Hospital. Is Ms. Reese available?"

She figured calling her "Ms. Reese" could only help her cause.

"I'll have to see if she has a moment," the man said. "Can you hold?"

"Gladly. Thank you."

The line went silent; she put it on speaker, and laid it down on the desk in front of her. You really could forget that the world had changed so drastically in moments like this one, she thought. She was sitting at her desk in her lab coat, making a phone call to check on a document for one of the doctors. Outside her door, she could see the occasional clipboard-carrying nurse, and she knew patients could be just down the hall sitting in the waiting area, maybe thumbing through an old magazine. The woman at the reception desk would still see her calling board light up just like before, though perhaps a bit less often since all the calls were coming from inside the building. They created this world of their own within the world outside, where they could pretend life had gone on without all the death and suffering, where they could keep trying to save every life they could. Anna was proud to work there, and rarely had much desire to leave. Walking outside the doors brought reality back to her like a baseball bat to the face, and it never failed to take her breath away when she walked around the town she'd known, and see it as a carcass on the side of the road. Alessandra was a husk of the place she remembered, and being in the hospital at moments like these allowed her a respite from that. She leaned back in her chair and smiled.

"Ms. Swafford?" the man's voice came back through the speaker.

Anna was jarred out of her daydream.

"Oh. Um, yes. I'm here."

"I'm transferring you."

"Okay. Thank you."

The phone clicked, then rang once. Twice. Three times. After the sixth ring, the ringing stopped.

"Hey," a different man's voice came through the line, deeper and more gravelly, as if he had a cold. "Who is this?"

"Um, this is Anna Swafford from Saint Francis Hospital. Who am I speaking to?"

"What do you want?"

"I want to speak to Ms. Reese about—"

"Audrey isn't here," the man interrupted. "This is Paul, her chief of staff."

Anna had heard Paul's name before. If she remembered correctly, he was Audrey's younger brother. She heard he grew up in some sort of private school outside of town, so she never had many dealings with him as they were getting older. She was fairly sure they never met, and she didn't even know he was working so closely with Audrey. And, given how few people Audrey could possibly have up there at her compound, Anna found it funny that she'd have a "chief of staff," since the "staff" was probably one or two people.

"Okay. Maybe you can help?"

"You never know."

"Are you familiar with Doctor Richard Giles' research on transmission of H6N1?"

"I'm…aware of it," he said. "Sure."

"Great. Well, I was trying to access the documents on it here, but the system says I need to get a password from Audrey's office before I can enter our password. So, double verification. Do you have the password I need?"

There was a long pause on the line.

"Why are you interested in looking at it?"

"I'm the Chief Research Clerk at the hospital. It's not terribly unusual for us to look through research documents."

"Yes, but why this particular one? Who's asking for it?"

"Is that important?" she asked.

"Is it important for you not to tell me?"

Anna pursed her lips and ran her fingers through her hair.

"Doctor Stephanie Sloan needs to review his findings for a project she's working on."

"S-L-O-A-N?"

Anna took a deep breath. "That's right."

"All right, then. That's all we need to know. For the password, try 'PROTECT226.' All caps."

Anna typed it in and hit Enter. The box went away, and she could type the department's password in.

"That worked. Thanks."

"Good," Paul said. "Keep in mind, that's a one-time-use password. Don't try to enter it after ten minutes is up. Tell Sloan the same thing."

"Um, sure. I'll do that," she said, but he'd already hung up.

Anna called up to Stephanie with the passwords, and told her she needed to get into the file within ten minutes for it to work. She hoped she hadn't just thrown her best friend into a pit of snakes.

37

Feeling adrift, Audrey walked into her room and closed the door. She took a drink from a glass of water on her bedside table; Father Hayden's words echoed in her head.

Am I that easy to read? I seriously can't believe he was actually channeling God there. How gullible would I have to be? But it's weird. In that moment, I felt more at ease than I've felt in months. I felt like someone was looking after me, guiding me in the right direction. I felt like everything was going to be okay, even if I don't know how. That felt good. Better than I've felt in quite awhile.

For so long, Audrey had battled doubt, and the nagging sensation that she was making the wrong decisions. She thought they were right. Or, at the very least, she'd convinced herself that she thought they were right. That didn't mean they were, though.

I have to separate the families, even the children. It's only for a few months until we can get everything straightened out. Then we'll move everyone back in together, and it'll be like nothing ever changed. There have to be sacrifices for the greater good, and every community is stronger when its citizens are giving up something important to get back something bigger. Shared sacrifice is essential, and that's what I'm implementing. I'm making sure we all have a stake in this. And, as a result, we'll all take ownership. And we'll all reap the benefits. Everyone has to feel the pain.

She fell to her knees, and rested her elbows on the side of the bed. She clasped her hands in front of her and, for the first time since she was a little girl with her mom kneeling beside her, she spoke to God.

"God, I know it's been a long time. I know I've strayed, and I've doubted. And, if you're there listening, I don't have to tell you that I'm still not quite sure what I believe. If you *are* there, watching over us, pushing us to carry out your plan, I fully admit I have no idea what you're trying to accomplish. This past year has been as much like hell on Earth as I can imagine. I've watched the town I love be spared the wrath of a terrible plague, only to see it succumb to a plague of a different kind. I thought I was the right person to lead them. I thought I was the rightful heir to this office. I pictured myself being remembered as the person who not only saved Alessandra, but someone who relaunched the human race. That's legendary. That's immortality. It was an opportunity, and I felt ready to take it on.

"Have I done the right thing, though? Have my decisions made the situation worse, or better? I sought the comfort of having my brother heavily involved, and I thought I could control him. But I know now that I can't. I'm not sure that anyone can. I don't think he has bad intentions, but he's not the boy I grew up with. That's not the kid I played in sandboxes with, and tackled in the backyard. This is a grown man, full of anger and resentment at something, or someone. Maybe me. I wish I knew what was driving him to this sort of behavior, but I'm clueless how to stop it. I've destroyed families. I've driven much of the town to depression, it seems. The palpable sense of relief, purpose, and belonging that existed as we were building the wall has evaporated. There's no energy here. I'm holed up in my mansion, overseeing a town that's died around me.

"God, I'm willing to cede control to you. I'm willing to admit that I don't have the answers, that I need someone's help. I need *your* help. I just need a sign. I need something to tell me that you're there, listening, caring. Anything. I'm on my knees here, willing to believe. Just give me one reason to. Please. Amen."

Audrey remained on her knees and bowed her forehead onto the bed, closing her eyes and staying silent except for the sound of the breath crossing her lips. She was waiting for God to do something to show his presence. She wasn't expecting something as dramatic as him standing beside her bed, slamming a scepter on the floor and declaring, "I am God!"—although the clarity of that would have been welcome. She was just looking for *something* that would help her. *Something* that would provide her with permission to give up and allow someone else with more knowledge to show her the way.

She kept kneeling, pressing her head harder against the mattress. Her fingers folded together on the back of her head, as she tried to blank out her mind. She wanted to hear nothing but the ambient sounds around her. The barely audible hum of the heating stove in the corner of the room. Footsteps pattering along in the hall outside her room, perhaps heading to the kitchen. The seconds she waited turned to minutes. Five. Ten. Fifteen. She kneeled, waiting for something she could possibly interpret as a sign that God was there to catch her and carry her to the finish line in this race.

After more than seventeen minutes, she opened her eyes and lifted her head, allowing her arms to fall to her side. She heard nothing. There was no one there. She was alone.

38

Stephanie scrolled through the study, looking for something that stood out to her. She was mostly scanning for keywords and phrases. She already knew the methodology was sound, and there was a lot of scientific jargon in any study like this. She'd read thousands of them, and they never got more interesting than reading the back of a bowl of oatmeal. To her, though, it was fascinating, reviewing the method of study Doctor Giles devised, remembering the conversations they had about how best to study a virus that was moving so rapidly and killing so indiscriminately. It was a terrifying time but, for a medical researcher, she had to admit it was also an exciting one. This was unlike anything any of them had seen, and they were getting to look into it first hand. Doctor Giles was the head of their Research Department, and he was determined to conduct this study himself, while the rest of the doctors just tried to save the lives of those he was studying.

What Stephanie wanted to see in this document was the final conclusion. That was what mattered in the end, because that was what Audrey and her people were going to point to in order to justify their extreme policies. That was what Michael was itching to see. If it was in line with what they claimed, then it would vindicate them for what they'd done. If not, Stephanie wasn't sure where that rabbit hole would lead. For this document, and all the others in their system, they also used an electronic signature system for verification, so she knew it should be clear that Doctor Giles himself signed off on the final result.

After several minutes of scrolling, she found what she was looking for:

Patient characteristics

A total of 227 patients (108 males) were included. At the time of inclusion, they had a median age of 43 years (range, 7 to 68 years old) and had been symptomatic for a median of 2 weeks (range, 2 days to 6 weeks).

Follow-up of the included patients

One hundred and three patients were tested more than once and were included in both the longitudinal and prevalence studies. The other 124 were expired prior to the longitudinal study's commencement, so they were tested only once. This resulted in an insufficient sample size for robust conclusions, but the limitations on subjects requires some latitude.

Incidence of seroconversion for H6N1 virus

During the 3-month period, the monthly seroconversion rate rose rapidly from 10.13% (23 of 227 patients at risk) to 41.85% (99 of 227 patients at risk) and 93.39% (212 of 227 patients at risk).

The 23 seroconversions observed during the initial month were detected in the most physically interactive units. The seroconversions in the subsequent two months were also detected in physically interactive units, encouraged to touch and behave toward each other in a familiar manner. Each month of the study, five subjects were isolated from all other people in order to gauge the impact of physical interactivity on H6N1 transmission. These were the only subjects that did not test positive for the virus.

Conclusions

While the lack of sufficient time and subjects cannot be discounted, this is a clear result that shows physical interactivity to be a likely hallmark of H6N1 transmission from human to human. We recommend isolation of all individuals to prevent the further spread of the virus.

That was the smoking gun she was looking for. It seemed that everything Audrey told the people of the town was true. Doctor Giles had not only made the determination that touch was the key factor in the spread of the virus, but had expressly recommended the policy Audrey chose. It was right there in front of her. He acknowledged the limitations of what he had to work with, but that was still a strong conclusion based upon a decent amount of data. Stephanie thought that, while it wasn't ideal, in a situation like this where the virus was so aggressive and deadly, they had no choice but to move forward with this as their guide. If she had been writing this, she thought she probably would have put something around eighty percent confidence that this was the correct course of action, and that was plenty when the stakes of not acting were as high as they were.

While she recognized Michael's frustration with Audrey and the state of existence in the town, she was relieved to have this firmly decided. The idea that the people of Alessandra had to live in such extreme isolation was a difficult one to accept, but she thought knowing their leader and friend was lying to them and destroying families in order to maintain her handle on power would have been far worse for everyone involved. If she was willing and able to do that, what else was she capable of? Stephanie was glad she wouldn't have to find out.

She moved her mouse up to close the file when she noticed something unusual. She'd never seen this on a document before. In the upper-right corner, there was a small red dot. It wasn't something she thought was normally there; if it was, she thought she would have noticed it on previous documents. In order to check, she opened up an earlier study she'd been reviewing and saw a small green dot instead.

What did that red dot mean? She knew plenty about research, but she was only a novice with this software they were using. Anna was the expert on this. She dialed Anna's extension and hit Speaker.

"Hey, Steph. Any luck with the Doctor Giles study?"

"Yeah. Everything looks good. Just one quick question."

"Shoot."

"If there's a small red dot in the upper right-hand corner of the document, what does that mean?"

"It means you probably hit a key or something," Anna said.

"What do you mean?"

"It just means there's been some change to the document since the last signature."

Stephanie could feel the hairs pop out on the back of her neck. She suddenly felt cold and couldn't speak.

"Steph?" Anna said. "You there?"

"Could you come up here? Like, now?"

"It's probably just—"

"Please? Now?"

"Um, yeah. Yeah. Five minutes. Just hang tight."

Stephanie's first thought as she hung up was that it was going to be a long five minutes.

"You probably bumped up against the spacebar or something," said Anna, sitting at the computer with Stephanie standing and watching over her shoulder. "It's happened to me a million times."

"I've never seen it before."

"Most people haven't. I'm surprised you noticed it. They should probably make it bigger so you know when you accidentally inserted a stupid typo into someone's study. Doctors hate that shit."

"I don't think I hit anything, but I guess it's possible. You said you can check the last keystrokes?"

"Ah. See, that's the great thing. If you know where to look, you can see the history of the entire document."

"Really?"

Anna smiled. "Yep. Most people wouldn't even know you could do that, but every change is stored right…Ta-da! Here!"

She turned to Stephanie while motioning at the screen. In front of her was a list of dates and times when changes were made.

"Anna, there hasn't been a change to this document in close to a year."

Anna looked back at the screen, and her face froze.

"Well, damn."

"What does that *mean*?" Stephanie asked, her hands clutching the back of the chair.

"Um, it might not mean much. Maybe just fixing a typo or something. But, ultimately, what the red dot and this series of dates and times means is that at least one change was made to this document between when Doctor Giles signed it, and when you opened it."

Stephanie's mouth went dry, and she swallowed hard.

"Can we see what the changes were?"

"Um, yeah. Sure. We can just click on the last date and time to pull up the doc prior to that change."

Stephanie sighed. "Do it."

Anna clicked, and another window opened with the same cover page.

"Scroll to the end of the document," Stephanie said. "The conclusion."

Anna hit the "End" button on the keyboard, and the final page came up. Stephanie scanned the words, looking for changes.

Patient characteristics

A total of 227 patients (108 males) were included. At the time of inclusion, they had a median age of 43 years (range, 7 to 68 years old) and had been symptomatic for a median of 2 weeks (range, 2 days to 6 weeks).

Follow-up of the included patients

One hundred and three patients were tested more than once and were included in both the longitudinal and prevalence studies. The other 124 were expired prior to the longitudinal study's commencement, so they were tested only once. This resulted in an insufficient sample size for robust conclusions, but the limitations on subjects requires some latitude.

Incidence of seroconversion for H6N1 virus

During the 3-month period, the monthly seroconversion rate rose rapidly from 10.13% (23 of 227 patients at risk) to 41.85% (99 of 227 patients at risk) and 100% (227 of 227 patients at risk).

The 23 seroconversions observed during the initial month were detected in the most physically interactive units. The seroconversions in the subsequent two months were also detected in physically interactive units, encouraged to touch and behave toward each other in a familiar manner. Each month of the study, five subjects were isolated from all other people in order to gauge the impact of physical interactivity on H6N1 transmission. These subjects contracted the virus at approximately the same rate as the physically interactive subjects.

Conclusions

While the lack of sufficient time and subjects cannot be discounted, this is a clear result that shows physical interactivity is not a likely hallmark of H6N1 transmission from human to human. We recommend not to isolate individuals, as it is unlikely to prevent the further spread of the virus. The conclusion of this study is that the key to H6N1 transmission is still unknown.

Stephanie and Anna stared at the screen for several minutes. Anna turned and looked at Stephanie with wide eyes.

"Holy shit," Anna said. "That's a pretty significant change. What do you think it means?"

"I'm pretty sure it means this right here is the real study Doctor Giles wrote and signed. And I'm pretty sure we both know who changed it, and who didn't think anyone would find out."

"My god," Anna whispered. "What are you gonna do?"

"I'm gonna tell Michael he was right," Stephanie said. "And then I'm gonna find Doctor Giles."

39

Dabbing her eyes with a washcloth in her bathroom, trying to clear up the redness, Audrey heard a knock on her bedroom door.

"It's Officer Greene," the voice said from the hall. "Can I come in?"

Audrey shut her eyes tightly, and gripped her vanity until her knuckles turned white.

"Not now!" she said, her eyes still clamped shut. "Please come back later!"

There was a short pause.

"Ma'am, it's about Michael. You asked us to track him for you. I think you'll want to hear this. We need your authorization to do anything."

She bent forward, resting her forehead on the periwinkle-colored marble around the sink, willing back the tears that came earlier. She took another long drink from the glass of water by the sink, then looked at herself in the mirror. She didn't feel ready right now. She felt scared, and helpless. She had half forgotten about Michael altogether; she just wanted to crawl into bed and sleep. But this was the responsibility she took on when she stepped into this role. Whatever she felt like at this moment, she had to let it slough off her like shedding a skin. She had to focus on her job, which seemed to be never ending.

Audrey grabbed a dry towel and wiped under her eyes, clearing some of the puffiness that was lingering. She picked up a bottle of Visine she figured was probably expired, but maybe it was the last bottle in existence, so…Oh well. She pulled each eye open one at a time with one hand, then carefully squeezed a couple of drops, blinking to let the chemical work its magic. Audrey gazed into the mirror again; she thought she looked more like she hadn't slept much than that she'd just cried for an hour. She'd take that. She took another swig of water and walked to the door.

"Okay," she said, as she pulled the door open. "Come inside. Tell me what you've got."

Paul followed closely behind the officer.

"We've been following Michael since he left here two days ago," Officer Greene said. "When we first spotted him, he was entering St. Francis Hospital, about twenty minutes after he left this building. That likely means he went straight there, given a regular walking pace over a mile. He was there for roughly an hour, then went to his house before going to old Towns High for the Watch meeting. Then, this morning, he returned to St. Francis. Within a half hour, he and a female exited the hospital with rings on and fled by bicycle."

Audrey looked at Paul, who shrugged.

"Who was the woman?" Audrey asked.

"Our officer wasn't close enough to get a certain ID on her, but he believe it was Doctor Stephanie Sloan."

"I thought they hated each other after the divorce," Paul said.

"I can't account for that, sir," Officer Greene said. "Like I said, it's not a hundred percent ID. But he said he was around eighty percent sure."

"What do you think they could be doing?" Audrey turned to Paul.

"No idea. But if he went straight there from here, you'd think there's a connection."

"So, Ms. Reese, what would you like us to do?" Officer Greene said.

"Do you have any idea what they were talking about, or what they might be doing together?" she asked.

"That wasn't part of our order, ma'am. We were just asked to secretly track his movements, so we've been keeping our distance. Any suggestion as to what they're doing would be pure speculation, and you could probably speculate on that better than we could anyway."

Audrey sighed and pushed her hair back from her face.

"What are our options?"

"Well, we don't have a ton of manpower, as you know. Right now, we're devoting a good bit of it to this, but we have other patrols that need to be completed. We can continue to track them from afar and keep you abreast as well as we can. Or we can send a force into the hospital to try to find out what they're doing. Someone in there likely knows."

Audrey put her fingers to her forehead and rubbed. She could feel a headache coming on. Too much had been thrown at her lately, and it was starting to take a toll. *What could Michael and Stephanie possibly be up to?* And, maybe more importantly, what did this have to do with her conversation with him shortly before that? They couldn't be unrelated. They challenged each other, and he'd left angrier than she'd ever seen him. She knew there was a possibility he'd do something rash, which was why she had him tracked to begin with. But where did Stephanie fit into this? He was mad about Nick being accused of murder, and Stephanie was a medical researcher. The two didn't seem to dovetail in any way she could see.

"What do you think?" she turned to Paul. He frustrated her sometimes—most of the time, maybe. But he was still the only thing close to a confidant she had in the world at that moment. And a confidant was what she needed in the worst way. He opened his mouth, then snapped it shut.

"I'm stumped," Paul said. "This Stephanie thing is out of left field to me. Up to you, but I'd keep tracking him. See where they go."

Audrey bit her lower lip and looked at the ceiling.

"Ma'am," Officer Greene said, "I don't mean to rush you, but —"

"I know, damn it!" Audrey snapped. "Just give me a second!"

She was feeling the weight of the decision on her shoulders, wishing she could rest. She knew it was what she needed. Maybe she could get some time to herself and just sleep if she could get them out of her room. Make this one call, and make it right. Do what's best for the people of Alessandra.

"Yeah," Audrey said. "Okay. Keep following him. I want to know what they're doing. Get me a report ASAP, you hear me?"

"Yes, ma'am. We'll get on it. Thank you."

Paul followed him into the hall and headed straight out the front door into the street.

Zac ran a dishcloth over the inside of a bowl, standing over the kitchen sink. These were some of the times he missed his kids and wife the most. Or ex-wife. He wasn't sure what to call her. When the virus was threatening Alessandra and Audrey had declared that no one could touch anyone else, and banned cohabitation, they dissolved all marriages. There was no federal or state government still functional enough to stop her from doing it, and she said it was to save the town. People complied. Eventually.

The one thing that government did do was set up a facility to house a limited number of people, Audrey said, as she told the town about how they'd execute the separation. When possible, wives and children would be evacuated and taken to a protective bubble facility, basically a large clean room protected from the virus. Space was very limited, though, and she could only afford to send the women and kids. The process ripped families apart, splitting husbands from wives, and children from their fathers.

When Audrey announced the plan, Zac and Karen vowed to fight. No one could get in the way of their family. Audrey told the townspeople that she'd prefer they comply on their own, but she'd be sending "counselors" to help them work through what needed to be done if they weren't ready to make a clean break of it with their spouses and children. When the counselors knocked on their door, Zac and Karen kissed for a long time, nodding at each other that they'd both insist to the counselor they would refuse to leave the house, that they'd have to be dragged out by a team of horses in order to go through that door.

Thirty minutes after the men arrived, Zac was as adamant as ever that this was his home, his family, and there was nothing they could say to change that. His time as a sniper in the military taught him patience, endurance, and discipline, but it hadn't taught him how to deal with power-hungry bureaucrats coming into his home, trying to rip his family apart at the seams. On the outside, he was trying to remain calm, but his insides were boiling over throughout the time they were talking. He just wanted them to feel sympathy for his situation. He understood the challenges Audrey and the rest of the people of Alessandra faced, and he recognized that it was only a temporary separation, but this family had given him something to live for when he wasn't sure he had anything. Karen had been his rock, through bouts of post-traumatic stress disorder and depression, following a difficult life growing up and a trying stint in the military. She had made him whole again, and he didn't want to see the man he would turn into without her.

But thirty-one minutes after the men arrived, Karen kissed him on the forehead then hung her head as she turned to walk out their front door for the last time. Two other men hustled their daughters—three and two years old—out the back door. Zac ran through the house, calling their names. How could they be gone? It happened so fast. But they were gone, and he had to

hope they would stay safe long enough for him to see them again
—and that he would too.

He had no way of contacting them, however, so there was no
way for him to be sure. He felt like there'd always be three holes
in his heart until they could be back together. The emptiness was
a toxic combination with the loneliness and isolation the town
was bearing down on him. He knew it was making him into a
different person than the loving husband and doting father of his
two little angels. He was morphing into a man he didn't
recognize. He didn't want to be this way, but he couldn't find
peace within himself. Everything he wanted in his life had been
living with him in that house, and now he had to bounce off the
walls that dripped like molasses with the memories they made
there. It all drove him further into a very dark place. Two years
earlier, he never thought he had it in him. He could never take
another man's life in cold blood, cradling the man's head in his
hands. Why would he want to? But slicing Trevor's neck had felt
so natural. Like it was the most normal thing in the world. He
victimized women. If Zac's wife or daughters were around, those
pictures could have been *them*. Trevor had earned his fate, and
Zac simply provided it. That had felt good. If life was going to
dole out punishment in large doses, Zac was ready to hand out
some justice of his own.

As he put down the bowl, Zac heard a banging on the front
door. That was what he thought he heard, anyway. That was
unusual. There weren't a whole lot of house calls those days.
People stayed in their bubbles unless there was some specific
reason to come out of them. So, this person must have had some
specific reason to be on Zac's front porch. But why?

He heard three more loud raps on the door, and there was no
mistaking it this time—someone was there, and they weren't
going to go away quietly. Zac laid down his dishrag and walked
through the hallway toward the door.

"May I help you?" Zac said, not recognizing the man standing in front of him.

"I'm Paul, Audrey's chief of staff," he said. "Can I come in?"

"I've never met you before, Paul. But if you really *are* Audrey's chief of staff, I'd think you'd know house visitors are against the law."

Paul rolled his eyes.

"Let's just say I've got clearance. Step aside."

40

"You guys are crazy," Danny said, placing a paper plate and plastic forks on the quarantine camp table. "This'll never work."

"Put yourself in our position," Nick said, trying to make eye contact with Danny. "We're sitting ducks if we just stay here. Should we wait until all of us are bludgeoned, rotting corpses in our tents, like the one twenty feet to your right?"

"Don't look at me."

"What?"

"Do. Not. Look. At. Me," Danny said, continuing to set the table up for dinner. "Anyone in the building beside us can look out and see the entire camp here. It's a perfect eagle's-eye view. If anyone sees that we're having some long, drawn-out conversation, I may get asked what we were talking about. And I'm not about to lie to save your ass."

Nick hunched his shoulders and looked at the table.

"Okay. Sure. But you've got to help us. You're the only hope we have."

"I don't have to do shit," said Danny, slicing the steaks into pieces because plastic knives clearly weren't going to cut through ribeye. "You're just gonna have to figure out a way to do this on your own. I can't be a part of it. I won't stand in your way. If you get the drop on Paul, I won't come running to help him. But that's the best I can do."

"But you've heard our plan. How does it work without you? You have a better idea?"

"I'm a cop. I don't do prisoner-breakout ideas."

"That's right," said Nick, looking around everywhere except at Danny. "You're a cop. You vow to protect the innocent. What, exactly, are we guilty of?"

"You violated the law. You knew the consequences."

"No, we fucking *didn't*, Danny, and you know it! Nobody knew what happened once you were taken to quarantine. We were *told* the consequences were that you get isolated temporarily to make sure you don't show signs of the virus, and then you get released back into the public. But that's not what happens, is it? Nobody's been allowed out of here once they go in. This is a death sentence, and you're helping to carry it out."

"Don't act like you didn't think this was a possibility. Maybe the early people had a case for ignorance, but not you. You'd seen nobody gets released, and you thought with your dick anyway. You're not the first man to have that bite him in the ass."

"But what did I do, really? Seriously. Bottom line: I was given a death sentence for comforting a rape victim. That's what happened. That's why I deserve to be here?"

Danny laughed. "And why were you going into her house in the first place, Mister Innocent? To sit across the room and stare longingly into each other's eyes?"

"I—" Nick fidgeted in his chair.

"We both know you were there hoping to fuck her. And we both know that's illegal for a good reason. So don't come to me with this 'I was just comforting a rape victim' blather. That's just what it turned into. This was a booty call. Don't act like it wasn't."

"Fair enough. You got me. But you think that deserves death?"

"Not up to me."

"But it is! Right here and now. If you don't help us, you're deciding that it *is* worth a death sentence, that you can't be bothered to help stand in the way of that happening. If you think we deserve our fate, fine. Finish setting this up, and walk away.

Eventually, you'll get to help mop up our blood. But if you think this is a gross miscarriage of justice, your only way to stop it is to help us do this."

Danny sliced the last few strips of steak and stood up, sliding the knife into his pocket. He nodded to the group and left without another word.

"Surely he's gonna help," Rachel said, as she piled Nick's clean plate on top of hers. "I can tell he's way more sympathetic to us than Paul is. I don't think his heart is in this."

"I think you're right about his heart, but we're asking a lot," Nick said. "We're asking him to put himself in harm's way in order to save our lives. If everything goes according to plan, it should work. But I'd be lying if I said there's no way for it to go sideways."

"I just don't see how this doesn't work, though," Omar said, some of the first words Nick and Rachel had heard the man say since they arrived in camp. Maybe having a plan to get out was perking him up. "Paul would be outnumbered and unarmed."

"I'm just afraid of what might happen," Nick said. "I don't know. Maybe you're right. Obviously, I think it's a good plan, or we wouldn't be pushing it on Danny so hard. I believe it absolutely *can* work. *Will* work, in fact. We can't let ourselves be lulled into the idea that it's foolproof, though. Underestimating Paul would be a mistake."

"That's only if Danny helps, though," Rachel said, collecting forks and tossing them into the bin on the table. "What if he doesn't?"

Nick looked at Omar, who stared back, expressionless. Theresa sat quietly, her legs crossed in front of her.

"You guys believe in God?" Nick glanced back and forth from Omar to Rachel and Theresa. "If so, that'd be a time to pray."

They heard the gate swing open, and Danny stepped inside. He walked in their direction and stepped around the far side of the table.

"I'm probably an idiot, but I'm in," Danny said, as he picked up the bin full of trash from dinner. "Tomorrow at dinner. Have your stuff together, and be ready."

He carried the bin back toward the compound, and stepped through the gate.

"You heard the man," Nick said. "Start gathering whatever you want to take with you. This is our shot. Let's make it count. We'll go over the plan one more time in the morning. Maybe we can beat this place."

41

Michael pedaled hard alongside Stephanie, trying to keep up. He had never been as strong an athlete as she was. Her ability to beat him in just about anything they did was part of what attracted him to her in the first place; she seemed to take a joy in showing her natural skills at everything. She could outrun him on the track, out-lift him at the gym, out-shoot him on the court, and outlast him in bed. And she was—it went without saying— smarter than him in pretty much every way someone could be smarter than another person. He was never sure whether or not that was what sent him over the edge during their marriage. They'd been through so much together, and he was sure she loved him. What he knew was he hadn't been ready to commit; he didn't want to stay with the first girl he slept with for the rest of his life. Now, the woman he was watching pull further ahead of him would never be his again. Watching her butt lifting gently off the seat, swaying back and forth as she pedaled forward, he couldn't help but lament that.

"Come on, slow poke," Stephanie said, looking back over her right shoulder. "Still plenty of doors to knock on."

"Can you…slow down? Just…a little, maybe?" Michael breathed hard between words, his legs starting to pump more slowly with each turn of the pedals.

Stephanie smiled. "Okay. Fine." She stopped her legs and coasted for several seconds, allowing him to pull up next to her. "Better?"

"Much. Is it really necessary to run this like the Tour de France, Lance Armstrong?"

"Necessary? No. Fun? Absolutely," she beamed, her teeth shining in pretty little rows. Michael thought about how much he'd missed that smile.

"So, where are we going next?" Michael said. "Nobody seems to know anything about this guy. He's a ghost."

"We've gotta try Walt's Bar one more time. Hopefully, he'll be there. I know Doctor Giles went there a lot after he was done here. Walt's known him for a long time. He's one of the guys I'd think would be as likely as anyone to know where he's holing up."

Michael nodded; they rode another couple of blocks and stopped outside the bar. They leaned their bikes against the side of the building, and walked inside. It was the early evening, and Walt was behind the bar, straightening some of the bottles of his homemade moonshine he brewed in a still behind the bar. Nobody else was there. Walt grabbed two shot glasses and laid them on the bar.

"Oh. Sorry, no," Michael said, raising his hands as he walked up to a barstool. "We're not here to drink."

Walt crossed his arms.

"This is a bar," Walt scowled. "*My* bar. Drinking is the only reason to be here."

He picked up one of the bottles of his moonshine and sloshed it into each glass, spilling as much on the bar as he got into the glasses, which were both so full a slight breeze would have overflowed them.

"Thank you, Walt," Stephanie said, laying her arms on the bar. "But we don't have a lot of time to drink. We just want to know if you've seen Doctor Giles around."

Walt straightened up and uncrossed his arms, cocking his head to the left.

"Richard?"

"That's right," she smiled and nodded enthusiastically. "Richard. You guys were close, weren't you?"

Walt paused and looked down. He glanced back up at Stephanie.

"Drink your shot, and I'll tell ya what I know."

Stephanie looked at Michael, who shrugged.

"I really don't drink, Walt," she said.

"Then I really don't talk, Steph."

She sighed loudly and turned to Michael again.

"When in Rome, I guess?"

"Bottom's up," he sipped a little off the top of his glass, then raised it to clink with Stephanie's. Then both of them tilted their heads back and drank. It immediately burned, like pouring battery acid down their throats. Both of them gagged, then shook their heads violently. It was as if a bundle of small needles tumbled down, scraping along the larynx and then into the esophagus before rolling into the chest and lungs, where it settled in, poking around and leaving destruction in its wake.

Stephanie coughed several times and pounded the bar with her fist. Michael closed his eyes and breathed slowly. He banged his chest with his open hand, trying to dislodge the needle bundle.

"Whew," Michael exhaled. "What'd you put in that glass? Sulfuric acid?"

"Special recipe," Walt said, his voice with the gravel from fifty years of tending bar and sampling the wares.

Stephanie rubbed her neck and grimaced.

"All right, Walt," she said. "We drank. Now, what can you tell us about Richard?"

Walt grabbed their glasses and tossed them in the sink behind him. He turned back to Stephanie.

"Richard disappeared a few months ago," he said. "Haven't seen him since."

Stephanie straightened her back, and her eyes got big.

"We know *that*. We need to know where he is *now*."

"Ah. Fuck if I know."

"What the—" Stephanie looked around the bar and raised her arms in frustration. "You said you'd tell us what you knew if we drank your shitty acid water there!"

Walt turned away and went back to straightening his bottles.

"And that's exactly what I did."

"I'm gonna knock those goddamn bottles off the—" Stephanie lifted her feet up on the barstool and got one knee up on the bar, scrambling to get over to the other side. Michael leapt off his stool and grabbed her ring, trying to pull her back.

"Come on, now," Michael said, wrapping both hands around the steel ring and straining to keep her from pulling herself over the bar. "It's not worth it. We'll keep looking."

"He knew what we wanted! He fucking *knew*!"

Walt barely glanced back as he lined the bottles up in alphabetical order, "Walt's Apple Brandy Cider" to the left of "Walt's Blueberry Nectar of Death" and so on.

"I know. I know, Steph," Michael said. "You're right. But let's just go. Come on."

Stephanie began to calm down, and let Michael haul her off the stool and down to the ground. He let go of her ring, and she straightened her shirt, adjusting the ring's attachment to her sides. She flipped Walt off with both hands, and they headed for the exit.

42

"Should I put on my ring since you're coming inside?" Zac said, as Paul barreled past him into the house. "I don't know what the official rules are on house visitors."

Paul waved his hand dismissively, then unclipped his ring from his sides, stepped out of it and reached inside to lean it against the wall just inside the door.

"God, I hate those fucking things," Paul said, as he stepped through the doorway, then into the living room, settling onto a green vinyl couch with a few holes in it where cotton was squeezing through. Zac stood a few feet away, looking down on Paul with his arms folded across his chest.

"So, to what do I owe the pleasure of this surprise visit?" Zac said. "I'd offer you a coffee but, ya know, the apocalypse and all."

"Yeah, I haven't had a good cup o' joe in a long time. I took it black. How 'bout you?"

"Plenty of cream. Plenty of sugar. My wife—who you and your boss tore from my life, along with my daughters and everything that made my life bearable—she took it straight black too. Said she liked to taste it."

"Sounds like a good woman."

"Yeah. She was. Now, tell me what the hell you're doing here, and why I shouldn't kill you right on that couch, because I'll tell you I don't give a shit about blood stains."

"Hey. Whoa, man," Paul put his hands up as if to show he was unarmed. "You've got me all wrong. I wasn't even around when all that happened. None of that was my idea. The rings? I had nothing to do with it. I'm just up there following Audrey's orders like a good soldier. I'm her brother, and she trusts me, so she brought me into her crew. But I was living in another town. I didn't even get here until the wall was mostly up. By that point, the wheels were already in motion on all this chaos."

"*That's* why I shouldn't kill you?"

Paul shrugged and leaned back against the armrest.

"Nah," he said. "That's just why whatever pent-up beef you've got ain't with me. And, hey, I get it. You've got a hell of a sad story. You're not nearly the only one in this town. Maybe not even the saddest one. But you're up there. Would I be angry if I were in your shoes? Hell yeah, I would. I'm not here to defend any of that. Not one bit. I mean, Audrey made the decisions she made, and I think we both know she had her reasons. Now, maybe they were justified in her mind, and maybe they weren't. Maybe she was just on a power trip and did it because she could. Ya know?"

Zac nodded, his arms dropping to his sides.

"I don't pretend to know the answer," Paul said. "She's my sister, but we don't share a brain. I can't tell you what she was thinkin', and I can't tell you to suck it up and play the good soldier for the 'good of humanity,' or some other bullshit. I can't tell you the sacrifice is worth it because, frankly, it probably isn't. If I were you, I'd have probably already offed myself. It's a fuckin' miracle you're standing here in front of me right now, as a matter of damn fact."

Zac sniffed loudly and tucked his chin under his shoulder blade, like he was trying to crawl into himself and hide.

"It hasn't been easy," Zac said, through gritted teeth.

"That's for damn sure. Not for any of us, but especially for you. You asked why I'm here. Well, let me be honest with ya. I'm not just here to blow smoke up your ass about how brave and miraculous you are. You're still a son of a bitch, just like the rest of us around here, and you killed a man."

His heart skipping a beat, Zac jerked his head up and looked at Paul.

"What was that?"

"We know you killed Trevor. You heard we thought Nick did it, right?" Paul laughed and ran his fingers through his hair. "That was just for show. You know Michael Sloan? He gave you up. Made a special trip to the compound just to tell us you killed the guy. I told him we didn't believe him, but he had a pretty good story, and we never really believed the Nick thing anyway. It was a stretch, but we knew we could sell it."

"If you knew I did it," Zac said, his head tilted and his eyes moving toward the ceiling, "why didn't you come after me instead of Nick?"

"It's not like we have a DNA lab these days. Detective work's a bitch when you're thrown back into the eighteenth century. We'd have had to build some sort of a case, find credible witnesses, look for hard evidence. Or we could just take a guy we already had in custody and have him read a statement. That was good enough for us."

Zac didn't say anything. Just stared at Paul.

"So, again, why am I here? I think our interests and skill sets may be coming together nicely."

"How's that?" Zac sat down on the edge of the coffee table in front of the couch.

"Well, you clearly don't have a problem with violence…for the sake of principle, we'll say. And you'd like to be able to have a nice little one-on-one powwow with Audrey. Am I right?"

Zac nodded, his hands clasped in front of him, leaning forward.

"I just so happen to need someone who's willing to get his hands dirty for the good of Alessandra. Someone, perhaps, without a whole lot to lose. And I have the access to get this someone as close as he wants to Audrey so he can have a little chat. How does that sound?"

"I think we can work something out."

"Good. Then it's time for your first assignment."

Paul was about to open the door to his bedroom to get some rest in before dinner when he heard quick footsteps from behind him and a familiar shrill voice.

"Paul! Where have you been?' Officer Greene said, in what seemed like a mini panic.

"Out." Paul looked at him with disinterest. "Something wrong?"

"It's Audrey. The door to her room is locked, and I've been pounding on it. She won't answer."

Smiling slightly, Paul put his arm around Officer Greene. Outside the compound, this sort of gesture would be met with shock, given all the anti-touching rules. But inside this house was basically Sodom and Gomorrah, relatively speaking, and people were pretty used to those rules being ignored.

"It's okay, William," Paul said. "It's all right if I call you William?"

"Um, sure. Of course."

"Great. So, William, this is my fault. I should have told you, she asked not to be disturbed this evening. You don't know her that well, so I don't know if you could tell earlier. But I know my sister, and she was really beat today. She's just been working too hard, ya know. I tell her all the time, 'You're doing too much. The people need you to be strong, and at your best. You need to sleep more.' Does she listen? Nope. Hardly ever. It's crazy. That's just the way she is, though. But finally, today, I talked her into lying down for awhile. That's a good thing."

"Well, yeah," Officer Greene said. "I just knocked so many times. How did I not wake her up?"

Paul laughed. "Well, another thing you wouldn't know is that, ever since she was a kid, she's been one of the deepest sleepers you could ever imagine. Ever know anybody like that? Our dad used to say a nuclear bomb could go off, and she'd barely roll over."

"I guess. Sure."

"Yeah, sure. You're a good guy, William. We do appreciate your concern. We really do. I know Audrey appreciates it too. But don't worry at all. She just said for me to handle anything that comes up while she's getting her rest. Were you wanting to update her on Michael?"

"Right. That's the thing. I knew she wanted to know what was going on with Michael after he left the hospital."

"You're absolutely right. We do want to know about that. What can you tell me?"

"Well, it's strange. They appear to be going door to door and asking people something. It's like they're canvassing the town for some reason."

"Interesting," Paul said. "And you don't have any idea what about?"

"Like I said before, all we've been instructed to do is follow without being detected. So we're keeping out of sight. We could follow up with some of the people they've talked to and ask what Michael and Stephanie talked about. But, for now, we're just keeping track of their movements. Should we go back to figure out what they're asking the people about?"

"No, just keep doing what you're doing, William. You're doin' a great job. You really are. I thank you. Audrey thanks you. And the town of Alessandra thanks you for your service."

"Well, thank you, sir. That means a lot."

"Don't mention it," Paul smiled.

Officer Greene turned to walk away, and Paul grabbed his shirt behind the shoulder and pulled him slightly back toward him.

"Just one more quick thing," Paul said. "You're not talking to anyone else about this, are you?"

"Anyone else?"

"Yeah. Besides me, and Audrey, and the officer who's following Michael."

"Um, no. Not that I'm aware of."

Paul nodded and tightened his grip on Officer Greene's shirt, stretching the fabric until he heard a slight rip in a seam.

"That's good. I think it'd be in everyone's best interest if we kept it that way."

Officer Greene nodded quickly, his eyes large and bright.

"Perfect. Then we should have no problems." Paul let go of the shirt, and Officer Greene jerked away from him, smoothing the back of his shirt out with his hand and avoiding eye contact with Paul. Officer Greene walked away. Paul spun back toward his room when he saw Danny coming out of the corner of his eye. *Now what?*

"Hey, Paul," Danny said, coming out from the kitchen. "You gonna handle dinner for the camp tonight?"

God damn it. Fucking forgot. Of course, Paul would never admit that to Danny.

"I'm pretty tired. I think I'm just gonna lie down for awhile instead. I'll figure something out later."

Paul opened the door to his room and stepped a foot inside.

"Because I was thinkin'," Danny said, and Paul paused without looking back. "I'm kind of in a cooking mood. I'd be glad to make everything and even help you set the table up if you'd just carry the food out. That's the one part I hate."

Paul stood halfway across the threshold to his room, looking at the floor. He blinked several times but wasn't saying anything. Danny stood, leaning against the wall.

"Yeah. Sure," Paul mumbled. "You can help me clean up that body too. Come get me at six."

Danny nodded once, then turned to head back to the kitchen and prepare the meal.

43

Stephanie shoved the bar door open with both hands and stormed into the street outside, balling her hands into fists and stretching her arms taut against her sides.

"God *damn* it, Michael! He was just screwing with us."

"Maybe we can circle back to him later or something. Let's calm down. We'll figure this out."

Stephanie wasn't ready to calm down, though. It was infuriating to look at Walt back there without a ring on, casually dismissing their cause when hundreds of people around them were suffering under this despotic system of government that was forcing them into isolation. She knew Walt could help. Just *knew* it. But if he wouldn't talk, there was nothing she could do about it. He was an old man. What was she going to do? Beat it out of him? They needed another plan. There was no telling how much time they had. It was possible nobody knew what they were doing other than her, Michael and Anna. But Anna had to call Audrey and let her know they were accessing the virus transmission file. So it was also possible that put a big, fat target on her back, and the cavalry might come any minute. It was a chance she was willing to take because she was a prominent person in the community who would have plenty of people defending her actions, but that didn't mean she was safe. Neither was Michael. And they needed answers.

"Hey," Michael leaned over and put his face close to Stephanie's. "Mister Chang's out sweeping the sidewalk over there. Let's talk to him. Then we can decide what to do from there."

"All right," she nodded slightly, then followed him across the street.

Liu Chang was another long-time Alessandra resident, who owned a small convenience store in town and lived in the apartment above it. His wife had been visiting her parents in South Georgia when the virus started spreading fast, and she called Liu to tell him her mom was sick, and she was going to stay there a little longer to help until she was better. That was the last conversation he had with her. Likewise, his son and daughter were grown and had moved away long before that. He had no way of knowing what ended up happening with them. He tried frantically to reach them, but there had been no answer. In the panic that gripped the country, next of kin weren't always notified of deaths; there were just too many of them, and not nearly enough staff that weren't already busy with more urgent tasks. That was part of the pain of a pandemic that spread so quickly and was so deadly. Many people never got closure with their loved ones. Liu carried on as ever after that, but most people who knew him could tell a part of him wasn't there anymore.

He continued to man the store because it was all he knew, and it kept him busy with something rather than sitting in his house and waiting to die. There were no national brands to carry anymore, so some residents donated homemade goods—socks, baskets, ironing boards, herbal teas, sewing kits—for him to sell, which usually meant either to barter or for them to owe him a favor, which he rarely called in. Some people still used U.S. dollars in transactions, but there wasn't much they could buy anymore.

Now, as he often was, Liu was sweeping the sidewalk in front of his store. Not because it was cluttered so much as because he just liked keeping his hands busy, and all his shop's shelves were probably as neat as could be.

"Mister Chang, how are you doing?" Michael said, waving as they crossed the street. Everybody in town called him Mister

Chang. Michael didn't know why, but it'd been that way since Michael was a kid.

"Doing fine," he said. "The world turns."

Michael nodded. "Nice day. Think the spring's starting to turn?"

Liu stopped sweeping and looked up at the sky.

"Oh, not yet. Sun's not ready." He went back to sweeping.

"So, Stephanie and I are looking for someone. We were wondering if you could help."

Liu stopped his broom and looked at Michael.

"You know Doctor Giles, right?" Michael said.

"Richard. Yes, I know him. Comes in the store a lot."

"He comes in the store? Like, recently?"

"Oh, no," Liu frowned. "Not recently. It's been a while. But he used to come by a lot. I'm not sure what happened. Now, the only time I see him is going into Walt's."

Michael looked at Stephanie, whose eyes lit on fire.

"What do you mean you only see him going into Walt's?" Stephanie said.

"Just what I said. Late at night. Walt's is about the only place in town that's lit up outside then, since he has a bit of a later clientele than a little ol' convenience store. So I'll see people duck in and out of there a decent bit when they can't sleep or just need a hit of devil water at two in the morning. One of those guys is Richard. Fairly regularly, actually."

"Are you sure about that?" Michael said, leaning forward.

"Oh, most definitely. What's weird about it—and why I've noticed it—is because he never comes from the street like everyone else. He always walks up from behind the bar, through that parking lot back there and goes in through the side door. He's usually not there very long, and leaves the same way he came. I can't figure out where he's coming from, or where he's going."

"That's gr—oh, shit," Michael said. "Stephanie! Wait!"

Michael turned to run, but Stephanie was already in a full sprint across the street, headed toward the front door of Walt's.

"Thank you, Mister Chang!" Michael yelled as he hit the asphalt, knowing she'd easily beat him to the bar, and wondering what she'd do when she got there.

44

Zac walked through the automatic doors of St. Francis Hospital, marveling at its high ceilings and large windows looming over the foyer. It was a beautiful building that seemed designed to help a person relax. He assumed that was part of the science of it. His military training in the deserts of Afghanistan didn't have any place this white, or this peaceful. Nor did Alessandra, outside of this building. It made him wonder what a day spent there might be like, rather than climbing the walls in his house, constantly bombarded by reminders of the life he once had. He thought about how he had struggled to adjust to the world back home after returning from active duty, but he'd done it. He put behind the war, the killing, the violence. He put behind that lifestyle, and embraced being a husband and father. And, four years later, look where it left him—alone, with fantasies of vengeance against the person who took it all away from him. Maybe the peacefulness of this place would rub off on him while he was there.

He approached Trish's desk, stopped and leaned forward against it.

"Hi! Welcome to St. Francis," Trish said, a smile spread across her face. "How can I help you?"

"Hi. I'm looking for…" Zac pulled a slip of paper out of the pocket of his olive-colored cargo pants and unfolded it clumsily. "Her name is Anna. In the Research department."

"Oh, Anna! Yes. Wonderful girl. Who can I tell her is—"

"Could you tell me *where* the Research department is?" Zac interrupted.

"Um, well, I have to call her first to tell her you're coming."

He leaned forward further, his face getting closer to hers.

"Why?"

She picked up the phone, but it hovered just above its stand.

"Because that's how we do things, Mister…?" her voice raised an octave in question.

"I just want to know where it is. Is that a secret?"

"Well, no. I guess it's not."

He leaned back on his heels and put his hands behind his back.

"So?"

"It's just down the hall here on the right," she pointed through a pair of double doors twenty feet away. "On the other side of those doors. Okay? I'm going to call her now. What's your —Sir! Wait!"

Zac began walking toward the doors. Trish yelled after him, but he didn't look back or break stride. For a moment, she was torn. Should she follow him to try and stop him, or should she get back to her phone and call to warn Anna? It was possible Anna wasn't even in there at the moment, though Trish knew the odds were good she was. She might not be right inside the door at her desk, but she was likely in Research somewhere. That girl basically lived in there. She was a Research rat, if there was such a thing. And, unless a doctor called her out to do something specific for them, she was lurking in there somewhere.

Trish had no idea what this man was up to, but she got a bad vibe from him before he bolted in Anna's direction. He didn't look outwardly angry so much as he looked like a man trying desperately to keep a lid on his anger, and perhaps failing. His veneer was paper thin. Was he angry at Anna? Normally, Trish might think he was a spurned lover, but did they even have those anymore? Alessandra was the most celibate town in the history of the world at this point, she'd guess. She rarely even saw people milling about if she wasn't at the hospital. Where would you even go to meet someone in this town? And what would you do with them if you couldn't touch them?

It worried her even more that she had no idea what this man's motivation might be, and he looked far too strong for her to physically stop, so she scrambled a few steps back to her reception desk. She grabbed the phone and hit Anna's extension as he pushed through the double doors. Trish knew Research was the second door on the right. He wouldn't know that, but he'd see the sign on the door. Trish's best hope was that the man wouldn't see it immediately. Every second she could buy Anna might help.

The phone rang once, twice, three times. Where was she? Must have at least been away from her desk. Part of Trish was hoping she'd get no answer. That would hopefully mean that Anna was out of the office, probably somewhere else in the building. If so, Trish would have time to summon security and get the guy removed from the building. On the other hand, it could also mean he already got to her, and she couldn't pick up the phone. Either way, Trish's next call was going to security.

Six rings. Seven. Trish was getting ready to put the phone back in its cradle when she heard Anna's voice.

"Research. This is Anna."

"Anna, it's Trish. There's a man on his way to you. You need to get out of there."

"What? I don't understand. Why would I…oh, wait. Hold on."

"No! Anna!"

Trish could hear mumbled voices, but she couldn't tell what they were saying. Time seemed to stand still, as she listened into the receiver, willing Anna to come back to the phone. Maybe it wasn't him. Maybe it was a doctor with a question. Maybe he hadn't found the room yet. Trish could feel the blood rushing from her face, her breaths getting thinner as she pressed the receiver hard against her ear, trying to pick up the words being exchanged only thirty feet away from her.

Then she heard what sounded like wheels scraping against wood, fading quickly, followed by a loud bang. Trish's heart quickened its pace, and she put her left hand to her mouth. What was happening? Then there was silence. Still standing, bent over the desk and waiting, hoping Anna would come back on the line, she saw the light on the phone for Anna's extension go out. Someone hung up. She disconnected the call and dialed security. The call went straight to a voicemail message.

"I'm sorry we missed your call. It's Wednesday, March first at three thirty, and the St. Francis security team has been called to visit Ms. Reese's office for a meeting with her brother, Paul, to discuss security measures for tomorrow's craft market event in the town square. We will return afterward, probably by seven. If this is an emergency, please follow normal protocol for securing the area until we return. Thank you."

Trish slowly hung up the phone and looked down the hall, wondering what was happening on the other side of those doors. Almost all of the doctors and nurses worked on the second or third floor of the building, so none of them likely heard if anything was going on in the room. That also meant that, to get help, Trish had three options: call random offices and hope to find someone at their desk; go upstairs and try to flag someone down in the hall; try to handle this herself. Her first two options might take a lot of time, and it was time she wasn't sure she had.

Hesitantly, she began walking toward the double doors, each step echoing ominously in her head.

Zac walked through the double doors, ignoring Trish's voice behind him. What was she going to do? Tackle him and pin him to the ground? He had a hunch he could take her if she tried. He

looked around. There were a few doors to his right, and a couple
more to his left, and then the hall turned right thirty feet away. All
she had told him was that Research was through those doors. He
tried the first door on his right, but it was locked. He was hoping
he wouldn't have to break a door down, but he suspected a
Research department door wouldn't be locked.

The door across the hall looked more like it would lead to a
closet than a significant Research area, so he decided to bypass
that one. When he turned to the next door, on his right, he saw a
sign on the door. From ten feet away, he wasn't entirely certain
what it said. It almost looked like it was scrawled there in pen, on
a small whiteboard. As he got closer, though, he saw it clearly
said "Research." He opened the door.

Just a few feet inside sat a short, waifish girl with dark pixie-
cut hair and glasses, holding a phone to her ear.

"What? I don't understand," he heard her say into the phone.
"Why would I...oh, wait. Hold on."

She laid the phone down and walked toward him.

"Hi. I'm Anna," she said. "I'm afraid the Research
department is just for hospital employees unless you have
authorization. Is there something I can help you with?"

He shoved his hands in his pockets and twisted his head,
sending a crack through his neck.

"Are you Anna..." he pulled the paper out from his pocket
again and glanced at it. "Swafford?"

"Um, yes. I am. And what's your name? I'm sorry for not
already knowing you, but I just don't get out of here much," she
smiled.

"You're friends with Stephanie Sloan?"

Anna felt a tingling sensation in her stomach. She crossed her
arms, and paused, shifting her weight from one foot to the other.
Her smile faded.

"Why are you asking?"

Zac reached down at his sides and began unhooking his ring. Four quick latches, and it was loose. He began dropping it to the floor.

"What are you doing?" Anna put her hands in front of her and began backing away.

He stepped out of his ring and walked toward her. The back of her left thigh hit her chair, sending it rolling across the room, spinning wildly. She stumbled, and he moved closer. She was losing her balance, her feet sliding out from underneath her, her momentum pulling her torso backward and down toward the floor. As her feet lost contact with the ground, her back slammed into her desk, sending a lightning bolt of pain up her torso into her shoulders and down to her hips. The desk rattled hard against the wall, jarring her computer monitor and knocking her jar of pens over, scattering several of them on the floor.

Zac reached her and hung up the phone, then unsheathed his knife and put his left arm around her back, pressing the tip of his M9 seven-inch bayonet against her skin. He cupped her mouth with his right hand, pressing it hard to her face. She could only breathe through her nose, and she could barely get enough air as her heart went into the red.

"I'm not here to hurt you," he whispered, his face an inch from her head, his breath warm on her ear. "I just need to know one thing: Why is Stephanie going door to door asking questions? What is she trying to find out?"

Anna's eyes were huge, and tears were forming. Her stomach was heaving.

"I'm going to take my hand off your mouth just a little bit," he said. "If you answer me, I'll leave. If you scream, I'll have to punch you. Now…"

He pulled his hand across her mouth and gave her enough room to breathe.

"Hel—!" she yelled as loud as she could before he covered her mouth again. He pressed his body against hers to pin her against the desk, brought his left arm around and thrust a fist into her ribs. She bent over and tried to clutch her stomach. She thought she was going to vomit on the man's shoes. He grabbed her around the neck and began pulling her toward the back part of the Research area, between the shelves of books in the library.

"Let's go back here, where we won't be so close to the door," he said. "I think we'll be more comfortable."

They weaved between bookshelves and got to the back wall. He shoved her against it, grabbed her shoulders and guided her carefully to the floor. She sat with her knees pressed against her chest. He reached into one of the pockets of his cargo pants, pulled out a cotton fabric and shoved it deep in her mouth. Then he grabbed some rope. He uncoiled it, cut off the length he needed, threw it around her back and began wrapping it around her midsection a few times, while sitting on her feet.

"So, I know you're hurt. You may have a broken rib or two. I punch hard," Zac said, as he started tying a knot, then got out a smaller rope to tie around her ankles. "But I warned you. That wasn't something I wanted to do, and I'd prefer not to do it again. I'm military, see. I follow orders. My orders right now are to get this information from you. That means it isn't optional. You're going to tell me, or I'll have to kill you; it'd be quick with this knife. I'd feel bad about it, sure. But I'd feel worse about not doing the job I was assigned to do. You understand? Nod if you understand."

Anna shook her head nervously.

He let out a small laugh. "Well, nevertheless," he said. "Here's the way this is gonna go. I'm going to pull out the cloth. Then you're gonna tell me what Stephanie is trying to accomplish with all this. I promise I'm not planning to hurt her. Or you. But I need to know what she's doing. Okay? You got it? Nod this time."

She did. He reached up to pull the cloth out so she could talk. In her head, she was trying to decide what to do. Should she continue to try to hold out? *Surely Trish realized something wasn't right. But why didn't she try calling back? Maybe she immediately called security. If so, though, why aren't they here by now? Surely they've had plenty of time to get here if Trish called right then. Is it possible Trish is so dense that she's just sitting at her desk playing Solitaire or something right now? I mean, what other possibility is there at this point? And, if that's the case, I'm fucked back here in the back of Research. Nobody can hear me from here. I might as well be on the fucking moon. And I believe this guy. He'll kill me right here. Somebody will find my bloody corpse slumped against this wall at some point when I start smelling too bad and don't answer when they call. If I just tell him about Stephanie, he'll leave. She's tough. She can handle herself a bit. And what's the worst that happens, anyway? I know I'm dead if I stonewall. If I tell him, at least we've got a shot.*

The cloth removed, he stared at her.

"Well?" he said.

"She's trying to find Doctor Giles," she said, immediately feeling disgusted with herself.

"You're sure?"

She nodded, grimacing, as much in shame as pain. Then she heard the door to Research creak open, and the man's head spun around. He shoved the cloth back in her mouth.

45

Paul scooped up the tray of food and cradled it on both arms, holding onto the handles underneath and trying to balance the bowls of macaroni and cheese with the carafes of tea.

"You don't fuck around with this food, do you?" Paul said. "You know they're just prisoners, right? This ain't the goddamn Ritz Carlton."

"Yeah, I don't know," Danny shrugged. "I just like having an excuse to cook."

"You can make me dinner anytime you like, man. Particularly if you want to load it up on this tray and bring it to me in bed."

"That's a tempting offer."

Danny led the way through the living room toward the den that overlooked the courtyard. With a quick glance as he walked, he could see the prisoners milling about, no doubt nervous about what was happening. By this point, they'd become pretty good at determining the time of day by the position of the sun, and they knew it had to be close to six. Everyone was getting in their places.

Danny wiped his forehead with his sleeve as he stepped onto the stairs, leaving the door open behind him for Paul to step through. It was a cool evening, but he didn't feel it. His body was pumping battery acid through his veins. This was a borderline coup they were marching into; it was unchartered waters for Danny, a lifelong cop who felt like he may have found his calling with Audrey in charge. Prior to post-plague Alessandra, he had learned some of the ropes of leading a group of officers, but now he was an unquestioned leader of the men—even if their manpower was limited. And leaders sometimes had to make tough decisions. Doing this was his toughest.

Part of him wanted to back out. The prisoners were going to follow his lead. If he didn't make a move, they wouldn't either. The plan was for him to gauge the situation and determine if the moment was right. If they didn't see his signal, they were to hold back and regroup for another opportunity later. A lot was on his shoulders, and he was trying to figure out if he was ready for it. It was hard to say for sure, but he thought he was ready. This was the just thing to do; these people were counting on him to give them hope, to give them freedom. They didn't deserve to be where they were, and he couldn't be a part of keeping them there any longer. He needed to do the right thing, and sometimes— often, even—the right thing was hard.

They reached the ground, and Danny walked to the gate. He pulled it open and held it for Paul to go in front of him. Paul walked through and closed the gate. It was unusual for them both to come at the same time, so that very fact got the prisoners nervous that this was actually going down. Danny could see them positioning themselves, all of them standing, ready to pounce when called upon. This was a numbers game, in a large way. Only Danny had a weapon, a small knife from a kitchen drawer. Danny figured it'd be enough to hurt Paul with a few quick stabbings while the rest of the people swarmed him, dragging him to the ground. Once he was pinned, Danny could finish the job by slashing Paul's throat. Nick would give Danny a couple of punches and maybe a quick cut on the leg or arm, and Danny would tell Audrey that the prisoners swarmed him and Paul, took their keys and fled. When Danny told Audrey about what Paul had done to them, and showed her the tortured prisoners remaining in the camp, he was confident he could eventually convince her to stand down, for her own good. The prisoners would take any of the weakest isolated prisoners with them if they were strong enough to move on their own. Maybe they could find a sympathetic doctor at St. Francis.

Danny didn't know their plan from there, but he didn't want to. The less he knew after that, the better. He hoped they could find someplace to hide, maybe at friends' houses, maybe somewhere in the depths of St. Francis. Who knew? But he hoped they could steer clear of Audrey's officers, and maybe this could be the start of exposing to everyone—not just Audrey—what Paul had done. Danny would be adamant that Audrey played no part in it. She'd bear some responsibility for ultimately being the leader, but Danny thought he could push the narrative that she hadn't known what was happening, and he'd eventually tell everyone the truth about how they put an end to it. Maybe he'd come out of this a hero in Alessandra. Just had to get a few breaks to go their way.

Danny could survey the scene from his vantage point, watching from six feet behind as Paul carried the tray of food. Danny could see Nick diagonal to his left, twenty feet ahead. Omar was flanked to the right. They'd be the first to grab Paul after Danny got his arms around him. Then, from over by the table, Rachel and Theresa would run over and help hold Paul's arms and legs down. They were up out of their seats and watching, thirty feet ahead. Everything was in place. Danny slowly pulled the knife out of his pocket and held it at waist height. If he was going to make the move, the time was now.

Yanking his arm backward to prepare to thrust it into Paul's side, Danny took a quick step forward. Out of the corner of his eye, he could see Nick and Omar tense up, ready to take Paul to the ground. Before he could get there, though, Danny saw Paul stop and drop the tray of food, flipping it forward in front of him. Paul half spun to his right, jerking his arm straight back, bringing his head around to see Danny charging his way. Danny felt a crater in his stomach when he briefly glanced what Paul had at the end of that arm—a black, military-style bayonet with a blade of at least seven inches, more than double what Danny had in his hand. It had been stashed inside the handle of the tray, and Danny had never known.

There was no time for Danny to sidestep it; Paul's pivot was ruthlessly efficient. He picked up his target and jabbed his arm directly behind him, thrusting it into Danny's neck, just below the chin. Blood squirted out in two directions, as the serrated edge toward the handle of the blade sliced the tissue in numerous places. With blood soaking his shoulder and streaming down his forehead, Paul turned back to look at Nick and Omar, who were frozen in place. Danny's face was quickly losing its color, his arms hanging loosely at his sides. Without looking back at Danny, Paul jerked the knife out, and Danny's body slumped into the bloody mud pit gathering at his feet.

Paul bent into a crouch and held the bayonet forward in his right hand, with his left hand mimicking the position.

"Anybody else?" Paul said. "Anybody else want some? Come on. Let's go."

Nick and Omar stared, not knowing what to do. They were unarmed, and he was holding a knife that looked like it could dice up a boulder. Neither of them was trained in hand-to-hand combat. They had been counting on Danny for that. But Danny's lifeless body was lying in a pool of blood, and they were staring down the man who killed him. Nick started taking steps backward, hoping to get back to Rachel before Paul did anything. Could Nick at least protect her? He didn't see how, if Paul decided he wanted to lay waste to all of them, but he was going to try. Omar joined him in backing away.

"Not so brave now?" Paul said, straightening his back and letting his arms hang at his side. "I thought not. This was a *bad* move, gentlemen. I could kill you now, but I'm gonna let you live long enough to really regret what you did here today. You don't even know how screwed you are."

Paul turned and walked back toward the gate, not even concerned that someone might charge him.

"Oh, and by the way," Paul yelled without looking back, "Dinner's canceled. For *good.*"

Nick fell to the ground on his knees, then onto his stomach, his arms pinned beneath him. He laid his head down and wept.

46

When Michael opened the door to the bar, he looked around but didn't see either Stephanie or Walt. It was silent. Where had they gone? She'd only beaten him there by a few seconds. They couldn't be far. He peeked on the floor behind the bar, but didn't see anyone. He walked through the place, glancing in long-unused booths as he went. Nothing. When he got to the back of the bar, it turned right toward the bathrooms, so he followed in that direction. As he got further down that hall, he could hear a sound that might have been feet scuffling on a linoleum floor. Then he heard a loud crash coming from one of the bathrooms. As he turned the corner, he saw a ring—he assumed it was Stephanie's —lying on the floor. He reached the women's room first and shoved the door open, then held it against the wall with his hand. He didn't see anyone, just one sink and a row of dingy stalls that looked like they could use a good scrub down. Then there was another bang, this time from the other side of the wall. There was no doubt now where they were.

He slid over to the men's room door a few feet away and threw his shoulder against the door as he ran in. Past the two urinals, there were two stalls, and the door was propped open on one of them. He could hear Stephanie talking to Walt.

"Tell me where he lives!" she said, followed by a small splash and the sounds of arms thrashing into the stall walls.

Michael ran back to the open stall and saw Stephanie's back to him, one foot on the floor and the other pressed into Walt's neck, holding his head inside the toilet.

"Are you really giving him a swirlie?" Michael said. "Jesus, Steph."

She looked back at Michael.

"You've got a better idea?" She pulled his head out of the toilet and held it above the rim, what sparse hair he had dripping down his cheeks and splashing back into the basin.

"Stop!" Walt said. "Please! I can't take this!"

"He's not a geek in high school," Michael said.

"No, *I* was the geek in high school," Stephanie said, looking at the back of Walt's head. "Tell me where Doctor Giles lives!"

"Okay, okay. Look," Walt gasped with water dribbling from his mouth. "I don't know much, and I'm not supposed to tell anyone anything. Paul said—"

"Paul?" Stephanie asked.

"Yes, Paul. Um, Ms. Reese's brother. He does a lot of stuff for her."

"Go on."

"Okay. Well, he told me I had to help Richard whenever he came here. Paul brings me some supplies at times, and gets me what I need to make the moonshine. In exchange, I don't tell *anyone* about this."

Stephanie looked back at Michael, who shrugged.

"Well, you've already broken that promise, so you might as well tell me everything," she said.

"No. No. You see, I don't really know that much. You have to believe me. I just help him when he comes. He was a friend before, but now we don't even really talk. He seems…different. I don't know. But I don't know where he lives. I just know he shows up at my side door a few times a week, and I give him whatever Paul brought for him. That's it. I swear."

Stephanie kept her foot on his neck, bracing herself with her hands pressed against both walls of the stall.

"Where does he come from?"

"What?"

She pushed his head into the water again. His arms pressed against the lid, trying to force himself back out. But she was too strong, pressing hard against him with her leg, watching bubbles rise to the surface of the water. Michael rolled his eyes and considered grabbing her from behind to stop her, but he figured he'd just get an elbow to the side. She pulled him out again.

"Where. Does. He. Come. From?" she said, carefully enunciating each word. "When he comes here?"

"I'm not sure," Walt spat water back into the toilet. "Oh, god. Just kill me. Seriously."

"I'm not going to *kill* you, Walt. But I am going to make your evening really goddamn miserable until you help me."

"Okay. Fine. I just know he comes from behind the bar. Back in the kudzu there somewhere. I don't fucking *know* any more than that. That's it! Really! Paul's going to fucking kill me!"

Stephanie glanced back at Michael and smiled, then paused for a moment.

"I believe you. I think that's all you know," she pulled him up to a full kneeling position and stepped around Michael out of the stall. "And I'm sure Paul won't *kill* you. You'll be fine."

Walt wiped both hands across his face, and across his mostly bald head.

"You don't know the guy," Walt said. "Can I get some paper towels?"

"Paper? Oh. Yeah. Sure," she said, looking at Michael. He gestured to the paper towel dispenser on the wall.

"Hey. The day I dunk some old guy's head in a toilet, I'll get the towels to clean him up," Michael said. "You do the dunking, you get the towels to mop up the mess."

Stephanie curled up the corner of her mouth and stuck her tongue out at him, then walked over and pulled out a large handful of paper towels. She handed them to Walt, who rubbed them all over his head. Stephanie and Michael began walking toward the door to leave.

"They say torture doesn't work, ya know," Michael said.

"Who says that?"

"They."

"Eh, what do *they* know anyway?"

Michael laughed. "But, seriously, how reliable is that? He'd have told you his mom flew Doctor Giles here on a unicorn that ran on fairy dust in order to get you to stop dunking his head in that nasty toilet."

"Doesn't matter," she shrugged.

"What do you mean it doesn't matter?"

"Because I was already pretty sure of that."

"What do you mean? Pretty sure of what?" Michael said.

"Where Doctor Giles came from."

"How would you know that?"

"When you were talking to Mister Chang, I looked back there. I could see where the kudzu was pulled apart and trampled. I'm betting there's a door back there."

"If you were already sure, then what was all that about?"

"I said 'pretty sure,' not 'sure,'" she smiled. "And, after all, that was fun."

47

Trish nudged open the door to Research and cringed as it creaked a bit. She wanted to push it just far enough open for her to slide through. But, after a point, every inch it moved brought another ache in its joints. She was wishing she'd lost a little more weight than she had in this post-apocalyptic wonderland, but she still had a weakness for frying fish and vegetables when she could get her hands on them.

She finally slid through the opening and stood in the front of the room, listening for any sound. She thought she heard something—or maybe someone—but she couldn't pinpoint where it was coming from. She glanced at Anna's desk, and it was a mess, which was unlike her. Everything was always in its place, the cup of pens on the right corner of the table, whatever stack of forms she was working on on the left, her octopus bobblehead doll staring at her from under the left corner of her computer monitor. But the pen cup was flipped over, with several of the pens scattered randomly across the floor. The folders looked jostled, and the octopus had face-planted on the desk. Trish didn't see Anna's chair at all. She knew something happened.

Once you got past the front area where Anna typically worked, the Research department expanded out and became much larger than most people realized. Even the doctors never spent much time down there. It was on the dreaded first floor; they rarely even stepped foot downstairs except to walk between the stairs and the front door. They'd smile to Trish as they did; she'd wave and say "Good morning!" with a cheery smile. But they didn't look at Trish and Anna as equals, and Trish knew that. The doctors were doing all the important work upstairs, while Trish and Anna took care of the paperwork down in the "basement." Most of them probably thought Anna was working out of a janitor's closet, but she'd organized this into an impressive medical library, especially for a hospital out in podunk. It was one of the things that Trish loved most about working at St. Francis—they might be a little community that few gave a second thought to, but the people there took pride in what they did. They took pride in being the best damn podunk hospital you'd ever seen. And this was the best damn podunk hospital research library they'd ever see.

Especially these days, though, it could get dark back in those stacks. Anna kept a flashlight somewhere, and Trish knew she'd need it. She went to the desk and opened the top-left drawer. She rummaged through some notepads, Post-It notes and index cards, but no flashlight. Switched to the top-right drawer and immediately saw what she was looking for—a very small flashlight. It worked for Anna because she basically knew where everything was and just needed to read the spine of a book or the note on a folder to make sure she had the right one. It'd be less than ideal for Trish, but she'd have to try to make it work.

She flipped it on and held it up by her head, pointed forward, between the eight-foot-tall shelves that lined the back part of the room. She peered down one aisle, but her little penlight was barely a match for the thick darkness in front of it. She could see her hand in front of her face, but not a lot else. Trish was quickly realizing that her ears were going to be her best friend. She couldn't see a lot, so she needed to listen. Until her eyes adjusted to the dark, that man would have the advantage—unless she heard him before he heard her. If he didn't know she was there, she might be able to help Anna with a sneak attack. She didn't know exactly what she was going to do, but she hoped she could spook him just by showing up.

Trish heard a sound, maybe a foot hitting the floor, followed by a voice. It sounded muffled, as if the person had something in their mouth. It was coming from at least two, maybe three aisles to her right. Then she heard quick footsteps, running in the opposite direction, toward the door to Research. Halfway down the first aisle, Trish turned and moved as quickly as she could back toward the door, trying to see who was there. She could see a shadowy figure grabbing a ring, then pushing the door further open and sprinting out. She started to run after him but slammed her hip into the desk, causing her to spin around, then stumble and fall. She was laid out on the floor, her arms and legs spread wide. She could still hear mumbling from behind her, and she struggled onto all fours. Trish wasn't sure how badly she was hurt, and she didn't want to risk standing up, so she crawled down the third aisle. She put the flashlight in her mouth, giving her just a little bit of light as she made her way to the back.

The further she crawled, the louder the muffled cries became. Her right hip groaned with each move forward, shotgunning pain like a hot poker through her leg and into her abdomen. It occurred to her that she was at least in the right place if she had broken her hip, but she needed to keep driving for now. Finally, she reached the back and saw Anna, a white cloth roughly jammed into her mouth, her wrists and ankles tied together with ropes. Anna was frantically trying to say something. Trish stopped and pulled the cloth out.

"He's going after Stephanie!" Anna said. "Damn it, he's going after Stephanie!"

"Paul...Paul, you there?" Zac said, into the walkie-talkie Paul had given him earlier in the day, getting no response for the third time. "Where are you, P—?"

"Yeah," Paul finally jumped in. "I'm here. I'm here."

"Where the fuck were you?"

"Let's just say it's been a long day. You got something for me?"

"Yeah. Anna said they're trying to find Doctor Giles."

Paul closed his eyes and breathed deeply.

"Shit. I was afraid of that."

"Is that a problem?"

"How are you with a rifle?"

Zac smiled.

48

Audrey rolled over in bed, her eyes creaking slowly open, the room around her still blurry like she was looking through a waterfall. Her head pounded, waves of pain reverberating through her skull, and crawling down her temples onto her jawline like liquid flowing through a sieve. There were aches throughout her body; her chest felt like it could pop at any moment, and her neck was a bundle of Boy Scout knots. She quickly found that even breathing was a chore; it felt like it was a conscious effort, as if her lungs would stop pumping if she didn't think, "Breathe in, breathe out. Breathe in, breathe out."

She put her hand to her forehead and shivered violently as she sucked in hard ("Breathe in, breathe out"). *What the hell is wrong with me?* She realized she didn't remember going to bed. *What's the last thing I remember? I remember the church, and Father Hayden. I came back here and prayed, but I don't think anything came from it. Then William came in and told me something about Michael. And Stephanie, I think. Is that right? Something about the hospital, maybe? Shit. And that's it. That's the last thing I remember, standing there, with William and Paul. Paul was there too. What the hell did they say? I feel like they told me something important. Why the hell can't I remember? And why do I feel like I'm just north of dead? Fuck me. I've gotta get up. Figure out what's going on.*

Audrey dragged her legs across the bed until they fell off the edge onto the floor, allowing her to sit up. The room spun; the walls were funhouse mirrors. She clutched both sides of her head with her hands, leaning forward, wondering if she was going to vomit. If so, she was hoping she could avoid the bed. The thought came to her that she didn't know how long she'd been asleep either. Was it two hours or twenty hours? She didn't know because she didn't have the first clue when she fell asleep. She thought it was the morning when she went to the church, and now it looked like it was around dusk. That wasn't helping her much. How much time had passed between her church visit, talking with Officer Greene, and crashing as hard as she'd ever crashed? She had no idea, and that scared the hell out of her.

I can't afford to be knocked out like that, and not know what's happening. What if something went wrong in the town? What if important decisions have to be made? I'm the one who makes them. I'm the one who commands the officers, and orders quarantines. I'm the one who prosecutes criminals. If I'm out of it, who's going to fill that ro—?

It came to her before she even completed the thought, like a jarring clap of thunder. If she was incapacitated in some way, who would everyone turn to for decisions? Paul. And Paul knew that. *Would Paul do something to get me out of the way for a while?* She would have liked to have immediately said, "No. He's my brother. Of course he wouldn't do anything to hurt me and undercut my authority," but she couldn't. After what she'd seen from him, there was no way she could dismiss the possibility. And now anger was starting to overshadow the pain, like a flash flood roaring through a plantation, wiping out the crops.

The aches and pains still lingered beneath the surface, but she drove through it, stalking to her bedroom door and flinging it open. Paul was standing in front of her, his hands at his sides. Their eyes met.

"Glad to see you're back with us, Sleeping Beauty," Paul smiled.

"What did you do to me?"

"What do you mean?"

"I know you knocked me out somehow. I don't even remember what the hell happened earlier! I don't remember going to bed at all, damn it! What did you do?"

Paul stepped closer to her.

"I think we should take this conversation into your room," he said, barely above a whisper. She turned and went back into her bedroom; he followed her, then closed the door behind him and locked it.

"You better tell me right the *fuck* now what's going on," Audrey said, and then turned around. When she did, the air was sucked out of her lungs as she stared down the barrel of a .357 magnum in Paul's right hand. "Whoa. Whoa. What are you doing, Paul?"

"Something that needed to be done a long time ago."

Audrey's heart was a jackhammer. She swallowed hard.

"I could scream."

"You do, and I'll shoot. Then I'll be in charge with no one to challenge me. And I'm probably not gonna have myself arrested."

"I don't think you want to kill me."

"Why not? Because you're my big sis? Because we played together in a fucking sandbox thirty years ago?"

"No. Because if you wanted to kill me," Audrey said, trying to control her breathing, "you'd have already pulled the trigger."

Paul was silent for a moment, keeping the gun pointed at her forehead.

"GHB," he said.

Audrey shook her head. "What?"

"That's what I gave you. GHB. Liquid ecstasy. I slipped it in your glass of water when you were gone."

"You roofied me?"

"Sort of."

"What the fuck, Paul? Why? And where did you even get that?"

"I've had it for a while. Shit has one hell of a shelf life. Why? Let's call it a trial run. I think I did a heck of a job in your stead."

"Oh, god," Audrey said. "What did you do?"

"I found out something your precious Keystone Cops don't know."

"What's that?"

"I know what Michael and Stephanie are doing."

"So it *was* Michael and Stephanie. Shit. What are they doing?"

"They're going to find Doctor Giles, because they apparently suspect something's bullshit with that study we forged," Paul said.

"Wait. What do you mean, 'forged'?"

"Oh, come on. You're gonna play ignorant again?"

"Seriously, Paul. Tell me right now what you're talking about, because I'm getting really scared."

"You honestly thought that study was real? You're telling me you didn't suspect a thing? You didn't think it was just a little too perfect, justifying the very policy you wanted to enact?"

Audrey collapsed onto the bed, her head cradled in her hands.

"The virus-transmission study?" She looked up at him. "You *forged* that, and never told me?"

"Once again, sis, you're as ignorant as you choose to be. I did it for *you*. You said you needed help, so I provided some. I assumed you eventually figured it out, but maybe not. It helped you and proved you right, so you just chose not to think too hard about it."

"Oh, god," she said, her breaths coming in short spurts, her chest heaving. "We did all that based upon that study, and it's all a lie. Do you not understand that? We ripped families apart! We took people's children! We sent people away, probably condemning them to death! And all because of a study *you forged*!"

"It had to be done," Paul shrugged. "And now Michael and Stephanie know. So I'm going to have them killed."

"The *hell* you are! We *do not* murder people just because their being alive is inconvenient for us. We'll figure this out."

"Not your call anymore, sis. This is my show now."

49

Stephanie pushed aside some vines that were clinging to the wooden wall almost as if they were glued there. The kudzu was thick in this part of the town, and it was tough to see if there was anything through the jungle-like maze behind Walt's Bar. Michael stepped gingerly behind her, ducking through some of the openings she created by forcing vines out of the way.

"I think I see something," she said, yanking on another vine, trying to force it to the side. "Really wish we had a machete, though."

"Your hands are doing a pretty good job."

"Maybe we could do a better job with four hands."

"Oh. Yeah, sure."

Michael stepped around Stephanie and grabbed the same vine her hands were on, helping her pull it to the right. When they did, they could see a slight opening running up the wall, though it wasn't easy to spot unless you were standing right in front of it. Unless you actually climbed back there and moved the kudzu out of the way, the odds were good you'd never know it was there. And there was no door handle either. Just a slight crack that let in very little light, spanning the height of the wall. Not all the kudzu was clear, but there was enough for them to get to that spot. And, because there was no handle, Stephanie reached out and pushed.

The gate swung open easily, with no hindrances on the other side. After a few feet, it scraped in the dirt and stopped, but there was enough of an opening for them to slide through. Stephanie stepped over to it and took off her ring, then turned sideways to fit through the gate. She kept her arms to her sides to make herself as thin as possible, which allowed her enough space to get to the outside. Michael followed behind her, using the same technique. They were both outside the wall for the first time in close to a year.

When Michael got through, he saw Stephanie looking to his left, into the woods. Dusk was approaching, so it wasn't easy to make out, but he thought he could see an angular shape that didn't look natural in the woods, maybe three hundred yards away.

"I guess we're headed in that direction," Michael said.

"Yep. Bring our rings out here. We don't want anyone seeing those. Then close the gate and follow me."

As they walked up to the structure they'd seen from the wall, they could tell it was a nice cabin, likely built long before the virus struck. Someone had been living out there, far enough away from everything to have a secluded spot in the woods, but still close enough to the comforts of Alessandra to swing by for supplies if they needed them. It wasn't a bad spot.

The cabin looked like it might have been built to be passive solar, meaning everything from the house's positioning to its window angles to its room designs were set up strategically to take advantage of sunlight and heat. There were also some solar panels lining the roof, and very few tall trees in this area of the forest. If done well prior to the virus, passive-solar construction could cut down significantly on the homeowner's energy costs. After the virus, it could greatly reduce the pain from not having much energy available at all. And what little energy you did want to use, the solar panels could probably provide that. The cabin also had a deck that fully wrapped around it, opening up to an expansive back deck that looked out over the massive ridge below, leading to the mountains not far in the distance. Off to the west, Stephanie thought the coming sunset would probably be gorgeous. But they didn't have time to enjoy it.

They went up the steps to the front part of the deck and approached the door. Stephanie leaned to her right and peered into the large front window.

"Keep in mind, he's not expecting us," she said. "And there's a reason he's all the way out here. Either he's hiding from Audrey and Paul, or they're hiding him from us. And, unless he created that gate himself, it's the latter. Either way, though, it may spook him to hear a knock on the door, and we don't know how he'll react when he sees *us* here."

"Right. You're the one who knows him, so he should see your face first. I'm not a complete stranger, but I only knew the guy in passing."

"Yeah. That's what I'm thinking," Stephanie cupped her hands around her face and pressed against the glass, looking for anything obvious to tell this was where Doctor Giles lived. "I know him well, so just follow my lead. Hopefully, this will work."

Stephanie slid back in front of the door and raised her fist. She froze for a moment, and took a deep breath. Hesitantly, she moved her arm forward but, before it could strike, the door swung open. Doctor Giles was standing in front of her, his head just below the door frame at six-foot-five, wearing a red and black plaid shirt and dirty indigo jeans with a pair of scuffed brown work boots. He had a full beard now, and it was mostly gray, but it was definitely Doctor Giles. He was staring wide eyed at Stephanie, his legs far apart, clutching the door with his right hand and not wearing a ring.

Stephanie opened her mouth, but Doctor Giles mouthed the word "No" and raised his right index finger, pushing it to her lips. He then curled that finger and wiggled it as he turned to walk toward the back of the house. Stephanie and Michael followed him.

"How'd you find me?" Doctor Giles said, leaning against the railing of his back deck and looking out over the woods below.

The sun had dipped below the tree line to his left, and the sky was a brilliant shade of tangerine, smeared across the tops of the jagged mountains that towered over the trees in front of him.

"A combination of conversation and intuition," Stephanie said, approaching him from behind.

Doctor Giles nodded. "I figured somebody would. Might have guessed it'd be you." He lowered his head, then turned to face Stephanie and Michael. "It's better to talk out here. When they come, I do my best to keep them inside. I have a hunch they're bugging the place. It's really not safe for you to be here."

"Safe or not, it's important," she said. "We know about the study."

He glanced toward Michael. "Who's 'we'?"

"Oh," she followed his eyes. "That's Michael. My ex. I think you two have met."

They both cocked their heads slightly.

"Anyone else?" Doctor Giles said.

"Only Anna," Stephanie confirmed. "She helped me navigate the doc."

"How'd you figure it out?" he asked. "No, wait. Never mind. It doesn't matter now." He turned and looked back out over the trees, resting his arms on the railing in front of him. "So you know none of it is true. I *tried*, Stephanie. I really did. I conducted the study as well as I could, given the circumstances. You saw the sample sizes and my methodology. It was sound. Or, at least, as sound as it could be; it was important that I give the town some sort of answer at the time. But when I completed the study and Ms. Reese's brother came to view the results, he said I screwed it up, that I'd missed something. I assured him that, while I could be wrong, I'd confidently stand by the results, but he wasn't having it. He said the public deserved direction from their leaders, and he wasn't going to have Ms. Reese tell the people again that we didn't know anything. It would make them look stupid and incompetent. So he made the changes. I just helped him with the terminology. I didn't mean to hurt anyone, Stephanie. You have to believe me."

"I do, Richard," she said. "I know you were in a tough position."

"He threatened to kill me. Then he threatened to blow up the hospital. He talked about turning it into a big bonfire. 'A blazing crater in the earth,' he said." Doctor Giles choked back tears, wiping his face with his sleeve. "It was mad. I couldn't let that happen. I didn't know what they had in mind. I really didn't think any harm would come of it. They'd get the answer they wanted, and we'd be able to go on with the important work we were doing. I didn't know what else to do."

Stephanie looked at Michael, who sighed.

"We understand, Richard. We're not here to blame you for anything." Stephanie walked over and draped her arm across his shoulders. "We're here because we need your help."

"Help with what?"

"You have the credibility to tell the people of Alessandra what you told us," she leaned in close to say the words. "You're smart. You're respected. You can give them their lives back. If you walk back through that gate with us, you can deliver them from everything they've gone through. You can reunite families, and provide people with a new reason to go forward, to get up in the morning. You can give people the gift of touch from a loved one that they haven't felt in so long. You can be a hero to Alessandra."

He bent his head toward Stephanie and swallowed hard. He had a look of fear across his face.

"They'll never let that happen," he whispered.

"We'll keep you safe," she said. "They'll never know until it's too late. We have camera equipment at the hospital. We can film you telling the truth and deliver it to the masses. You just have to come with us. Please. Come."

Stephanie took her arm off his back, then stepped back and extended the hand toward him. Doctor Giles looked down at the wood-paneled deck floor, then back up at Stephanie. He took his arms off the railing and stood a bit straighter.

"How are you sure you can keep us safe?" he asked. "Do you understand who you're dealing with?"

"We'll be *really* careful. The hospital isn't—"

Doctor Giles' head exploded in a bright flash of light and burgundy liquid, like a burst balloon, as Stephanie watched. The sight of his head ripping apart came before the sound of the shot from the FN FAL, one of the most powerful rifles in the world. Stephanie fell to her stomach and looked to her left to see Michael's left shoulder jerk backward, and he fell to the deck while the sound of the shot reverberated through the woods.

That one was meant for me.

Staying low, Stephanie crawled toward Michael. As she did, she took a quick glance at Doctor Giles, whose skull was mostly gone, revealing a quarter of his brain intact while blood poured out through the slats in the deck. She paused for a moment, then kept crawling while shots continued, some buzzing by into the side of the house. Others were glancing blows off the deck, sending splinters flying high into the air. Judging from the initial sound delay, she knew the shooter was some distance away. She guessed it was at least a few hundred meters. She needed to hope Michael was in decent enough shape to run out of there with her, because she figured the shooter wouldn't be that far away much longer.

"Shit, Michael. Are you okay?"

"It's my left shoulder. Damn, it hurts!" he winced and banged the deck with his right hand.

"I know. Let me look."

She crawled around to his left side and lifted his arm slightly; he let out a brief scream. His shirt was torn at the shoulder, and blood was beginning to soak the sleeve, pooling around the back of his shoulder. She took off her light jacket and button-up shirt, then used that to wipe away some of the blood to get a better look at the wound.

"The bad news is, there's a lot of blood, and I'm not sure how bad you're hurt," she said. "The good news is, this looks like more of a glancing blow than a direct hit. Otherwise, judging by what happened to Richard, you wouldn't have a shoulder left."

He nodded, and she started to wrap her shirt around his shoulder and under his arm.

"Also, the shots have stopped. That either means he's given up, or he's advancing this way. We don't have time to wait around and find out. You feel like you can run with me? I'll get you somewhere where I can help, but we've got to get back into town."

"Yeah," he said, through gritted teeth. "Let's get outta here."

Zac carried the FN FAL in front of him as he walked up to the front steps of the cabin, peering through the window that spanned the front of the house. The door was open, and everything seemed quiet. He could see glass scattered across the living room floor, and there was no obvious sign of Stephanie or Michael.

He looked behind him into the woods, but it was getting dark quickly, and he couldn't see very far. All he could hear was crickets. He stepped through the doorway, keeping the gun's barrel pointed forward, in case one of them was lying in wait. From the 400-meter distance he had set up, his accuracy hadn't been perfect, even given the amazing gun he was using. He loved that thing. The U.S. military never officially sanctioned its use for combat, but there had been extensive tests to determine if it was an investment they wanted to make. Dozens of other countries used it, but the United States ended up being one of the few holdouts. Still, the guns were around, and one of his Lieutenants handed him one toward the end of his tour in Afghanistan, saying it was a gift. He knew the significance of what he was holding, and he'd looked forward to the right moment to use it. This had been his chance.

The first shot, he'd basically nailed. He didn't consider himself a murderer, but he'd placed himself into a military state of mind at that point—Paul was his commander, and he had a target to snipe. That's all it came down to. He wasn't there to question, or wonder why. That wasn't his job. His job was to fulfill this task, so he could get his revenge against the woman who ripped his family and life to shreds. If these people were standing in his way, they might have to be collateral damage. That's what happens in war sometimes. It sucks, but war is hell, and this was too.

He knew the most important target was the tall man with the beard, so that was who he made sure to hit first. When Zac arrived at his perch, the three of them were already on the back deck, just as Paul told him they would be. It was set up well. Zac was able to settle in, get comfortable, and take his time sighting in, then locking on his target. He could see through his scope that the shot had been perfect, even if he'd gotten a little cute with it. The chest is a bigger target to hit, but he wanted to show off the FN FAL a little by making the head shot, and that red explosion in his sights gave him a warm shot of adrenaline. He couldn't help but try for it again with Stephanie, standing to the tall man's right. He had to get there quickly, though, and he didn't have time to set up the shot. She also ducked right as he was pulling the trigger, throwing his aim off even more, and the bullet whizzed past her into Michael's left shoulder.

Then Zac panicked a little, thinking he was going to fail at his mission. He tried to rely on the strength of his weapon, thinking if he fired enough rounds toward the house that some of them would be bound to hit the remaining two targets. After a minute or so, he stopped and had to decide whether to stay there and continue firing, or try to move closer. He had never been comfortable firing at close range. There was something about being in a sniper's perch, hundreds of meters away, that took away much of the personal nature of the killing. It turned it into a video game, looking through your sight, almost like looking at a TV screen while fighting the Germans in "Call of Duty." You could distance yourself from the results of your actions. But up close, looking at the person in the eye, you had to face it. He'd used the knife on Trevor, but he wasn't sure he could have shot the guy if that had been his only option for the kill. Up that close, a gun felt to Zac like it was sucking the humanity right out of a person. It was hard for him to explain.

This was a mission, though, and you have to do what you have to do sometimes. So, hesitantly, he emerged from his perch and made his way down to the cabin. He hoped they were already dead. Absent that, perhaps they were hobbled, and he could just finish the job. If they were gone, he was screwed.

Zac stepped lightly through the living room, being careful not to step on the broken glass, and reached the door to the back deck. He nudged it open and pointed his gun through the crack, with his head following behind. He saw nothing at first, just a deck covered in dozens of wood shards. Then he noticed a headless body lying in a pool of blood and brain matter. He walked closer and was certain that was the tall man, with his gray beard still tickling what was left of his chin. He turned around and scanned the deck. Behind him, he noticed another pool of blood. This one was much smaller than the one under the tall man, and he saw no other signs of anyone being there. As far as he could tell, they were gone.

Reluctantly, he pulled out his walkie-talkie, and pressed the button to transmit.

"Paul...Paul, you there?" Zac said.

"Yeah, copy that. Is it done?"

Zac took a deep breath. "Yes and no."

"What the hell does that mean?"

"Number one target, confirmed kill. Secondary targets, at least one wounded, but I cannot confirm their status."

Paul paused for a moment.

"So you got Doctor Giles? He's dead?"

"Yes. Should I pursue the other two?"

"No, it doesn't matter. They don't have the credibility, and we don't need to be causing chaos in the streets. I do have one more job for you, though. I'm gonna keep these hospital security guys busy a little longer. After this job's done, come on up to the mansion."

50

By the time they reached the gate to re-enter Alessandra, Stephanie could tell Michael was getting weaker. The shirt she wrapped around his wound would apply some pressure, but she hadn't had much time to do it properly, and her white shirt was already a deep maroon. She knew he was losing a lot of blood, and he needed more help than she could give him without some better equipment.

"Should we go to the hospital?" Michael said, still jogging but losing energy as he went.

"We can't take that chance. If he's right behind us, we can't just lead him to the hospital. It's the most obvious place for us to go, and there's no telling who he'd hurt to get to us. Once I get you settled, I'll go there on my own. I can move quickly and slip in through some of the underground areas of the building. You'd slow me up in this condition."

"So, what do we do?"

"I think I know. Stick with me."

Stephanie fastened her ring back on, then slid Michael's up to his waist as well. She knew they'd be far easier to transport if buckled to themselves than if she tried to carry the bulky rings. After going back through the gate, Stephanie led Michael in the opposite direction from most of the town, including the hospital. She wasn't sure if she was being paranoid, but watching a man have his head blown off and then being shot at repeatedly had a tendency to do that to a person. Assuming the shooter was following them but didn't see which direction they went, she figured he'd guess they were going to the hospital, especially if he knew Michael was wounded. If so, she just had to hope he wouldn't be trigger happy when he couldn't find them. That worried her, but the more immediate concern at that moment was Michael.

After five minutes of walking as fast as Michael could go, she spotted what she was looking for—an old abandoned warehouse halfway to the lake. It hadn't been used for years, and seemed to still be standing by the virtue of hand-holding termites. The last time she remembered it storing anything, old farmer Claude Skinner had been filling it with bales of hay back in the 1980s, piling them in the rafters and any other empty crevice he could find. Nobody was sure who owned it, so Claude just sort of took it for himself, and nobody ever stepped in to claim it. Claude once told Stephanie it had been overflow storage for a local car dealership, but she never knew if that was actually true, or if that was just one of those stories old people told kids because they wouldn't know any better. But Claude died in 1992 and, by then, the kids in town were convinced the old warehouse was haunted. Whether the adults thought it was haunted or not, none of them had any reason to go near it, so they didn't. With the owner unknown, the building fell into disrepair. At this point, it creaked and swayed with high winds, its brittle metal skeleton wavering but not falling, helping to hold up a a creaky wooden shell. It had an expansive bottom floor, with a large loft overlooking it, and lengthy openings on the top floor that rose up six feet and gave a view out over the adjacent street and the grassy hill opposite it. That loft was where she figured she'd store Michael until she could get him better help.

They walked up to the garage door in front of the building, and Stephanie bent down to grab the handle while Michael sat on the curb. At first, it didn't feel like it was going to budge, but Stephanie put both hands on it and got into a low crouch, hoisting it off the ground to give them three feet of clearance before it lodged into place. That was going to be good enough. She took Michael's hand and led him over. They both bent and walked inside; she reached back and pushed the door closed with a reverberating crash.

It was almost fully dark by then, and it was difficult to see, but those upstairs openings gave them just enough moonlight to make out shapes and solid objects in the warehouse. The place was larger than Stephanie remembered, and there were still rectangular brown spots on the floor where Claude had kept his bales of hay. Stephanie squinted and saw stairs on the far end of the building. She pointed, and Michael headed toward them. When they got to the second floor, she took both of their rings off and told him to lie down.

"How are you feeling?" she said.

"A little light headed. Kind of hot."

That's not good. Rapid blood loss can bring on anemia, and those are warning signs.

"Okay. Just relax. Try to control your breathing. Deep breaths: in through the nose, out through the mouth. Got it?"

"Yeah. Deep breaths. Got it."

"Good. Quick question…Are you wearing underwear?"

"What? I mean, um, yeah. Boxers."

"Great. I would have hated to have to leave you up here half naked. Particularly *that* half. Just lie still."

Stephanie unbuckled Michael's belt and slid it off, then unbuttoned his jeans, pulling them down over his knees. He bent them up to help her get the pants past his feet. She unwrapped her shirt from his shoulder and snapped it in the air to straighten it out.

"This thing's pretty nasty, but it'll help keep you warm until I get back," she said, as she laid it across his legs. "You probably won't feel hot too long."

The wound was still bleeding, so she stretched the pant legs in opposite directions, then rolled them up like a cigarette. She stretched the fabric taut underneath his arm and wrapped it tightly around his shoulder, tying the loose ends to hold it together. She grabbed the belt and pulled it around the outside of the pants, yanking it to its last hole before threading through the prong.

"I feel like you've done this before," Michael said, his head resting on the wooden second floor of the warehouse.

"The makeshift bandage, or taking off your pants?" she smiled, and he stifled a laugh.

"Well, both, now that you mention it."

"Just rest over here," she pointed toward the wall a few feet away. "You'll need to press your back against that wall so you can keep the shoulder elevated above your heart. And don't move around. This should hold you from bleeding *too* much until I can get back with some stuff to stitch you up."

"Am I gonna be okay?"

"As long as I'm on the case, you are."

"Then you better be careful," Michael's eyes were welling with tears. "I can't lose you."

"Not again, you mean?"

Michael turned his head away from her and sighed loudly.

"Have I ever told you I'm sorry about the way everything worked out with us?"

"Nope. But apology accepted. No time to reminisce right now, though. I've gotta save your life, mister."

He half smiled, then bit his bottom lip and nodded. She strapped her ring back on, then jogged down the stairs, and out into the night.

51

"This waiting is killing me," Anna said, pacing the floor of the St. Francis Research department, her ribs sore but not hurt as badly as she'd feared. "What if he finds her?"

"We're not expert trackers, honey," Trish spoke in her most soothing receptionist voice. "I love Stephanie too, but what are we gonna do? We have no idea where any of them are headed."

"I know. I just can't stand the idea of her being out there, and not knowing he's coming after her. And it's all my fault."

Trish hobbled over, her hip still aching, and grabbed her by the shoulders, turning Anna to face her. She pressed her face close to Anna's.

"I'm not gonna hear that anymore from you, ya hear me?" Trish said. "Nobody's gonna blame you for what you said, and you can't keep blaming yourself. That guy was gonna kill lots of folks if you didn't tell him what ya knew. You saved lives back there, and I'm proud of ya."

Anna's head dropped, and Trish pushed it back up with two fingers under her chin.

"You know that, right? I'm proud of ya. Always have been."

Anna nodded.

"You're my girl, and I'm not gonna let nobody say anything bad about what you did. They'll have to answer to me if they want to talk all ignorant about it. You're a hero, girl. Okay? Now, the best thing we can do is wait here. This is the most logical place for Stephanie to return to when she sidesteps that asshole. She's one tough cookie. Hell, *he's* the one who should be afraid of *her.*"

Anna laughed at that. "She *is* a superhero."

"Damn right, she is. Super Steph. Leaps tall buildings. All that. She'll be fine. We'll all be laughing about this when she calls down to say she's sitting in her office, and that guy's tied up and tossed into the woods somewhere."

Smiling, Anna pressed her back against one of the library shelves and slid down it until her butt hit the floor, her knees bent in front of her. She wrapped her arms around them and tried to relax. Trish had just carefully settled into the desk chair when the doors to Research flew open, slamming into the walls behind them.

Zac walked through the doors of St. Francis hospital, with one direction on his mind. This time, he already knew how to get to the Research department. He was thankful Paul had let him off the hook for not taking out all three of his targets at the cabin; at least he nailed the big fish in a spectacular way. Now, if he could just complete this last job, he'd get the confrontation he'd been looking for.

He left his gun at the cabin because he expected combat in close quarters if it was necessary here, and he felt better with a knife in those situations. So there was his M9, sheathed and ready in case it was needed. With Paul chatting hospital security up at the compound, though, Zac felt like this could go pretty smoothly.

There was no one at the reception desk, which was a good sign already. Meant he didn't have to deal with that lady getting hysterical—and possibly having to slit her throat—on his way back down the hall. He didn't prefer to kill anyone on this visit, but he'd do it if he had to.

Everything seemed quiet. The first floor of the hospital was cavernous during the day, with the large windows overhead allowing the sun to flood the building with light, but it felt much smaller at night. The stars shone overhead, and you couldn't see the expansiveness of the second floor above you, only the shadows thrown from the limited lights they kept on in the halls in the evening. Zac thought it gave the hospital a bit of a spooky feel.

He strode down the hall, through the double doors and beyond the first two rooms past that. He reached Research and didn't break stride, shoving the doors open with both hands, crashing them against the walls and stepping inside. Anna and Trish were sitting in front of him, staring wide-eyed. He hadn't been counting on that, but he figured it might save him some time on this mission, so he figured he'd take advantage of the situation.

Anna stumbled to her feet and ran between large shelves, toward the back of the room. Trish tried to quickly get out of the chair, but it rolled out from underneath her, sending her sprawling onto the floor. Pain struck her body like a bucket of water splashed on her—full and enveloping. She screamed, and clutched at her side. It dawned on her that she couldn't run even if she could get to her feet.

Zac walked over to Trish, bent over and slid his knife out of its sheath. He put his left arm around her midsection and lifted her into the chair, then slid the knife around and across her neck.

"Hey, Anna!," he yelled into the darkness. "I'm sure you know those stacks better than I do, so I don't wanna chase your ass in the dark. But you should know I've got your nice friend here with a knife to her throat, and she doesn't look like she's moving too well. I don't want to hurt her, but I'll start taking fingers off if you're not out here in thirty seconds. Starting... Now. One Mississippi. Two Mississippi. Three Mississippi..."

Anna reached the back of the room and slammed against the wall, huddling in the dark when she heard Trish cry out.

Shit. Trish can barely move. First I hung Stephanie out to dry, and now I left Trish behind. You're turning out to be quite a friend, Anna.

Anna started to shiver, wondering what she could do. Run back up there? And do what? Tackle the guy? He had a big knife before; it stood to reason that he still did. She had her fists of fury, but not much beyond that. And Trish wasn't exactly a fierce warrior, even with two *good* hips. What would he want with Trish anyway? Maybe he didn't want anything to do with her. If he let her go, Anna figured she could hide pretty well in the darkness of the Research library, which she knew like most people know their birthdays.

Then she heard Zac's voice. He had Trish. There was no way to keep hiding. If he was back, that might mean he already found Stephanie; she might even be dead. She couldn't let Trish die too —or listen to her as her fingers were sliced off one by one. When he got to "Twenty-six Mississippi," Anna emerged from between the shelves.

"Okay, I'm here," Anna said. "Let her go."

"Why would I do that? She's my insurance that you'll do what I ask," he wheeled her away from the desk.

Anna glanced at the desk, then at them. "What do you want me to do?"

"Wake up the computer, and pull up the virus-transmission study."

Anna walked over and jerked the mouse, and the monitor sprung to life, glowing blue in the darkness of the room around them. She opened up the records system and went to "Open Recent" on the pulldown menu. It was the first file on the list.

"It's up," she said. "Now what?"

"Go to File, and 'Delete Record.'"

Her eyes grew large, and she hesitated. "But..."

"Don't play games with me. I'm not making a request. Do it, or we'll find out what sorts of sounds your friend makes as I remove her fingers. Bone's pretty hard, ya know. Even with a knife this sharp, it'll take several good saws to slice all the way through."

Anna shivered at the thought, then turned back to the computer. She clicked on "File," then "Delete Record." A window popped up asking her if she was sure. She paused, then clicked "Yes." It processed for ten seconds, then said it was completed. She sighed.

"Good job, Annie," Zac shoved Trish and her chair, and it crashed into Anna.

Zac hit the doors and sprinted down the hall toward the exit.

52

Stephanie walked as fast as her legs could pump through the streets of Alessandra, making her way to the hospital. She was in good shape, but she knew she'd exhaust herself trying to run the whole way. She figured it would be a ten-minute trip each way, and she could probably gather up the necessary items from the hospital basement in another five. Twenty-five minutes wouldn't be enough for the bleeding or the cold to kill Michael—she was pretty sure, anyway.

She wasn't sure what her feelings were about Michael at this point. The divorce had been hard on her; he was the first—and the *only*, really—man she loved, and she always envisioned spending the rest of her life with him. She didn't care that he didn't graduate college, or that he had a modest job compared to her. But she could see he was never comfortable after they got married. He grew more distant each year, it seemed. It probably didn't help that she worked crazy hours, sometimes overnight, sometimes pulling thirty-six-hour shifts, because patients needed her and she was a young doctor trying to make an impact. Stephanie pushed herself, and maybe it had taken a toll on their relationship. Between her absence from home, and his discomfort with her making five times what he did, maybe the marriage had always been doomed to fail. Maybe they never should have tried.

Stephanie didn't want to become the woman so obsessed with her own career that she never had a family of her own, though. She *was* driven, and she *did* want to be successful in the medical field, but she didn't think that meant she had to compromise on her life outside of the hospital. She could have it all—the lucrative career, and the enviable home life with a loving husband, 2.5 kids and a picket fence. After the divorce, though, she threw herself even deeper into medicine, taking on research projects and neglecting nearly everything in her life for the sake of the hospital and her patients. Even before the virus, she couldn't count the number of nights she had spent sleeping in her office. She had the most comfortable brown leather couch she could find installed in the corner just for that purpose. And now that she really *was* spending pretty much every night there, that couch had come in handy. She had the most comfortable bed in the place. Sometimes, she'd walk into her office and hear snoring from another doctor catching a nap in between patients.

There was no time to meet anyone else, even if these rules weren't preventing that from happening anyway. She wasn't sure she was prepared to start over with someone else, but she was sure she was using work as an excuse not to try. It was just simpler to throw herself into her job rather than deal with the rigors of starting a new relationship from scratch. She had been with Michael forever; she didn't even know how adults met people in a place like Alessandra. Before the virus, some doctors asked her out, but she always fell back on "I don't date people I work with." She didn't even know if that was a valid excuse, since she never tried. But it was a good way to shut down the conversation, and remain focused on the job. Now, she was approaching her late thirties, though, and, to whatever extent she had a proverbial biological clock, it was ticking louder than a cheap wristwatch. She always imagined while growing up that a traditional family life was in her future, that it was everyone's dream. Did she still want that? She didn't know. At that moment, all she wanted was to keep Michael alive, and then pull off a revolution of sorts. Babies and biological clocks were going to have to take a backseat for the time being.

As she approached the hospital, she turned down the adjacent alley and jogged beside the building to the back, then down into the old loading dock. This was where deliveries of all sorts of supplies—medicine, rubber gloves, bedding, surgical masks, and many others—had come in before the virus, but it hadn't seen a truck in more than a year. During a normal day then, this area was bustling with life most of the time, but it was dark and silent right now. Stephanie was glad for that, because she didn't want to encounter a soul on this visit. She still worried that the shooter might come to the hospital, but that wasn't a concern she had time to deal with. Michael's life was hanging in the balance, and it depended upon her getting in and out of there as quickly as possible. She hopped over the concrete barrier and walked down the bay into the basement storage center for the hospital.

Zac was sprinting into the dark, around the side of the hospital and turning in the direction of Audrey's compound when he saw some motion flash across the corner of his eye. There was practically no light at this point beyond the moon and stars, so it was hard to tell for sure, but he thought he saw a woman jogging down the alley beside the hospital. And if there was a woman going down the alley next to the hospital, who was it more likely to be than the woman he had been assigned to kill earlier that evening? She worked there, and she probably needed something to treat the man he shot. Zac hadn't come there to find her, but this might be good luck. If he could kill her, that'd be two of the three Paul had asked him to take down. And if she was stashing the wounded man somewhere while she came back to the hospital to fetch some treatment for him, there was a pretty good chance he'd bleed to death while he waited for her to return. Zac hated leaving a mission unfinished; maybe this was karma's way of giving him another shot at wrapping up the job.

He slipped his knife out of its sheath and stalked down the dark alley, the knife gleaming in the scant moonlight. He wasn't familiar with the basement of the hospital, but he was glad she was headed into the dark, out of sight. After he killed her, he would have time to determine what to do with her body. He got to the corner of the hospital and hopped over the concrete abutment, then climbed in through the back dock and entered the hospital's storage area.

To his left was the check-in station, with a computer and desk where the receiving supervisor would register the delivery trucks as they pulled into the loading dock. To his right was a large open space, where lines of wooden pallets would have typically covered the floor, waiting for boxes of supplies to be piled high upon them. Each box would be unloaded from the truck and inventoried, then confirmed to carry the items on the invoice. From there, it'd be stacked and set to be unloaded either to the basement storage shelves just above his sightline toward the stairs to the main part of the hospital, or brought out to the supply closets on the first and second levels of the medical building.

He could see most everything around him, and there was no sign of anyone. That likely meant she was on the second level of the basement storage department, with the stairs thirty feet away against the far wall. He didn't hear anything, but he knew he had to make the rounds up those stairs.

When he reached the top, he stopped and listened. He wanted to hear something that would justify his being up there, hoping that following her hadn't been a waste of time. For a few seconds, he heard nothing. Just the occasional creak of the stairs behind him, and the massive sliding doors that hung from the rafters of the docks down below. Finally, though, he heard the tapping of shoes striking the hard floor, between some shelves less than forty feet away from him. There were six rows of shelves up there, and he couldn't be completely sure which row they'd come from, but he didn't think she knew he was there, so he figured he had the element of surprise on his side.

Zac walked over to the first set of shelves and pressed his back against it, his head turned to the side and his knife held just below shoulder height. Quickly, he gave a glance into the aisle without revealing much of himself, then darted back behind the shelf—nothing. She was further in. He hopped across the opening and pressed against the next set of shelves, trying to remain under cover as much as possible. Again, he took a peek into the aisle between shelves and didn't see anyone there. One more time, he heard a couple of taps on the floor, and he could tell he was getting closer.

He hopped across another aisle and set up against the next shelf. Based upon the sound of her feet on the floor, he thought she was on the next aisle. He thought this should be his chance to pounce on her. She was cornered in this cramped second-floor basement, and Zac knew he had the advantage of surprise.

Zac glanced into this aisle and—again—didn't see anyone. He was confused. He was running out of aisles, and he was sure this was where he heard her feet tap across the floor seconds earlier. He jerked his head back and listened, waiting for some sign of where she might be, his knife in his right hand.

He was preparing to hop across one more aisle when he felt a piercing pain on the left side of his neck and reached up to slap at a syringe stuck deep inside his skin. He screamed and tried to pull it out, but a large hunk of stainless steel slammed into the side of his head, sending him stumbling backward. It hit him again, and he fell to the floor, writhing in pain.

The drug in the syringe was etorphine, an animal tranquilizer. In the movies, he would have slumped to the floor unconscious within seconds, but Stephanie knew that wasn't the reality of what happens with chemicals like this. The etorphine needed time to work into his bloodstream. It helped that she thought she'd gotten it into his carotid artery, but that was never easy; in an emergency room situation where it was essential, she would have used ultrasound to be sure she hit the right spot. Here, though, she had to trust instinct and some twenty-twenty eyesight to hope her aim was true. If so, it could improve her induction time by ten-fold.

As a guard against that, she figured a few shots on the side of the head with a stainless steel bedpan couldn't hurt. Besides, that was the best weapon she had at her disposal on such short notice in these tight quarters, so that was what she was going with. She saw the man had a knife, but it was slumped at his side at this point. She swung the bedpan twice more, connecting hard with the side of his temple, and he showed no signs of movement. Whether the etorphine or the concussion had knocked him unconscious, she didn't care. She had the equipment she needed, so she tossed the bedpan aside, ran toward the alley and began jogging up the street to make up some time in getting back to Michael. She was twenty feet down the alley when she stopped and thought for a second, then turned back and re-entered the loading dock, jogging back into the storage area. Stephanie crouched beside Zac's body and yanked the knife out of his limp hand. She slid it into the back waistband of her pants; it occurred to her that it might be useful.

Light snuck in through his cracked eyelids as Zac stirred awake, lying on a cold concrete floor, looking at a series of what appeared to be storage shelves. His head was a jackhammer, thumping against his temples, sending shockwaves down the base of his skull to his spine. He didn't immediately remember the encounter with Stephanie, but it came back to him gradually like the fade-in scene from a movie—following a noise up the stairs, trying to track that noise for a sneak attack on her between the shelves, then feeling a sharp pin prick and a metallic smack upside his head.

So, he remembered what happened, but he had no idea how long he'd been lying unconscious on the floor. Paul had been expecting him at the compound within an hour or two after they last talked, but Zac didn't have a watch to know what time it was. During the day, he mostly estimated by where the sun was, but he found he rarely needed to care at night; he was usually resting at home alone by the time the sun went down. He might drink if he had some of Walt's moonshine handy, the warm tingling of the brown liquor helping dull the pain of the memories of his wife and daughters that his house drowned him in. Those were the memories he carried with him always. Getting his skull smashed in might have been worth it if he'd been able to forget them. Maybe he could let go of this pain and anger. Just trying to re-assemble the puzzle of his brain, this is where his mind went— straight to his family. Or, his former family. They were why he was lying where he was. They were ripped from his life, like tearing at a piece of fabric and leaving the seams hanging loose. He knew he'd always be damaged; he would never be whole. He couldn't be fixed, but he needed to take a pound of flesh from the person who did this to him. He needed to get to Audrey. And, to do that, he needed to get to his feet.

He rolled onto his stomach and pushed with his hands, raising his torso off the floor and then sliding his knees underneath him. He rose into a kneeling position, and got one foot on the floor, then the other. He wobbled, and the room spun. Suddenly, he was six years old on a carousel, the world rocketing by around him. For a moment, he was happy, clutching onto the head of a ceramic horse, its mouth open and eyes laughing. He wore a blue coat with a bright yellow lining. His dad was sitting on the unicorn next to him, and they weren't quite in sync, his dad starting down just as he was reaching the top of his rocking motion. Little Zac was squealing, waving each time they passed his mom smiling from the ground, holding his baby brother in her arms. His dad reached over and grabbed little Zac's arm, pulling it back inside the ride.

"You've got to hang on with both arms," he said. "Don't want you to get hurt."

There was no way of knowing all three of them would be dead within the next three years—first, his mom from breast cancer, which metastasized unusually rapidly, destroying her liver and eating her lungs before it dutifully killed her six months after the diagnosis, and then his dad and brother in a car accident when they plowed into the back of an eighteen wheeler. The truck stopped unexpectedly when his dad was trying to get them to behave in the backseat. Zac's brother didn't like to be strapped down, and had figured out how to unbuckle his harness. He was crawling across the backseat toward Zac when their car hit the truck. Zac's dad turned around just in time to see the brake lights and get his foot to the brake pedal, but they barely slowed down at all before impact. They hit it at more than forty miles per hour. Zac's dad was killed instantly when the roof crushed in on his head, and Zac's brother flew forward, his tiny three-year-old body embedded in the shattered windshield glass. Zac sat in the back seat and screamed.

The memories flooding back to him like a thousand stabbings to his chest, he collapsed back to the floor.

53

Stephanie walked up the stairs to the loft of the warehouse, carrying the medical equipment for Michael in a small backpack. She wondered if the man who had attempted to attack her at the hospital was the same man who had shot at them earlier in the evening. If so, why was he only carrying a knife, and how did he track her to the loading dock in the basement of the building? And if not, how many people were being deployed to kill them? She was catching a glimpse at the lengths Paul and Audrey would go to retain their hold over the town, and it made her hair stand up on the back of her neck. She was just a normal doctor with a bent for research. How'd she find herself in this position?

"It's me, Michael!" Stephanie yelled as she reached the third step on the staircase. "I've got everything I should need. How ya hanging in there?"

There was no response, and she stopped for a second to listen. The silence hung in the air like an eclipse blotting out the sun, blocking everything around it. Her stomach sank, and she sprinted the rest of the way up the stairs.

When she reached the top, Michael's body lay slumped to the side, his right arm hanging limp against the floor, and his left laying curled across his midsection. His head was hovering inches from the hard floor, supported by his right shoulder. His mouth was open, and saliva was seeping out of the corner, dripping onto the floor below him.

Stephanie flung the backpack off her shoulders and tossed it to the side. She hit her knees next to Michael, then placed her right index and middle fingers against his neck, feeling for any hint of a pulse. With her other hand, she pinched his earlobe to see if he'd wake up.

"Michael! Are you all right? Wake up! You can't leave me like this."

After a few seconds, she felt a beat, though it was faint. She spun him around, turning his feet toward the wall and propping them up by pressing his heels against it to encourage blood flow to his brain. She lifted his chin and tilted his head back to make sure his airway was open, then put her ear to his mouth to listen for breathing while keeping an eye on his chest for expansion. She was a doctor and had dealt with unresponsive patients hundreds of times; she knew this should come as second nature, but she was barely containing panic.

He's lying here because of me, the thought raced through her mind, trying to muscle out the decision-making impulses she needed to save the man lying in front of her. *I'm the one who said we had to go find Doctor Giles, and I'm the one who led him back there. I already got Doctor Giles killed, and now I'm on the verge of losing Michael too. I should have known. If they were determined enough to alter the study and lie to everyone, I had to know they'd make every effort to keep this quiet. Anna told me they knew I was looking at the study, but I plowed forward anyway. Maybe I just couldn't fully accept that they'd go this far. Maybe I was too stubborn and impatient to sit back and come up with a more deliberate way to approach this. Bull in a fucking china shop, that's you, Stephanie. Every damn time. You can't ever stop and think; you have to go with your gut instinct. And this time, the collateral damage is all around you. One man is dead, and a second might be lying here in front of you.*

Her muscles tensing up and time turning into a surreal blur, she began CPR as if autopilot finally kicked on. The chorus to "Staying Alive" played on repeat in her head—Ah ah ah ah Stayin' alive, Stayin' alive—as she pushed to the beat on Michael's chest, twenty times, twenty-five, thirty. Then she opened his airway, pinched his nose, took the deepest breath of her life, and blew into his mouth. She pulled up and turned to listen. Nothing. She prepared and breathed into his airway once more, then turned to listen. How long had he been unconscious? She had no idea. Should she have just taken him to the hospital in the first place? She was beginning to question that. It wasn't that cold a night for March, and he was protected from the wind, but she could tell he was cold. He was counting on her to save him after the gunshot, and she didn't know how she would live with leading him to his death.

Most of the times she performed CPR before, there was near chaos around her. Often, family members of the unresponsive patient were in the room with them. Maybe it was an emergency situation. There were machines beeping repeatedly. Nurses were being called over the intercom. The cacophony of noise helped to focus her—all eyes were on her, and her training took over. She was always confident she knew what to do, and she'd save the person's life.

Sitting here next to Michael, though, her legs crumpled beneath her body, there was no sense of emergency anywhere but in her head. The crickets chirped around the building just as on any normal late-winter evening. The warehouse was quiet, a silent witness to a dying man and the desperate woman trying to pull him back from that precipice. No nurses were scrambling to bring her a defibrillator. No mothers were gasping. No fathers were being escorted from the room. The tranquility was the most maddening part for Stephanie. It was her staring into the abyss, and the uncaring world staring back, resolute and unyielding. Mother Nature was indifferent to Stephanie's crying pleas. No one was there to save Stephanie from her own decisions, except for herself.

Wiping tears from her eyes, Stephanie shifted to do another set of compressions when Michael's chest rose slightly, and a throaty cough slipped from his mouth. It was the most wonderful sound Stephanie had ever heard.

"Oh, thank god," Stephanie scrambled to turn Michael slowly onto his side, into the recovery position. "Thank fucking god, Michael. Now just lie here. Be still. You're gonna be okay." She hoped she believed that.

He continued to cough as she folded his body into position, and then she laid herself down facing him. She kissed his forehead and hugged him lightly.

"You scared the crap out of me, you know that?" Stephanie said, a smile crossing her lips. "I'm not losing you like that."

Michael coughed again. His head was a little fuzzy, but he was coming around.

"How long was I out?"

"I have no idea. It doesn't matter now."

"Well, thanks for saving my life, I guess," Michael sighed.

Stephanie choked back tears and folded her hands to her mouth as if in prayer. She nodded and looked away.

"One thing I remember thinking before I blacked out," Michael said. "We're gonna need a new plan."

"It's okay," Stephanie ran her hand over his head. "I'm just glad you're alive. There'll be time for that. Let's not think about it right now."

"No, I already did," Michael said. "And I'm pretty sure I know what we can do. Not sure you're gonna like it, though."

54

Carrying a small basket of potatoes, Paul walked down the stairs to the courtyard. He got to the fence for the quarantine area and dropped the basket on the ground at his feet. He reached in and grabbed two potatoes at a time, then tossed them over the fence into the dirt on the other side. They thudded as they landed, and tumbled in various directions, each one eventually wobbling to a rest until the basket was empty.

He'd gotten the potatoes from one of Alessandra's two farmers, just outside the wall. They were Red LaSodas, harvested in the summer and stored for several months. Because they weren't fresh, the farmer was happy to let Paul start taking them off his hands, as spring was approaching and he'd need the storage space soon. Potatoes were one of the hardiest crops available to the area, and they were a big part of the diet for everyone in post-plague Alessandra. And, at this point, they were the entirety of the diet available to the people left alive in quarantine in Audrey's courtyard. Their days of well-prepared meals and dining like civilized humans died with Danny. The gate hadn't opened since Paul dragged Danny's lifeless body out, and he had no interest in changing that any time soon. For Paul, that wasn't out of fear, but out of punishment: "You come at the king, you best not miss."

Nick heard the thumps of potatoes dropping to the ground near the fence and wondered what time it was. There was no telling what sort of cadence Paul would have in feeding them now. They landed and tumbled through the dirt, leaving him,

Rachel, Theresa, and Omar to gather them up and eat as best as they could. Beset by hunger and despair, the four of them hadn't talked since the previous day, choosing to spend most of their time huddled alone in their tents, sleeping, reading one of the books still circulating around the camp, or just thinking in silence.

Nick hoped that wasn't sustainable, but someone was going to have to make the first gesture, and that wasn't easy for Nick to do. The rebellion had been his idea, and this was where it had gotten them—they were indisputably worse off now than they had been before. The last thing Rachel said to him was minutes after Paul dragged Danny's body out and locked the gate.

"You just couldn't leave well enough alone, could you? We were well fed and rested! You had to go screw with that, and now he's gonna slowly kill us! That's what you've done!"

He didn't think that was fair. She agreed to be a part of it. She had every opportunity to tell them she thought it was crazy, or to come up with a new plan, but she never did. But Nick understood where she was coming from. She wanted freedom as much as any of them, and she had latched on to the plan as a life raft, as the hope of something bigger. Her role wasn't all that large, so she decided she'd trust Nick, Omar and Danny to execute the plan. She didn't want to be the one to squash their one chance at freedom without even taking a shot. Then she saw them get played by Paul; she knew her world was going to crumble around her, and she needed someone to blame for that. It was Nick's plan that failed, so he took the brunt of her anger. He understood. It was hard to accept, but he got it.

So he wasn't sure if he even could make the first move. Should he apologize? Admit he screwed up? In the end, Danny was the one who had really let them down—not realizing there was a knife concealed in the tray he gave Paul—but there was rarely much satisfaction in pointing the finger at a dead guy. Nick couldn't figure out how to move them past it, though. Was there anything that could be done at this point, or were they going to waste away in their single tents until there was little human left of any of them? Was this permanent?

Nick unzipped his tent and trudged toward where the potatoes landed, spread across several feet of dirt near the fence. The other three tents in his part of the yard were zipped, and he hadn't heard any of them emerge to get their food. There were ten potatoes that he could see, and it was hard to know how many to take. Theoretically, there was nothing stopping him from gathering as many as he could carry back to his tent, but he'd essentially be stealing from Rachel, Theresa, Omar, and whoever might be alive in the smaller tents nearby. They were still shackled inside those tents, so Nick thought he might toss a potato into the tents where it looked—and, maybe more importantly, smelled—like someone might still be living there. Occasionally, one of them would push an empty bucket in front of their tent to signal they needed a refill on water. Nick could fill that up from the hose at the fence, then deliver it back to their tent. If Paul wasn't going to take care of the people in the camp, it was up to the people themselves to do it.

Nick tossed potatoes in their direction, then bent over and picked one up to try to gnaw through the dirty skin in his tent. When he turned to walk back, he saw Rachel standing in front of him.

Her expression was blank, almost staring through him. Her eyes looked glassy and faint. There was little sign of the life that had drawn him to her months before, of that irresistible girl who sat on the edge of the fountain and twirled her hair around her fingers, urging him to make a wish. That smile had kicked off what seemed like a million dreams for Nick, thinking about touching her, what it might feel like to caress the small of her back, the swell of her ass. It hadn't exactly been love, but Nick thought it was more than mere lust. There had been *something* there. Something *real.* Nick was sure of it. And, had they met in another time, another place, he would have found out. But that was so much of the tragedy of this time and this place—he knew he almost certainly would never find out. They were different people standing in this place, looking at each other like strangers, despite all the time they spent together. She didn't cross her legs and tease him. The corners of her mouth didn't curl, and her eyes didn't dance with splashes of the water cascading behind her. She just stared. Then walked to her left, picked up a potato, and walked back to her tent. She bent, crawled inside and zipped it closed. Nick stood motionless for another minute before going back to his.

55

Paul opened the door to his bedroom to go inside and relax when he saw Officer Greene out of the corner of his eye, walking up the hall carrying a person in his arms. Paul squinted and leaned toward them, trying to make out the identity of the person.

"Paul! Sir!" Officer Greene said. "I found Zac Latham lying on the street a hundred yards from here. When I spotted him, I ran up and rolled him over on his back. He was barely awake, but he kept repeating to bring him to you. He said you'd know why."

"Shit, William. Why didn't you call me on the walkie-talkie? That's what those are for."

"I did, sir. There was no answer."

Paul paused and looked up at the ceiling. Then he cracked the door to his room and leaned his head inside. His walkie-talkie was sitting on his dresser, turned off.

"Okay, then. Fair enough." Paul shut the door. "Can you maybe put him on the bed in the guest room just down there to the left?" Paul pointed behind Officer Greene, down the hall. "I'll keep an eye on him."

"You're sure?"

"Y—Yeah. Sure. Thanks for tending to him. It's good to have you around."

"Yes sir."

He carried Zac into the room, dropped him on the bed, and Paul saw him exit and start to pull the door shut.

"You can leave it open," Paul said, half yelling. "I'm gonna wander down there in a second."

Officer Greene nodded and then walked down the hall in the direction he had arrived, headed toward the exit to take him back out to the street. Paul took a deep breath and walked to the guest room. He went in and closed the door behind him, then slowly walked to the edge of the bed. Zac's eyes were closed, but he was clearly breathing; he had a lump and a nasty bruise on the side of his head. Paul knelt beside the bed and rested his elbows beside Zac.

"Wake up, Zac," Paul used his hands to nudge Zac in the side. "Time to have a chat."

Zac's eyes opened slowly, like an automatic garage door with a broken motor, opening just a little bit, then stalling. A little more, then fluttering a bit, the world coming into focus tiny bit by tiny bit. After several seconds, he realized Paul was kneeling in front of him.

"What happened?" Paul said. "Haven't heard from you for awhile. I was getting worried."

Zac tried to adjust into a more upright position and winced, then fell back on his back.

"Um, no. No reason to worry. I'm fine. Just a little woozy. I hit my head on a tree limb when I was running through the woods. Guess I was hurt worse than I thought."

"Did you get rid of the study, like I asked?"

Zac had to stop and think for a few seconds. "Oh…Yes! Yeah, I did. Got done everything you asked for."

"Except Stephanie and Michael, that is."

"Yeah. Sure. But we've been over this. You were okay with it. The tall guy was the one you really wanted."

"Sure," Paul patted Zac on the shoulder. "Sure he was, Zac. You did fine. Just rest here for a bit. Looks like you took a nasty knock on the head while you were out there. I'll come check on you in a little bit. Sound good?"

"Yeah, I could use some sleep," Zac rubbed his head, and recoiled at the pain. "Damn. She really got me."

"She?"

"Um, I mean, it's just an expression. 'She.' Like Mother Nature."

"Mother Nature?"

"Sure," Zac shrugged and gave a dry laugh. "Mother Nature can be a real bitch sometimes, ya know?"

"Oh, yeah. I know. Lie back and get some rest. I'll be back."

Zac laid his head on the pillow and closed his eyes. Paul walked out of the room and closed the door.

"Mother fucking Nature, my ass," Paul mumbled to himself as he walked to his room.

Audrey woke up and tried to roll over before remembering her arms and legs were tied to the bedposts. There was a rag jammed in her mouth, which was drier than Phoenix in July. She tugged at the ropes holding her in place, but there was very little give. She could feel the rope's threads digging into the skin of her wrists, and the start of a bright red rash was forming.

After several seconds of thrashing about, she stopped and lay still, staring at the ceiling. Her head throbbed, and her shoulders felt like horses had been pulling her arms in opposite directions for hours. Had Paul drugged her again? She wasn't sure. She remembered him pulling the gun on her, and the betrayal and fear she felt at that moment. After everything else he'd done, she convinced herself that she could control Paul's darker side because he looked up to her, and wouldn't do anything to hurt *her*. Sure, he might do something horrible if left to his own devices, but the fact was that she was the one in charge, and she was his sister. She knew he had his flaws, but her being his sister had always been enough. He respected her, and looked up to her. When she needed someone she could trust to do right by her, she could always turn to him. He might not be trustworthy to most, but she was confident he'd help her accomplish her main goals, and she'd be able to keep him in check on his more base instincts. Staring down the barrel of that gun, it was finally clear to her that she underestimated him, and he was the one in control.

Maybe it had been a craven move to bring him into her inner circle in the first place. Maybe she should have known that he was too unpredictable, too manic to keep in check, but she hadn't. Lying on the bed with her limbs strapped tightly to the frame, she knew that was a decision she was going to have to live—and, perhaps, die—with.

She tried to consider what might happen next. Would he actually kill her? She didn't think so, but she was done underestimating what he was capable of when it came to her, or anyone else. The one saving grace was that he hadn't done it *yet*. And if that was what he was planning, why not do it immediately? Why go through this show of tying her to the bed? He wasn't Snidely Whiplash, chaining the damsel to the train tracks while twirling his handlebar mustache. This wasn't some Steven Seagal movie, where the bad guy had to keep the girl alive just long enough for the hero to save the day. If he wanted her dead, he already had every opportunity to make that happen. So she thought he must have something else in mind. At least he hadn't made a firm decision to kill her, which meant she still had a chance of getting out of this. She just had no idea how.

What would become of Alessandra in the meantime was also unpredictable. She knew she hadn't been perfect in her decisions up to that point. Maybe the people of Alessandra would have been better off with a different person leading them. But none of those people stepped up to the plate. She was given the task of keeping these people—perhaps the last organized colony of humans on Earth—alive, and allowing them to thrive as much as they could in such a dire situation. And she felt like she did that, albeit with some challenges. But she thought she could be forgiven most of the missteps she made, because they were in service of the people. She hadn't known the virus-transmission study was forged; hopefully, the people would believe that if the time came to explain. She did what she thought was best, and that was the most anyone could ask for. In the end, she was proud of the work she had done for Alessandra, and she wept for what might happen to it next.

Paul clearly wanted power; he wanted to be the one making decisions about the town. What were his objectives? She didn't know. She thought he shared her goals of keeping everyone alive until they could confirm they were safe from the virus, and then rebuild the fabric of society while beginning the slow, arduous task of repopulating the planet. But a mutiny wouldn't seem to serve that goal. If he truly shared that as the chief objective, talking to her about how best to get there would have seemed like the play. This was a power move, of someone who wanted a radical change in approach. He wasn't going to listen to her, and her agenda was out the window. With the cocking of that gun, he was putting his own plan into place, and he would lead her and Alessandra down an uncertain path.

What she wasn't going to do was simply lie there and wait for it to happen. The people of Alessandra needed her at that moment, even if they had no idea how much. She needed to find a way to get out of that bed and do something. She couldn't say what at that point. But she was ready to fight if necessary.

56

Stephanie led Michael through the front door of the hospital, and they headed for the stairs to reach the second floor.

"Do you really think this'll work?" said Michael, still a bit weak and favoring his heavily bandaged left shoulder, but otherwise feeling far better than he was earlier.

"Can't be sure of anything, but it's a good idea, Michael. I've told you that."

"I know. I just like to hear it."

He smiled, and she turned back to return the look as she hit the top of the stairs.

"And besides," she said, "there's no telling how much time we really have. At this point, just about any plan is better than no plan. So don't let your head get too big."

She walked down the hall, easily outpacing Michael. To her right, she pushed open a door and ducked in, coming out with a large yellow "Caution" cone. She carried it with her as she walked, and Michael watched it swaying a bit as she did.

When she reached the set of bathrooms another fifty feet down the hall, she placed it in front of the women's room to block it off, then hurried into another room two doors down. Michael always enjoyed watching her work. When she got her mind fixated on making something happen, she was a woman of action. Nothing stopped her. He had a tendency to get sidetracked and lose focus, but he never saw that happen to her. Also, after what she told him happened when she came to the hospital earlier to get the equipment to help him with, he was just glad to see her alive. If she hadn't made it back, he knew he would have died on the wooden planks in that rickety old warehouse.

While she gathered what they needed, he made sure no one was looking and slipped into the women's restroom. He walked to the stall by the far wall, went inside and locked the door behind him, then climbed up on the toilet and sat on the back of it to stay out of sight in case someone ignored the caution cone.

He waited there for several minutes, nervously rocking back and forth, keeping his head ducked down between his knees so it wouldn't peek out from above the stall and give him away. They discussed on the walk to the hospital how important it was that he kept himself out of sight as much as possible until they could get this done. They still weren't sure how big a target was on their backs, and they couldn't afford for both of them to get shot or captured. Nobody else knew about the plan, and so at least one of them had to be free to execute it.

Michael heard someone slap at the restroom door, then push it open. There were two footsteps on the linoleum, and then he heard the door bump closed.

"We good?" Stephanie said, bending to look for feet under the stalls.

"I think we're set," Michael raised his head up to peer down at Stephanie, who stood nude before him, her pale skin almost reflective in the harsh light of the room; she gave him a shy grin. She was holding a small hand-held camera, and she walked toward his stall. Her hips swayed, and he could see the muscles stretching as she moved.

Suddenly, Michael's nerves were replaced by excitement—it was the anticipation of a 17-year-old virgin on prom night. But this wasn't even about sex; he wasn't sure exactly what was going to happen. It was about taking back what had been denied to them for too long. Humans are a social species, and being artificially denied a significant part of that social nature was like having a limb removed—you could still feel the tingle of that need, as if you had felt the warmth of an embrace just yesterday. But that didn't change the fact that it was gone.

She pushed open the stall door and stepped inside, then gave him a come-hither finger to beckon him down from his perch; whatever differences they had when they were married, she was sure to get her way this time. If his heart had been bongo drums earlier, it was the climax of a fireworks show now, exploding at the idea of Stephanie's hands on his body—*anywhere* on his body.

They stood face to face, breathing in each other's air. After all the time Michael had spent at arm's length from everyone, standing this close to someone was invigorating, just sharing a space so intimately. Being this close to Stephanie was at once unfamiliar and very familiar. They'd spent eight years in wedded…not bliss, exactly, but it was a life together. No kids, and the ups and downs were hard, but he had certainly been this close, and much closer, to her before. This was a feeling of reclaiming what was his, of the greyhound finally reaching the dummy rabbit kept just out of his reach for the race.

They stared at each other with quivering lips and eyes for thirty seconds…one minute…ninety seconds…and a smile broke on Stephanie's face. She reached down and helped him pull his shirt over his right arm and shoulder, then tugged it over his tilted head, guarding his left shoulder. Every touch of her fingers to his bare skin was a shot of electricity, an almost debilitating boost of endorphins. There were stabs of pain as they worked to remove the shirt, but his adrenaline shoved them aside until she draped the shirt over the stall door. He stood, vulnerable and visibly shaking in front of the person he trusted most in the world. They set up the camera on the toilet basin's lid, and turned it on.

Slowly, she reached both hands up beside her head and placed them flat on his chest. Michael was an appliance plugged into the wall after sitting in the attic collecting dust—the wiring may have been frayed, but it quickly sprung to life with this surge of power. Feeling his shudder, she crept her hands down his chest, to his navel and stomach, tracing a familiar path over a midsection less bulbous and muscles more apparent than she remembered. The "Survive a virus that kills millions of people" diet had worked for them both.

She bent and kissed his stomach, looked up at him and smiled, then laughed—it was a sound he hadn't known he missed so much during their time apart, and he followed suit. They laughed while trying to hold in the sound, muffling the noise with their hands. Finally, she said "No more noise," stood and softly kissed him on the lips, lingering there for a few moments; it was the first kiss he ever had, and it was life affirming. It was amazing this had been stolen from them all. It wasn't that they'd gone too long without the feel of another person's lips against theirs, or the physical intimacy that comes with connecting with another person in that way; it was that they'd been denied even the possibility of that connection. They'd been robbed of the hope that they could feel that with another human being, to have skin touch skin, for Michael to have a woman's hand slide gently down the front of his pants, then slipping them to the ground, for Stephanie to feel the jolt of a man entering her body. They held onto each other tightly, attacking one another with tongues dancing, teeth clumsily clacking together in their excitement. He spun her around and set her down on the toilet lid, and he bent over her, thrusting and wrapping his arms underneath hers. Her mouth was wide, but she would only allow muffled moans, twice biting her fist to fight the urge to scream. Sweat poured down Michael's forehead, dripping down Stephanie's breasts and swimming down her sides.

It was like meeting up with an old dance partner—even if the bodies are a different shape, many of the moves are still the same. You remember the person's rhythms, and that hitch in their step. Michael knew Stephanie liked to feel his fingernails grinding against her ass, and she had no trouble recalling how he shook and arched his back at climax.

He collapsed across her body, and she tried to get into a somewhat comfortable position, leaning against the stall's wall. She kissed his forehead and rubbed the back of his neck.

"I didn't…" Michael said, pausing to catch his breath, "… think we'd really go all the way."

She laughed silently. "Lies."

57

The morning sun cut lines across his bed, and Paul stirred awake, stretching his arms above his head as he rolled over to his back. He laid his arms on top of his blanket and settled deep in his pillow, unready to get to his feet and start the day. The annual craft fair was that evening, and it was one of Audrey's biggest priorities to keep having that in order to maintain people's spirits. In past years, everyone would come, and many would bring paintings, photographs, ash trays, Christmas ornaments, or whatever other random artsy hobby they happened to have, and peddle their wares to the masses. Audrey had been adamant that this was going to go on, even with everyone wearing rings, and even at a much smaller scale. She didn't care, because she wanted people to have that escape. It was also the perfect time to play Nick's confession for the public for the first time, since so many would hear it. And Paul was pretty sure he didn't care enough to stand in the way.

After all, if nothing else, it had given him a good pretense for pulling the St. Francis security team out of the hospital for a good portion of the day, and busying them with blather about planning for the event. He said they'd need all hands on deck to make sure they maintained order during the fair. He didn't honestly care whether or not they helped, but it made them feel important, and it gave Zac the run of the place when he went to do the work Paul needed, so it was worthwhile. And, honestly, Paul wasn't dumb; he knew that throwing the common people a periodic bone, where they felt like they were allowed to mingle, enjoy their hobbies and be entertained, was hugely valuable when it came to making them deal with orders they might not like in the future. You were never going to get a kid to eat his Brussels sprouts if you didn't tease him with a bowl of ice cream afterward, and your average set of citizens were the same way. Might as well let the festivities run their course, and use it as a platform to show the people that they could conduct a successful investigation and catch a murderer. Because he'd like to have the credibility to make a public example of some people the following day—starting with Stephanie and Michael.

Paul didn't think of himself as a killer. Not by a long shot. But he knew it was important that a leader show strength. If someone took a swing at you—as Stephanie and Michael did when they snooped around at the H6N1 transmission study, then hunted down Doctor Giles—you had to swing back twice as hard. Maybe ten times. If you were going to garner the respect of the people you were trying to lead, how else could you reasonably conduct yourself? If the people saw you as weak, you might as well be a guy on the street corner begging for change—there's no way you can lead. You have to be strong, resilient, and a fighter. You have to show that no one will get the better of you, and you'll fight to make sure your followers are safe from every enemy.

To that end, Paul knew that examples had to be made from time to time. He regretted that Audrey never could stomach that; she seemed caught up in the idea of conducting themselves based upon some semblance of objective morality, but he knew that was an incoherent concept. God or not, everything was relative. The people involved, the circumstances, and the potential outcomes all had a hand in determining what was moral. Thou shalt not kill? What if there's a man sprinting toward you with a knife ready to stab you? Thou shalt not steal? What if you took a loaf of bread from the grocery store because you were broke and had a starving family at home? Paul knew there was a set of events that could justify pretty much anything. And, in the circumstance where killing two people might help save a town of hundreds, he was confident that was one of the times when "Thou shalt not kill" flew out the window—whether you were religious or not.

The question of what to do with Zac and Audrey, though, still hung over his head. Zac had been a loyal servant the previous day, doing solid—though imperfect—work toward what Paul needed. Paul thought he might make a suitable errand boy for his administration once he was recognized as the town's leader, but he wasn't sure he fully trusted him. Paul's problem there was similar to Audrey's—there was only one person in the world they truly trusted. For Audrey, that person had betrayed her. For Paul, he had drugged that person and tied her to a bed across the hall. He had promised Zac a chance to go in there and confront her one on one as a way of convincing him to do some dirty work, but Paul hadn't been totally sold on actually doing that. He just figured he'd make the deal, then hope Zac never made it up there to collect. Now that he was there, Paul wasn't sure whether he wanted to risk further problems by blowing Zac off, or if he just wanted to make good on his promise for convenience's sake.

Paul swung his legs over the side of the bed, placed his feet on the floor and stood. He walked to the door and cracked it open to look down the hall. The two big problems he had to figure out were behind doors number one and two, and he didn't plan to drag out the decisions. By the end of the day, he suspected at least one of them would be dead. Whether it'd be at the hands of him or each other, he figured he'd find out soon enough.

58

Anna's eyebrows peaked high above her eyes, and she nearly broke into laughter.

"You did *what*?" she said, sitting with Trish in front of Michael and Stephanie, hearing the end of their story from the previous day.

"I know, I know," Stephanie said, hands up in front of her. "But it's important as part of the plan. We need to show people that touching isn't going to kill them. And tonight may be our only chance to do that."

"I'm just not sure, Steph," Anna said. "The plan isn't terrible, but I don't think just you two is gonna be enough to convince people."

Stephanie looked at Michael, then back at Anna and smiled. "You read our minds. That's why we need your help."

Anna swung her head left, then right. "*My* help?" She pointed at her chest.

"You're still friendly with Dennis, right?"

"I mean, we're friendly, but you're not suggesting that we…"

Stephanie and Michael nodded.

"Oh, come on," Anna said. "This is nuts."

"It's the only chance we've got," Stephanie walked over to Anna and kneeled in front of her. "I've thought about this, and I don't know of another way to spread the word. We need something dramatic and impactful. And, after everything that's happened, I don't know that Michael and I have much time left. They've sent someone after us twice already. We're gonna have to be careful just to make it to tonight. That's why it's even more important that you get involved. If something happens to Michael and me, you have to carry this plan forward. You and Dennis can do it if you need to. But the timing's perfect. We'll hopefully have most everyone in the same place at the fair—assuming people actually wander out of their houses for it, out of habit if nothing else—and we can get our message out to lots of people at once rather than trying to go door to door.

"So we have to have your help, Anna. You don't have to go any further than just touching. It's not like you have to go all the way. But the more couples we can march up there to show everyone, the more easily we can say, 'This is a farce, and we're healthy standing here in front of you. We're not afraid, and you shouldn't be either.' Can we count on you?"

Anna sighed. "I doubt I'll have any trouble convincing Dennis. But I'll be damned if I'm letting him ram his tongue down my throat."

"That's fine. Go talk to him, and then come back here. The camera is still set up in the bathroom. And tell anyone you trust to do the same," Stephanie turned to Trish. "You got a Romeo somewhere you could recruit for this?"

Trish smiled. "I'll have to narrow the list down first."

"Knock 'em dead, girl," Stephanie's shoulders heaved as she laughed.

Trish walked away, and Stephanie looked at Michael, who shrugged and then winced, grabbing his left shoulder. They both laughed.

Stephanie hadn't slept much the previous night, with "What does this mean?" doing laps in her head. They didn't sleep together; she took the couch in her office, and Michael curled up on the floor in the corner of the room, next to a stand with a houseplant on top. She heard him snoring what seemed like most of the night, so she figured these thoughts hadn't been bothering him in quite the same way. Did he want them to get back together? Did *she*?

There was so much history there, so much comfort and familiarity. In an uncertain time, it was easy to fall back on what was comfortable. Would she have sought Michael out if he hadn't come to her? Probably not. But she couldn't rule out that the thought would have crossed her mind. Of course, if he hadn't come to her, they wouldn't be standing there trying to topple Audrey's regime, fearing for their lives, and convincing their friends to screw on camera in a public restroom. Strange times often call for strange measures.

What did she really *feel*, though? She wasn't sure. Did she love him? She thought she always would, at least to some extent. But that didn't necessarily mean she wanted to make a family with him when this was all over—*if* this was ever all over. She couldn't deny that the sex had been mind blowing, but she hadn't so much as felt a man's hand on her thigh in more than two years; he could have been a wrinkled ninety-year-old with one functioning hand, and maybe it would have still made her squeal like a sorority girl at a mixer. Still, they always had good chemistry. Whatever problems they had when they were together, they were never evident when they were in bed together—or, alternatively, in the stall of a women's restroom while balancing on a hospital toilet in post-apocalyptic Alessandra. That part of their relationship had always worked. It was everything around it that had fallen apart, and she wasn't sure whose fault that had been.

She had no idea if they were destined to trek down that road again, stupidly assuming that this next plan would go any better than their previous one. If it was going to work, they needed people to show up in big numbers at the fair. Looking out the hospital window, she could see some people starting to set up tents around the fountain. That was a good sign. This would be the first one since the virus struck, and there were no guarantees, especially with the extent to which people had fallen into their little personal bubbles in recent months. That was why Audrey had made it a point to keep the fair going, though. People used to come from towns all around Alessandra to walk around and buy homemade crafts. They'd stroll through the square, munch on a corn dog on a stick, sip on a Coke, and probably see an old friend or two. People in the area considered it one of the signs that winter was ending, and warmer weather was on its way.

Of course, there'd be no visitors from other towns this year. This was the All-Alessandra craft fair. She hoped that people would remember the fun they had there before, and want to come back to relive it. The bigger the crowd, the easier it'd be to pull this off. It was going to be a risk either way, but she didn't see any way around it. There was nowhere for them to hide. They couldn't exactly hop a plane and get the hell outta Dodge. They were stuck. And, if Audrey, Paul and his minions wanted them dead or locked up, that was exactly what they'd be sooner or later. So there was no time to wait. Hiding wasn't a viable option. Doing something was a risk. But doing nothing was even riskier.

59

Audrey was trying—and failing—to sleep when she heard the lock on her bedroom door click. When it swung open, Paul stepped inside. He turned and locked it behind him.

"Morning, sis," he said. "How'd you sleep?"

The words formed in her head, but the rag stuffed in her mouth limited her to muffled consonants out loud. She thrashed her limbs around on the bed with a brief burst of energy before slumping onto the mattress. He walked to her with his hands clasped behind his back.

"Sorry. Can't understand you," he leaned over her, his face hovering above hers. "Didn't mom always say not to talk with your mouth full?"

She stared up at him, breathing loudly through her nostrils, like wind blowing across a car window with an imperfect seal.

"I could take it out, but I'm not sure I can trust you. What do you think?" He pulled a butcher's knife out from the back waistband of his pants and raised it up in front of her. "Can I trust my big sis not to make a racket so we can chat?"

Her eyes grew large as she nodded.

"All right, then. Open wide." He reached into her mouth and yanked at the damp cloth, pulling it out and tossing it on the bed. "God, you made a mess of that thing."

Audrey stretched her jaw in every direction.

"Water," she tried to say, but it sounded more like "Otter."

"What was that?" Paul cupped his hand to his left ear.

"Need otter!"

"Why do you need an otter? And what did I tell you about keeping your voice down?"

Audrey closed her eyes and took a deep breath, then tried to swallow, but it just dryly scratched her throat.

"W—Water," she said softly, trying to enunciate with cracking lips and a tongue made of sandpaper. "Please...get...me... water."

"Ohhh, water. That makes more sense." He put up his index finger and walked to her bathroom. Her glass from the other day was still by the sink. He rinsed it out, then filled it nearly to the brim from the tap. He walked over and tilted it toward her lips. She pulled on the ropes holding her wrists to get herself in as close to a sitting position as she could, leaned her head forward and drank. He kept it tilted toward her, and she swallowed in large gulps, the water cooling her mouth as it slid across her tongue and into her throat. It was the best glass of water she ever tasted, and she attacked it voraciously. Audrey breathed through her nose as the water kept flowing; she didn't want it to stop. As the glass got near empty, she still wasn't done; she had no idea when she might get another drink, and she wasn't going to waste a drop of what he was willing to give her. When the water was gone, Audrey gasped for air, and Paul set the glass down on the bedside table.

"Better now?" he said.

She nodded, and allowed herself to slide her head back onto her pillow.

"Good," Paul leaned over her again. "I was hoping we could have a chat. Quietly, of course. Let's use our inside voices."

She agreed.

"I hated to have to do this to you, you know," he said, beginning to walk around the bed. "Don't think I did it on some spontaneous whim or something. I didn't just wake up one morning and think, 'Hey, let's drug my sister and tie her up to the bed today.' A lot of thought went into this. I looked at my options, and the town's options, and I just didn't see another choice. You may be more experienced at all this government stuff, but I don't think you understand the people. We've talked about this before, of course. You just aren't willing to make all the tough decisions that have to be made. You're not willing to get your hands as dirty as they have to get, and the people are going to suffer for it. I can't let that happen."

"Or maybe you're just a psychopath."

Paul's eyebrows arched. "A psychopath? No, that seems unlikely to me. Just because you're weak and lack the stamina and fortitude to carry this town where it needs to go, that doesn't make me a psychopath. I mean, look, I'm not saying you've done everything wrong. The whole ring idea was a stroke of genius. But you were going to let a fucking doctor ruin that whole thing before I stepped in. Then when I said that meant separating families, you did what you needed to do. But, even after that, you can't accept that sometimes people have to suffer and die for a cause larger than themselves. It really shouldn't be a difficult notion to grasp."

"Simple notions are often the least likely to actually be true. It's like with God."

"What about God?" Paul asked.

"Well, I used to want God to exist. Our parents made us go to church for the longest time. Remember? We had to participate somehow when we were growing up. I did the children's choir for years. Practices after school once a week. I thought I actually got to be pretty good. And mom was so proud when you became an acolyte, up there in your robe, carrying the flame to the altar."

"Yeah, I remember. If there had been phone cameras back then, she'd have been snapping pictures like crazy. I hated those robes."

Audrey laughed. "Yeah, you fought every time you had to do that, but you did it anyway, because you didn't want to disappoint mom. And maybe because you didn't want to disappoint God. I think we believed then, at least in the way a little kid believes, almost because they think they're supposed to and everyone else does rather than because they have much of a concept of what it is they're believing. Hell, maybe that childlike belief isn't all that different from the adult one, come to think of it. Once we got too old for mom to push us into church, though, we all stopped going, and I'm pretty sure we both drifted away from faith too. That bothered me, though. I looked at all the people happily going to church, sharing Bible verses, praising Jesus's name, and I sort of missed that childlike innocence I had when I was doing that. I wanted God to be there. I wanted someone to be in control. I wanted this world to have some meaning beyond what I gave it.

"I went and prayed the other day. I walked down to the church and kneeled at the altar. The priest found me there, and seemed to know exactly what I needed to hear. It was kind of surreal, actually. I thought that maybe I'd found what I was looking for. Maybe it had been there all along."

"But it wasn't, was it?" Paul said.

"No," Audrey looked away from him. "No, it wasn't. God is a simple notion, wrapped up in the trappings of something complex, just like what you're talking about. It's comforting to think there's a powerful truth out there that just happens to conform to your own beliefs about the world. And that you're one of the strong ones for believing it. How did this all come to be? Well, God made it, and poof! There it is! I used to want that to be true. But I'm seeing things in more grays now than blacks and whites."

"But that's just what I'm telling you," Paul said. "You're right that there's no god. And morality is one of those grays. 'Murder' is a legal term. Forget about that. Lose the baggage that comes along with it. Our lives only have the meaning that we assign to them as individuals. We get to choose our own path. Morality only matters in terms of the community in which you're living. We're starting over in Alessandra. We get to set the rules. We get to determine right and wrong. We get to determine what's true and false. It's a blank slate. There is no ultimate arbiter. *We* are the ultimate arbiters."

"Saying there's no objective morality doesn't mean there's no morality," she said. "Societies have been built for thousands of years on the notion that indiscriminate killing for the sake of consolidating power doesn't work. It doesn't keep the order; it breaks it down. We don't get to establish some new world order just because we happen to hold the keys to power for the time being. We don't get to destroy lives just because we *can*. These are human beings, and we have to treat them with respect. We stand on the shoulders of those who came before us; we don't supplant them. But you never were all that good at history, were you? *I* was the smart one who everybody actually *liked*."

Paul ran his tongue along his teeth and picked the soggy rag off the bed. Audrey's eyes opened wide, and she began tossing her head violently back and forth. She started to scream, and he punched her in the jaw, then jammed the rag into her mouth. Her screams turned to barely audible mumbles as Paul exited the room.

Paul paced the hall, his footsteps getting louder, his chest tightening. He stomped back to his room and picked up his walkie-talkie.

"William, come in," he said.

"Officer Greene here, Mister Reese. What do you need?"

"You know the quarantine area we have in the courtyard at the compound?"

"Yes. I believe so, sir."

"I need you to go in there. You'll find a key in the gate. Inside to the right, you'll see a pile of arm shackles. Get Nick from his tent and secure him with those. Forget playing the tape tonight. I want him down there to show everyone what happens if you screw with us. He can read the confession himself."

"Um, okay, sir. What about if he tries to escape?"

"If he even hints at running, shoot him. As many times as necessary."

60

"Do we have enough?" Michael said, walking into the hospital's Research lab as Stephanie, Anna, and Trish turned toward him.

Stephanie smiled. "There's some hot stuff on here, but we unfortunately cut most of that out. Anna took it down to just a short clip of each of the four couples."

"We got four?" Michael's eyebrows raised. "Who?"

"Well, these two scamps, of course," Stephanie pointed her thumbs at Anna and Trish flanking her. "And Anna brought in another couple. I think one of them's a friend of yours."

"Oh yeah?"

"Yep," Anna pointed toward the back of the room. "He's wandering through the library right now. His ex has been a girlfriend of mine for a while. Said he's a member of that Watch group you organize."

Michael walked toward the shelves of books and paperwork that lined the back of the Research lab. As he walked, he glanced down each aisle, looking for someone. On the fourth aisle, he saw a man flipping through a thick book. The man saw Michael, looked up and nodded once.

"Hey," Hank said, then swiveled his head to look around him. "Quite a setup here."

"Yeah. I'm told Anna does a good job keeping this place together."

Hank looked at the floor, then closed the book and placed it on the shelf. He raised his chin and took a deep breath. Michael tried to meet Hank's eyes.

"Look, man…" Michael said. "About what happened before…"

"I know. I'm not gonna pretend I wasn't pissed. Maybe I still am. I didn't agree with the way you handled Trevor." Hank took a couple of steps toward Michael. Neither was wearing a ring. "But this is a good thing you're doing. They said you pushed for this to happen, and you've really risked a lot to get us this far. I'm not anywhere near the only one who lost a family in all this mess. Zac, Andy, Benjamin, the list could go on for a while. You and I are lucky that our exes were needed at the hospital, so at least they're here. Lots of these men may never see their wives or kids again. We've all paid a heavy price to survive this long, and it's a price we didn't have to pay. It's a price we paid so others could have dominion over us. And we let it happen because…what choice did we have, really?"

"I don't know, man. I wish there was more we could do."

"*This* is what we can do right now, all right? We can't erase the past, but we can start over again tonight. We can make a stand, and start fresh tomorrow, with a new Alessandra. Somewhere that family and fellowship matter again. We're stronger together. And that's exactly why they don't want us to *be* together. So this is a good thing you're doing. It doesn't mean I agree with everything you've done," Hank paused and looked at the ceiling, then returned his eyes to Michael's. "But let's say it means I'll accept that your intentions are good. And I'll work with you on the next step."

Hank extended his right hand, and Michael shook it.

"Good to have you, man," Michael said. "Let's just not go in for a hug." He gestured with his head at his left shoulder. "This other shoulder nearly got taken off by a bullet. Doubt I'll be lifting it much for awhile."

Hank laughed and slapped Michael on his good shoulder; they walked back toward the front of the room. Hank's former wife, Leslie, had joined the three other women at the computer.

"Is everybody ready to start a revolution?" Michael said as he approached them.

The crowd was gathering on the square when Michael approached with a bulky brown bag slung across his good shoulder, and his ring settled along his waistline. Dusk was approaching, as the sun began touching the upper reaches of the violet mountains in the distance, sending cascades of color dancing into the valley below. It was his favorite time of the day, and it was why this was the only place in the world he ever wanted to live. The trees leading to the jagged mountains, and the crisp late-winter air, feeling just a kiss of spring. On his walk, he noticed a flower or two trying to wake up from their months-long slumber in the ground. Alessandra had to be one of the most beautiful places in the world at this time of day and year.

And, for the first time in months, the town had a bit of a buzz to it. This used to be Alessandra's biggest event of the year, and it was good to see people still wanted to do it. The event was far smaller than it had been in recent years, but the community was clearly still on board. Lots of residents had booths set up, talking up whatever they'd been making over the previous few months. Some of them would barter for items other residents had, like fresh winter herbs and vegetables, or give them to people as a gesture of friendship. It was the most people in one place Michael had seen in many months, and the crowd meant he'd occasionally hear the clanking of rings deflecting off one another as people squeezed through tight spaces.

A handful of Audrey's officers were lingering, watching over the event, but he suspected that was more a formality than anything. This was a night for the people of the town to enjoy themselves, and he didn't think Audrey would do anything to disrupt that. No one would be quick to pay much attention to Michael, as he wandered over to the fountain in the middle of the square and sat down on its rim.

He faced the bandstand, with cobalt blue paint around the outside, lining a silver roof, topped by a cherub dancing on a blue point. The railing around the perimeter was criss-crossed with ironworks, designed by the grandson of one of the town's founders in the 1940s, and there were entrances on both sides of the structure. Behind the bandstand was the long, weathered wall of the old courthouse, a building that had fallen into disrepair in recent years. On the outside, it still looked like it could hear cases, but the building wasn't sealed well after being abandoned, and the interior was infested with rats and pigeons looking for refuge from the cold. For years, the town had put focus on keeping the exterior looking presentable, an artifice to its decaying state on the inside. Even its green dome stood tall above it, sparkling in the sunlight on bright days as a reminder of the beauty Alessandra was once proud of; meanwhile, the clock beneath it had sat stuck on 7:27 for eight years.

Prior to the virus, there had been a campaign to save the courthouse and return it to its former glory, when it was the focal point of the town for more than 100 years, but the resources dried up once everybody began getting sick. Everything they had was poured into building the wall and fitting everyone with their rings using the steel that would have gone into supporting new walls to replace the ones that had deteriorated inside the building. The front door was locked up; they moved city services to a newer building in 1992, so no one had been inside it for years— save the occasional looter or bored resident who wandered through the rooms looking to connect to the town's past.

That wall was also prominent next to the square, and that was where Michael's eyes were focused. He shrugged the bag off his shoulder, opened it, and pulled out a battery-powered projector, then set it on the spot Trish marked earlier in the day with a Post-It note stuck on the fountain's rim. That was where it needed to sit to throw their little home movie onto the wall where everyone would be able to see it. The setup was perfect, and the crowd was filing into the square around Michael. The security guys were munching on popcorn and chicken on sticks, so they didn't look like they were going to provide any obstacle to him. No one was paying attention to him, which was exactly what he wanted. Out of the corner of his eye, he could see Stephanie and the rest of the group from the hospital walking into the square, and blending into the crowd. Once the sun dipped below the line of the mountains, they'd gather to the left of the bandstand, and Michael would flip the projector on, then join them. By the time the security guys figured out what was going on, they wouldn't have time to stop it. Then it would be up to Michael, Stephanie and the others to sell the people on the truth.

For the first time in several days, Michael felt he could take a breath and relax for a moment. He was nervous about whether or not this plan would work, but there would be time to worry about that. At that moment, seeing everyone gathered together, sharing their work with others, enjoying each other's company, looking out over the mountains slowly swallow the sun in the crisp evening air, he felt at peace. They were taking action, not just sitting back and accepting their fate. Maybe by the next time he saw those mountains turn to violet, they'd have a new town, with a new chapter in its history starting. If nothing else, sitting there on the fountain, there was hope that a new day might change the course of their community, and end the separation that had crippled Alessandra over the previous year. Behind him, Stephanie and Anna were gathering the others to set up next to the bandstand.

From his right, Michael noticed two men walking away from the crowd and toward the bandstand. One of them was wearing shackles on his wrists, and the other appeared to have a gun in the man's back, nudging him forward. With the gathering dark and lengthening of the shadows, Michael wasn't sure who they were; he leaned forward and squinted, trying to identify the men. As they traipsed up the steps to the bandstand, his breath grew thin, and his heart raced. He knew who the man in shackles was, and he feared he also knew what was coming next.

When the men reached the bandstand platform, the officer yelled for everyone's attention, but few were looking in that direction, and the din of the crowd made it difficult for them to hear him. Michael could see clearly now who stood thirty feet in front of him, but it was difficult to believe. Nick was shackled like a common criminal, perhaps a show so everyone knew he was dangerous. In the commotion of recent days, Michael had almost forgotten about the approaching incrimination of Nick, and it looked like Michael and his crew weren't the only ones who found a night when everyone was gathered together on the square to be a convenient time for a big announcement.

Nick didn't look too different; he appeared to be reasonably well fed, but he was dirty. It looked like there was mud caked on his cheeks and arms, as if he'd rolled around in a swamp on his way up to the stage. Michael imagined that if he were closer, unspeakable odors were probably wafting off his old friend. Alessandra was lucky to be able to pump a good amount of water out of Lake Chatuga, but that resource wasn't unlimited, and it looked like bathing the quarantined group wasn't a high priority for Audrey and her team. Michael was at least happy to see his friend alive, but Nick didn't look like himself at all. From that distance, it was tough to tell exactly, but there was something distant in his stare, as if he wasn't entirely there in the moment. That look worried him; what were the people in quarantine going through? Now he knew just how great an injustice that quarantine really was, and he hoped to wrap Nick in a bear hug later that evening.

The officer yelled for a third time, and whistled louder than a train horn; finally, everyone's head spun toward the bandstand, and he motioned for people to gather closer. People filtered over from whichever booth they'd been browsing to hear what he was going to say. Michael's heart beat madly, and his finger sat anxiously over the projector's power button. Everyone was in place.

"Ladies and gentlemen, thank you for giving me a moment of your time," Officer Greene bellowed, holding one hand in the air above his head. "First, I want you to know that your mayor, Audrey, is watching the festivities through that camera you see perched on the outside of the square. It's a wonderful piece of technology that transmits the signal straight up the hill behind it to her home. She so wanted to be here, but she was feeling ill. She'll be back on her feet in no time, though. Everyone, wave to the camera and say hi to her. That'll lift her spirits, I'm sure."

Most everyone turned and waved, but it wasn't Audrey they were waving to; Paul was the one sitting by the window facing down to the square, watching the events on a small monitor. Even the officer didn't know that much, though.

"Thank you all," he said. "Beside me here, I think many of you will recognize Nick Dyerson, a native Alessandrian who had to be isolated because he came into contact with a woman named Rachel Iles. I assure you they're both being treated well, and will be released back to the town as soon as possible. However, we have come upon some distressing news about Mister Dyerson that we both wanted to make you aware of while you're all here. You're all familiar with the tragic death of Trevor Kites, a week ago. I know we all had difficulty dealing with something like that happening in our beloved town. We promised you we'd find who did it, and make sure they were brought to justice, because your safety is what matters the most to Audrey. I'm happy to say that Audrey led the investigation to find the murderer, and Mister Dyerson has a statement to read you all tonight."

He turned to Nick and gestured toward the crowd.

"Go ahead," he said quietly.

Michael sat watching this, and weighing his options. He wasn't sure he could stand to listen to Nick confess to a murder he didn't commit as the town watched on in horror. The safest move, though, would be to wait until they were finished, and moved well clear of the bandstand before playing the video. That was the safe play. *But fuck safe. If I wanted safe, I wouldn't be here in the first place. I could have just let this lie, and continued going about this meager existence if I was interested in what was safe. I left safe behind the moment I walked into Stephanie's office and convinced her to investigate this scandal. There's no turning back now. This all started with Nick's confession, and that's where I'm ending it.*

Nick lifted a slip of paper just below his chin. He tilted his head down, lowered his eyes and began to read.

"I, Nick Dyerson—"

Light flashed in front of Nick, momentarily blinding him and Officer Greene. It flickered and shone in their direction, seemingly right into their eyes. Michael watched as they put their arms in front of their faces and turned away. Michael's video began to play on the wall to their left, and he sprinted to join Stephanie and the other couples.

"What are you doing?" Stephanie said. "We need to wait until they're finished. I think that guy has a gun."

"I can't let Nick do that. This is happening now."

The speakers were attached to the side of the projector, and they blared as the video began.

"Hello, friends and neighbors," Stephanie's voice boomed through the speakers. "I'm Doctor Stephanie Sloan. You've been lied to in order to justify policies that isolated each one of us. There is nothing wrong with touching one another; it will not spread the virus, as you've been led to believe. The study was forged, and the doctor who was duped into lending his name to it was murdered. I know. I was there. The following video should show our confidence in this fact."

As the voice played, Officer Greene stumbled and tried to get clear to where he could see what was playing. The other officers were still standing around the perimeter of the square, not fully comprehending what was happening. Paul couldn't hear the words—there was no audio on the camera—but he could see Stephanie's face projected on the wall.

"What's happening?" Paul's voice came through the walkie-talkie on Officer Green's hip. "Come in, Officer Greene! Come in and tell me what the hell's going on!"

Officer Greene could barely hear Paul's voice over the sound of Stephanie and the commotion of the crowd around him. Bright flashes of white still cut across his field of vision, and he kept rubbing his eyes, trying to get them to adjust. He was stumbling forward, trying to get enough distance between him and the wall to be able to see what was playing there. Meanwhile, he lost track of Nick, who was wandering in the opposite direction, near where Michael and Stephanie were standing.

As Stephanie's face disappeared from the wall, she quickly appeared again, this time with her breasts pressed against Michael's bare chest, her hair dangling messily across her forehead while they kissed. Michael and Stephanie walked out in front of the crowd and unfastened their rings, then let them fall to the bandstand floor with a metallic thud. They locked hands and held them toward the sky. The people were looking from one to another, many not fully processing what was happening.

After Stephanie and Michael's video, Anna and Dennis flashed onto the wall with a shot from the side as he gripped her bare ass with both hands, lifting her in front of him while she tossed her hair back and laughed in a way she hadn't in years. They walked up beside Michael and Stephanie. Anna gave Stephanie a smirk, and they briefly locked eyes before Anna and Dennis dropped their rings to the floor and locked hands in the same way as Michael and Stephanie.

The buzz in the crowd was growing. People were talking with each other and mumbling to themselves. They had become so accustomed to people keeping their distance from one another that this was a stunning breach of protocol.

When Officer Greene got far enough to see the video on the wall, his heart leapt into his throat. It was the same time that he realized he didn't know where Nick was, and Paul's voice was screaming through his walkie-talkie. He had to pick it up.

"I'm here, Mister Reese!," Officer Greene said. "I don't know what's going on, exactly."

"God *damn* it, William! Get that video stopped right fucking *now*! Do you hear me?"

"Yes! Yes, sir. I'm on my way."

The last couple was walking onto the bandstand as Officer Greene made his way to the projector, his shadow flashing across the picture on the wall when Hank and Leslie dropped their rings to the ground and locked hands. Officer Greene slammed the power button, and the light flickered out like a movie projector flipped off in the middle of a film. Everyone was still transfixed on the four couples, standing defiantly on stage in front of them all, risking their own freedom in order to regain it.

"Join us!" the eight of them yelled in chorus, lifting their locked hands higher toward the sky. "Drop your rings! Drop your rings! Drop your rings!"

They began the chant as just the eight of them, but it grew louder with others joining in. It became loud enough that Paul could hear it echoing up the hill to the compound, bouncing off the walls and fluttering through the eaves of the mansion. His blood boiled at the betrayal from all of them, that they'd question the decisions he made. He had done everything he could to keep them alive, and their pettiness over this issue had him shaking in his chair, gripping the armrest tighter with every word of that chant. He switched to the channel for all the officers on his walkie-talkie.

"Kill them!" he screamed.

One of the officers looked down at his walkie-talkie as if surprised it was still there. He lifted it to his mouth.

"What did you say, Mr. Reese?"

"Kill them! All of them!"

Rings were dropping all around the square, thumping to the ground, clanking against each other, with people stepping out from inside of them and embracing. They were pulling each other into group hugs, smiling and hopping together like the energy they were feeling was too much just to stand still.

The officers looked at each other, and many of them wanted no part of where this was headed next. But they knew if they turned their backs on Paul, they'd be some of the first ones being shot. It was time to just follow orders.

"Kill...*everyone?*" Officer Greene asked, hoping he misunderstood the order.

"Now! Every single goddamn person there! Fire your weapons!"

And the gunshots began to ring out in the night air, breaking through the thickness of the March evening, blasts popping among the terrified screams. As bodies collapsed limply to the ground, some with their arms wrapped each other, people scrambled for cover.

"Run!" Stephanie shouted to the other couples, and anyone else who happened to be within earshot. "Get to the front of the courthouse! Go! Go!"

The four couples were further away from the armed officers than almost anyone else, and were able to make it to the side of the building. Stephanie was breathing heavily when they pressed their backs against the tan siding of the courthouse's facade.

"Is everyone okay?" she asked as she looked to her right, counting heads. She counted seven, so she had her group intact. They all looked left and right, nodding. There was chaos in the square to her left, with screaming and people running in every direction. "We're pinned down here, guys. We could make a run for it, but that puts us right out in the open. Any ideas?"

There was silence from the group, with gunshots ringing out through the night. Then they heard "Michael!" from back where they'd come from. They all looked at Michael, whose eyes narrowed as he paused to listen more closely. They heard it again, and he shrugged. Stephanie jerked her head to her left to signal Michael to come over and take a look.

Nick was crouched behind the bandstand, clutching a gun resting against the floorboards. The chains on the shackles were loose enough that he could bring his hands together to hold the gun firmly.

"I got Officer Greene's gun when he was staggering around the stage!" Nick yelled to Michael. "They don't know I'm back here. I nailed a couple of the officers."

Michael looked, and there were two uniformed officers whose bodies were lying between the bandstand and fountain.

"We could get their guns and walkie-talkies," Stephanie said to Michael. "That might allow us to get ourselves enough cover to get out of here and regroup."

"Yeah. You and I could grab the stuff as quickly as we could, then get back here to cover."

"No, wait. What's this 'You and I' stuff? You're hurt, and you're not the world's fastest sprinter when healthy. One of the others can go."

"It's my shoulder, Steph. I don't have a torn Achilles'. I can run just as fast as ever. I bet I'll even beat you."

They both smiled, and she bowed her head to laugh.

"Don't get carried away with yourself. All right. You ready to do this?"

"Yeah. Hold on just a sec." He poked his head around the corner of the courthouse. "Nick! We're gonna try to get their guns and walkie-talkies! Can you help keep our path clear?"

"You got it, brother!" Nick extended the thumb on his right hand. Michael returned the gesture. Meanwhile, Stephanie told the group what they were doing, and for them to stay where they were.

"All right. On three," Michael looked at Stephanie and breathed deeply. "One…Two…"

He took off, getting a few steps ahead of Stephanie. The bodies were thirty feet from where they stood, which made it ten running steps and a quick slide to get low and grab the equipment. Michael's arms churned as he focused his eyes on the body to the left. He could see muzzle flashes in the distance, cracking in the darkness like flickering lanterns. He barely beat Stephanie to the bodies, which lay four feet from each other, and he slid on his side next to it. He snatched a .357 Magnum from the holster on the man's right hip, along with four ammo clips he slid into his pockets, then slipped the walkie-talkie out of its sleeve on his left hip. He looked up, and Stephanie was already sprinting back to the courthouse. *Show off.*

As Michael pulled his feet underneath him to stand, he noticed another gun out of the corner of his eye. It was fifteen feet further from the courthouse, but another gun could make the difference between them getting out of there alive and losing one or more of the group. Maybe it was worth the risk. He made eye contact with Stephanie, who was motioning for him to hurry back to where they were, but he pointed behind him at the gun and raised his right index finger in front of his face. It was shaking.

He wasn't sure he could carry two guns and the walkie-talkie, so he left the walkie-talkie by the officer's body. That'd be a nice luxury for communication, but the gun could save a life. He turned his back to Stephanie, stood and ran toward the gun. He dove and slid head first to it, and he heard a shot from behind him, near the bandstand. He wrapped his right hand around the gun, turned and stood to run back when he felt a piercing pain in his right calf like being stung by a nest full of hornets, and he collapsed to the ground, slamming his head hard into the dirt. Two more shots fired behind him, toward the bandstand. Nick ducked for cover; the hammer was locked back on his gun, indicating he was out of ammo. Leaning out from around the courthouse wall, Stephanie fired three times at the man, who was able to crouch low enough for the bandstand to mostly protect him. He fired back, and Stephanie spun back, the bullets clanking off the side of the building, sending shards of wood scattering into the air.

The officer grabbed Michael's feet and began dragging him away, Michael's face skipping off the rocky ground as he was pulled further from Stephanie and the others. When Stephanie saw Michael's body being taken, her blood turned cold, and she felt frozen in place. Was he already dead? She only knew he was shot, but she had no idea where he was hit. His body looked limp, though, as it bounced across the dry ground. Whether he was alive or dead, she couldn't let them take him away. Her breath was short, but she turned around the corner and screamed from deep in her chest, a guttural roar that she didn't think she was capable of producing. It was the sound of rage, of hopelessness and desperation. Of hate rushing through her veins, extending out through her arms, taking hold of her body.

She pulled the trigger rapidly, emptying the clip in seconds. As her finger kept pushing the trigger, she heard no sound. The gun was empty. As her eyes focused, she could see nothing from where Michael had been except the lines in the dirt where his head and arms had dragged the earth. The chaos of earlier was over. Several bodies lay strewn across the ground. Tents with bullet holes had collapsed upon themselves, buckling and falling to the ground around their owners' bodies. Silence hung like a pall over the square. Stephanie's knees buckled, collapsing her to the ground; she sunk her face into her hands.

Nick crouched and put his shackled right hand on Stephanie's back, then placed his head on her shoulder.

"I'm sorry I couldn't do more," he said. "My bullets ran out, and I was stuck."

She wiped the back of her hand across her cheeks, the cold of her tears chilling her skin.

"I know," she threw her head back, and her hair splashed against the middle of her back. "I know you did your best."

Anna walked up behind her and sat next to Nick. Stephanie looked at her and tried to force a smile.

"I can't believe that happened," Stephanie said. "Look at this." She lifted her arms to motion at the dead bodies piled up across the square.

"I don't know what to think. It's insane."

"Is he dead?" Stephanie said, to no one in particular. "Is Michael dead?"

"No. No. I'm sure he's fine," Anna said, rubbing her back. "We're gonna find him. Right, Nick?"

"Yeah. I couldn't really see from behind the bandstand, but Michael's a fighter. We'll do anything we have to in order to get him back."

Stephanie hung her head and threaded her fingers through her hair, tucking it behind one ear at a time. She wiped her face one more time.

"I know where we can go," she said.

Anna looked at Nick, then to Stephanie. "What?"

"We can't stay here, and I know where we can go," Stephanie said. "They'll come back if we stay."

Nick shrugged. "Okay, then. Lead the way, boss."

He stood and grabbed her left arm as best as he could. Anna scrambled to the other side and reached for her right. They helped Stephanie to her feet, and she wiped the dirt off her jeans.

"I'm a total mess," she said.

"We're gonna keep you anyway," Anna smiled and winked at her. Stephanie cracked a small smile, perhaps more like a smirk. Anna would take it.

Stephanie walked toward the rest of the group, still waiting by the front of the courthouse.

"Do you guys know the old abandoned warehouse off of Juniper?" she saw a few nods of recognition, but mostly blank stares. "Well, whether you know it or not, I think that's where we're headed. It's got good vantage points, and a second story where we can get high ground on anyone who approaches us. Anyone got a better idea?"

She looked back and forth at the group, and no one spoke up.

"Then it's settled. That's where we'll meet. Anyone got any guns at home? Raise your hand."

Hank, Leslie, Trish and her man, Quinn, all raised their hands.

"Okay. You guys take the walkie-talkie Nick grabbed and gather up whatever guns you can carry, then meet us at the warehouse. Also, grab something to cut Nick loose with. Keep in touch with us on channel three. The officers are apparently using channel two, so steer clear from that."

Nick handed Hank his walkie-talkie, and he motioned for the other three to follow him. They set off in one direction, and Stephanie began walking in the other, with Nick, Anna, and Dennis in tow.

Stephanie called for Nick, and he jogged up beside her. She tossed him a pair of magazines for his gun. He juggled but caught them.

"Nice catch, considering you're handicapped," she said. "Grabbed these off the dead officer back there. Figured you might be able to use them."

"Cool. Thanks." They took a few silent steps before he spoke again. "How ya doing?"

"Trying to keep all that shit off my mind, to be honest. If we don't stay alive ourselves, I guess it doesn't much matter what happened to Michael because we won't be around to help him."

He nodded. "Michael's a brother to me, and I know how… important he is to you. We're gonna get him back."

"Yeah," she looked up into the black sky. "I hope you're right."

They walked for a few more minutes before Anna walked up beside Stephanie.

"Hey, Steph," she said. "Remember you were talking about channels on the walkie-talkie back there?"

"Sure. What about it?"

"You said the officers were on channel two."

"Right."

"Well, I was thinking, maybe they're still on channel two. And, if so, we just might be able to make that work for us."

61

Officer Greene and the eight other remaining officers trudged through the mansion's front door, carrying Michael's body, and the stench of death entered with them.

Not a word had been spoken on the walk back up the hill from the square, where they'd together killed forty-three men and women of Alessandra, their friends and neighbors. People they used to invite to their pool parties and share a drink with before the virus struck were now lying across the cold ground, their bullet-ridden bodies twisted and mangled together. They not only had to watch these people die, but they had to participate in their destruction.

Most of the men knew it wasn't the right course of action, but they were sworn officers. When the leader is crazy enough to make an order that violent and radical, not to follow it would be to sign a suicide note. The gun would turn on you in the time it took to lower your weapon. They weren't willing participants in Paul's vengeful ambush, but they also weren't strong or organized enough to mount a resistance. Collective action dilemmas are real. Who's going to be the first to bring up the possibility of fighting back against the order? How does that person know that even the question won't get him killed? Easier to go along with it, and try to pretend the targets aren't human. Your conscience may never let you off the hook, but at least you'll live long enough to have those sleepless nights where you wake up screaming.

As they walked through the hall and into the house's den, they saw Paul sitting by the window, overlooking the square. Officer Greene scanned the room.

"What should we do with Michael? You said we should bring him."

"He's still unconscious?" Paul said without taking his eyes off the window. "Just dump him in that room to your left and lock the door. The key's in the lock."

The men who were carrying him followed the instructions. Officer Greene turned back to Paul.

"Where's Audrey?"

Paul rose from his chair and began stalking toward Officer Greene. "Fuck Audrey. Where's Nick?"

Officer Greene opened his mouth, but no sound came out. He bowed his head.

"Jesus, William," Paul rolled his eyes. "Could you guys have fucked this up any more? What the hell happened down there?"

"I don't know, sir. Everything was fine until the projector started. The light was so bright, and I was so close to the wall that I couldn't make sense of what was happening for a few moments. I think we were all stunned."

He looked at the other men, and many nodded in agreement. Paul turned and began pacing back and forth before speaking.

"Well, *something* needs to be done. This is an uprising. More than that, this is a goddamn *coup*. Look at the lives they cost us today. Their act of recklessness killed those people on the square this evening, including your fellow officers. I even watched them loot those men's bodies. That was a horrifying act of *betrayal* of Audrey, me, and all of you. *They* killed those people, not *you*. Make no mistake about that. You had no choice in the face of their foul act of rebellion than to put it down with force. The only alternative is anarchy. The only alternative is *madness!* You did your duty, and you should hold your heads high for that. Mistakes were made, no doubt. But, when the moment called, you all acted valiantly. You put your emotions aside and did the difficult work *required* of those of us who want to make this experiment in governing, in *living*, function.

"I know that couldn't have been easy for any of you, but that's the point. *Nothing* worth doing is easy. Save simplicity for elementary school. We're adults. We're *men*. And we're trying to keep order in a community that's trying to unravel before us. We're the only ones equipped to arrest that unraveling before it gets out of control. They're storming the gate, but they're gonna meet hell when they get there."

Paul stopped pacing and looked at the men, his eyes darting from one to the other, making eye contact with each one individually.

"You men are the hell Audrey and I are unleashing to ensure the future of Alessandra, your home. We're proud of you. We know you stand with us to protect and defend. This place cannot only live on but *thrive* going forward, once we can quash this. I just need you to stay with me a little longer tonight, and we'll wake up tomorrow with a new morning. I'll issue a directive that the rings are no longer needed, and people can reunite with their families as desired starting immediately. That should give people the morale boost they need to get past tonight. They'll be thankful for what you've done as well. We all will bring freedom to them. It'll be a beautiful day. Are you ready to help me get there?"

The men affirmed that they'd stick with this through the night, some enthusiastically, others with some reluctance but wanting to find a way to buy into what Paul was saying. Could he be right? Could they be the good guys in this? His seeming certainty was at least a little inspiring. Almost all the men were distraught on the walk to the compound, with women's terrified screams echoing through their heads, but most were now feeling righteous, like they had a holy mission. This wasn't just following orders; it was fighting for a cause. They would do what they had

to, even if that meant taking lives. Kill a dozen to save a hundred.
This wasn't a battle they asked for, but they were prepared to
fight it all the same.

Paul started to speak again when all of their walkie-talkies
crackled to life.

"Hank…Come in, Hank."

"That's Stephanie!" Officer Greene said. "I remember that
voice from the video."

"Shut up," Paul said. "Listen."

"Copy that," Hank said. "Where are we meeting up?"

"There's a big abandoned warehouse on Juniper. Two doors
east of that is a house I think we can hole up in and fight if
needed. Wish we had some ammo, but we're out. We'll have to
draw them in. I'm not sure who lived at the house, but there's
some food and water to last us for at least a day or two. It's not
gonna be easy."

The officers looked around at each other, and Paul was
smiling.

"Ten-four," Hank said. "We got some food too, so at least we
won't starve. If we can get them close enough, we'll have a
chance."

"Yeah. God help us. See you guys in a few?"

"On our way. Over and out."

Paul laughed and clapped his hands several times.

"They forgot to switch the channel. That's too perfect. Okay,
gentlemen, we know where they are, and we know they're
unarmed. But don't get complacent. An animal is most dangerous
when it's cornered. Be ready for a fight, but know you have the
upper hand. Go!"

Several of the men thrust their fist into the air as they turned
to leave.

"William," Paul said, and Officer Greene turned around. "A
moment, please. Let them go on. They can handle this for now."

After weaving their way through the halls of the mansion, Paul led Officer Greene into a study, where they sat in high-backed chairs with thick upholstery in forest green. The room had an expansive Persian rug spanning most of its length, and two large glass-cased bookshelves that were full of mostly nineteenth-century literature—Officer Greene spotted Thackeray, Dostoyevsky, Spyri, Goethe, and Turgenev on a quick glance, and he guessed most all of them were gathering impressive amounts of dust. As they sat, Paul placed his hand on Officer Greene's shoulder.

"William, how do you feel things are going? With you and the officers, I mean?"

"Today, or generally?"

"Let's say both."

"Well…I didn't expect to have this role. But I've been doing what I could to fill in since Captain Bray passed away." Officer Greene spoke of Danny, who Paul told him was killed by the people in the quarantine camp while he was delivering them food. "It hasn't been easy, but I think we've been doing pretty well, considering."

Paul nodded silently, then placed a finger to his lips.

"I know it's been difficult, but I appreciate you sticking it out. What happened with Nick down there wasn't good, but maybe I've pushed you too hard too quickly. Still, I'm confident you'll get a chance to make that up to me soon. And I'm confident you won't fail."

"No, sir. I won't fail. I'm ready for whatever you need me to do. I do have a question, though, if you don't mind."

Paul leaned forward. "Go ahead."

"Is there something…*wrong* with Audrey? I haven't heard anything from her since the morning when she wouldn't answer her bedroom door when I knocked, and the men are starting to get worried."

Paul sat back in his chair and folded his arms across his chest. "Are they?"

"Absolutely, they are. It'd be great if there was something I could tell them."

"Well, what do you all *think* is wrong with her?"

"Um, I'm not sure what you mean."

"Surely the men must have speculated. You must have discussed it, right?"

"It's not really our place to guess, sir."

"But you *have* guessed. Yes?"

"I…I don't understand why you're asking this," Officer Greene stuttered. "What difference does it make?"

"I'm looking to you to potentially be a leader for me. Us," he said, putting a hand on Officer Greene's back. "And I need unquestioned loyalty from anyone who's going to lead for me. I need to be able to trust you fully. One hundred percent. When I tell you to do something, I don't need you asking for my motivations, or psychoanalyzing me like I can see you doing right now." Paul's stare was getting colder, his eyes seeming to melt into pools of blue, and his hand was sliding up to the back of Officer Greene's neck and squeezing. Tighter every second. "When I say jump, you ask how high. And when I tell you how high, you say you'll go higher. 'Why?' is not a viable or welcome question. When I ask you for something, I expect to get it. Capiche?"

Officer Greene winced as he tried to nod, but could only barely rock his head against the grip of Paul's left hand. The piercing pain felt like vertebrae were going to start popping like a string of firecrackers set alight with a long fuse. Finally, Paul let go.

"But you're right," Paul said. "It doesn't make any difference. Except that you failed a second test. That's two strikes. If there's a third, I'm confident neither of us will be happy."

"I'm sorry. I won't let it happen again. What do you need me to do?"

Paul reached into a basket by the wall and pulled out some rope. "Take these, and go secure Michael in that room, assuming he's still alive. If he needs water or food, go ahead and get that taken care of. Then join your crew. Hopefully, they'll have already finished the job, and you can just high-five them on the way back."

62

"You guys weren't fucking around when you said you had guns," Stephanie said, as Hank handed her a metallic gray AR15 Model 1 rifle. "This looks like something from the movies."

"Basic perimeter defense, my friend," Hank laughed. "You comfortable handling that thing?"

"I think so. What are those you're carrying?"

"Mossberg Blaze twenty-two LR. Since you can't just go to your local gun shop and buy an AK forty-seven in this freedom-loving country of ours, these are basically the next best thing."

"Jesus."

"Jesus or not, you're glad we have this stuff now, aren't you?"

"Abso-friggin-lutely."

Stephanie saw Nick out of the corner of her eye walking over. She turned back to Hank.

"How'd you get Nick out of the shackles?"

"Big-ass bolt cutters. Lying over there by the wall," he gestured behind him with his thumb.

She smiled. "Nicely done. Now go get everyone armed to the teeth."

Nick approached. "Nice thinking with that deke on the walkie-talkie. Think they heard it?"

Stephanie shrugged. "It was Anna's idea. And, no real way of knowing. I'm sure they'll switch channels now, and they're gonna be cautious, as should we. These things aren't all that powerful, and there are only a few channels we can use."

They looked away from each other, and Stephanie curled her head around the corner to look up the street from the warehouse second floor toward the town square, and Audrey's compound beyond it. The streets were quiet. She figured they'd hear the officers coming. But, even if they didn't, hopefully no one would be expecting Stephanie and the others to be in the warehouse, looking down on them as they passed.

"You still think we're gonna get Michael back?" she said.

"I've gotta think so. Something's gotta keep us going."

Stephanie nodded.

"There are others, ya know."

Stephanie snapped her head back in, and turned to look at Nick.

"Others?" she narrowed her eyes. "Oh, the quarantine. Shit."

"Yeah. I know people got so caught up in getting through every day that we were pretty much forgotten about up there. It's hell. And now we know…I mean, is it true? What you said in that video?"

"I'm sorry to say it is," Stephanie exhaled. "I found the original study and talked to the doctor who conducted it. The whole thing was fabricated as a facade for maintaining control over us."

"So now we know for sure just how great an injustice it is that they're up there. That *I* was up there."

"You're right. It was always wrong the way they handled it, but yeah. They locked people up and destroyed lives because they didn't want to give up the hold they had over us. The only good thing about tonight is everybody knows it."

"Well, the ones who *lived* know it, anyway."

Stephanie bowed her head, fighting off tears that were inevitably going to come again. This wasn't the time to reflect on everything that had happened, though. She knew she needed focus.

"Let's get into position," she said. "It's dark, so we may not have a lot of warning if they come. It's not like we're gonna see them from a mile away. We're gonna have one shot once they get here."

Stephanie looked at the rest of the people and raised her arms wide overhead. They all stopped and looked at her. She put one fist in the air and spun her arm around, signaling everyone to get in position. The warehouse's second floor had been blown out over time, and it was mostly open to the elements along the front facing the street, and the back facing a field of grass in the direction of the wall.

During the day, they'd have been at an even bigger advantage because they'd be able to see a good distance in all directions. The dark made it harder, though. They were fortunate the moon was nearly full that night, so they got some light reflected from there, but it was mostly shadows straight into town after twenty feet or so. In the opposite direction, Stephanie could see that moonlight sparkling off Lake Chatuga, a couple hundred yards away.

The "Man your positions" signal doubled as a "Be very quiet" signal, given the lack of light. Their best bet was to hear the officers coming. Maybe they'd catch boots hitting pavement along Juniper Street. Or maybe they'd hear the men talking. But even more importantly, nothing was going to give Stephanie and the rest of them up faster than making noise themselves. They were well positioned if they stayed as still and quiet as possible. One wrong move or sound, though, and they didn't have the firearms training to win a fair fight with these guys.

Stephanie was looking out over the street side, and Anna was set up to watch the back of the warehouse. Stephanie's mouth was dry, and she could feel sweat beading on her forehead despite the cool March night air. She was a doctor, not a soldier. She was trained for emergency rooms, not foxholes; saving lives, not taking them. The stillness was unnerving. She was being hunted, like a wild animal. It wasn't a human feeling. Her skin crawled, and her heart fluttered, anticipating the piercing of a bullet at any moment. In the dark, her life could end without her ever realizing it. Everything she did, erased with the snapping of a trigger. Maybe the muzzle flash would ignite in the cold blackness below her, and that would be the last thing she'd see before everything went black, and nothing mattered. She wondered if the others, crouched in their ready positions, guns resting at their sides, felt the same anxiety—that this could be where their lives end. She thought of all those people on the square earlier in the evening. Did they see it coming? Did they have time to think once more about their loved ones, to reflect on a life lived, or did a switch just flip, sending them careening into the ultimate void, feeling nothing? *Being* nothing? The next second was far from guaranteed to any of them, enveloped in this darkness. This quiet.

She suddenly saw shapes, nearly below her, at the corner of the warehouse, swimming through the dark. She turned and saw Anna motioning that she saw the same thing. They were approaching the warehouse from both sides. It was time.

Stephanie crouched, pressed against the partial wall that looked over the street to her left, as she watched the shapes become more fully formed, looking like humans, their legs pumping in quick intervals, their rifles clutched to their chests.

They moved close to the warehouse, directly underneath her. She sucked in a deep breath, determined to hold it in her lungs until the men passed. If the officers heard any noise and looked up, there was little preventing Stephanie from being spotted and giving away the rest of the group. They had the high ground, but most of them had little to no firearms training, particularly in a life-or-death gun battle in the dark. The sooner they were spotted, the more bodies Stephanie was going to see laid out on that second-floor landing.

Every noise was magnified. Her own breathing rattled against the inside of her skull, the percussion making it sound like it was reverberating into the air around her. It was hard not to think they heard it. Surely her rapid heartbeat carried its *thump thump* down to the men making their way through the blackness that surrounded them. How could they not hear it? But there was no reaction from the men. No eyes turned upward. No heads looked around in confusion. They appeared determined and resolute. They knew their prey were two buildings beyond the warehouse, and their focus remained in front of them.

As they began to clear to Stephanie's right, she raised her right arm, and everyone lifted their guns, cocking them into place. Anna followed suit, her left arm skyward, signaling that the officers below were also clearing past her. Stephanie and Anna gazed across the warehouse at each other, both of them holding their arms high, waiting for the right moment to tell their team to fire.

The weight of the moment blanketed Stephanie. Her arm and Anna's were the only fulcrums standing between a group of eight men and their likely death. The men had been tricked, and were perfectly positioned for her team's considerable firepower to take down quickly with a few accurate shots. Her worries about her own death were sliding out of her mind, replaced by the concern over what it would feel like to command the death of eight other people. She knew they wouldn't hesitate to kill her if given the chance, but that was an intellectual stance—emotionally, she wasn't sure how this would affect her. She had never killed anyone, but she'd sure as hell come close a few times in recent days.

The men were in a tight group and reached nearly to the far corner of the warehouse. Stephanie took another look at Anna, and they both nodded. At the same time, both raised their arm slightly, then brought them down like pulling a rip cord.

As if they'd pulled the trigger themselves, guns immediately rang out, shattering the quiet night like a hammer smashing a set of China, the pieces scattering across the floor. Stephanie could see shapes flay about, then fall to the ground, still and lifeless. Some shapes moved, but then staggered and collapsed, just short of cover. Smoke floated in front of her, from her own gun and that of others, filling up the sky like fog and setting a filter between her and the men below. It took several seconds for the firing to stop, and the quiet to once again invade.

Stephanie tried to scan the ground below, but it was tough to see. How many bodies lay there? There had been four men on each side of the warehouse. Were there four bodies on her side? Were there four on Anna's? Stephanie leaned forward, scampering across the open facade to try to count.

"How many did we get?" she whispered to Hank, crouched along the other end of the opening.

"I know I got two. I can see them down there. Pretty sure I see another one to their left. Do you see a fourth?"

Stephanie looked toward Anna, raising up four fingers with a shrug. Anna's head pivoted, and she held up three fingers. Stephanie's stomach turned to knots, and she swallowed hard. Unless they just couldn't see, there were still two armed men below. And now the element of surprise was gone.

She heard a shot, and a large splinter flew off the partial wall in front of her, somersaulting through the air and clipping off her shoulder to the floor. Another one pierced the wall above her, and took out a three-foot chunk.

"Get flat on the ground!" Hank said, motioning downward with both arms. "Everyone!"

People started to flop on their stomachs, but then there was a shriek from Quinn, and he was clutching his chest. Leslie crawled over to him and rolled him over on his back, pressing a hand to his chest as blood began to soak through his shirt. Trish covered her mouth and began to scream, then ran toward Quinn. She knew CPR, and she thought she could keep him awake. Then a bullet entered through her right ear, tearing off part of her skull and sending her body limply to the floor. Four seconds, and three people dead. Everyone was prone. No one dared move.

Hank looked at Stephanie and caught her eyes. He motioned with his right hand for her to move to his left. Then he pointed down and behind him, signaling where the shots were coming from. Stephanie nodded and did as instructed. She could see in Hank's eyes that he was struggling to hold it together after seeing Trish and Quinn killed, but he knew the people around him still needed him. He then waved to get the attention of Nick, Anna, and Dennis, and swung his right arm wide around his body to signal them to walk around the outside of the building and set up on the street side at the other partial wall. Crouch-walking with guns clutched in front of them, they did just that.

Hank held up two fingers first to Nick, Anna, and Dennis, then behind him to Stephanie and pointed downward. Stephanie understood he meant there were two shooters left. Then Hank held an index finger to his lips, and everyone held still. Listening for any sound that could offer a clue where the men were. The wait was interminable. Stephanie glanced at the bodies lying on the other side of the floor. She hadn't known Quinn very well, but seeing Trish there was difficult. *How did she get wrapped up in all this anyway? She just wanted to brighten people's days a little bit. She didn't have a mean or violent bone in her body, but half her head is blown off. She didn't deserve this.* Stephanie thought about Trish's friendly voice that always gave you a warm feeling whenever she wished you good morning. Patients talked about Trish all the time; the doctors used to theorize that a lot of the patients weren't even sick when they came in. They just wanted to see Trish. How could a life like that be snuffed out so unceremoniously, with an unfired AR15 leaning against her stomach? It wasn't fair. She deserved to die at home, surrounded by friends and family. In this chaos, who even knew if she'd get a burial?

Stephanie still hadn't heard a sound from below, but Hank's head lifted, and he motioned to Anna, pointing behind her and to her right. She looked, but turned back and shrugged. Hank bent and straightened his arm a few times, imploring her to walk back that direction. When she did, she found a tennis ball. Stephanie didn't see it at first either, but once she started to pick it up, she didn't know why she missed the bright yellow orb in the first place. Anna held it up at Hank, and he nodded. Then he pointed her toward the stairs on the other side of the floor, and held out two hands, pressing them downward to signal for her to take it easy. Walking slowly on her tiptoes, Anna made it to the stairwell. Hank looked in her direction, held his right arm straight out in front of him with his hand balled up in a fist, then opened it. She nodded.

Anna held the tennis ball over the top step, and let go. It dropped, bounced a foot off the stair, then skipped to the next one, clipping that one once more before hitting the next stair down. It hit nearly all of them on its way down to the bottom floor. While it did, Anna quickly made her way back to where she'd been, next to Dennis and Nick. Again, they all waited silently.

Stephanie heard footsteps. Light, but unmistakable. They were converging on where the tennis ball had bounced, guns drawn, no doubt. Hank slowly spun and stood, his guns pointed at the thin wooden floor. He paused and listened again; Stephanie couldn't breathe. The tennis ball could draw the shooters into Hank's sights, but it also brought them inside the building, where there was no way to see them. They were trained for firearm combat. What if they charged up the stairs after seeing the tennis ball lying there? How many of Stephanie's team would survive that sort of assault? She watched Hank, and hoped.

Suddenly, Hank fired, the sound so much louder than she remembered it from earlier. He pumped the gun, round after round, tearing through the wooden floor, sending shards of twisted maple careening around him. She could see the floor beginning to rip into pieces not far from his feet, and could almost swear it was going to collapse, and he would shatter most of the bones in his legs on impact with the floor below. But he kept firing until the AR15 clicked, and the echoes died down, leaving Stephanie's ears with a persistent hum that morphed into a light ring. Other than that, there was quiet. No return fire.

Hank stepped lightly toward the stairs, and Stephanie watched him from behind. She glanced at Anna, who looked like she didn't know whether to stay where she was or jump to the street and run screaming into the night. Nick wrapped his hands around his gun and sat against the partial wall, his knees shivering against his chest.

When Hank reached the top of the stairs, he swiveled his gun and pointed it toward the floor, its butt pressed hard against his right shoulder. Slowly, he began to descend. Where the tennis ball bounced, he used a deft touch, his feet dropping like feathers upon each stair as he walked to the ground level, his finger twitching in front of the trigger of his AR15. From Stephanie's perspective, Hank's head descended closer to the floor with each careful step, bobbing slightly as it went down a few inches at a time. After a few steps, all she could see was his forehead and dark hair, curled atop his head. Then, with another step, he was gone.

She braced for a burst of gunfire, pressing her hands to her ears. It was a roll of the dice at this point. If guns blazed, there was a solid chance the next head she'd see poking above the second-floor stairs would be the one of the man who would kill her, along with Anna and Nick. Whether she had time to get off a shot or not, the odds of any of them being able to get a headshot on a trained police officer in the dark were just north of zero.

Just when Stephanie thought the quiet wouldn't break, there was gunfire, and her heart skipped a beat. Her muscles tightened as she squeezed her head, trying to muffle the sound as at least one gun roared through the building, echoing off the floorboards and soaring into the eaves. When it stopped, she nearly screamed. What lay next was beyond her control. She scampered across the floor to Anna, Dennis, and Nick, huddling together with them. Anna wrapped her arms around Stephanie from behind, and Nick placed his AR15 across Stephanie's left shoulder. They trembled in the night air, petrified at what would happen next. They could jump from there, but the landing was uncertain in the dark, and there was little reason to think they'd get far. They were cornered.

Stephanie heard feet hit the stairs, faster this time, ascending with purpose. Nick raised the gun and pressed against the trigger as a head emerged.

"Whoa, guys! It's me," Hank said, raising his left arm. "I thought I saw some movement in the street out there, but it looks like it's all clear. The shooters are dead."

Relief washed over Stephanie like a warm shower, rinsing her body of the debilitating fear it was harboring. Moments before, her life had seemed fragile and temporary, but now she had a new start. She had survived the most difficult night of her life, and she did it with trusted friends at her side. She turned to face Nick.

"This night isn't over, is it?" she said.

"I don't know about you, but not for me. We can't let them regroup. We've got to go to the compound tonight."

Stephanie nodded. "Yeah. We don't know how bad off Michael is. We can't just leave him there overnight. They're short on men, and they won't be expecting us. We need to take advantage of that."

Nick rose to his feet and walked over to Hank. He extended his hand, and they shook.

"I don't think we could have made it without you, man," Nick said.

"Did what anybody would do. Glad we got out of it alive," Hank looked away, then back at Nick. "You're going up there to be a hero, aren't you?"

"I don't have a choice. There's no point in saving myself if I leave everyone else behind."

"I'll come with you."

"No. Anna and Dennis need someone to stay with them and help them get somewhere safe. Let us take care of this. You've done plenty."

Hank nodded solemnly. "All right. I'll keep the other walkie-talkie. You guys let me know if you need backup. I'll come runnin'."

"You bet," Nick reached his arms out and wrapped them around Hank's shoulders, slapping his back as they embraced.

Meanwhile, Anna tried unsuccessfully to convince Stephanie not to embark on the rescue mission.

"Michael better be worth it," Anna said. "Because if something happens to you up there, I swear to fucking God…"

"I've got this, Anna. I won't take any chances I don't have to, but I can't leave him up there. We've got too much history together. He's too much a part of my life."

Anna sighed. "Just promise you'll be careful."

"Pinky swear."

They hugged, and Anna held Stephanie for several seconds, squeezing her like she didn't want to let go. Stephanie knew this could be the last time she'd feel the embrace of her best friend since childhood. She knew she might not return from trying to rescue Michael. But everything they had been through that day had meant nothing if they just left their friends to rot in custody of the leadership. She didn't know what tomorrow would bring, but she couldn't chance that they'd double down and come out fighting. She wasn't going to let Michael be a pawn in that. If that meant she didn't live to see the next day, she was comfortable with that.

Nick tapped Stephanie on the shoulder, and she pulled away from Anna. She waved briefly and joined Nick heading down the stairs, then out the back side of the warehouse and into the night, toward the compound.

Five minutes later, Hank, Anna, and Dennis were about to descend the stairs when they found themselves staring down the bullet of a rifle pointed at their heads.

"Hey, guys," Officer Greene said. "Drop the weapons."

They let go of their guns, and they slammed to the wooden floor with a hard clank.

"Why don't you all raise your hands and come down the stairs," Officer Greene said. "You're gonna want to come with me."

63

Paul opened the door to Zac's room and stepped inside, shutting it closed behind him. Zac sat up in a chair by the opposite wall, reading a book.

"Whatcha reading'?" Paul asked. Zac looked up.

"*Paradise Lost.* Found it on the desk over here. Did you know it's actually a poem?"

Paul ignored the question. "Looks like you're feeling better."

"Yeah. Headache's pretty much gone. No more swimming around and blurry vision. The words on the page even make sense."

"Good to hear."

Zac paused a moment, then closed the book and laid it down on the desk.

"So, thanks for helping me. Maybe I'd have ended up dying in a ditch out there if you guys hadn't brought me up and got me better. I appreciate it."

"Sure. You helped me, so I figured it was the least I could do. Couldn't just watch you die out there."

Zac nodded. "Now that that's out of the way, you and I both know why I did all that. And we know why I was on my way up here last night. Is that deal still on the table?"

Paul lowered his head and leaned against the wall by the door.

"I think we can work something out. Do you know what you're gonna do?"

"The anger is deep. *Really* deep. I've buried it—or, at least, tried to—for what seems like a long time now. That seems like another life ago, ya know? It seems like that husband and father couldn't have been me, that I'm a completely different person. And maybe that's not even wrong. Maybe I've changed so much that I basically am. I feel like the old Zac would have sympathized with her. Maybe would have seen all this more from her perspective, tried to make sense of it. Why she did what she did. The pressure she must have been under. I think he'd try to find a way to forgive her."

Paul pushed himself off the wall and began walking across the room. "And the new Zac?"

"That's what I don't know. It seems like it's been forever, but I really haven't gotten to know this version of me yet. I've fantasized about the opportunity to come face to face with the person who destroyed my old life and led me here. But that was never *real*. That was in my head. And it could play out however I liked it. If I'm actually in the same room with her? Alone? No repercussions?" Zac took a deep breath, staring at nothing in particular. "I just don't know. I might snap. Break every bone in her body. I might just break down and ask her why. Seek to understand. Or I might walk in, slit her throat, and walk back out with a smile stretched wide across my face. It makes me nervous, honestly. Is that something I want to learn about myself? What will I do if confronted with the source of all my pain and suffering? 'I don't know' is the only answer. If you'll hold up your end of the bargain, we'll find out soon."

Paul dug into his pocket and pulled out a key. He laid it on top of the book next to Zac.

"Walk out of this room and down the hall to your right. Her room's the third one on the left. This key will get you in," Paul said, his hand still on top of the key. "And this is important: Don't let anyone see you go in or out. Okay? Nobody."

"All right. I'll be careful."

Paul walked back to the door and opened it, then paused before exiting. He looked back toward Zac.

"Take your time. Go over there whenever you're ready. Also, I left a knife in your dresser if you want it."

"Thanks for the chance to work this out; I needed it. I know she's your sister—"

Paul interrupted, "Not anymore she's not." He walked out and shut the door.

Sitting in his room, Paul ended his walkie-talkie conversation with Officer Greene, who told him Stephanie and Nick weren't there when he arrived at the warehouse, but he had the others who remained alive under his control. They hadn't been willing to say where Stephanie and Nick were—at least, not yet. Paul thought he had a way of figuring it out, though. Officer Greene told him Hank's walkie-talkie had been set to channel four. Paul got up and walked down the hall through the den, and stepped into the room where Michael was lying on the floor, his arms and legs strapped together with rope. Paul took a gun out of the waistband of his pants and held it to Michael's head; Michael began writhing and mumbling through the cloth threaded between his teeth.

Paul switched his walkie-talkie to channel four and pushed the button to talk.

"Stephanie. Come in, Stephanie. We need to have a chat."

Paul heard nothing, and waited. Five seconds. Ten. He pressed the button again.

"Stephanie, I have Michael. I'm willing to work something out. Talk to me."

Almost immediately this time: "Who is this?" she said.

"I think you know who it is. You want to get your boy back?"

"He's my ex-husband. Do what you want with him. I'm gonna save myself and my friends out here. We're in good shape."

"Oh, come on, Steph. Don't play coy. I saw you two in that little porn you made. You look like you work out."

"That was just for show, so we could make it clear what a fraud you and your sister are. You and your little henchmen are through, asshole."

"Fair enough. Then I guess you won't mind if I pull the trigger and kill Michael right now?"

Silence.

"Great! He's taking up valuable space anyway. On three. One…"

"Wait! Fuck."

"That's what I thought. You give a shit. We both know it. Fortunately for you and Mikey here, I'm not a monster. I'm willing to let him go."

"Then do it. Let me talk to him for a second, and release him. I'll meet him somewhere out here."

"It's not gonna be quite *that* easy. Come on up. Alone. Unarmed. We'll negotiate. Rap a little."

There was a long pause.

"My patience is wearing—"

"Fine! Yeah. I'll come. Give me thirty minutes."

"You've got five before I start firing bullets into him."

"But I'm at least ten minutes away."

"You better hustle then. See you in five."

He turned off the walkie-talkie and looked at his wristwatch. It was 9:52.

64

Stephanie clipped the walkie-talkie to her belt and started jogging. Nick followed suit.

"Doesn't really change our plan," she said. "Just got to pick up the pace a little."

"Yeah. We'll stick with it. You gonna be okay going up there alone?"

"Not much choice, is there? I wish he didn't have Michael, but he does. And I'm not leaving him behind."

They kept jogging, picking up the pace. Stephanie figured they were three minutes away if they moved quickly.

"There is one thing that's bothering me, though," she said.

"What's that?"

"Paul seemed to know I was alive."

"Yeah, maybe. Could have been a guess."

"It's possible. But I thought he sounded awfully confident."

"What's your point?"

"Well, why wouldn't he assume his men killed me? He's probably the one who sent them, or at least knew about it. And if so, how would he know I survived?"

"Maybe he didn't know about it?"

"Maybe. Or maybe someone told him. Another officer who found the others."

"Shit, Steph. We can't think about that. Even if it's true, there's nothing we can do about it right now. Let's try to think positive. We've got enough to deal with in front of us."

"Yeah," she shook her head, and her breathing was getting heavier. "I just wonder."

They churned their legs harder as they reached the final hill up to the compound, and were both bending over with their hands on their knees at the top.

"Good...luck...in there," Nick said, between breaths. He held out his fist, and she bumped it with hers.

"You too."

Nick jogged down the side of the hill around the north end of the compound. Stephanie pushed the doorbell. It was 9:57.

The door opened, and a bald, thin man in a dark suit stood inside it. The expression on his face seemed sullen, with his sunken cheekbones and large lips curled into a frown. His weak chin was nearly concave, turning underneath his mouth.

"Welcome, Doctor Sloan," he said. "Mister Reese is expecting you. I'll show you to him."

He walked ahead, and she followed down a long hall toward the den. This was the most well-lit building she'd been in for at least a year, far more even than the hospital. The rhythm of their steps nearly matched as they walked across the marble floor. The hall was almost palace-like. She had never seen anything like it, especially in a place like Alessandra. There were columns rising ten feet in the air along the walls, flanked by floor-to-ceiling windows and gold-flaked trim that twirled amid a cream backdrop. Standing on a hill above a town full of people who could barely find food to get them to the next day, the opulence was breathtaking.

They turned a corner, and she could see the den ahead of them, with Paul standing behind Michael, who was sitting in a chair, his arms tied behind it and his ankles tied to the legs. There was a small television set up in front of them, facing away from Stephanie as she approached. Paul was smiling broadly, and Michael's mouth was sealed with a rag wrapped around the back of his head.

"I see them," Stephanie said. "I'll take it from here. Thanks."

"As you wish," the man said, then spun and walked back the other way. Stephanie kept walking and reached the hardwood floor of the den.

"Happy to see you, Stephanie," Paul said. "Michael's not all that talkative right now, but I'm sure he's glad to see you here too."

Getting closer, Stephanie could see Michael's face was a purple-spotted mess of jagged cuts and scrapes, one swollen eye and a cheekbone that looked out of place. His eyes were only partially open; he looked like he'd just emerged from a heavyweight boxing match.

"What did you do to him?" she said.

"Relax. I haven't done anything. This is how he was when he got here. I'm not sure if it's from his head bouncing around on the ground, or if my guys had to rough him up a little," Paul shrugged. "I don't really ask questions like that."

She walked quickly over to him and put her face an inch from his, looking into his eyes.

"My god, Michael. Are you okay?" she put her hands against his cheeks and kissed him. She could tell his bottom lip was swollen. "We're gonna get you fixed. All right? It's gonna be fine."

"The reunion's touching, but we need to talk. You should turn around and look at the TV screen behind you."

Stephanie pulled away from Michael and slid around to his right side, placing her hand on his shoulder. Paul touched a button on the remote control, and the TV flashed on. Anna, Dennis, and Hank were on their knees in the town square, facing the camera. The terror in their eyes bore through the screen at Stephanie, whose knees nearly buckled. She gripped the chair to keep her balance. An officer she didn't recognize stood behind them, holding a handgun.

"I'm gonna let you decide what happens next," Paul's said.

Audrey didn't know how long she'd been tied to her bed, but she thought she counted two nights, and at least one full day. She was losing track of the hours, and the pins and needles in her arms had given way to a sort of dull ache. She tried to reposition often to keep some blood flowing to her extremities, but it wasn't easy, contorting her body in various ways to get temporary relief.

She was experiencing a level of hunger she had never dreamed of—she thought it had been somewhere around forty-eight hours since Paul had brought her food, but that was a pure guess—and the hunger also eventually subsided into a consistent stomach ache that was nearly unbearable. It was amazing how quickly the body adjusted. When pain was the body's normal, the pain became more and more tolerable by the hour.

So she lay there on her back, her arms fully extended away from her body past her head, her legs spread slightly and the knees with just enough room to flex an inch or so. The ropes on her arms were tied around her wrists. She tried unsuccessfully many times to wiggle free from them, but it was difficult to get any leverage in that position, and she couldn't collapse her hand enough to pull it through. She'd rubbed raw the skin around her bones at the base of both hands from trying to squeeze it out.

That left her feet to try to break free. When Paul tied her up, she was wearing her long black boots, tucked inside the legs of her jeans. The rope was tied just above the cuff of her jeans, wrapped around the boots. As she looked at it and shifted her weight, she realized the rope had likely loosened a bit during the past two days. No longer was it squeezing the boot's leather hard against her skin. Her leg didn't move freely, but she could turn it just a bit, and she knew that hadn't been the case before. And, if it were loose enough for that, she wondered what else might be possible.

Because the rope was tied around her jeans and boots, there had always been some amount of space she had to play with between her skin and the rope. That didn't help her much when it was extra tight, but even a little bit of slackening meant that much more room for maneuverability. It was still tied well, and it wasn't going to come completely loose; she wondered, though, if there might be another way.

Propping her torso on her elbows, she pressed her heels into the bed, trying to bend and flatten out her feet. Her teeth ground against each other while she worked one foot, then the other, looking for a bit of leverage to slide her feet down deeper into the boot. Gradually, her toes inched downward, as her heels slid back toward her, almost imperceptibly, but she could feel herself making progress. It was painful, though. The boots fit her well, and the top of her foot was pushing hard against the boot's instep; it took every ounce of energy she had to hold it there, and not allow it to slide back where it started. Her eyes squeezed shut, and she grimaced in pain, fighting every urge to allow her feet to slide back into the boot. She knew she couldn't let the pain deter her. This might be her only chance to get out of the bed.

Finally, her right heel dislodged, and it slid upward in the boot, flattening against the back of the shoe, and she flexed her calf uncomfortably. She clutched the side of the bed and made another hard push with her left foot and got it to slide free as well. The tops of both feet throbbed, and she thought they were bleeding, but they were free. She began to slide her feet out toward the top of the boots when she heard the key turning in the latch of her door. She kept her feet flat inside the boot and lay on her back, sweating. It had been awhile since Paul paid her a visit.

The door opened, and it wasn't Paul. At first, she wasn't sure who it was. She only caught a quick glimpse of him as he entered, then turned to close and lock the door. After he did, he walked toward her bed.

"I've been waiting for this, Audrey," he said. "You have no idea how long I've waited for this."

She saw a large knife in his right hand. The light in the room was dim, but she thought she recognized him.

"Zac...Latham?" She remembered him from living in the town, but she was confused about why he was there. "What are you doing here?"

"You don't even know?"

"Should I?"

"Do the names Karen, Brittany, and Corinne mean anything to you?"

"Those are your wife and daughters, right?"

"They *were*. Until you ripped them from my home. Ruined my life. When are they coming back? *When?*"

"I'm truly sorry for that. We all are. Paul and I had to make a lot of difficult decisions that—"

"Shut up! Shut. Up. I'm not gonna hear excuses! Tell me now when they're coming back!"

Audrey stared up at him and her eyes dropped. She closed them tightly.

"You have to understand," she shivered, her words shaking restlessly off her lips. "I was trying to do what was best. For Alessandra."

Zac straightened his back a little, stiffening his shoulders. His eyes widened.

"Wait. They're not coming back, are they? None of them."

Audrey's throat howled as she swallowed. Her eyes filled with tears. She had no words.

"Tell me the fucking truth!" Zac screamed as he stabbed his knife into the bed, inches from Audrey's head, ripping through the mattress and clinking off the springs below.

"Oh god," she said, sniffling as tears streamed down her cheeks. "I wanted to do what was right. You've gotta believe me."

Zac pressed his nose against hers, his eyes drilling deeply into hers.

"I won't ask you a-fucking-gain," his teeth clamped together, his lips curled in a snarl. He spoke slowly. "Where. Are. They?"

Audrey's body shook as she began to speak. The tears continued to come, but she couldn't feel them. She was numb.

"There was never a safe facility," Audrey's words came out in a near whisper, and Zac's mouth fell limp. "We just needed to reduce the population. We couldn't handle it all. We figured the men would be more useful to keep, and keeping the women and children together was a good story. It was only a handful of families. Ten. Twelve, maybe. We had to save the town. The resources weren't there to keep everyone alive."

Zac's arms fell limp at his sides. He stared at the wall behind the bed.

"But," he began, his eyes searching blankly ahead. "What did you do with them? They're not *here*."

"We loaded them in vehicles and drove outside the walls. We had them blindfolded, told them it was required. Then we drove each group in a different direction. Fifteen, twenty miles away. That was it."

"Jesus," he stared ahead, expressionless. "You're a fucking monster."

"Paul! Paul pushed most of this forward! Go after him. I'll help you."

Zac looked down at her. "Who do you think gave me this knife?"

He climbed onto the bed, swinging his right leg over her and straddling her knees. He leaned forward, holding the knife inches above her face. It glistened in the dull light that lingered above the bed. She squirmed, writhing back and forth, each time kicking her boots a little further away, and bringing her feet a little closer to freedom. He leaned his elbows on her arms, pushing down and leaning her forearms backward. Her shoulders groaned as he did, and she screamed at the needles of pain grinding against her collarbone. She was glad he was focused on her upper body, though, so he wouldn't notice the boots sliding down the footboard, lilting to the right, very loose and hanging well off her feet.

Zac lifted the knife and showed it to her again. He pressed the tip against her chin until it pierced the skin, bringing blood bubbling to the surface, streaming down across her neck to the bed. She gasped, and he dragged it, tracing the line of her cheekbone and opening a flap of skin along the side of her face, and blood poured out in streams onto her neck, pillow, and bed sheets.

She knew she was close, and she yelled as she yanked her feet out of the boots, bringing her right knee up in the same motion, connecting hard between Zac's legs. She held the knee there, pressing with as much energy as she could muster, trying to lift him in the air if she could. His mouth fell open, and he dropped the knife to reach for her knee, wanting to push it away or pivot off. As he did, she brought her left leg back and then lifted it, kicking him underneath the chin and sending him backward off balance. The back of his head collided with the corner post on the footboard, and his body went limp, slamming loudly onto the floor.

For a moment, she was terrified someone might come in to check on all the noise. Maybe it would be Paul, or one of the officers. But ten seconds passed, and there was nothing. Twenty, and she felt she was safe. The knife lay on the bed, near her waist. She lifted her butt off the bed and bent her left knee to get her foot up to the knife. She kicked it lightly, and it slid toward her torso, its handle tucking underneath her back. By lifting off the bed and pressing again repeatedly, she was able to move the knife gradually closer to her shoulders, then her head. Blood was still gushing from her face and pouring over her pillow. She shoved that out of the way with her head and elbow, then opened her mouth and grabbed the handle of the knife in her teeth. She sat up for the first time in a couple of days, and pulled the knife out of her mouth with her right hand.

She still needed another contortion. By twisting to her side and bringing her right arm over and across the side of her head, she could reach the rope with her knife. She pulled it taut with her left arm, pressed and slid the knife across the rope's threads. Several snapped on the first hard tug. She slid it again, and most of the rest gave way. One more slice, and the rope broke free from the headboard. The other one was easy, now that her left arm was free. After more than two days, Audrey could shake her arms to get feeling back, and she bounced out of the bed. She pressed her hand to her cheek and scampered into the bathroom, rifling through drawers as blood poured from between her fingers in slow, thick waves. Finally, she found a box of large bandages and pulled one out, stretching it taut to stick onto her face. She stuffed the rest of the box into her jeans pocket. She suspected she'd need stitches, but that was going to have to wait.

She had no idea what was happening outside of her room, and what hell Paul might have unleashed. She slid on a pair of loafers from her closet and opened the door to the hall; she could hear Paul talking just around the corner from her room, in the den at the front of the house. But she wasn't sure she was ready to deal with him yet. What she knew was that Zac wasn't entirely wrong. She *had* made her share of mistakes, some of which might even have been unforgivable. But she could start trying to make up for them. First on her list were some people she owed a visit.

65

A boulder sat in Stephanie's stomach as she blinked at the image on the screen in front of her, trying to will it away. Had they missed one of the shooters somehow? Was there a straggler? It was all getting close to being too much for her. Her mind wrapped itself like tentacles around the idea that every decision she was involved in over the past couple of days led to someone dying—from the trip to find Doctor Giles to showing the video at the fair to going to the warehouse. And now, leaving with Nick left them two people down. Could having five instead of three people have made a difference? She didn't know. But it occurred to her that they might have been waiting for her to leave the group. They knew she'd come after Michael. Paul was going to make sure that happened. She was just a pawn.

"What do you mean that you're gonna let me decide?" Stephanie said, her hand rattling the arm of Michael's chair.

"I mean it's up to you who dies. You see there are three people on the screen there, and then we've got Michael in the chair beside you. All you have to do is pick one, and this'll all be over."

Her breath shortened and her lips trembled as she tried to speak. "Pick one...*what?*"

Paul frowned. "You're not listening. I thought I was pretty clear. Pick one to die. The rest will live. That's it. Easy."

Stephanie's heart raced, and the room spun around her, the world pixelating itself. Paul's words slowed to a crawl; they trickled out of his mouth in baritone dribbles. They couldn't be real. Her mind didn't want to accept where she was, or what was happening. It was all too much. She tried to speak, but it came out as a whisper. Or maybe nothing came out at all. She wasn't sure.

"What was that?" Paul said, but she didn't react. He walked closer to her. "Stephanie, I can't hear you."

Stephanie felt a hand on her shoulder, and she jumped, her breath coming quickly in staggered, ragged intervals. Her head spun left, right, then back left again. Her hands balled up into fists, then flexed, fists and flexed. She saw Paul's eyes, and they were calm.

"It's okay, Stephanie," he said. "Take deep breaths, all right? Let's try it. Inhale…Exhale…Inhale…Hold it…Now, exhale. Good. That's good. We don't want you overheating here. You're too important right now. Are you gonna be okay?"

She closed her eyes and faced the floor at her feet, nodding.

"Excellent!" Paul said. "So, I really am going to need your decision within…let's say twenty seconds." He held his watch up to eye level.

Stephanie's head snapped up. "Wait! No, I don't understand. Why do I need to pick someone to die?"

"Because I want you to make a tough decision. Fifteen seconds!"

"But I can't! What if I pick no one?"

"Then I'll pick someone, and then we'll go round and round until you pick, or all of you are dead. Whichever comes first. Ten seconds!"

Stephanie swallowed hard, but there was nothing in her throat; her chest felt like it was collapsing in on itself. She was so thirsty, but there was no time for water. She needed to concentrate.

"This is insane! I'm not doing this!"

"Then you'll all die. Suits me fine. Five seconds!"

Stephanie's mind raced faster than she could keep up. *Is he serious? Surely he can't be. I can't do this. I can't order someone's death. He's bluffing. He has to be, and I'm calling him on it. I refuse to play this game. When I won't participate, he won't know how to react.*

With that, Stephanie's chin stiffened, and she raised her shoulders, standing straight up, her arms tight at her sides. She was resolute, and ready to see what Paul's next play would be.

"Time's up!" Paul said, and turned to look at Stephanie. They made eye contact. "I'm disappointed you didn't make a decision, but I guess there are three more rounds."

He picked up his walkie-talkie and pushed the talk button. Stephanie's tongue was sandpaper in her mouth.

"William…Kill the girl first. Stand by for the next name."

Stephanie's eyes grew, and her chest tightened into knots.

"No, you son of a bitch!" She sprung from where she was and lunged toward Paul. He sidestepped Michael's chair and slid around in front of him, his gun held firmly at Stephanie's head. She stopped, her breath labored, and her lips pressed firmly together. She was shaking uncontrollably.

"There's nothing I can do now. You had the chance to pick someone, and you deferred to me."

Keeping his gun pointed at Stephanie, Paul stepped to his right so she had a view of the screen. Officer Greene stepped behind Anna and held the gun to the back of her head. Stephanie turned away, pressing her hands to her ears, her head trembling violently. There was no sound on the video, but this was happening not far away on the town square. Even with her hands covering her ears, she heard the echo, reverberating through the glass and against the mahogany walls around her.

She fell to her knees and collapsed on the floor, her head between her legs. She cried out with a dry, cracking wail, feeling broken and empty. Her back and shoulders heaved as she wept on the floor, doubled over and spent, physically and emotionally.

She wanted to curl up and disappear, have a hole open in the Earth and swallow her into its depths. She didn't want to exist and, at that moment, she couldn't imagine how she'd ever want to again. Anna, her best friend for as long as she could remember, who used to set up a camera to film them playing dress up as a kid—Anna always let Stephanie be the princess, because she wanted to be some sort of superhero, or an astronaut—was dead. Stephanie would never see her hunched over that computer in the Research lab again, coming up with some new way to organize the hospital's files, or some new encyclopedia article Stephanie had to read. It wasn't possible. It simply wasn't possible.

"Stephanie," Paul tapped her on the back with the barrel of his .357 Magnum. "Oh, Stephanie. I know you're upset, but I've got a schedule to keep. I'm gonna need you to buck up and pick someone. It's Hank, whoever that other guy is, and—"

"Dennis!" she looked up, her throat throbbing with soreness, her face damp and red. "His name is Dennis, you motherfucker! He's Anna's husband!"

"Ah. Then Dennis, it is! So, Hank, Dennis, and Michael. Pick one, and we're done. Or I will, and we'll do this again. You know the drill. Twenty seconds, starting..." he made a dramatic show of snapping his elbow as he lifted his wristwatch to his face "... Now."

"No!" Stephanie pushed herself onto her knees, then to her feet. "I refuse to play this game! This is bullshit!"

"Your option, I guess. Fifteen seconds."

"How can you expect me to make a decision like this?"

"Sacrifice one to save three, including yourself. Sometimes leaders have to make tough calls. Ten seconds."

"Kill me instead! I'll sacrifice myself!"

"Not an option. Seven seconds."

She couldn't look at the screen. She faced the back wall, her head pounding, her chest aching. He wasn't bluffing. He proved that when he killed Anna. Stephanie either had to directly order the murder of one, or tacitly allow the murder of three, likely ending with her own death. The biggest question might be if she thought he'd follow through with letting them all walk away if she made a choice. What reason did she have to trust him? He was a maniac. It was entirely possible she'd say a name, and he'd kill them all anyway. But what choice did she really have? He was the only armed one in the room. All the leverage was his. She could either make a call, or watch them all die one by one.

"Dennis!" she cried out, then buried her face in her hands.

Nick came around the corner, between two large pillars, and entered the front end of the large courtyard in the center of the compound. He could see the fence that imprisoned him for too long, and he wasn't going to let it hold anyone past this night.

He walked toward the fence and spotted the gate to his left. When he got to it, it was locked. It occurred to him that he should have brought Hank's bolt cutters. Going back would take too long, though, and be too risky. He was here. He needed to find a way in.

He grabbed the lock with both hands and tugged on it. In the dark, it was hard to see much, but it looked like a fairly standard Master key lock. With the right tools, it could be broken. It was going to take something stronger than his hands, though. He looked around for something he might be able to use. The lack of light made it difficult to pick much out, but he finally spotted something that looked promising. Nick walked over and picked up a large rock that was lying by the main building. It was jagged and a little bit larger than his hand. He thought it would do the job; his one concern was the noise it would make. If he could break the lock in one or two swings, he might be okay. But the more times he had to slam this against the metal lock, and have the gate rattle on its hinges, the more likely it would be that Paul or someone else in the building would hear it and come out with weapons drawn. He had to be careful.

Nick walked back to the gate and raised the rock above his head; he paused, trying to will himself to swing with all the strength he could muster. He took a breath and crashed it into the lock. There was a metallic ping, and the gate shook, the twisted metal vibrating against itself to create a loud hum, moving down the fence in both directions like a wave. It took ten seconds for quiet to return.

When it did, he grabbed the lock in one hand and lifted it a bit, bending over to get a closer look at the damage. As far as he could tell, the first attempt made almost no impact. There might have been a small nick on the top front of the lock, but it looked otherwise unscathed. He thought he might have underestimated the lock's strength. If the rock was going to work at all, it was going to take a lot more than two hits. And he knew Paul was somewhere not far away with Stephanie and Michael.

Nick heard a creaking noise from the top of the stairs behind him, and his heart jumped. He didn't immediately see anywhere to run. He was caught in the open courtyard. Someone must have heard. He took off, heading toward the corner of the building. Being on the move would at least make him a tough target to hit, and maybe he could get to the corner of the building.

As he ran, he heard no shots, and he got around the corner, tucking himself out of sight. Had the person not seen him? He wasn't sure. But he could hear the person's footsteps hitting the stairs as they descended to the courtyard. He waited, and there was silence. Whoever it was came down, but he didn't hear them go back up. He didn't dare take the chance to look and possibly expose himself in case they hadn't seen him. Then the voice came.

"Is that you, Nick?" Nick felt chills at the sound of his name. Was that Audrey? He thought so. Not only had she seen him, but she recognized him. "Not sure how you got out, but it's okay. I'm unarmed. My hands are up; go ahead and look. I know you're hiding around that corner over there."

Nick leaned just far enough to let one eye see into the courtyard, and Audrey was standing there, hands raised above her head, a large bandage that looked appeared to be soaked through with blood affixed to her cheek. She was walking toward the fence. He ducked back behind the wall.

"I know you don't trust me," she said. "I wouldn't trust me either if I were you. What I did to you, and to everybody, was wrong. I had my reasons. I thought I was doing the right thing. I really did. But I got carried away with what was possible for me to do, rather than what was necessary, and I let myself be fooled into doing it. I exempted myself and my team from the stipulations I was visiting upon everyone else. Deep down, I probably knew I had taken it too far, but I just didn't know how to pull it back. I thought that if I did, I'd lose control. I'd be blamed for doing it in the first place, and then I'd be blamed if the virus crept in after. I honestly set out at the beginning with good intentions but, somewhere along the line, that changed.

"I know words can't make up for any of that. I know I have a lot to answer for, and a lot of atoning to do. I can't make up for it all in one night, but I want to start trying. I don't know how you got out in the first place, but I'm assuming you came back to free the other quarantined people. So I'm unlocking the gate."

He looked again, and he saw her placing a key in the lock. She turned it, and the lock unlatched. She pulled it off and dropped it to the ground, then opened the gate.

"Is this for real?" Nick said, turning to look at Audrey. "Are you really going to help me?"

She motioned for him to come to her. "Yeah. Come on. It's past time they got out."

He jogged over and picked up the lock, then threw it as far as he could into the black sky, disappearing into the trees.

"No need for that anymore," he said.

"Agreed," she smiled and nodded. "Ready to get them out?"

"After you."

He walked inside behind her, and they walked toward the back, where Rachel, Theresa, and Omar were still set up.

"You go check that one," he pointed to Omar's tent. "I'll get Rachel and Theresa."

He unzipped Rachel's tent and saw her huddled inside, asleep on the ground. He jostled her shoulder, and she stirred. She looked surprised when she opened her eyes and saw Nick.

"It's okay," he said. "I'm getting you guys out of here. The gate's open. You're free. It's over."

"I didn't think I'd ever see you again," she threw her arms around his neck, and tears welled up in his eyes as he wrapped his around her waist. He thought he had lost her after Danny's death, when it looked like she would never forgive him. To feel her arms around him again was energizing.

They exited the tent, and Audrey was sitting at the old dinner table with Omar. Theresa heard the noise and crawled out of her tent to see everyone there. Audrey was smiling.

"We weren't sure how long you guys would be in there," Audrey said to Nick. "Thought we'd give you a little space."

"No time for that," Nick said. "We'll also need to check those smaller tents up front. I have no idea if any of them are still alive, but they're going to need medical attention if so. We'll come back for them. First, though, I know Paul's in the house with Stephanie and Michael. You have any idea where, Audrey?"

"I heard him. Pretty sure they're in the den. No idea what's going on, though."

"Okay," Nick nodded. "You talked about atonement. For your next act, any chance you'd be willing to help us take out your brother?"

Audrey smiled again. "What do you have in mind?"

66

"See? I knew you could do it," Paul said. "That's because you're a leader, Stephanie. You know that difficult decisions have to be made for the good of the group."

Stephanie rubbed her eyes, trying to clear the tears that were coming, but they wouldn't stop. She sniffed repeatedly, wanting to hold back the avalanche of sadness and shame that was washing across her. She wanted to be strong, for Michael if for no other reason. In a few minutes, she hoped she'd be walking out of that building with him, and they could try to forge ahead. Maybe salvage something approaching a normal life. First, though, she had to live with condemning Dennis to death, shortly after her indecision led to his wife—her best friend—being murdered.

Paul grabbed his walkie-talkie and was about to press the talk button when Stephanie heard a noise from back down the hall, behind them and to the left. There was a commotion of some kind at the back of the house. Paul and Michael followed Stephanie in turning to look in that direction.

They couldn't see much that way, because there was a wall between them and the hallway. Stephanie didn't know much about the layout of the building, so she didn't know what—or who—might be back there. From the look on Paul's face, though, she didn't think he did either.

The noise was getting closer. There were footsteps, definitely. But something more. A low murmur, perhaps. She wasn't sure. But these people were making their presence felt, whoever they were. And they sounded like they were coming toward the room Stephanie was in.

Paul put down the walkie-talkie and walked hesitantly toward the corner, leaning to see around the wall. The murmur grew, reverberating against the floor and walls of the hall they were on, carrying into the large den and floating ominously around them. Paul got near the edge of the wall and peered around it. Stephanie didn't know what he saw, but she watched him raise his gun to point it in the direction of the noise. As he did, the hum expanded into a roar, of quick, hard footfalls and almost primal screams of anger and frustration, lashing out in one direction. Suddenly, it dawned on Stephanie who it might be. *Nick. They came for us.*

Stephanie sprang from where she stood and ran to Paul, sliding the knife she took earlier from Zac out from her rear waistband and thrusting it into his side. Paul's back arched as he screamed in pain, trying to spin and fire at Stephanie, but she pivoted away and he fired with his eyes squeezed shut. Two bullets hit the marble floor and made black marks, chipping it and ricocheting off in some direction. She got behind him and wrapped her arms around him, pinning his arms against his side. Paul writhed, trying to get his gun pointed toward her, but she refused to loosen her grip. Nick was wielding Audrey's knife, and he was leading five of them—Audrey included—in charging toward Paul. As Nick approached, he lifted the knife high above his head, grunted madly and lunged as he brought it down hard into Paul's chest. The woman and man who were with him came around to the sides, and Stephanie backed away as they slammed into him hard enough to knock him to the ground. Nick leapt on top of him and continued stabbing, driving the knife repeatedly into Paul's chest, abdomen and neck, covering himself in Paul's blood. The other three stopped punching Paul and were standing over them, watching the carnage. They reached down and grabbed Nick's arms. Stephanie heard one of them say, "That's enough, Nick. We're good."

She reached over and grabbed the walkie-talkie, then pushed talk.

"William…This is Stephanie. Paul's dead. Drop your gun and leave now, and we'll let you live. Otherwise, we'll hunt you down and make you wish we'd killed you quickly."

Stephanie looked at the monitor in time to see Officer Greene look around, then lay his gun down and run. Hank and Dennis looked at each other, and then Dennis crawled to Anna and lay beside her. Stephanie quickly looked away.

When she did, Audrey was standing there, her hand extended. Stephanie shook it.

"As I told Nick earlier, I'm sorry about all of this," Audrey said. "It never should have happened this way."

Stephanie nodded and turned to Nick, who was crying on the girl's shoulders.

"I'm Stephanie. I only know Nick out of the four of you, but thanks. I don't know how that would have gone if you hadn't shown up. We've already lost so many people."

They all introduced themselves and exchanged handshakes.

"Also, I know it's pretty bloody, but could I borrow that knife?" she said, and cocked her head toward Michael.

Nick raised his head and handed it to Stephanie. The knife dripped blood in ribbons onto the floor and her shoes. She used her shirt to wipe it so it wasn't quite so messy, then began slicing the ropes that strapped Michael to the chair. When he was free, he stood and threw his arms around Stephanie. They held each other for a long time.

They didn't know what lay ahead. Alessandra was a ship without a captain, and there were bodies—so many bodies—that needed to be buried and memorialized. The people of the town needed that. They most certainly deserved it. They also needed leadership, and that vacuum was going to be tough to fill in the near future. Audrey's administration might have survived it all—study forgery, rings, separation of families, quarantine camp, framing of Nick, and even the mass killing of so many in the square—if she could have reversed policy and reunited the families after Paul's death. The clamoring for her to do so came almost immediately in the morning light following the massacre in the square. Many of the people who were left marched to the compound to confront her, but all they found was a disoriented Zac stumbling around her bedroom.

He told them there was no safe place for the women and children; Audrey drove them out into the Georgia wilderness to die. And, in the winter without anything but the clothes on their backs, that's most certainly what they did. Men wept, pounding the ground at their feet, praying it wasn't true. Many had suspected as much, but the shock of hearing their suspicions confirmed still left them shaken. Around 3 a.m., Audrey had decided she didn't have the strength to face a town that knew what she did, and she fled quietly in the night. Stephanie led a group to check Doctor Giles' cabin, but there was no sign of life other than the doctor's body being picked over by wildlife on the back deck, his blood congealing into a black pool around him. The group carried his body back into town to be buried.

Personally, Stephanie knew the road in front of her was going to be a difficult one. Nothing in her life prepared her for what she saw and did over those days after Michael returned to her life. As a doctor, you can grow accustomed to seeing sickness and death happen before your eyes, but it's not something you ever want to grow complacent toward. And the sheer scale of the death and destruction left in the wake of her quest with Michael to press the issue of the dishonesty of the town's leadership left her shaken.

Over the coming months, the phrase kept returning to her head, "Was it all worth it?" There were people in the town who thought it wasn't. Stephanie and Michael weren't hailed as heroes by many. A number of people blamed them for causing the massacre on the square by showing that video. Even though Stephanie and Michael thought it was clear that the people of the town were isolated in their individual prisons, many of them liked their prisons. They liked the day-to-day routine of it, the *normality* of it. Stephanie and Michael not only crushed that normality, but their actions resulted in dozens of their friends and neighbors being killed. Of course, Paul was the one who ordered the killing, but he wasn't around to answer for it, and Stephanie and Michael took the brunt of the blame from those who didn't want change —or, at least, not at that cost.

So, was it worth it? She couldn't say. Michael and Stephanie talked about it a lot, and neither of them had a definitive answer. He leaned toward yes, because he felt like the price of freedom was always high; someone has to be willing to fight to keep it. In this case, they were the ones who did. At some point, the people of the town would understand that, and appreciate it. Stephanie wasn't sure, though. Freedom always had a cost, but had this one been too high? The lives they lost couldn't be replaced. So many of the children who had remained in the town and survived— being raised by town officials in the back part of the compound for close to a year—had no parents to return home to when they were released. Sorting through that alone was heartbreaking. There was nothing worse than telling a little girl that her friends got to go live with their parents again, but hers had died. There's nothing that erases those tears from your memory.

Another question that popped into her head a lot was, "If you could go back, would you do it again?" To that question, she always said yes. Even knowing what she knew later. The clock doesn't go backward; only forward. And freedom does have a high price. She could accept the consequences of what she'd done, because she knew she did it with the good of the community in mind. She did what she felt she had to do. Mistakes were made, and she wished it had ended differently. But she'd do it again. She'd pay that price to reclaim her life and make sure when she died, she would do so with her hands unbound.

ACKNOWLEDGMENTS

Any story a writer can be proud of is far from a one-man piece of work, and *The Solitary Apocalypse* is certainly no exception. It's been more than a year since I began writing, and I never could have gotten it to this point without a tremendous amount of support along the way.

First and foremost, my wife, Jamie, has been my biggest cheerleader, idea generator, supporter, and scrutinizer along the way. Her intelligence and willingness to call me on my bullshit is invaluable for someone who knows he needs a check sometimes. I know that nothing I write would be remotely as good without her here to help shepherd me along the way, and forgive the nights when I hammer away at my keyboard upstairs for hours at a time, trying to work out that one scene. She's basically the fuel that makes this all happen.

Secondly, thanks to my editor, Liz Hurst, and my book cover designer, Monica Haynes with The Thatchery. Both are consummate professionals that put many hours of work into helping to put a nice sheen on this story I've tried to make suck as little as possible. Without them, the errors definitely would have piled up, and I'd have a cover drawn badly in MS Paint. Nobody wins there. Liz helped to guide me through multiple revisions, and helped to make sure I didn't wander from the story pace I was trying to set. Meanwhile, Monica poured everything into digging into my mind for answers that helped her narrow her focus until the perfect cover came into view — the sign of a true artist. Their contributions can't be overstated on this story. And, as always, if you do find any errors, those are all mine. If you don't find any, thank Liz.

Next, my friend Mike Holcomb really went beyond what was asked to help me push this book to the finish line, not only offering terrific feedback as a beta reader, scrutinizing the full manuscript, but taking this city boy to the gun range to school me on handguns. It was an education that — frankly — was sorely needed, and hopefully helped to make the book's scenes that feature guns much more realistic and true to the way the individual firearms actually function. I could research all I wanted via the web, but there's no substitute for loading, holding and firing the weapon with my own hands. Anything I still got wrong is the result of my own lack of paying enough attention, as I was in really good hands there.

I also need to thank beta readers Leslie Levine and Oliver Boudreaux, who offered helpful critique and suggestions at a critical juncture for getting the story as right as it could be. Good beta readers are always some of the heroes of making a good novel great, and here's hoping that's what they helped to accomplish with this one.

Finally, thanks to all my friends and family who have been so encouraging as I ventured down this road to authordom. It's not the easiest (or most sane) transition from journalism to fiction writing, but the support I've gotten from everyone around me has been a big motivator, and they've been a good source of accountability for me to stay focused on getting the manuscript completed. When everyone knows you're writing a book, that's even more reason not to let that book slide away from you, so it's great to have everyone there to make fun of me if I screw stuff up.

And, of course, thanks to you for getting all the way to this point. I'd probably be writing something whether the readers existed or not, but knowing there are people who actually care about and look forward to diving into these worlds that are created in my mind is pretty damn cool. If you liked the book (or, hell, even if you didn't), I'd appreciate it if you'd like a review on Amazon. Reviews are some of the lifeblood of drawing more readers into the fold, so more people can take a shot on reading an indie author they've never heard of.

If you did enjoy the story, don't forget that I have one other novel and two novellas for sale on Amazon now. You can also get a free original short story called "The Trolley Problem" if you sign up for my newsletter at my website. I'd love to have you on board. Thanks.

MORE BOOKS BY JEFF HAWS

<u>Novels</u>

The Little Tragedy — For the past twenty years, every child has fallen into an endless coma on the night of their 10th birthday. Families are broken apart. Society is forever altered. And now, the human race itself is marching toward extinction. Until Kevin Fraser wakes up. With one Fraser child awake and the other rapidly approaching his 10th birthday, his family -- and the world -- holds its breath. Is this the sign of the plague finally ending, or will the walls start closing around the Frasers as the burden becomes too heavy for them to bear?

Killing the Immortals — Would you murder for god? Would you stand in the way of those who would? Cain and Hannah have to decide what side they're on in this fast-paced thriller about the dangers of fanaticism in a world where people are living indefinitely.

<u>Novellas and Short Stories</u>

Tomorrow's News Today — When Walt suddenly discovers that anything he writes at his small newspaper job will come true, he believes he has the power to reshape his crumbling marriage and career. But he also has the tools for his own destruction. Which path will he choose?

The Slingshot — Taylor's a typical geeky teenager who just wants to fit in with the cool kids for once. But soon, events spiral out of his control, and his moment of mischief threatens to tear apart his life, and his family's along with it. His older brother is the only one he can trust to save him.

FREE WITH NEWSLETTER

SIGNUP

The Trolley Problem — Andrea will do anything for her son. She wants what's best for him, so she's doing her best to work a custody arrangement with her husband, and juggle a relationship with her new boyfriend. But now her ex wants to cut her out of her son's life, and she has to decide how far she's willing to go to keep her boy in her life.

REVIEW AND RATE *THE SOLITARY APOCALYPSE*

Now that you've finished *The Solitary Apocalypse*, please consider posting a review and rating on Amazon and Goodreads. This serves both as invaluable feedback for the author, and as social proof to other readers that this book is worth their valuable investment of time to read. Also, if you liked what you read, follow Jeff on Amazon and Goodreads to interact, and be among the first to know when he writes something new.

ABOUT THE AUTHOR

Jeff Haws is a long-time journalist who has turned his writing eye to fiction. This is his second published novel and fourth published book. His first novel, *Killing the Immortals*, was published in 2016, along with the novellas *Tomorrow's News Today* and *The Slingshot*. Over the past 20 years, his writing has appeared in the *Washington Post, Atlanta Journal-Constitution, Miami Herald, Arizona Republic, New Orleans Times-Picayune*, and many other publications. He lives with his wife in Atlanta, Georgia.

SIGN UP FOR NEWSLETTER FOR UPDATES:
jeffhaws.com/newslettersignup
TWITTER/FACEBOOK/INSTAGRAM: @ByJeffHaws

www.ingramcontent.com/pod-product-compliance
Lightning Source LLC
Chambersburg PA
CBHW051941240626
47153CB00005B/1581